DEFYING

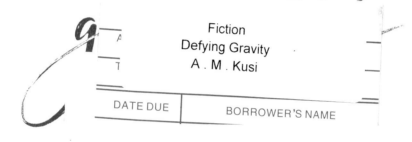

Fiction
Defying Gravity
A . M . Kusi

DATE DUE	BORROWER'S NAME

Fiction
Defying Gravity
A . M . Kusi

Published by A. M. Kusi 2020

amkusinovels@gmail.com

Visit our website at www.amkusi.com

Editor: Anna Bishop of CREATING ink

Sensitivity Edit: Renita McKinney of A Book A Day

Proofreader: Judy's Proofreading

Cover Design: Regina Wamba of ReginaWamba.com

ISBN: 978-1949781175

OTHER BOOKS BY A. M. KUSI

A Fallen Star (eBook FREE on all retailers)
(Shattered Cove Series Book 1)

Glass Secrets
(Shattered Cove Series Book 2)

The Lighthouse Inn
(Shattered Cove Series Book 4)

His True North
(Shattered Cove Series Book 5)

The Orchard Inn
(Book 1 in The Orchard Inn Romance Series)

Conflict of Interest
(Book 2 in The Orchard Inn Romance Series)

Her Perfect Storm
(Book 3 in The Orchard Inn Romance Series)

For a complete list of all our books, visit:

WWW.AMKUSI.COM/BOOKS

"If you are neutral in situations of injustice, you have chosen the side of the oppressor."

- Desmond Tutu

"It just takes one conscious individual to recognize their wounds, recognize ancestral patterns, see dysfunction and trauma and think 'maybe I can stop it here.'"

- Unknown

This book is dedicated to all those out there who've been through trauma and decided to not let it define you. To those who do the hard work to break the patterns.

GET A FREE SHORT NOVEL

Join our newsletter to get a FREE short novel that's not available on any retailer. Plus updates about new releases, giveaways, pre-orders, sneak peeks, and more.

Visit the website below to join now.

WWW.AMKUSI.COM/NEWSLETTER

A NOTE TO READERS

This book has sensitive subject matter that deals with abuse, mentions rape, but does not go into detail. This story takes on the subject of racism and police brutality. It was a very emotionally challenging story to write, but we feel the story needs to be told to help shine light onto the injustices, and micro-aggressions, that happen every day in America. We hope you fall in love with Bently and Belle just as much as we did. Their love story is real and raw and it just had to be told. Enjoy!

TABLE OF CONTENTS

1

BENTLY

Bently winced at the bitter aftertaste coating his mouth. He lifted his cup of coffee and swallowed again. Nope. Still terrible. "Should have stopped by Remy's," he said aloud to the empty truck cab as he set the brown sludge passing for java in the cupholder.

The radio crackled. "Squad one, what's your twenty and status?"

Bently picked up the radio as he turned into a side street and pressed the speaker to his mouth. "This is squad one. I'm on Everton Street. Status ten-eight."

"Unit one, take the suspicious person walking with a bike on Shell Ave."

He pressed the button once more. "Ten-four."

Bently put his blinker on and went left at the stop sign, scanning the sides of the road. After making a series of turns, he ended up on Shell Avenue. Slowing, his gaze focused on a kid pushing a bike on the side of the road. His blue school backpack was nearly bursting at the seams. Bently scanned the upscale neighborhood for any signs of a threat.

"He's just a kid walking home from school." He shook his head and notified dispatch that he was on the scene before pulling up beside the kid.

He hopped out. Squinting at the sun, he grabbed his aviators from his pocket and slipped them on as he greeted the kid. "Good afternoon."

The teen kept walking with his head down, swaying slightly. The flapping of deflated rubber slapping against the cement sidewalk brought Bently's attention to the tires of his bike.

Bently stepped next to the boy. White earbuds stuck out of his ears, contrasting with his light brown skin. He moved into the young man's periphery to get his attention. "He—"

Wide frightened brown eyes stared up at him as the boy's trembling hands flew towards the sky. The bike crashed to the ground. Bently swiveled around searching for the danger that had the guy so riled up, but they were alone on the street.

"Sir, I don't want any trouble. I'm just walking home from school." The young boy's voice was steady. His eye was swollen and bruised.

Bently furrowed his brow. *He's scared of me?* Smiling in hopes to set the boy at ease, Bently motioned to his headphones. "Can you take those out for a minute?"

Slowly, the boy plucked the headphones from his ears, the steady thump of hip-hop pouring from the tiny speakers.

"Nice tunes." *Smooth, Bently.*

The young man remained silent. His eyes were glued on Bently. His shoulders nearly touched his ears with tension.

"I'm Sheriff Evans. What's your name?"

"TJ . . . uh, Thomas Jones, sir."

Bently nodded, looking over his bike. "What happened to your ride?"

TJ looked down for a moment before he shrugged. "Flat

tire."

"May I?" Bently asked, reaching towards one of the wheels.

"Okay?" TJ's answer was more like a question.

"I know a thing or two about bikes. This is a nice one."

"I didn't steal it if that's what you're thinking," TJ said, his jaw tense.

"I never assumed you did. You can put your hands down, you know." Bently ran his palm around the outer tire, finding the source of the leakage—a long slice between the folds of black rubber.

"The person who slashed these tires the same one who gave you that black eye?" Bently asked, standing to his full height.

TJ shifted nervously. "Why do you care?"

Bently sighed. "Because this is my town and I care about the people in it. If someone is being harassed or assaulted, I want to know."

TJ nodded hesitantly.

"Do you want to file a report?"

TJ's eyes grew wide again as he shook his head vehemently. "Nah, it was just a misunderstanding."

"If you're sure." Bently knew better than anyone else that you couldn't help someone until they were ready to be helped.

A flash of movement caught his eye. One of the residents stared out the window of her two-story home at him, her hand clutching the fabric of her shirt.

"Where do you live?"

"Maple Street."

"That's still two miles away. Why don't you hop in and I'll give you a ride? I'll throw your bike in the back." Bently picked up the metal frame.

"You don't have to," TJ said.

"Wouldn't want you to have any more misunderstandings on the way back. Besides, I'm headed that way anyway. I have a friend who lives in that neighborhood. *And the last thing I need is another phone call to dispatch about a kid walking home from school. Since when did that become a crime?* "Would you like the ride?"

"Uh . . . okay." TJ opened the passenger side and climbed in.

Bently hefted the bike into his truck bed before climbing in the driver's side. Geez. Had anyone ever sat farther away from him and still managed to be in the same car? The kid was practically crawling out the window.

He wasn't blind. The kid was terrified of him, and unfortunately, Bently guessed the badge across his chest had something to do with it. There were so many news stories, seemingly a story every day about clashes of police and people of color. How could Bently assure him that wouldn't happen here in Shattered Cove? He was not a racist, and no one in his department was either—at least he didn't think so. Maybe he should slip in the fact that his sister-in-law was Black? No, that'd be awkward.

"You play any sports?" Bently drove towards their destination.

"Basketball."

"Oh, my kind of guy . . . You lived here long?" Bently tried to keep the strain out of his voice.

"Just a few months. My sister got a job at the hospital."

"What about your parents?" Bently turned down the end of the street.

"It's just us. There, the blue one on the right is ours." TJ pointed out the window to a small duplex. The burlap wreath over the door said "welcome."

Bently pulled in along the side of the street and put the truck in park. TJ hopped out, quickly shutting the door, and

Bently followed suit. He walked around to the back to grab the bike just as a door slammed behind him.

"Oh, shit," TJ said.

"What the hell happened to your face, TJ?" a strong feminine voice growled.

Bently turned. The breath ripped from his lungs. The woman before him was the most beautiful person he'd ever laid eyes on—and he'd laid eyes on a lot. Big ringlets of curls danced around her brown glowing skin in the breeze. Her dark eyes flashed at TJ with worry before she targeted him with those stormy spheres. Fear tinged the edges of her furious glare. Her bright red lips moved as his ears rang, blood rushing to his groin.

"Did he do this to you?" She grabbed TJ's face, checking him over like a mother hen. TJ turned away from the unnamed beauty.

"Nah, just some kids at school messing around," TJ said. "Sheriff Evans gave me a ride."

"You got in the car with a cop?" she snapped.

Bently closed his mouth, embarrassed that he'd been standing there gawking. Wiping invisible drool from his mouth, he cleared his throat and extended his arm, offering the smile that he'd been told melted most women's panties. "Hi. I'm Bently."

She stared at his open hand like he'd just stuck it in a public toilet. "Is my brother in any trouble?"

He frowned and straightened from the rejection. "No. Of course not."

"Good, then we're done here." She grabbed TJ's arm and pulled him into the house while Bently stared, utterly confused. *What the hell just happened?*

"Belle! My bike—" TJ protested.

"Get inside!" His sister shot him a look and TJ shut his

mouth and complied.

It needs the tires fixed anyways. I can do that.

The woman shoved her brother in the house and whirled around. Her powerful gaze met his before she slammed the door shut.

Damn, she was something.

* * *

A few hours later, Bently pulled the bike from his truck bed, admiring his handiwork. This fresh set of tires and the tune-up he'd performed would be the perfect icebreaker. It wasn't unusual for him to go above and beyond the call of duty for his fellow townsfolk. But none of them had a sister who was hotter than sin and feisty as fuck either. *Does this count as breaking my no-hooking-up-with-locals rule?*

Nah. This was just good old-fashioned flirting and helping a fellow community member out. It wasn't like he would follow through.

Bently knocked on the door, noting the older model Ford Focus in the driveway that had seen better days. Red flowers bloomed at the base of the porch, a discarded pile of pulled weeds off to the side. Several potted plants were spaced around the small area and a few baskets hung from the rafter hooks. He swiped the sweat from his brow and drew in a deep breath. Nerves scattered through him as he shifted his feet. Since when was he this off-kilter over a woman?

The energy shifted as the knob twisted. His heart beat faster as he swallowed.

The door opened and Belle's smile quickly morphed into a frown.

"What do you want?" Belle said, her chin rising.

"Good evening." He smiled and waited a beat. Her scowl

only deepened. *Have I lost the touch? Did cancer steal this from me too?* He cleared his throat. "Uh, I just wanted to return TJ's bike."

She looked at the metal object as he set it on the porch. "Okay."

"Is he home?"

"He's doing homework," she answered with a hint of suspicion in her voice.

"I'll only be a second. If you don't mind, can I come in and ask him about who gave him that shiner one more time?" *Maybe she'll see I'm just trying to help.*

"Do you have a warrant?"

"E-excuse me?" he asked, baffled. He was used to not being everyone's favorite person as an officer of the law, but this was something more.

"Unless you have a warrant, you cannot come into my house or search my property. I know how *you people* work."

What the fuck?

"You leave my brother alone. He's smart and he's going places. He's a good boy. We don't want any trouble, *officer*." Belle's voice was steady, but her trembling hand gave it away. He glanced at her dainty fingers shaking at her side.

Belle balled them into fists before he considered her face, the fear in her eyes. *She's scared of me.*

"I never intended to cause trouble. Just wanted to make sure he got home safe. Have a good evening, ma'am." He turned and walked back to his truck, utterly speechless.

Defeated, he started the engine and shifted into gear. He needed a good strong drink. A woman's company wouldn't hurt either. Visions of sucking on those red lips and fisting those dark curls made his cock jerk. He gripped the steering wheel until his knuckles turned white.

Too bad it would only be a fantasy and his hand tonight.

2

BELLE

Belle pushed the door open to the locker room and strode past the row of metal closets, then sat on the lone bench in the center of the room. She rubbed her hands over her tired face. It had been another long shift that made her body ache. But this was what she'd worked so long and so hard for since she was eighteen. An education and a job to take care of her and her little brother, so they never had to end up on the streets again.

"Long shift?" Katy asked, hanging her lanyard in her locker before shutting the metal door with a screech.

"Very," Belle answered the woman who'd seemed friendly the few times they'd worked together.

"You should come out with the girls from first shift and me. You've earned a drink after this hellish week. I know I did." Katy pulled her hair down from the tight ponytail.

When was the last time Belle had let loose? Had a drink with girlfriends? She'd been stuck in survival mode for so long. Maybe it was time she took a moment to let out the breath she'd been holding since childhood. TJ was old enough to look after himself, and wasn't he always bugging her to go out or find a hobby?

"Text me the details. I think I can make that happen." Belle stood and opened her locker, quickly switching out her lanyard for her keys.

"Woo-hoo! 'Bout damn time we show you this town. Maybe even get you *some*." Katy smiled and winked.

"That won't be necessary." Belle cringed. She had no want of a man. She could fulfill her own needs—she always had. Life had taught her some valuable lessons the hard way. Men only wanted one thing from a woman, and the second they got it, they were gone. Instead of stuffing down the anger that boiled up inside her, she inhaled long and deep through her nose before exhaling out her mouth. *In with light and love, out with the negative.*

Katy patted her shoulder before reaching for the door. "You say that, but you haven't seen all that this little seacoast town has to offer. Unless I read you wrong and you're looking for some female company?" Katy asked.

"No. I just like being single. Relationships . . . complicate things." It was a canned response that got most well-meaning friends off her back.

"No one said anything about a relationship, girl." Katy giggled and led the way into the long hallway of the hospital.

Belle wasn't that type of girl either. Not that she judged women who were able to separate feelings from sex. God, she wished she could. She just wasn't built like that.

The automatic double doors to the emergency entrance opened and summer's floral fragrance enveloped her, wiping away the sterile hospital scent that always burned her nose.

"See you tonight," Katy called out as Belle opened the door of her car. She took one more pull of clean air before climbing inside and buckling up. Her old Ford rattled to life and a silent ping of gratitude flitted through her. One more thing to be grateful for today. Her car had started. TJ was safe. She had a job that she enjoyed. And now, a potential night on the town with a friend.

* * *

Belle walked in the house and hung her keys on the notch. "TJ?"

"In here," he called from the kitchen. Several books lay open in front of him and he held a pencil in his hand. Upbeat music bled into the room from his earbuds.

She smiled. He had grown up so much, survived hell and still come out such an amazing human being. She loved him more like a son than a brother. It was only fitting because she'd raised him since birth, when she was only seven. Sure, her mother had been "there," but never emotionally, and sometimes she was even physically absent for days at a time.

She reached and plucked one of the white pods from his ear and listened in. "American Funeral" by Alex Da Kid and Joseph Angel blasted through the tiny speaker.

"Studying hard?" she asked, taking a seat across from him at the small table and handing him back his earbud.

"Aren't I always?" He gave a cheeky grin.

"Have you heard anything about the early graduation?"

His grin widened. "It's all set for December before Christmas break. I'll be in college by January."

She flicked the cap off his head. He was cocky, but it was well-deserved.

"Hey!" He picked up the hat and adjusted it a little to the side.

Pride and love welled inside her chest. "That's amazing. What about the scholarships?" Even if he didn't get them, she'd work two full-time jobs if it meant her brother could get through medical school and achieve his dreams.

"Working on finalizing the submissions with the guidance counselor."

She patted his arm, now bigger than hers. She studied her brother's face. The dark purple bruise under his eye made her stomach dip. Concern furrowed her brow. If only he could survive just a few more months in high school, then his life could start as he pursued his own dreams.

Light black scruff shadowed his chin and cheeks in spots, while others were left bare. TJ was somewhere in the middle of the transition from a boy to a man. More gratitude welled inside her, warm and bright. She thanked the universe every day that they had survived.

"How about pizza for dinner? I'm too tired to cook," she suggested.

"I'll never complain about pizza. Pirate's Pizzeria?" He pulled out his phone and punched the contact.

"Get two large and we'll have leftovers." She stood before heading towards the stairs. Worry cinched her chest. "Money is in my purse. Oh, I was gonna go out for a few hours tonight. Stay inside, okay? You can have someone over, but——"

"I know the rules." He waved her off.

She didn't have many, but staying inside from dusk till sunrise was one of them. She didn't want to come home one day and see her brother on the news mistaken for a criminal. One visit from the police, however innocent it seemed, was more than enough.

"I was going to have Mark come over in a couple hours to study. When are you leaving?" TJ asked.

Belle smiled, grateful he had at least one friend in this small town. She pulled her phone out of her pocket and checked her messages.

Katy: *Shipwreck at 8:30.*

"At eight-fifteen. I'm gonna go shower and get ready. Let me know when the pizza is here."

"Will do."

"I love you."

He rolled his eyes. "You too, sis."

As corny as he might have thought her constant reminders were, she wanted him growing up knowing there was always one person in this world he could count on—her and her fierce love.

* * *

Belle checked her reflection in the car mirror as she applied a heavy layer of her favorite fire-engine red lip stain. Her curls were loose around her face, stopping just before her shoulders. She'd squeezed into a pair of white skinny jeans and picked a black off-the-shoulder top. It was nice to dress up in something besides scrubs for once.

Taking a deep breath, she got out of her car in the already full parking lot. Alternative music grew louder each time the front door to the club opened. The stars glittered above in the humid summer night. She walked towards the neon signs and stopped in front of the hulking man with scars on his face and tattoos peeking out from the collar of his shirt.

"ID, please," he said, his deep voice gruff but kind.

She pulled it out of her pocket, and after a quick inspection, he handed it back to her and opened the door.

The place was like something out of a movie. Fish tanks were built into the wall with lights reflecting off the water, bathing the place in a warm blue glow. The timber bar was surrounded by a group of men laughing, most likely on the hunt for someone to keep their bed warm.

"Belle! Over here." A shout from the side had her turning to find Katy surrounded by four other ladies she recognized from the few times she'd worked first shift.

As Belle approached the table, Katy patted the seat next to her. "You look hot, girl. Who knew that body was hiding under those scrubs?"

Belle's cheeks grew warm. She shifted uncomfortably. "Right back at ya, girl. What are we drinking?"

"Shots!" a blond woman yelled loudly enough that Belle assumed she'd already had a few.

"Tina picked the last round. Tawny picked Fireball before that." Katy motioned in a circle, naming the ladies. "Sue picked boring old beer."

"Hey!" Sue whined.

"Now it's Amy's turn."

"Okay, I'll be back, bitches." Amy stood, wobbling a bit. She grabbed the table to steady herself before walking to the bar.

Sue was sitting on the other side of Belle and turned abruptly. "I love your hair. I wish I could get mine to do something creative like that. Is this your real mane?" Sue reached out her hand and Belle's shot out to stop her.

"Don't. Touch. My. Hair . . . please," Belle added with a forced smile.

"Oh, I—uh. I'm sorry. I was just curious," Sue said, draining the few drops left in her empty glass.

Katy laughed. "What about you, Sue? Are those your *real* boobs?"

Sue looked down and then back up at Katy, her cheeks scarlet. "Of course they are."

The other ladies laughed, breaking the tension.

Belle chuckled too. *Maybe this was a good idea after all.*

"Okay, I hope you all like whiskey," Amy said, balancing the glasses on a tray. She handed out one to each woman.

"At this rate, I'm gonna be puking before the end of the night," Tina complained.

"Too bad we can't bring the banana bags home for personal use," Katy joked.

"Don't all look at once, but guess who I saw at the bar?" Amy squealed.

"Who?" Tawny yelled as every one of them turned their heads towards the last man Belle wanted to see.

Cerulean-blue eyes, alert and narrow, he scanned the room—a contrast to his jet-black hair that was slicked to the side. Dark stubble peppered across his strong jaw. The man was *GQ* model-worthy. He looked as if he should be on a billboard selling rare artisan whiskey rather than walking among mere mortals. The almost permanent smirk on his face told her he knew what kind of power he held and how to wield it for his benefit. She swallowed, her eyes traveling to where the T-shirt stretched against his wide muscular chest. His toned arms were not bulky, but defined. The kind that you had to work out regularly for. He obviously cared about how he looked. *He's probably shallow and vain.*

"The sheriff?" Belle confirmed.

Katy turned back to her long enough to answer. "He's, like, only the hottest playboy in the entire seacoast."

"Many women have tried to tame him, but none have succeeded," Tawny added like she was speaking of a mythical creature.

Belle shook her head. So, the man in uniform *was* a player. That was no surprise.

"It was like a rite of passage in high school to sleep with Bently Evans around here," Tina said, dreamily.

"No one's worried about the diseases he could be spreading?" Belle asked bitterly before she drank the liquid that burned her throat.

All five women turned to look at her as if she'd just said the pope was dead.

"He's got a reputation, that's for sure. But, honey, I can tell you from experience that he's worth the heartbreak. That man has magic fingers, a mouth that should be considered illegal, and a heart of gold." Tawny eyed her.

"Not to mention, rumor has it that he has a ladies-first policy," Amy added. "And he gets regular checkups. Because of HIPPA, I can't tell you anything, but let me just say, I'd do him."

"Sounds like the perfect guy." *Perfection isn't real.*

Her skin tingled, prickling with awareness. She glanced up and Bently's ice-blue eyes locked with hers. He smirked and her pulse quickened. She may have been angry at the male species, with good reason, but she was still a woman. Her body reacted to his six-foot-something frame, with his white shirt stretched taut against those bulky muscles. The man was pure lust, and she wanted none of it. He was just like all the rest, looking for another notch on his bedpost. Hell would freeze over before she became one.

Belle focused on her drink, draining it quickly.

The woman tending the bar approached them and switched out their drinks with a round of Sex on The Beach. "From an admirer."

"Come on, Charli, put us out of our misery and tell us it was from Prince Charming," Amy begged.

Charli rolled her eyes. "From the flirt himself."

"Seems like someone's piqued his fancy." Katy eyed Belle suspiciously as Charli walked away.

Belle didn't give him the satisfaction of looking up for the rest of the night. Katy's round was next, and she chose something fruity and potent. They all laughed together about antics from work.

"That's nothing. Once I had a patient come in because she didn't think she had to remove a tampon before putting another one in." Katy shook her head.

"Where did she think they would go?" Tina asked.

"She thought they just dissolved!" Katy laughed.

Belle cringed.

"Bently keeps staring over here," Tawny said.

"Maybe he wants round two after all with you," Belle suggested.

Amy shook her head. "Bently hasn't dipped his pen in Shattered Cove ink in years, to many single ladies' dismay."

"And some married ones." Tawny giggled.

"Ever since he became sheriff," Katy clarified.

"All we get is his grade-A flirting. I heard he goes to the city for company now." Tina sighed.

I wonder why.

No. Belle had no business giving that man any precious real estate in her mind.

"I gotta get home to my husband and boys. I'll see you ladies at work next week." Tawny stood.

"Do you mind if I catch a ride with you?" Tina asked.

"Sure thing. Good night, ladies."

"Good night."

"I'm gonna go say hello to that fine-looking man over by the stage. Don't wait up for me," Sue said, pushing her breasts a little higher.

"Just us left?" Katy motioned to Amy and Belle.

"Looks like it. I'll run to the bathroom and grab another round," Belle said, sliding off her stool. The room swirled around her as she reached out her hand and steadied herself on the table. It had been a while since she'd had a few drinks, and three of them had her tipsy. *Guess I'll be hailing a cab tonight.*

It didn't matter, because for the first time in a long time, she was relaxed and happy.

Belle went to the bathroom and washed her hands. She smacked her lips together, happy her lip stain hadn't budged in hours. Heading out the door, her foot caught and she stumbled. Two strong arms caught her before she could face-plant and embarrass herself. Electricity tore through her. Her body hummed with heat. She gasped.

"Thank you." She looked up at her savior and her breath hitched. *Whoa. He's even hotter up close.*

"No problem, beautiful," Bently said, the smirk on his mouth reaching pantie-melting territory. *Pantie-melting? What the hell is wrong with me?*

"Oh, fuck."

He chuckled.

Shit, I said that aloud.

"I like that idea." His hungry gaze raked across her skin like hot coals, blistering her with need.

No! This man is a man. A tragic flirt. And he's a cop. And he's a white-man-cop. Her brain worked overtime to reason with her drunk self.

She jerked out of his grasp, quickly righting herself. The pulsing energy fizzled to a simmer between them, giving her at least some clarity.

"I hear there isn't much you don't like," she said, but kept her tone as even as she could, without the heat of the anger that lurked deep within her. *Men like him in power have very big egos that are highly fragile.*

"I think we got off on the wrong foot. However, I'd like to help you wake up on the right side of the bed." He chuckled and his grin widened.

Anger rose, quickly morphing into fury. How dare he think she was just some easy one-night ride that he could use up and turn back onto the street? He had a whole queue of willing participants, so why target her? Bently was just like all the other men of her past.

"Does that line actually work on women?" she snapped.

His smile faltered.

"Look, buddy." She poked his chest as he frowned. Damn, even that was hot. "I'm not sleeping with you. There are several ladies in here who are looking for what you have to offer, but I'll never be one of them." She turned on her heel and walked away with her head held high.

Damn that man and her traitorous body that craved to know what his hands would feel like on her skin.

But after one night with him, there was only one emotion she would be feeling—regret.

3

BELLE

Belle's back ached as she walked down the hall towards the break room. She'd been on her feet for almost twelve hours now and was in desperate need of coffee.

"There's my favorite nurse." The deep voice had her glancing to her right.

"Doctor Stanley, what can I do for you?" She smiled at the good-looking doctor, fighting the urge to check her watch to see how many minutes were left on her shift.

"Room six needs your competent hands."

She nodded. "No problem."

"Thank you," he called after her as she rounded the corner, finally giving into the temptation to look at the time on her wristwatch. Twenty minutes left.

She knocked on the door and Doctor Burton called her in.

Belle had seen her fair share of blood and broken bones in the emergency department. But nothing prepared her for the sight in front of her. Her breath caught and tears prickled the back of her eyes, but she kept her expression void of the violent reaction wreaking havoc inside her body. The woman lay on the hospital bed, both eyes so bruised they were black, and so swollen they were shut. Her arm lay at an odd angle as she tucked herself in a ball. More bruises marred her arms, and legs. Belle forced a slow inhale to steady herself as she got to work helping Doctor Burton. This was why Doctor Stanley had sent her in here. Belle was one of the few in the hospital trained as a Sexual Assault Nurse Examiner.

"Okay, Brynn, Nurse Belle is going to help me set that arm so we can get it in a cast," Doctor Burton said, adopting a more soothing tone.

The patient nodded slowly and winced as if even that small movement was too painful. "My son. Is he . . ."

"I had Nurse Katy bring him down to the cafeteria. He's getting some food in his belly," Doctor Burton answered.

"Thank you," Brynn said.

"Brynn, honey, we have to ask with injuries like this—were you sexually assaulted?" Belle asked.

Brynn's body began to tremble. Belle laid her hand gently on her shoulder, careful to exert only enough pressure so that her patient would know she was not alone in this.

"Not this time," she whispered.

Belle grit her teeth together as her heart broke for this woman. It was better not to wonder how she got stuck in this type of situation. She didn't need her medical degree to know that one in four women would experience violence from their partner, and nearly one in three women would be sexually assaulted in their lifetime. She'd experienced firsthand the dangers of domestic violence and how easy it was to believe that you were trapped. *If only I could have protected myself.* Just one more reminder that she'd promised herself she'd learn self-defense and never got around to it. If TJ ever had to see her like that . . .

"Would you like to talk to an officer and press charges?" Doctor Burton asked.

Brynn tensed as she sat straighter and shook her head vehemently, then cried out in pain. "No! No cops."

She shifted to the edge of the bed while Belle reached out her other hand to steady her.

"I shouldn't have come," Brynn hissed through gritted teeth.

"Yes. You should have." Belle spoke up. "You did the right thing. Your arm needs to be set and your injuries checked over. It is your right to refuse to report this. And it's our job to offer you confidentiality. We can help you so you can heal, and if you are interested, we can offer you resources so you never have to go back." This was the hardest part of the job. The moment when the abused might return into the arms of their oppressor.

Belle waited, holding her breath.

"Are you sure? There won't be *any* police?" Brynn asked hesitantly.

"I promise." Belle nodded.

Brynn took a deep inhale, wincing before she let it out. "Okay. I—I can't go back. He'll kill us. I need help. My son . . . he deserves better," Brynn said, easing somewhat back onto the bed.

Belle motioned to Doctor Burton that she was ready to begin.

After her patient's arm was wrapped in a cast, Belle took a few pictures of the injuries with Brynn's permission to keep in her file.

"Are you hungry?" Belle asked.

"I could use a cup of tea, and maybe some crackers."

"Coming right up." Belle glanced at the clock on the wall. She was past quitting time, but it didn't matter anymore. This was why she'd gone into medicine. To help women like this.

Because I couldn't save my mother.

Rounding the corner, she dug in her pocket for her credit card.

"Good evening." The deep voice rumbled, sending a bolt of lust through her body. She snapped her head up to find the sheriff in a pair of jeans that clung to his muscular thighs and a T-shirt that said "Seaview Construction" across his broad chest.

"Like what you see?" He chuckled, and her cheeks flushed hot.

"Are you stalking me now?" she hissed.

His brow furrowed and he held up his hands as if to placate her. "Darlin', I'm the man who catches the criminals, and from what I can tell, the only crime being committed here is that scowl across your beautiful face."

Heat flooded over her. Her head rang as she tried to form a sentence that made sense enough after a response like that. Irritation prickled her skin. "Why are you here, then?" She crossed her arms over her chest.

His eyes dropped before flicking back to her gaze, his sky-blue spheres darkening.

"Katy called about a DV situation."

Right. *My patient.* Brynn had made it very clear she didn't want to talk to the cops, something she had in common with the woman.

Belle held out her hand and shook her head. "You wasted a trip, officer. My patient doesn't want to press charges or report anything."

He sighed, the concern on his face seemingly genuine. "Let me at least try."

"I can't allow you in there. She's already refused."

"Will she speak with a female officer?" Bently's eyebrows came together to form a triangle.

Belle shook her head. "No."

His fists clenched at his side. Belle took a step back from him. Was he violent?

"I hate these calls," he said as if sensing her fears and offering up an explanation.

"She's agreed to use our resources. She's going to leave the situation. But really, what could you do for her?"

"I could arrest the son of a bitch who thought it was okay to put his hands on a woman," he said, his voice rising.

His answer earned a little respect from her, but she wouldn't let him know that. "Would it stick? If it's his first offense, he might get a pass or minimal time in jail. What if he's got money? He could pay his way out to make this all disappear."

"So, we should do nothing? We shouldn't even try? Is that what you're saying?" he growled, anger emanating off him in waves.

"No, what I'm saying is every situation is unique. We can't help someone who isn't ready to help themselves. I'll make sure she gets counseling and a safe haven. I'm trained with how to deal with these types of situations. I'm a SANE nurse."

Bently just stared at her, the corner of his eyes wrinkling as he studied her.

"A SANE nurse—you know, a Sexual Assault Nurse Examiner."

"I know what that is."

"Okay. Well, even you have to admit that the system isn't very good at helping victims. She has to have her reasons for fearing for her life and not making a report. My money is on her survival instincts. She did the hard part already, by leaving. Now I'll get her the support she needs to stay gone."

He ran a hand over his face, and sighed, drawing her attention to his overgrown five o'clock shadow. God, that was sexy.

"I guess I'll head home then, since there's nothing for me to do here." He raked a hand through his messy hair, his shoulders slumped.

There was that niggling feeling of disappointment again.

He took one step forward and leaned in, invading her space. Bently smelled like coffee and oak. Woodsy. Manly. The energy between them crackled as she stood frozen in place. His gaze locked on to hers as he glanced at her lips. Her brain was screaming at her to do something, move away, tell him off, but her body wasn't budging—too caught up on fumes of lust and intoxication of some sort of magic pheromones.

"Have a good night, darlin'." He turned away and walked towards the exit.

Her heart thundered in her chest as anger burned her veins. How could she have been so weak? He'd come close to kissing her! Fuck!

"Don't call me darlin'!" she snapped, trying to regain some semblance of control of herself and the situation. What was this man doing to her?

Brynn was admitted for the night. Belle got her settled with her son in a room before finally clocking off. She was dead on her feet, drained from the long shift, her last patient, and her run-in with Sheriff Hotness.

"Ugh," she grumbled, opening her locker. Thank god she had the next two days off. It would give her time to relax before she came in and did it all over again.

"You heading out?" Katy peered her head inside.

"Yeah."

"You up for a self-defense class with me tomorrow? It's free," Katy asked in a singsong voice.

"Self-defense?" Brynn's battered face popped into her mind immediately. It was time Belle made her own safety a priority. "When is it?"

"Tomorrow at seven."

"I'll be there. Send me the address," Belle agreed. It might feel good to sweat and punch things for a little while. Not to mention hone the skills for survival as a woman.

Maybe then she'd be able to fight off these urges a little better.

4

BELLE

A gust of warm wind blew against Belle's skin as she adjusted her sports bra and grabbed her water bottle from her front console.

"You ready to kick some ass?" Katy asked from across the parking lot.

Belle glanced up and shut her door. "Sure am."

She walked beside her friend towards Tidal Gym. "Have you ever taken a self-defense class before?" Katy asked.

Belle shook her head.

"Well, this one will be fun *and* educational." Katy opened the door for her.

Belle entered the brightly lit, large room. Various workout equipment lined the edges of the space. A full-size boxing ring was staged off to the far corner where two women sparred in head gear and taped hands.

"Kickboxing. I've always wanted to learn." Katy pointed. "The lockers are through there if you ever need them. There's a room across from them for private classes. That's where we're going."

Excitement and nervousness weaved a tangled web in Belle's belly. This was something new for her to conquer, a challenge and a goal she'd set for herself long ago. But life had always seemed to get in the way.

She walked into the room as a gaggle of other ladies all turned towards her entrance. Disappointment flitted across their faces before they swiveled back to each other, resuming their conversations. *Sorry to rain on your parade.*

Katy dropped her water bottle near the edge and Belle followed suit. Her reflection stared back at her in the mirrored walls. A few pieces of bright red equipment lay stacked neatly in the corner.

"How often do you come to these?" Belle asked.

"As often as I can. The Shattered Cove police department puts them on for free for women in cycles of six weeks. They also run a separate class for kids to deal with bullying and trouble at home." Katy leaned against one of the mirrors with her arms crossed.

"Wow. That's a really great resource." It was sure to change lives. How much better would her childhood have been if she'd had a place like this to go to for help?

"Yeah, the instructors are volunteer-based and the department does fundraising during the year to pay to rent this space," Katy continued.

"I've never heard of a town doing this—at least not this often."

"I don't think there is one. Luckily for us, the topic of women and children's safety is a priority for our sheriff." Katy smiled.

Bently had organized this?

"Well, hello, ladies." The deep voice confirmed her thoughts. She cut Katy a pointed look. Her friend just winked at her.

A chorus of "hellos" answered him back as several women crowded his space. One woman touched his arm as she spoke. Bently stepped out of her reach as another woman all but shoved her boobs in his face. Belle shook her head as her stomach flipped uneasily. Bently smiled and nodded politely to the group as he made his way into the room. Another lady followed him inside, her dark hair pulled back into a tight bun.

"Ladies, you remember Deputy Vargas. She's going to be helping me today," Bently said, scanning the room.

Belle stood tall. She was here because she wanted to learn. She wasn't going to let some playboy sheriff take that from her. His eyes met hers before a smile broke out on his perfectly chiseled face. She hated how her breath faltered.

She gave him her best disinterested expression while holding his stare, willing her eyes not to scan over his muscle shirt to ogle those perfectly toned arms.

"Alright, everyone, let's form a wide circle," Bently said as he and Vargas walked to the center.

"How many of you have taken a self-defense class before?" Vargas asked. Several of the women raised their hands.

"Okay, what we're going to do is run through a few scenarios that could happen, and show you how you can best protect yourself," Bently said, turning around. Belle's eyes slid down, swallowing hard at the view of his firm backside.

"Could bounce a quarter off that ass," Katy whispered in her ear.

Belle couldn't argue. The woman spoke the truth.

"Who wants to be the first volunteer?" Bently asked.

Every woman's hand in the group went up except Belle's. Vargas shook her head.

Bently chuckled. "Glad to see so much enthusiasm."

His eyes locked on hers again. A tingle of fear swept through her. She just needed to put everything else out of her mind, ignore the way he sent a hurricane of different emotions swirling inside her, and focus on the task at hand.

"Katy," Bently called.

Belle sighed with relief as her friend walked over and stood next to Bently. "Let's say you're walking down the street and some guy grabs you like this." He placed his hand over Katy's forearm.

"To get out of his hold, you'll want to put your own hand over his knuckles, like this." He moved Katy's free hand over his. "Then you'll need to swing your arm around to grab his wrist."

Katy did as he said.

"Now push down," Bently directed.

Katy shifted. Bently fell to his knees with his arm held back at an odd angle. "Very good."

She smiled as she let him go and then took a small bow.

"Now, you all break up into teams of two and try it yourself," Vargas instructed.

Katy returned to Belle's side and grabbed her wrist. Belle moved through the steps and had her friend on her knees quick enough. She'd had to be a fast learner in order to survive.

Bently and Vargas walked around the circle, guiding the women through the moves.

"Nice form," Bently said, smiling at her. She nodded before he continued on. Belle gripped Katy's arm as they switched turns.

A redhead sidled up to Bently, pushing her large breasts against him. "Can I try on a real man?"

"Sure, Marcy." Bently grabbed her arm, putting some distance between them. Marcy went through the moves, and he obligingly bent to the ground.

"I love when a man gets on his knees. Makes me want to return the favor." She winked.

Katy snorted as Belle's cheeks heated. Why should it bother her that the woman was throwing herself at Bently? He was a player and she had no interest in him. But it grated on her nerves anyway.

Bently stood. "Vargas, why don't you take over here and show Marcy the next position."

"Marcy's been throwing herself at him since high school," Katy whispered.

"Probably sniffing around for seconds," Belle mumbled.

Katy quirked her eyebrow.

"What?" Belle asked.

"You like him."

Belle rolled her eyes. "Don't be ridiculous."

Bently and Vargas demonstrated another evasive move that had him on his back, pinned to the ground.

"Honey, there's no shame. He's more godlike than man."

"He's nice to look at, but that's it," Belle conceded.

"He's also never given Marcy anything but a polite smile. So, you can sleep well tonight knowing the man has standards." Katy laughed.

Damn the flutter in her chest and the relief that washed over her like a tidal wave.

"I'm gonna run to the bathroom really quick," Katy said before scampering out of the room.

"Okay, ladies, now you try," Vargas said. The teams of women sprang into action. Belle stepped back, waiting for her friend's return.

Bently stood next to her. "Looks like you need a partner."

Belle took a longing glance at the door before she nodded. "I guess I do."

"Get down."

Belle lay on her back on the mat flooring.

Bently knelt between her thighs and reached out his hands for her throat. She shuddered. It had been a long time since any man had been this close to her. Everywhere his body gently nudged hers, zings of electricity shot through her. Her breathing grew more uneven as she tried to get a hold of herself.

"Now wrap your legs around my lower back in a close guard to secure me." His voice was gravelly. She followed his directions, bringing his face close enough to notice the small scar separating the rough stubble on his chin. His woodsy scent made her head dizzy. He smelled good—too good.

It's just biology. He's a hot guy, and our bodies are close. And it's been a really long time.

"Then lift your arms and secure them around my elbows by pushing them closer together."

Sucking in a shaky burst of oxygen, she did as he said. She was glad to have his directions because with him touching her like this, it was hard to remember her own name. The movement pressed her breasts against his arms. Her nipples hardened and peaked. Heat rose to her cheeks, blanketing her whole body as the sensitive buds rubbed against him. There was no way he couldn't feel it through the thin material of her sports bra. His eyes bore into hers rather than glancing at her cleavage. His restraint earned him a little bit of her respect. His body trembled as if he too was struggling to remain in control.

"Now what?" she asked, her voice breathier than she'd intended.

"Uh, now you release my waist and throw your legs around my shoulders and squeeze. Then lift up with your hips."

She did so and he released her before sitting back on his heels. "Good."

She panted, as she burned from the inside out.

"Bently, can you show me too?" Marcy asked in a seductive tone.

His gaze remained on Belle as he answered her. "Yeah, I just need a minute."

"What did I miss?" Katy asked, rejoining Belle.

"Belle can show you." Bently got up. "I'll be right back," he said, before leaving the room.

"Damn, girl. I leave you alone for ten minutes and you gave the teacher a hard-on."

Belle's attention snapped to her friend. "No I didn't!" *Did I?*

Marcy glared at her from across the room.

"I'm just joking," Katy teased.

Was it possible Bently was just as affected by her as she was by him? Then again, it probably didn't take much to get a man like him going.

Belle got up and grabbed her bottle of water. She took long gulps of the cool liquid in hopes it would help quell the fire inside.

I need to order a new vibrator.

"Okay, ladies, let's move into the next position," Vargas instructed.

Bently came back in a few minutes later and they resumed class. He gave every woman the same attention, smiling and being polite and professional. He either ignored Marcy's come-ons or used Vargas as a buffer. Though his gaze found Belle's several times over the course of the class, and lingered.

Bently didn't quite fit the original view she'd had of him. He didn't seem arrogant, but rather humble and confident. He knew how to work a room of women, but he was respectful. He hadn't made one flirty comment the whole class. Not to mention the fact that this whole thing was his idea. Why was protecting women and children a priority for him? Was it just because he was a good guy? Or was it something more personal than that?

Maybe they did have something in common after all.

5

BENTLY

Cold water rained down on Bently's slick skin. The bite was needed to calm his arousal. For the second week in a row, Belle had come to his class in a sports bra and leggings that left almost nothing to his imagination—and he had a vivid one. He prided himself on his professionalism, and having to leave class to deal with his hard-on was anything but appropriate. That had never happened during a lesson for him. He was supposed to be showing these women how to defend themselves against attackers, not fantasize about how Belle would look on her hands and knees while he pounded into her from behind that sweet, shapely ass.

Damn. He was at full mast just thinking about her. The way she smelled like vanilla and cocoa butter. Her full red lips that he just wanted to bite. His palm wound around his hard cock. If a cold shower wouldn't work, then he had to take matters into his own hands.

He closed his eyes imagining her dark curls swept onto the mat. They'd be the only two people in the classroom. She'd pant with him on top of her, her body trembling with her own need. He'd lean close, his lips brushing hers lightly. She'd squeeze her legs around him, pulling him closer. His hand pumped faster, envisioning it was her reaching down to stroke him. His spine tingled with the building pressure. Those brown eyes would look up at him as she said, "I want you. Fuck me, Bently."

His self-control would snap. He'd tear off her leggings, and she'd be bare underneath, already so wet and ready for him. He'd slip inside with one quick thrust. They'd moan together because they felt so good. He tightened his fist around his shaft, moving it faster and faster. His abs clenched as his release spurted all over the tile wall. Bently groaned as pleasure shot through him. He took a moment to get his ragged breathing under control, switching the water to nearly scalding.

What was Belle doing to him? He never obsessed about a woman like this. He just needed to fuck her and get her out of his system.

Fifteen minutes later, he was staring at the array of police reports on his bed. He had just enough time to browse through the cases again before leaving to meet the boys at the bar. He dried off his hair, then tied the towel around his waist. He'd brought work home because he'd hit a dead end with all of them. Muggings, break-ins, and some minor complaints with very few witnesses wasn't a lot to go on. There'd been no trace of the perpetrator. Whoever was responsible knew how to avoid being caught. They were like ghosts.

Smash! Beep! Beep! Beep!

What the hell?

Bently rushed over to the window that overlooked his dark front lawn. He pulled on a pair of sweatpants and grabbed his Glock before he rushed down the stairs and out the front door.

"Fuck!" His truck's windshield had a large hole in it and spiderweb cracks weaving through the smashed glass.

Adrenaline coursed in his veins. He turned around, searching the area for any movement. Nothing caught his eye except a few nosy neighbors whose porch lights quickly flicked on as their curtains moved.

Bently ran inside and grabbed his keys and phone from the bowl by the door and shut the alarm off.

"Everything okay over there, Sheriff?" Nosy Nancy Plotts asked from across the street.

Why was this happening in his town, and now to his own property? Why would someone do that? He ran a hand through his hair. Plenty of people disliked the police—but in Shattered Cove, things were generally quiet. Well, until recently.

"Sheriff?" Nancy asked.

"Yes, ma'am. Nothing to worry about."

After dialing Vargas, he called in the incident. He went back inside and got dressed properly before dialing his brother.

"What's up?" Mikel answered.

"Can you pick me up before you head on over to the bar?"

"Sure, I can't stay too long tonight though. It's my turn to put the kids to bed."

"No problem."

"See you soon."

Ding-dong.

He buttoned up his shirt and jogged down the stairs to open the door.

"Vargas," he greeted her.

"Evans. Looks like you've had some trouble."

He headed outside with her, careful to lock his front door. "I didn't ask the neighbors if they saw anything, but by the time I made it out, there was no trace of the dickhead that did this."

"I got Lincoln on his way to tow it to his garage. Said he'd have it fixed up quick for ya." She walked towards his driveway shaking her head. "Any theories?"

"Probably some punk kid who thought he'd show off to his friends and smash the sheriff's truck," he said dryly.

"You sure you didn't piss off any woman in class tonight? Marcy get tired of being shut down time and time again?" She smirked.

He shook his head. "I've been a choir boy. Besides, you know I don't shit where I eat." *Until Belle, I've never been tempted.*

She laughed. "You, Bently Evans, are many things, but a choir boy will never be one of them. You forget I've known you since junior high."

"I've grown up a lot since then," he argued.

"That's true." She eyed him up and down.

"How's Millie?"

Vargas beamed. "Millie is successfully halfway through her pregnancy."

"That's awesome. You two will be great moms. Do you know what you're having yet?"

"A human, hopefully," she deadpanned.

He chuckled. "Guess I walked into that one."

"We find out if it's got a sausage or a taco at the appointment next week."

"That's exciting. I went with Jasmine when she found out with Zoey—it was definitely something special." His chest tightened at the memory. His sister had been through so much, and now she was a damn good single mother.

"Looks like your brother's here." Vargas pointed over his shoulder.

"I'll see you in a couple hours at the station." He waved goodbye and hurried to get to Mikel.

Sliding into the passenger side of the truck, Bently sighed.

"What happened?" Mikel asked, backing out onto the street.

"Someone smashed my windshield into smithereens."

"Why?"

"Let's not talk about it. I'm already pissed off enough. I just need a drink and to relax."

Mikel chuckled. "Is it just the car that's bothering you?"

Bently shook his head.

"Rough week?" Mikel asked.

"That's the understatement of the fucking century."

* * *

Once they arrived at The Shipwreck, Bently found a seat at the bar and Mikel took the one next to him.

"Andre still coming?" Bently asked.

"As far as I know."

"Good. I got a little something special planned for him."

Mikel's eyebrows formed a triangle.

"Mia is meeting me here soon."

"What can I get you guys tonight?" Charli asked.

"A very large, very cold beer, please," Bently said.

"Pepsi for me." Mikel gave Bently a once-over as Charli got to work getting their drinks.

"What?"

"You don't seem like your usual self. Something wrong? Is it the car thing?" Mikel asked.

"Nah. That's probably some kid with an issue with authority. Maybe I gave him a ticket or something. Hazards of the job."

"So, what is it?" Mikel wasn't dropping the subject.

Bently sighed. "There's this woman."

Mikel clapped a hand over his chest. "Thank god. I thought you were gonna tell me you had cancer again or something."

Bently shook his head. "Nope." The reminder stung. One more reason he wasn't a whole man.

"Well, don't leave me hanging," Mikel said, as Charli delivered their drinks. Bently handed over a twenty, then shrugged. "Not much to tell. She's *fine*. I mean a ten out of ten."

"Is she married?"

"No. Nothing like that. She just won't give me a chance. But I can't get her out of my head. No other woman even sparks my interest anymore." Bently took a long sip of his beer. He wouldn't tell his brother this lack of interest had been going on long before he met Belle.

"She immune to the Bently Evans charm?" Mikel smirked.

"Seems to be a bit more than that." He sighed.

"Why'd you invite Mia, then?"

"To get Andre's stubborn ass back into enjoying life."

Mikel glanced up. "Look what the cat dragged in."

"What are you two troublemakers up to tonight?" Andre asked, taking a seat next to Bently.

"Bent is having a bit of woman trouble," Mikel supplied.

Andre exaggerated his shocked expression. "The myth, the legend, the man-whore of Shattered Cove is having . . . woman troubles?"

Bently punched his arm hard enough to leave a bruise. "It's not like you could help. You've been a fucking priest for the last year, unless you hooked up with that blonde awhile back?" He smirked.

Andre shook his head. "Nah, I don't have it in me to take the kind of risks you do."

"What risks? My heart isn't ever involved. I think you might be defective—you are the only man I've ever known to always get his heart involved when he uses his dick. Don't you know they're separate organs?" Bently chuckled and took another swig of his beer.

"I meant risks like herpes, you dumb fuck." Andre smacked his friend's back.

"What can I get you, Dre?" Charli asked, interrupting their chiding.

"I think I need the hard stuff tonight," Andre answered.

"It's probably the only thing that gets hard for you anymore." Bently chuckled and Mikel burst out laughing. He needed to poke the bear for his plan to work.

"Bently likes a woman who won't give him the time of day," Mikel said, changing the subject.

"What? Your charms are not working on someone for once?" Andre's smug smirk brought a wave of defeat crashing over Bently like a bucket of ice water.

"They seem to have the opposite effect on her actually," he grumbled.

A very beautiful woman with dark hair entered the bar, her gaze scanning the room until it locked on his and she smiled. He grinned as a spark of determination lightened his chest. "You know what they say though, try, try again. I think I'll practice a little more with Mia." He laughed.

Mia approached them with a hesitant smile directed at him. Andre's body tensed beside him. *Jackpot.*

"Hey, baby," Bently said, standing up to give Mia a hug.

"Another." Andre waved to Charli, having downed his first whiskey already.

"Sorry I'm late," Mia said, adjusting the strap of her dress. The woman was gorgeous, but she still did nothing for him. Her touch didn't elicit sparks. Mia's closeness didn't make breathing difficult. He saw her the same as Charli—as a friend.

"You're right on time and my you look delicious." He put the flirt on extra thick, knowing it was going to drive his friend nuts.

Mia laughed. "Is he always this much?"

Mikel answered her. "Bently never changes. His ego is bigger than anyone else I know."

"That's not all that big, unlike some of my other body parts," Bently said, purposely revving up his buddy.

Andre scowled.

"Don't mind our rude friend—he's just cranky because he hasn't gotten laid in a loooong time," Bently joked as Andre turned around to face them.

Mia's eyes darted from Andre to the dance floor, her cheeks glowing with a slight blush. "That's okay. How about a dance?" she asked Bently.

He hooked his arm around her waist and led her towards the other couples. Mikel was talking to Andre while his best friend glared daggers at him.

He spun Mia and nodded to Mikel who got up and winked on his way out. She felt good against him, but as beautiful as she was, she didn't make him want to throw caution to the wind and . . . and what? Break his rule for one night that was sure to be amazing, just to get her out of his system, and then? It wasn't like he could do more than one night with Belle anyways. Maybe he needed to make that clear to her.

She may not like him very much, but the way her body reacted to his told him she was attracted to him too.

"How are you enjoying Shattered Cove so far?" he asked Mia. He could ask Belle for a brief encounter—a short and dangerous hookup.

"It's nice. And small." She smiled.

"It sure is."

She chuckled before resting her head on Bently's shoulder as they moved to the slow music. Bently slid his hand down her waist to the small of her back, knowing full well it would drive his friend crazy. The man was too stubborn for his own good. Anyone with two eyes could see these two had a thing for each other. If Andre wasn't going to man up, it was Bently's duty as his best friend to push him into the deep end.

A rough tap on his shoulder brought a smile to his face.

"Mind if I cut in?" Andre said brusquely.

"About damn time."

Mia looked between the two men.

"I gotta get going anyways. You'll make sure she gets home safe?" Bently asked.

"Of course." Andre wrapped his arms around Mia as they started to dance.

At least he could still do something right. Now, he needed to man up and ask Belle if she'd be interested in fucking this out of their systems for one night only. The sooner he had her, the sooner he could move on with his life and get out of this funk.

A knock sounded at Bently's closed office door. "Come in." He shuffled the papers on his desk into a neat pile as Officer Luke Parsons walked in. The older man nodded and pulled out a seat for himself across from Bently. "Good afternoon, Sheriff. Man, after all these years, it still seems weird that the same newbie I trained is now my boss." Parsons tapped his fingers on Bently's ancient wood desk.

"Tell me about it." Bently smiled.

"I heard your truck got done in last week."

Bently sighed. "Yeah, probably kids. What can I do for you today?"

Parsons sighed and leaned back in the metal chair. "I had a run-in with a group of kids spray-painting those abandoned buildings on Kent Street."

Bently nodded. "Did you catch 'em?"

"I may be old, but I'm still light on my feet." Parsons chuckled.

More like your partner is. Bently eyed the man's bulging belly.

"We caught two of them."

"You got them fingerprinted and booked?"

Parsons sat a little straighter. "One kid was Mary Braxton's boy. I gave him a warning and brought the other one in for booking."

Bently's brows furrowed. "Why not give both of them a warning, or book the lot of them?"

"It was just kids being kids. Abandoned building and all, I didn't think there was much harm done. Scared the shit out of them when we blared the sirens."

"So why arrest just the one, then?"

"I just had a feeling that this one was trouble. Maybe you want to consider him for that mugging involving Andre Stone. Fits the description he gave us." Parsons set a file on his desk. Just one more in the seemingly endless pile of paperwork.

"Why didn't you bring this to Deputy Vargas?" Bently asked.

Parsons rolled his eyes—something no one else in the small department would dare do. But the man was old enough to be Bently's father, and taking orders from a man young enough to be your son was hard on most people. "The princess was not in her office. Probably getting her nails done. Besides, she tends to be lenient with *these* types of cases."

"Vargas is a damn fine officer—that's why she's my deputy," Bently said, hating that he had to say anything at all. Sure, ribbing was normal on the job, but it still didn't sit right with Bently.

Parsons held out his hands as he laughed. "No offense, snowflake. Didn't realize it was that time of the month for you. I just wanted to make sure this crime was solved. Excuse me for trying to do my job."

Bently raked a hand over his face and stood. "Alright. I'll call Dre in to see if it's the same kid who mugged him."

Parsons grunted as he got to his feet, seeming to take extra effort.

Bently should really talk to him about retirement, but a small-town sheriff had to take what he could get for help.

"Alright, I'll have Owens put the kid in holding until you have your friend make an ID."

After Parsons left, Bently picked up his phone and dialed his best friend.

"Hey, man. What's up?"

"Dre, can you come down to the station? Just need you to look at a picture and confirm if someone we got into custody is your mugger's accomplice."

"Be there in ten."

Bently opened the door, finding Betsy his secretary blowing her nose into her handkerchief. Her platinum-gold curls were never out of place, though she was nearing seventy. She touched the same strand of pearls around her neck she wore every single day as she smiled up at him. "Mister Evans, do you need something?"

"How about you order us both some lunch from the High Tide Diner. It's on me." He handed over his credit card.

"You want your usual?"

He nodded. "Yeah, but have them add a chocolate milkshake this time too." He gave her a wink.

"Absolutely." She opened a drawer and pulled out a tan purse before heading out the door.

The office was silent. Bently walked back to his desk, not bothering to close his door, and pulled open the folder. A picture of a young boy who couldn't be more than thirteen stared back at him. He shook his head. So young and already in the system thanks to a bad decision and Officer Parsons's gut feeling.

A few minutes later, Andre's voice called out. "Bent?"

"In here."

Dre peeked his head inside before walking in. His dark-brown skin was spotted with a mixture of sawdust and white flecks of plaster.

"Came from the worksite?"

Dre nodded. "Yeah. Your brother is driving me nuts, so I could use the break."

Bently chuckled and gestured to the metal chair across from him. Andre sat and scooted forward, his elbows rested on the worn wooden desk. Bently pushed the array of images towards Andre, studying his reaction.

Andre shook his head. "Not him."

"You sure? None of them?"

Andre pointed to each photo. "Nope. No. Definitely not. And this kid is way too young. He's just a baby. Was he arrested?"

Bently glanced at the face of the kid that Parsons had arrested. "Yeah. For resisting arrest after being caught vandalizing the abandoned buildings on Kent."

Andre shook his head. "No one cares about those eyesores. Hell, we used to do it. Who brought him in?"

"Officer Luke Parsons and his partner."

"Figures."

Bently frowned. "What is that supposed to mean?"

Andre sat back in his chair. "Oh, come on, Bent. You know that guy's got a hard-on for targeting a *certain* group of people. He's pulled me over more times than I can count. You can't let him get this kid into the system."

"Are you saying he's racist?" No way. The man had been a

cop longer than Bently had been alive. He was one of the good guys.

"Are *you* saying you really don't know?" Dre shot back.

"Parsons is from a different generation. He likes to joke around and give everyone a hard time. That's just who he is. But he's a good cop."

With all the racial tension peaking in the country, he understood why Belle reacted the way she had towards him. He didn't have to like being lumped in with the few bad apples and others who hid behind the badge to sweep their misdeeds under the rug.

I'm one of the good ones and so are my team.

"Sure, that's why I came in here to look at a boy who doesn't fit the description of the mugger's accomplice except for one thing." Andre held out his finger. "The color of his skin. But all Black people look the same to some."

Is Parsons racist? The man had been his mentor. Parsons was a prickly old bastard, but he gave everyone a hard time. "Doesn't he have coffee with your dad every week at the diner?"

"Yeah. You're right. He has a Black friend, so he can't be racist," Andre said, sarcasm dripping from every syllable.

"That's not what I meant."

"It's alright. You wouldn't understand anyways." Andre waved him off.

"You need to get laid and let off some steam, my friend."

Andre growled, "And you need to mind your own fucking business."

"Ooh touchy subject." Bently chuckled. "Thanks for coming in. And for your thoughts on Parsons. I haven't seen it myself, but I'll definitely keep it in mind."

"No problem." Andre stood just as Betsy returned with her hands full.

"Miss Betsy, you have a nice day. Don't let this guy work you too hard," Andre said, nodding as he left.

"Have a good one yourself, young man." Betsy set Bently's food containers in front of him before carefully placing a plastic fork on top along with his credit card.

"Thank you, Betsy."

"I don't know how you can stand that rabbit food every day," she mumbled, motioning to his Caesar salad before walking slowly out to her own desk.

He didn't much care for it either, but his health was important. Too many people were counting on him and he couldn't afford to get sick again.

Unfortunately, his lunch would have to wait a little longer. First, he needed to sort out this mess Parsons had left on his desk. The kid had no prior record and the few hours he'd spent in holding should be enough to deter him from future bad decisions involving a spray can. Bently would call in a favor and get the charges dropped in exchange for the kid agreeing to work with Aaron at Hope Facility. This kid deserved a fighting chance. It also cleared his conscience and the niggling feeling that Andre was right about Parsons. Bently would keep an eye on Parsons's future arrests and see if there was a pattern. He picked up his phone and pressed the contact info.

"Just when I thought my day couldn't get any better," the husky female voice of ADA Lucy Millstone answered.

"Hey, Miss Millstone, I need a favor."

She chuckled. "It's about damn time, Sheriff. I knew I'd wear you down one of these days."

He smiled. At least some women were not immune to his charm. "I got a boy in lockup who I believe would benefit from some community service rather than a stint in juvie."

"All work and no play, huh?" she teased.

He'd enjoyed their flirtatious banter back and forth for years. He'd never crossed the line because he was the sheriff and she was the prosecutor. There was too much of a conflict of interest in the powers at play, and above all, Bently respected the office. That was why, once he'd become sheriff, he'd ventured outside city limits when he needed some female company. *Until Belle.* He'd never wanted a woman as much as her before. If she elicited such a reaction from him with the brush of a touch, how much more amazing would the sex actually be?

"Sheriff?" Lucy called, bringing him back to the issue at hand.

"Yeah, sorry. Been a long day. I'll send you over the details in an email."

Later that evening, he drove to the public courts parking lot. He'd run home long enough to change into some long shorts, a muscle shirt, and his sneakers. He parked his truck and grabbed the basketball out of the bed as he walked towards the near-empty courts. A lone figure caught his eye dribbling down the side before shooting and scoring a basket.

"Nice shot," Bently called out.

The boy turned, his demeanor changing the instant his eyes met Bently's.

It was the kid with the bike. "TJ, right?"

TJ nodded. "Sheriff."

Bently dribbled his own ball as he approached the young man. "You can call me Bently. I'm off duty."

TJ searched the empty lot behind them.

"You up for a little one-on-one?" Bently asked.

TJ hesitated, turning his head to scan the area.

"I promise I'll go easy on ya." Bently smiled, hoping to set him at ease.

TJ faced him again. "Alright. Let's see what you got."

Bently set his ball aside and situated himself at the half line. "First one to five wins."

TJ didn't waste a second as he faked left and swerved around, narrowly missing Bently's block. He had to hustle to keep up with him. The kid was quick. TJ lined up the shot. Bently swiped his hand out, knocking the ball from TJ's grip. The ball bounced out of bounds. TJ ran over to get it. Bently crowded the line, shifting his weight from side to side in anticipation of TJ's move. The ball bounced between his legs and TJ disappeared around his left, quickly catching the ball and making the shot. Nothing but net.

"Damn. You're good at this," Bently said, his blood pumping. This was going to be more of a challenge than he'd thought. "I let you have that one, so get ready for my A game." He chuckled.

Forty-five minutes and three games later, Bently crashed onto the metal bench out of breath. He stripped off his shirt, now soaked with sweat. He'd won two out of three, but TJ was good.

"You play on the school's team?" Bently asked.

"Nah. I'm graduating this semester and I don't have time for team sports."

"How old are you?"

"Seventeen."

"Ahh, so you're like super smart, then." Bently wiped his head with his shirt.

TJ shrugged, and smiled as if he was shy. "I'm starting January classes at the local college. I want to be a doctor someday."

"Wow. Well, I'm sure you'll get there. You seem like a good kid."

TJ nodded. He seemed more relaxed around Bently now that they had spent some time challenging each other and laughing.

"Thanks for my bike. Sorry about my sister the other day."

Belle. The woman was an enigma. She'd gotten under his skin.

"No problem. Happy I could help . . . Is she always so . . ." *Uptight? Rigid? Angry?*

TJ laughed. "Protective?"

That was a safer answer. "Yeah."

"She has good reason," TJ said seriously, as his eyes grew dark. "She's like my mom more than my sister."

"Where are your parents?"

TJ shifted his gaze to the ball in his hands. "Not in the picture."

"Mine either," he confessed.

TJ looked up at him. "Why are you hanging out with me?"

Bently shrugged. "I came here to play ball."

TJ nodded, seemingly accepting his answer.

"You made any friends yet?"

The kid hesitated. "One."

Bently pulled his phone out of his pocket. "Give me your phone number and I'll send you the link to a pretty cool place my friend Aaron runs. A lot of teens in the area hang out at his facility. They have basketball courts, game rooms, people your age."

TJ took his phone and typed in his information before handing it back. Bently sent him the link to Hope's website.

"You really got it bad for Belle, don't ya?" TJ asked.

Bently cringed. "What do you mean?"

"You're not the first to try and fail to get with my sister. Besides, you left a puddle of drool in our driveway." TJ laughed.

Bently pushed his shoulder playfully. "I did not."

"You sure seemed speechless." TJ smirked.

"Well, she's made it clear she doesn't want anything to do with me. I can respect when a woman tells me no." He wasn't a total asshole.

"You're not really her type."

A pang of disappointment rippled through him. "She prefers doctors?"

TJ laughed again. "Something like that."

Bently stood and stretched his tired limbs. "You want a ride back home?"

"My sister's at work."

"What's that got to do with my question?" Bently asked, confused.

"So, if you're using me to get to her, it won't work." TJ eyed him warily, though he still had a smile on his face.

"That's not the kind of guy I am," Bently assured him.

The distrust in TJ's eyes seemed to waver.

Bently picked up his ball and headed back towards his truck as he called over his shoulder, "You coming?"

This kid was almost as hard to win over as his sister. But Bently had never backed down from a challenge before, and he wasn't about to start now.

7

BELLE

August turned into a crisp September. The leaves changed to vibrant reds, yellows, and oranges. There was nothing like fall in New England. Belle inhaled the cup of cinnamon apple tea before taking a sip. The sky seemed as if it were on fire with its vivid hues blending into the increasing darkness. Each day was getting shorter than the last as they inched towards winter.

She placed her mug back into the center console before grabbing her water bottle. This was the last self-defense class in this six-week cycle, and then they'd start over from the beginning next week for any newcomers.

Belle was glad she'd stuck it out, even though she had to deal with the incessant flirting and banter between the ladies vying for Bently's attention. She'd quickly taken a spot on the sidelines, just trying to learn the skills and get out of there before she combusted. Bently's searing gaze burned her skin often. She had resorted to racing from class as soon as it was finished, and she waited until one minute before class started before she went inside.

This would be her last class. Then she could be free of Bently Evans.

"Hey, girl." Katy waved.

"Hello." Belle set her water next to her friend's.

"You ready for the test?" Katy asked.

This was the moment she'd been waiting for. A chance to see if her new skills measured up.

"Hell yes," she said, her veins thrumming with adrenaline. *I can do this.*

Bently walked in, followed by a few other dangerously handsome men. "Good evening, ladies. These here are my volunteers. You get to test out your abilities on taking them down. I bet them each a hundred bucks that you ladies could do it, so don't fail me now." He smirked.

There was a collective moan throughout the room.

"You got this. You've trained for this. Now you can see how it would be with a man," he finished.

Belle's stomach fluttered with nerves. These guys were *big.* She was only five feet two inches. How could she take down one of these giants?

Bently nudged the scarred, tattooed man she'd seen outside the bar.

"I'm Mason," he mumbled.

"Mason is a former Navy SEAL," Bently added.

The handsome man next to Mason said, "I'm Rife Owens, an officer with Shattered Cove PD."

"Look at the man candy," Katy whispered in her ear with a giggle.

Belle gave her a polite smile. Her friend was right—these men were sex on a stick.

"Okay, let's clear the floor. We need the first three volunteers—each one of you will go up against one of us. If you don't get it on the first time, don't worry. We'll walk you through the steps until you're confident in your abilities in a lifelike simulation. Your attacker won't be as lenient as practicing with your fellow partners," Bently assured the ladies in the room.

"I call dibs on the SEAL." Katy nudged her.

As long as I don't have to spar with Bently.

Bently turned on a speaker and "Queen" by Loren Gray blared through the sound system.

She tapped her foot as the first three women went. Marcy sidled up to Bently, shoving another woman out of her way with her hip. Belle rolled her eyes and took a seat. She'd wait until the room calmed down. One after the other, the women took their turns, grappling with the beefy men. To see the uncertainty on their faces grow to confidence by the end of their session was the most exciting part. She and Katy cheered on the ladies as they practiced their moves on the men.

Katy chuckled. "This is how the world should be—each woman supporting the other to take down the patriarchy."

"With the help of our allies of course." Belle nodded towards the three men taking hit after hit, and willingly coming back for more.

"I have to admit, if I was cornered by those three, I'd probably beg them to do their worst."

Belle burst out in warm, light-filled laughter. For the first time in a long while, she was relaxed and having fun. Her eyes caught with Bently's and her smile quickly faded. Marcy took advantage of his distraction and twisted out of his hold and had him on his knees. Bently said something to her and then she released him with a smile as she jumped up and down. Belle averted her eyes to the other groups, drawing in a deep breath.

Some women left after they finished their turns. Katy went up against Mason. Belle cheered her on. When she was finished, she high-fived the giant and went back to sit with Belle.

"Who's next?" Bently asked, searching the few women left against the mirrored wall. Belle looked over her shoulder. Everyone had gone except her.

Shit.

She stood to her shaky feet. "I guess I'm up."

Awareness prickled her skin. The room suddenly seemed a lot warmer. She stood in front of him.

"Ready?" he asked.

Not really. "Yes."

Bently grabbed her arm. Even though she'd come to expect the current of energy that snapped between them, it was still a shock to her system. There was no preparing for the onslaught of feelings that erupted from his touch—fire that promised devastation. Raw, unbridled sexual attraction spun her up like a tornado, whipping her around until she lost all her senses except one—fear. His eyes darkened with dense storm clouds blurring between them, crackling her synapses. She forced her breath in and out slowly and focused on the task—getting his hands off her.

Channeling her anger at the power this man held over her body, she grabbed his knuckles and swung her arm like he'd taught her. He didn't go down quite as easily as he had when she'd first learned this move six weeks ago. She used her weight to push him.

He fell to his knees. "Great."

She dropped his hand like it was on fire, but the blaze was inside her. She sucked in a staggered breath, wiping the beads of sweat that had formed on her brow. He directed her through a series of grabs that they'd learned as the dreaded choke hold drew nearer. Her muscles strained and flexed, shoving him to the ground again and again. Each position added fuel to the tension that wound around them.

"Perfect," he commented, staying on his knees. "Last one."

She steeled herself and lay on her back. Exposed and vulnerable, her skin lit with anticipation. He moved closer, situating himself between her thighs, every point of contact magnified by whatever this thing was between them. His hands reached for her neck as his scent washed over her. Oak and sin. She licked her lips, tasting it on her tongue. His eyes darted to her mouth. Her inner walls clenched. Arousal thrummed through her, so powerful, she worried he'd feel the vibration. His focused blue eyes locked on to hers—bright and pure and edged in darkness. Breathing came in pants as she fought the urge to grind against him. He leaned in closer still. Her mouth went dry. Was he going to kiss her? She wanted him to.

No! What had this man done to her? She was out of control. Anger swelled. No one could take that from her again.

Belle wrapped her legs around him and grabbed his elbows closer together. She used every bit of a lifetime of deep-seated anger to ignore the fact that she was now pressed against the hard ridges of his abdomen. She swung her legs over his shoulders and lifted her hips, making his arms bend at an unnatural angle as he released her.

She rolled away from him quickly. A few other women in the group laughed. Mason skirted past, almost as if he was running from the room, nodding to Bently before he exited. Katy's mouth turned up into a knowing smile as she handed her water bottle over. Belle didn't bother to say anything—she grabbed her keys and hoodie and darted out of the room. She needed air—fast.

Pushing open the door to the parking lot, she inhaled, filling her lungs with crisp oxygen. Wood smoke with a hint of salt. She jogged to her car, her hands trembling so hard, she dropped the keys.

As she bent over to retrieve them, a shadow loomed over hers. *Oh god, he followed me.*

"You okay?" Katy asked.

Belle whipped up to standing, choking on her relief. "Uh—yeah. I'm fine."

"It looked like you two had a moment," Katy pressed.

"Nope. Definitely not. Hate to break your bubble, but he's not my type." She forced a strained laugh.

"You look terrified." Katy's brow furrowed as if concerned.

Belle wiped her forehead with her arm. "I'm just high on adrenaline from the workout." *More like rattled to my core.*

"You sure you're okay?"

Belle nodded. "Yeah, absolutely."

Bently burst through the gym doors, his gaze locked on her.

"I should go," Belle said.

"Okay, well, I guess I'll see you at work later in the week." Katy waved and walked away. Belle jiggled her key into the lock again as Bently stopped only a foot from her.

"Hey, uh, I wondered if we could talk?" He shoved his hands into his pockets.

The key found purchase and she inserted it and twisted. "I really need to get home."

"I just wanted to know if you'd have dinner with me sometime. Now that I'm no longer your instructor," he added with a smile.

"I don't think that's a good idea, Sheriff." She used the title like a shield.

He frowned. "We all gotta eat sometime. I promise, just dinner and a little conversation. I'd like to get to know you better."

Like she couldn't see straight through that invitation. Did he think she was born yesterday? "Men," she grumbled under her breath as she opened the door and threw her water inside.

"We men are good for some things." He winked and smirked.

What part about this was funny to him? "I don't need a man," she grated.

"I'm not proposing marriage—just dinner." He shrugged.

There it was. He'd spelled it out for her. He wanted sex, company for a night, and then he'd be on his merry way with no care in the world for the devastation he'd leave behind. Here was another man, trying to *take* from her. "That's exactly why this will never happen. I said no, *Sheriff*. Isn't that what these classes are about? To help women deal with men who don't take no for an answer?"

He stepped back as if physically struck. As if he'd never heard the word no directed at him before.

Maybe he hadn't earned the jab, but her anger for every man that had ever hurt her bubbled to the surface. She would burn this bridge and move on. "You're a pig."

Bently's jaw tensed. His body turned rigid. The vein in his neck pulsed rapidly under the light of the streetlamps. Anger radiated off him in waves as his eyes narrowed. "Because I'm a man or because I'm a cop?" he asked, his expression grim.

"Both." She climbed in and shut the door before quickly

starting the engine. He turned around and walked away, each step tugging at her chest.

"Fuck!" she yelled. Her mind and body were so mixed up. Had she taken it too far? It didn't matter. She wanted nothing to do with that man or the feelings he stirred up inside her.

It was better she was left alone.

8

BELLE

Belle walked towards the nurses' station.

"Belle, patient in room one needs stitches, so get the suture kit set up, please," Doctor Stanley said.

"Sure thing." She got to work preparing everything the doctor would need.

She checked her watch—four in the morning. Three more hours to go. She'd offered to cover third shift for a nurse. Belle yawned. She'd need coffee to make it through.

"Belle, they need a SANE nurse in room six. I'll take over here," an older nurse said, slipping on a pair of gloves.

"Okay." She walked back into the hall, her stomach knotting as she prepared for the worst and hoped for the best.

She peeked in the empty room. After picking up the chart, she reviewed the information. Patient's name was Charlotte Reed. Brought in via ambulance after she was attacked.

"Oh good. You're already here," Doctor Stanley said as two men pushed the hospital bed inside. Belle stepped out of the way as they maneuvered it in the middle of the room.

Dried blood streaked down her patient's face from a gash

on her eye and nose. Her lip was swollen and purple, but she was still familiar.

The woman from the bar.

Charlotte winced in pain and held her side with a bruised and scraped hand. She'd fought hard by the looks of it.

Doctor Stanley lifted the X-rays to the lightbox. "Looks like a couple cracked ribs. No internal bleeding. We'll get a few sutures on the cut by your eye.

"Okay," Charlotte said, her voice hoarse.

Doctor Stanley looked at Belle, giving her a nod.

Belle walked over and adjusted the IV bags. "Charlotte, is there any chance you could have been sexually assaulted?"

Charlotte closed her eyes tight. Tears mingled with the dried blood, spilling down her cheeks. "I don't think so. I passed out at some point. But my clothes were still on me when I woke up. I'm sore everywhere, so it's hard to tell."

"Okay." Belle put her hand gently on hers to comfort her. "Is there someone you'd like me to call for you that you'd like to keep you company?"

"My husband is deployed in Afghanistan. There's no one else."

"I'll be here with you the whole way. My name is Belle. You're going to get through this, sweetheart. You survived, and now you can start to heal."

"Okay. Please call me Charli—everyone does. Can I have some water?" Charli asked.

"Of course. I'll be right back." Belle slipped out of the room and grabbed a cup of ice water with a straw before heading towards her patient's room. The sight of the tan uniform made her do a double take as a stampede of wild horses stomped all over her heart. "Sheriff?"

Bently turned towards her, his shoulders tensing and his jaw set. Butterflies of apprehension tumbled in her belly. It had been a week since their last encounter, and her unease had faded. She'd thought life had returned to normal.

"What——" she said, at the same time Bently said, "I——"

They both stopped, Bently's eyes looking anywhere but her it seemed.

"I'm here to see Charli," he said.

Belle shook her head. "Wait. I have to ask her if she even wants you here." She darted in front of him, expecting to have to fight for her patient's privacy.

"That's fine. Can you just make sure to tell her it's me that's come? If she prefers Deputy Vargas, I can call her in. She might be more comfortable with a woman." He backed down.

It wasn't what she'd been expecting at all. "I—uh . . . yes."

His thoughtfulness threw her for a loop. Belle went into the room and handed the water to Charli. "The sheriff is outside. He wants to know if you would like to speak with him. He offered to call the deputy if you would rather have a female officer."

"Bent is fine." Charli nodded.

Belle went back out. Bently was leaning against the opposite wall, his arms crossed. His black hair was tousled like he'd just crawled out of bed. He looked up at her expectantly.

"She'll talk to you."

Bently walked past her, going immediately to her patient's side. "Charli, what happened?" Concern emanated from him as he sat in a chair next to her. His big hand reached out to hold hers.

Belle got to work checking Charli's vitals.

"I had some trouble with a few guys at the bar an hour before closing. Mason kicked them out. He usually stays and walks me to my car after my shift. But his nanny called—his daughter was throwing up, so I told him to go on home."

Charli took a breath before she continued. "I locked up and walked to my car. I had this feelin' like I wasn't alone. I hurried to my car and unlocked it. As soon as I got the door open, someone grabbed me from behind. It all happened so fast. I'll never forget that voice." She shuddered. "He was angry that I embarrassed him in front of his buddies. He . . . threatened to . . ."

Bently rubbed her tattooed arm soothingly. "It's okay. Take your time."

She looked down. "He said he'd teach me a lesson and pulled at my pants. I bit him, and that's when he gave me this." She pointed to the gash on her face. "I fought so hard." She began to sob.

Bently wrapped his arms carefully around her as best as he could from her side. "Shhhh, it's okay. It's over. You're safe now."

Belle's chest tightened. Seeing this caring, nurturing side to Bently made her heart prick with guilt over their last exchange. Was she wrong about him?

"Did he get that far?" Bently asked, his jaw tensing.

"I don't think so. I passed out at some point." She pointed to the ring of bruises around her neck. "When I woke, my clothes were on."

Bently nodded. "I'm so sorry this happened to you. I'm gonna find the man who did this," he promised, his voice full of conviction. "I'm going to step outside so Belle here can finish examining you. I'm gonna need your clothes as evidence, and tomorrow I'll come over to your house and get a full statement if that's okay with you."

Charli nodded. "Okay."

"How long until Lieutenant Reed gets home from deployment?" Bently asked.

"Just a few more months now." Charli's lips turned up into a watery broken smile.

"You're almost there. Listen, if that ever happens again, and you don't have Mason to walk you to your car, I want you to call me. No matter what time it is." Bently nodded and left the room.

Belle walked Charli through every step of the exam. She wanted to make this process as gentle as possible. Unfortunately, she'd had plenty of practice in her few years of nursing—sexual assault on women was so prevalent.

"Bently is going to catch him," Charli said, staring at the wounds on her hands. "He always comes through on his promises."

Belle nodded. "He seems to really care about you."

Charli took a sip of water. "We've been friends since high school. He stood up for me when I came to class in rags. A lot of the other girls wanted his attention, but he zeroed in on me. Because of him, high school was tolerable. He was like the big brother I always wanted and never had. Then he introduced me to my husband, Finn."

"Sounds like a good guy," Belle said, and for the first time, she meant it. Apparently, she hadn't worked through her anger as much as she thought. Maybe she'd let her experiences with men taint her opinion.

Guilt blanketed her shoulders. She was woman enough to admit when she was wrong. She'd judged him before she got to know him. Why did she react so viscerally to him of all people?

Because I'm scared I could fall for him and he'd leave me rejected and alone.

She'd already ruined any chance they could be friends. The distance between them was evidence of that. The usual smoldering energy felt more like the churning sea in a storm now. Everything seemed off and unsettled.

Maybe it was for the best. They could both go on with their lives and stay out of each other's way.

If only she could believe that.

9

BENTLY

Scrolling through the news article, Bently sighed and shook his head. Another police shooting of an unarmed Black man. Video had surfaced, and it was obvious that there was no excuse for the officer to use deadly force. The man was on the ground, complying with the officer's demands, and he was still shot in the back.

Bently raked a hand over his face. This was a problem—there was no doubt about it. But things like that didn't happen in his small town. These were good people, his fellow officers were servants of the law and *for* the people.

"Knock, knock," Vargas said as she opened the door.

"Kind of defeats the point if you don't actually knock and let yourself in anyways." He set his phone facedown on the table.

Vargas chuckled and sat across from him in the empty chair, sliding a folder onto his desk. "It's not like you're up to anything in here. You forget I've already seen you naked," she teased.

He chuckled. "I've changed a lot since we were fifteen and skinny-dipping."

She popped her gum. "Seeing you, Dre, and Mikel streaking your bare asses down the beach was one of the funniest things I ever laid eyes on."

"Good thing we didn't have camera phones back in those days."

Vargas tapped her forehead. "It's forever burned in my memory."

Bently chuckled. "Enough about my sexy body. What did you bring me?" He flipped open the file. Joe Canoby's mug shot was paper-clipped to the top, along with several photos of his lifeless body and crime scene photos. The scene was still so fresh in his mind, he could smell the tang of blood in the air.

Rushing through Remy's back door with Mikel hot on his heels, hoping with every fiber he wasn't too late to save his niece and her mama. Charging in, gun drawn, searching the rooms for any sign of life. Joe Canoby staggering back from Remy's seemingly lifeless, bloody body. The glint of a knife as the man surged forward as if to strike Remy again.

A millisecond of time elapsed between identifying the threat and pulling the trigger. One shot.

Bang!

Bently jumped in his seat.

Vargas eyed him warily. "You okay?"

"What did you find?" he asked, avoiding the question.

"We know Canoby was a low-level dealer and loan shark. What we don't know is who he was working for. We've spoken to June Simpson, as you know. She mentioned a name that she'd heard once—Carelli."

"Carelli, as in the mob boss?" Bently clarified.

Vargas nodded and popped her gum again. "The trail stops there."

"The FBI are going to want in on this. This crosses state lines if he's involved."

She raised her hands as she sighed. "My other leads here have all but dried up."

Bently nodded. "Thanks for giving me the update. Go ahead and call our friends at the Bureau."

"Yes, sir." Vargas got up and collected the file before leaving his office.

He glanced at the clock. *Quitting time.* Bently organized his desk before heading out. Betsy was already gone for the day. Officer Rife Owens was at his desk.

"How you doing, Owens?"

The officer sat up a little straighter. "Just fine, Sheriff."

"You settling in here nicely? It's been what, three months since you finished the academy?"

"Yes, sir."

"You're doing a good job so far."

Owens smiled. "Thank you, sir."

"I'm heading out for the day. I'll have my phone on me if you need anything at all. Parsons will be in shortly." Bently pulled his keys out of his pocket.

"Have a good evening, sir."

"You too."

Bently pulled his truck into the gravel parking lot in front of The Lighthouse Inn. Warm pride filled his chest as he took in the large house. Fresh white paint decorated the old building making it seem much younger than it was. His sister had finally made her dream come true.

He walked to the front door, not bothering to knock as he entered the foyer. A rich, savory smell wafted from deeper within the house. He continued along the dark gray-stained wood floors, past the cameras that he'd installed himself so that Jasmine would be alerted on her phone of movement. Couldn't be too careful when it came to two of the most important women in his life.

"Bent, I'm in the kitchen!" Jasmine called out.

He passed through the lobby area into the large kitchen. Mikel and Andre had redone it for her too.

"This doesn't even look like the same house old Mrs. Jenson lived in," he mused.

Jasmine tucked a strand of her black hair behind her ear and handed the baby in her arms over to him as she answered, "No, it doesn't. Still a lot of work to do though. Just need the money to do it."

"You'll get there." He tilted his head to smell his sleeping niece's forehead before he kissed her. "Zoey is getting so big."

"She certainly is. I can't believe it's been seven months since she was born." Jasmine stretched her back.

"What are you making me for dinner?" he asked.

Jasmine stirred the pot. "Mom's chicken noodle soup recipe."

Bently nodded. There were so many memories clinging to even the simplest mention of their parents. Good and bad shadows lurking behind triggers of trauma past.

He cleared his throat. "You doing okay?"

She smiled. "I'm doing a lot better. I started to go to a group thing once a week. It's really helping me deal with . . . everything."

"You mean for single mothers?"

She shook her head, storm clouds dimming the light in her green eyes. "No, for survivors."

"Oh. That's good. If it's helping you." He shifted in his seat. Talking about the past was uncomfortable. He preferred to leave it where it belonged, and avoid the topic altogether. "You never told me who Zoey's birth father is."

She added a pinch of salt to the pot and stirred it again. "How are you doing?"

"One of these days, you're going to have to tell me," he pushed.

"Today isn't that day," she said firmly.

"I just want to make sure you and Zoey get the best in life. If I need to kick some deadbeat's ass, I will," he assured her.

Jasmine rolled her eyes. "It's nothing like that. Just drop it, Bent."

"Fine," he grunted, turning his attention back to the sleeping bundle in his arms. Zoey had her mother's angular eyes, but his niece's were a stunning gray blue.

"You never answered my question," she said, ladling some of the soup into a bowl and setting it on the table.

"Which one?"

"How are *you* doing?" she repeated.

"I'm fine."

"You ever think about talking to someone about Mom and your dad?" she asked, making a bowl for herself.

"Why would I? They're gone. Nothing to discuss anymore." The smell of the savory soup wafted over to him. His mouth watered and his belly grumbled.

"Just because it's over, doesn't mean the wounds aren't still there. Until you deal with them, they'll fester." Jasmine took the seat across from him.

"You been watching Oprah?"

"The therapist in the group told us that. It made a lot of sense to me." Jasmine scowled.

He put his hand on his sister's. "Look, I'm really happy this is working for you. But talking about shit I can't change doesn't do me any good." In fact, it made him angry. He'd failed his mother, his sister, and his brother. He couldn't protect them when they'd needed him most.

"Thank you, Bently. I know I haven't gotten the chance to ever really say it. But you've always been there for me. You're the only one who never ever left. I appreciate everything you do for me, and now Zoey."

His throat grew tight. He didn't deserve this. He could spend his entire life in servitude of his sister and it would never make up for the time he'd failed her so horrifically.

Turning his attention back to Zoey, he said, "Who could say no to this cutie? She's the only girl who will ever have Uncle Bently tied around her finger."

Zoey's pink rosebud lips moved as if she was suckling in her sleep. Her little eyebrows frowned and then relaxed. Peace and calm swallowed him up as he held his niece. All was right in the world, at least for the moment.

10

BELLE

The windshield wipers were on as fast as they could go and it was still hard to see the road in front of Belle. Thunder rumbled and lightning flashed.

She parked at the library. TJ was under the eaves with another boy around his age. They seemed to be in deep conversation. TJ hung his head low as he fidgeted with his backpack strap—something he did when he was nervous.

She honked the horn twice and both boys' heads jerked towards her. TJ's friend smiled and waved. Something about him felt off.

"This is some storm," TJ said sliding into the passenger seat.

"That your friend from school?"

TJ swallowed and looked out the window. "He's in my science class."

"What do you want for dinner tonight?"

"Chinese?" he suggested.

"But it's your night to cook," she pointed out.

"Please?" He smiled and flashed his puppy-dog eyes at her.

She chuckled. "Alright."

After a few moments of silence, TJ asked, "You ever goin' to date?"

A triangle formed between her brows. "What kind of question is that?"

"Well, I'm gonna be going to college and then medical school, and you'll be here all alone. Wouldn't you like some company? You know, someone to watch your back?" TJ asked, almost too innocently, but there was a tinge of fear in his voice.

She shook her head. "I appreciate your sudden interest in my love life, but I'll be fine on my own."

"The sheriff seemed like a nice guy."

Belle turned her head and glanced suspiciously at her brother. "You met him once. And he's a cop."

"I know. Just seemed like maybe he was into you."

"More like he wants to be *into* me." She laughed.

TJ grimaced. "TMI, sis." He shook his head. "I don't know, just appeared you two had some . . . chemistry."

More like the whole damn lab exploded. "You got all that from a few minutes of me finding you outside the house getting out of a police car? Me yelling at you to get your ass inside. You scared the shit out of me, TJ. And besides, that was two months ago." Her voice rose.

"He was just giving me a ride home because my tires were flat."

She gave him the side-eye.

TJ shrugged and popped his earbud in.

She turned down another street. "What the——"

An object lay on the side of the road. The rain was pouring too hard for her to make it out clearly. She squinted as they drove closer, the figure coming into view. Belle screeched to a stop and gasped. "It's a person."

She opened her door and dashed into the freezing rain. It soaked through her jacket in seconds. Belle checked the woman's pulse. Her skin was hot to the touch despite the cold temperature outside.

"Help me get her in the car."

TJ just sat there, staring at the woman.

"TJ!"

He snapped out of it and raced from the car before bending to grab the woman's feet. Belle directed him into the back seat of her car.

"Let's get her to our place and I can check her over there," she said, driving towards their destination.

When they got home, TJ helped her carry the unconscious woman across the wet grass and into the house where they laid her carefully on the couch.

TJ's hands raced across his phone screen as she took the woman's pulse. *Too fast.* "Stop messing on your phone and go get my kit."

You'd think a kid who wanted to be a doctor would be more helpful in this situation. TJ disappeared upstairs. Minutes passed by. Belle huffed and followed him. "What's the holdup?"

"I can't find it," TJ said, coming out of her bedroom.

"Because it's in the bathroom, not my bedroom." She grabbed the kit and ran down the stairs.

After pulling out the thermometer, she checked the woman's temperature. *One hundred and three.* Next she used the stethoscope and listened to her lungs. *Not good.*

"I'm going to go upstairs and get out of these wet things and get her a change of clothes. Keep her covered for now and then we'll take her to the hospital." Belle didn't wait for her brother's reply as she ran back up the stairs.

Belle changed and grabbed another set of dry clothes. The woman was a lot taller than her, but they'd have to make do.

A knock sounded at the door. *Who could that be?* She grabbed a towel on her way down, freezing halfway.

Bently Evans was in her house, in uniform. Fear wound around her. How had he known to come here? Was he watching her? TJ's earlier questions and the sheriff's sudden presence made the hair on the back of her neck stand up.

"Mia?" Bently gasped, rushing over to her now awake patient's side.

"What is *he* doing here?" Belle snapped, focusing on her brother's guilty look.

TJ shrugged.

"Don't act like you're not happy to see me," Bently said frostily.

Had Bently used her brother to get to her? She rolled her eyes. "Has hell frozen over?"

"TJ called and let me in. Seems he rescued my friend." Bently turned his attention back on the woman lying on Belle's sofa. "What happened?"

"I just need to go home," Mia rasped, before coughing.

Putting her distrust for this man aside because someone else needed her, Belle interjected, "No, she needs a hospital. Her lungs sound like they have some fluid and she's running a high fever. She was passed out in the freezing cold, soaked to the bone. No idea how long she was exposed to the elements, but she could have pneumonia."

"Let's go, Mia. Doctor's orders." Bently took her hand as she stood up.

"I'm a nurse," she deadpanned.

"Home. No hospital." Mia coughed again, seemingly unable to stop before she went limp in Bently's arms.

"She needs to go to the ER," Belle commanded. "TJ, take my keys and meet me there."

Bently hooked his arm under Mia's knees and carried her out while Belle held the door open. She ran to his truck and climbed in the extended cab seats, opening her arms for Bently to hand Mia over. He obliged, shutting the doors before climbing in the driver's side.

The rain had let up, only sprinkling now as he pulled onto the road and raced towards the hospital.

"She's a friend of yours?" Belle asked, regretting the tinge of jealousy in her voice.

He glanced in the rearview mirror, meeting her eyes briefly. "She's my best friend's girl."

"Oh."

Bently handed her his phone. "Could you text him for me? It's under Andre Stone."

"Sure." She took the phone from his hand, while balancing Mia's unconscious body against her lap. She found his contact information and typed out the message before handing the phone back to Bently, her fingers grazing his. The skin tingled where he'd touched her.

He picked up the radio and alerted dispatch to notify the hospital that they were incoming.

"How did TJ tell you about Mia?"

Bently's brow furrowed. "I gave him my number. Wanted to send him some information about Hope Facility that my friend Aaron runs. It's for homeless teens and kids from troubled homes mainly, but it's open to all kids in the community. They have basketball courts and a game room. It seemed like he might be having some trouble making friends, and I just thought it might be useful. Sorry if I overstepped."

Her stomach knotted. *When did this happen? And why didn't TJ tell me?* She wasn't expecting Bently's honesty, and it was just one more piece of the conflicting puzzle of Bently Evans.

"I'm sorry I called you a pig, Bently. It was uncalled for. I apologize for reacting so harshly."

His gaze flashed to hers once more in the mirror.

"Thank you for that." Switching his blinker on, Bently turned down the road leading to the hospital. "I'm sorry if I made you feel unsafe at any time. That was never my intention." His voice was gruff.

Bently didn't say another word or look at her again before they pulled in front of the emergency department doors.

A line of nurses, all of whom she recognized, were waiting with a gurney for Mia. The doors opened and they got Mia out and rushed into the hospital. Belle climbed over and then Bently shut the door. She tilted her head to the sky and closed her eyes. It had stopped raining. Eyes still shut, the damp cool air clung to her and sent a shiver through her. When she opened them, Bently's gaze dropped to the ground as if he'd been staring.

"Do you want a ride home? I'm heading that way to get Mia's family." He only stood a few feet away, leaning against his truck. But it felt as though he was smothering her.

It seemed the tension between them had returned, making it hard to breathe. Why had things changed? Was it TJ's questions in the car earlier? Or the way he'd jumped in and cared for this woman so readily? Could it be the fact that he wasn't pursuing her anymore? She forced in a lungful of crisp, wet air. "TJ should be along soon."

Bently nodded. "Do you want me to wait until he gets here?"

The kind gesture was yet another reminder of how unfair she'd been to him. The more time she spent with him in different scenarios, the more she could see the makings of one of those rare good men.

"I'll be fine, but thank you."

He stood and walked to the driver's side before climbing in and offering her a wave as he left. His red taillights glowed in the cloudy afternoon.

"What did you do, Belle?" she asked herself aloud. Maybe she'd let her fear dictate too much of her life.

And just maybe, she'd ruined her shot at happiness because of it.

11

BELLE

Warm sunrays made the crisp wind tolerable. Colored leaves rustled in the breeze as Belle walked down Main Street. The epicenter of the small town, the little shops were clustered together on this stretch of road. A far cry from the inner-city streets she'd grown up on.

Cinnamon and spices wafted through the air, no doubt from the Stardust Café on the other side of the street. Oh, she could kill for a good coffee. And perhaps a good book to distract her from all the confusion Bently had created in her head.

She ducked into the bookstore to grab some reading material, then walked to the café. She adjusted her bag of purchases and pulled open the door with her free hand as a gust of wind blew, making her hair fly in her face. She went inside and pushed the door shut as the bells rang together from the disturbance. Sweet baked goods and the earthy fragrance of coffee melded together, enveloping her in a scented embrace.

Picking her hair from where it stuck to her ChapStick, Belle walked to the counter, studying the colorful chalkboard menu on the wall in the otherwise empty café.

A little girl dashed in front of her. "Is that a present?"

Belle glanced at the bag in her hand and then to the little girl. "I guess it kind of is." *A gift to me from myself.*

She smiled, showing off a few missing teeth. "I love presents. Christmas is only two more months away. Then I can get presents!"

"Lyra, I asked you to stay in the back room while I finished changing your brother."

Belle glanced up as a dark woman walked through the back door, adjusting a baby on her hip.

Lyra's head lowered as she crossed her arms behind her back. "I'm sorry, Mama."

"Go get your coloring book and set yourself up at one of the tables, and I'll bring you a hot chocolate and cookie, okay?"

Lyra's eyes brightened as she ran off.

"I'm sorry about that. My mom usually watches them while my husband and I work, but she's sick and my brother-in-law won't be here for another thirty minutes. I'm Remy, by the way. What can I get you?"

Belle smiled. "It's no problem at all. I understand what it is to have to juggle little ones and life."

Remy grinned and adjusted the baby into a carrier on her back. The little boy protested, kicking out his chubby little legs and crying.

Remy blew out a frustrated breath as Lyra came back, coloring book and markers in hand. "Can I have a chocolate-chip mermaid cookie, Mama?"

"Yes, sweetheart." Remy grabbed a small cup and poured

hot water inside. "I'm sorry. Just give me one minute to get her settled and I'll be right with you."

"It's really no problem at all. I'm in no rush."

Remy hurriedly mixed the hot chocolate, dolloping whipped cream and a dash of cinnamon on top as she jiggled up and down, trying to ease the crying baby on her back. Brushing a few stray braids from her face, she blew out an exasperated sigh and came over to the counter, smiling at Belle. "What can I get you?"

"A latte with two of those—"

The baby's cries grew more insistent as the bells jingled above the door and a group of four people walked in.

Remy glanced at the clock while she pulled the baby off her back before tucking him into her front. "I'm so sorry. It's his nap time and he only likes to be held a certain way when he's this overtired."

Belle reached out her hand. "Stop apologizing. There is no need. Your baby's needs come first. I get it. If I was capable of jumping in behind the counter and taking over, I'd help out until your brother-in-law gets here. But my skills are in taking care of people. Would you feel comfortable with me entertaining these two while you deal with your other customers? I can sit right there where you can see us." Belle pointed to where Lyra was happily munching on cookies.

Remy looked between her and Lyra, her forehead wrinkled in the dilemma.

"Here's my badge from the hospital. I'm Belle Jones—a nurse in the emergency room. If you want to hang on to this, I totally get it." Belle held up her hospital ID.

Remy narrowed her eyes on the plastic and then back to Belle, the lines on her forehead disappearing. She smiled. "I don't need to keep it, but I'll take you up on your offer."

Remy walked around the counter and pulled the fussy

baby from her front. Belle tucked him against her chest and started to bounce from side to side.

"He's eaten and been changed. He's teething and missed his morning nap. Yes, just like that."

"I got him. You go do your thing," Belle assured her.

"Thank you," Remy said before dashing back to the counter to take care of the growing group of customers.

Belle hugged the baby boy close as she hummed and moved closer to Lyra's table, swaying back and forth. He quieted, clutching a strand of her hair in his tiny fist. She smiled. It had been a long time since TJ was this little, and she was not much older than Lyra when she'd taken care of him by herself. Something about holding a sleeping baby made everything calm and peaceful inside her.

"Is he asleep?" Lyra asked, whispering.

Belle lifted her head and sure enough, his eyes were closed, his tiny fist partially inside his mouth. Drool slid down his hand, no doubt spilling onto her jacket.

"I think so," Belle said, sitting across from the little girl. "What are you coloring?"

"Tiana from *The Princess and the Frog.*"

"Oh, she's very pretty," Belle said.

"She's the only princess with skin like me. Well, except for Moana and Pocahontas. They're light brown too."

Belle nodded. The little girl had already noticed the vast underrepresentation of people of color in the media. Why was it so hard for most adults to see? What child didn't want to see someone who looked like them saving the day and finding their happily-ever-after?

"What about *Doc McStuffins*? Have you ever seen that show?" Belle asked.

Lyra stopped coloring and smiled at her. "Yes! I love that show. And *Nella the Princess Knight.*"

Belle nodded. "Can you draw me your favorite character? You are great at coloring."

Lyra took a sip of her hot cocoa, leaving a mustache of chocolate on her upper lip and a dab of whipped cream on her little nose. She grinned. "When I grow up, I'm going to be an artist."

"I bet you will." Belle handed her a napkin.

"What do you want to be when you grow up?" Lyra asked, her face serious as she wiped her mouth, leaving the spot on her nose.

Belle bit back another smile. "Well, I am pretty grown up. I'm a nurse."

The little girl's mouth dropped open. "Do you work with *Doc McStuffins?*"

Belle chuckled. "Not exactly."

Lyra scribbled across the page, her little body hunched over in focus as her pink tongue stuck out the side of her mouth in concentration. Lyra turned the page upside down to put what appeared to be the finishing touches on her drawing. Belle breathed in the scent of the baby as his little chest rose and fell.

The bell jangled as a couple of patrons left the café. Remy set a steaming latte in front of her. "This is on the house. Along with my eternal gratitude. Did you want anything else?"

"I would love a couple of those mermaid cookies. But I insist on paying."

"It is the least I can do." Remy left and quickly came back with a bag full of the dessert.

"Thank you." Belle grabbed one cookie and bit into it. "Delicious."

"I don't suppose you want to keep him for a little while

longer, do you? If I move him, he'll wake up and then be miserable the rest of the day." Remy bit her lip.

"I'd love nothing more. I've got an adorable baby on my shoulder, caffeine, cookies—heck, I should be paying you to enjoy this." Belle smiled, hoping to set Remy at ease. Taking care of people was what she'd done for as long as she could remember. It made her feel needed and appreciated.

"You are a godsend."

"She's a nurse, Mommy! She works with *Doc McStuffins*," Lyra added excitedly.

Remy smiled, eyes widening towards her daughter. "That sounds super fun." Remy kissed Lyra's forehead before grabbing another chair to sit by them. "Are you new to town, then?"

Belle took a sip of the latte before she answered. "I moved here a few months ago with my younger brother after I got the job."

"How do you like Shattered Cove so far?"

"It's a nice place," Belle said honestly. The town was nice—and Remy was nice too. Maybe she was another potential friend—someone outside of work. The other nurses had been kind but, aside from Katy, she hadn't really bonded with any of them. Remy was different. There was a feeling of *potential* here.

The bells jingled above the door behind her as a gust of wind blew into the café. Her skin prickled in anticipation as Lyra's face broke out into a wide grin.

"Uncle Bently!"

No.

12

BELLE

Belle froze, the blood draining from her face. Bently? As in, Bently Evans? Sheriff Bently Evans was Lyra's uncle and Remy's brother-in-law?

"Hey, sweetheart. You ready to go to my house? I thought we could play with that new dollhouse I set up for y—Oh. Hi, Belle." Bently looked as surprised as she felt.

"Hi," she said, much steadier than she was. His gaze was fuel to an instant ache. Those blue eyes sent her tumbling, plunging into darkness so she didn't know which way was up or down. Longing and uncertainty clamored in her chest as she took a wavering breath.

"You two know each other?" Remy asked, pulling her from the trance as more customers entered the café.

"She's the one who found Mia," Bently's gruff voice answered.

"Oh! You did? You're just an everyday heroine, then, aren't you?" Remy joked.

Bently cut Remy a questioning glance before focusing on the sleeping babe on Belle's shoulder.

86

"Can you wait until Phoenix wakes up before you go? I know it's not ideal, but if we move him, he'll be in a horrible mood for the rest of the day. He's already been asleep for thirty or so minutes," Remy asked Bently.

"Uh, sure. Whatever you need," he said.

"Color with me, Uncle Bently," Lyra directed.

He grabbed a chair and sat beside his niece, his tan police uniform clinging to his muscled shoulders. A few stray locks of black hair tumbled over his forehead.

"I'm going to go help those customers. Does anyone need anything?" Remy stood.

Belle shook her head.

"Coffee would be nice." Bently smiled appreciatively.

"Coming right up." Remy left them alone with the kids at the table.

Bently got to work coloring the prince after Lyra handed him a marker. Seeing this tough ladies' man being so gentle and loving towards his niece made Belle's ovaries ache. Not that she wanted children—at least not anytime soon. But witnessing Bently talking about playing with dollhouses was such a stark contrast to her first impressions of him. She'd been very wrong about Bently Evans.

"How'd you meet Remy?" he asked, shaking her from her spiraling thoughts.

"I came in for some coffee and she was having trouble managing the kids and running the whole café by herself." She sipped her latte again.

He nodded. "Thanks for helping her out."

"Of course . . . I had no idea you were related to her."

"Yeah, my brother, Mikel, and Remy got married last year. But they had a long history before that," he explained.

The urge to say something built, but she wasn't sure what to start with. She'd already apologized. "She seems nice."

"Did you know Belle is a nurse, Uncle Bently?" Lyra interjected.

He turned his attention back to the little girl. "I did know that, ladybug."

"That means she saves people like you saved Mommy and me," she said matter-of-factly as she continued coloring.

Bently winced. Belle wanted to ask, but it wasn't exactly her business.

Remy set a cup of black coffee in front of Bently. "I have the perfect way to say thank you, Belle. We're having our annual pumpkin picking hayride and then a bonfire after-wards with some hot cider and food at my house. Bring your brother and I'll introduce you to everyone. What's your number?" Remy pulled out her phone.

"Uh . . . I don't know if—" Belle glanced at Bently who kept his attention glued to the paper he was coloring.

"I won't take no for an answer. I'm sure Mia would love to see you and thank you properly."

Maybe it was time to stop holding back so much and let the walls down. Remy seemed lovely. Why not? Belle rattled off her number.

"Great. I'll text you the address and information. You bring your pretty self and that brother of yours, and I'll worry about the rest." Remy scurried away with Lyra before Belle could respond.

Bently's jaw was set, his blue eyes flashing as he glanced at her.

"Is it okay with you if I go? I don't want to intrude," she said.

"You were invited," he said as if that would answer the questions swirling around inside her. *Does he want me to go? Is he mad at me? Why does it matter so much?*

* * *

88

Days later, Belle parked in front of the large home among the several other vehicles already in the driveway.

"Nice house," TJ commented from the passenger seat, the edges of his mouth turned up like he knew something she didn't.

She swallowed her unease, and shut the engine off. Getting out of the car, she pocketed the keys in her jacket.

"I forgot to tell you the woman we helped, Mia, will be here tonight."

TJ snapped his head towards her, before looking away and shifting on his feet.

"Is that okay?"

"Yeah." His voice cracked. "Why wouldn't it be?"

"Why are you acting all antsy?" *What secrets are you keeping from me now?*

He sighed and tipped his head up. "I'm not. I just don't like surprises—you know that."

She nodded. "You know you can tell me anything, right?"

TJ smiled, which set her somewhat at ease. "I know, sis. Now, quit your stalling and let's go see your *boyfriend*." He started walking across the lawn.

"You little shit," she grumbled.

The smell of wood smoke and the sound of laughter drew them around to the backyard. TJ walked by her side as they approached the group of friends.

"Belle!" Remy called, waving her over.

TJ's steps faltered as they grew nearer. She looked back at him questioningly. Fear flashed through his expression as he eyed the small crowd.

"It's okay. I'm sure they don't bite," she joked.

He cleared his throat, eyes widening.

"Hey—" a man started to say.

"Andre!" the woman she recognized as Mia growled and

89

sprouted a flurry of Spanish at him as she tugged him away from the group.

Everyone watched them go until they were out of sight.

"What was that about?" the man asked. Surely, with such a similar face and build, he had to be Bently's brother.

"I don't know. But I'm sure Dre deserved it." Remy pulled her gaze back to Belle. "I'm so happy you could make it."

"Sorry we couldn't do the hayride. My shift only ended an hour ago," Belle explained.

Remy waved her off. "No problem at all. I'm just glad you could come. Let me introduce you. This is my husband, Mikel. You've already met Lyra." She pointed to the little girl on her husband's shoulders.

"Hi again, Lyra." Belle gave the little girl a high five.

"Hi!"

"And you got to know Phoenix. And this handsome man must be your brother." Remy motioned to TJ.

"TJ, good to see you again," Bently said with an easy smile as he stretched out his hand to her brother. Her heart fluttered. Damn, she needed to get a hold of herself. Heart palpitations could be a sign of a serious medical problem. But they only happened in his presence, which was scarier than the potential medical issues.

"You too." TJ's voice smoothed out.

"This is Jasmine, Mikel and Bently's sister, and her adorable daughter, Zoey." Remy opened her arm to welcome the other woman over.

"Hi." Jasmine waved, a little more reserved than the rest of the group.

"The two lovebirds in the house are Mia, whom you rescued, and Andre, my brother," Remy finished.

"I'll admit, I'm terrible at names, so please forgive me if I don't remember them all." Belle smiled and they all laughed.

"I know it's a lot to take in. Can I get you something to drink? Food is almost ready."

"Sure, cider would be nice."

Jasmine and Belle made small talk as TJ joined a game with Bently, Mikel, and Lyra. The easy way TJ interacted with Bently gave her the feeling that the two had grown closer than either of them had let on. *Why would TJ keep this from me?*

"Belle?" The accent in the voice made her name sound more like "Bella."

She turned as the familiar face of Mia came into view. Blue yoga pants hugged her curves, and she wore a gray hoodie that said "Shattered Cove, N.H."

"Yes? Mia, right?"

The man she'd come to know as Andre stood by her side, his arm protectively wrapped around her as he watched the other guys play.

"I am. And I just wanted to thank you for, well, saving my life." Mia smiled.

"No need to thank me. Really, I'm just glad you're okay."

"Dinner!" Remy called.

They all filed into Remy's house. The natural wood flooring added to the warm and inviting atmosphere. They turned left into the dining room with a long table set with various savory dishes. The smell of the delicacies made her stomach grumble with hunger. She'd only had time for a quick smoothie for lunch today.

"Mia, you sit here, and TJ will sit on the other side," Remy directed them. "Bently you're here."

"Since when do we have assigned seating?" Mikel asked as Bently took the empty chair beside Belle. She inhaled slowly, taking in the hints of oak, campfire, and him.

Remy cut her husband a look that had him changing the subject. "How's the studio, Mia?"

"Oh, it's great. My classes are so full, I've had to add an extra one on the weekends," she answered.

"Do you do yoga, Belle?" Remy asked.

"I've never tried."

"It's really fun. We girls should get together and have a class sometime," Remy suggested.

Belle nodded. She'd never really had friends before, but it seemed that was possible in Shattered Cove.

Bently handed her a platter of vegetables and she served herself some before passing it on to TJ as everyone made polite conversation. She'd never seen so much food at one table in her life. Once everyone was served, Mikel lifted his glass of what looked to be hot cider. "To family and friends."

The group of adults lifted their own cups and repeated the sentiment before taking a sip. Belle glanced at Bently's plate, at the similar array of vegetables and seafood before she tucked into her own. Flavors exploded in her mouth, rich and savory. "This is fantastic." She nearly moaned. Bently seemed to sit a little straighter next to her, his jaw tense.

"So, how did you two meet?" Mia asked, motioning between her and Bently.

"I thought they met because of you," Remy said, narrowing her eyes at him. Belle didn't like being the center of attention. She glanced at Bently nervously, pleading with him to answer.

"Yeah, I'd like to know too," Andre said, eyeing TJ.

"I gave TJ a ride home. His bike had flat tires. Belle was there when we got to his house," Bently answered.

"And?" Remy prodded.

Belle shifted in her seat.

"And we've seen each other at the hospital a few times because of work," Bently supplied, taking a sip of a beer.

The fact that he'd left out how rude she'd been to him,

saving her the scrutiny of his friends, brought a sharpness to her chest. She'd never had anyone stick up for her, or try to protect her besides TJ.

"What aren't you telling me?" Remy asked, her gaze boring into Bently's.

"I took his self-defense class too. How old are you, Lyra?" Belle asked, changing the subject.

"I'm six!" the little girl said around a mouthful of asparagus.

"So, you've known each other for a couple months, then?" Mikel asked, eyeing his brother suspiciously.

Bently grunted.

Mikel smirked and nodded to Andre. "Seems like Bently here is speechless for once in his life."

Bently sighed and drained the last of his beer. He covered Lyra's ears beside him and said, "Enough, you two dickheads. Eat your dinner and shut the fuck up."

He returned his hands to the table and took another bite. His friends were grinning but she was really out of the loop.

"How's business at the inn, Jas?" Mikel asked.

"Pretty good. I'm saving up to finish the reno downstairs," Jasmine answered, nursing her little one.

"You own an inn?" Belle asked.

"Yes." She beamed. "The Lighthouse Inn. It's right on the coast—a couple miles from town."

"That sounds like a pretty cool job to have."

"TJ, you up for a game of hoops after dinner? You and me against Dre and Mikel. A hundred bucks says we can take 'em," Bently asked. Her chest tightened again.

"I'm game," TJ answered.

"How about we make it two hundred?" Andre asked, smiling while eyeing TJ.

She wasn't sure she liked that man. It would be nice to see TJ wipe that smirk off his face.

"You're on," Bently agreed.

After dinner, the guys went outside to play while the women popped a bottle of wine. Both babies were asleep, and Lyra was watching a cartoon about an ice princess and her sister saving the kingdom.

This was so easy, so comfortable. The ladies talked, laughing and making jokes. She felt right at home, like everything just clicked. This was her new tribe.

Belle sipped the crisp white wine.

"So, Belle," Jasmine started, and Belle gave her new friend her full attention.

"Did you fuck my brother?"

13

BELLE

B elle choked, spurting alcohol onto the table in front
of her.

"Jasmine!" Remy scolded.

"Did she?" Mia asked.

Belle accepted the paper towel Remy handed her as she
cleaned her face and table.

"No. She's the one that he was talking about. The one
who wouldn't give him the time of day," Remy clarified.

"Ohhhh," Jasmine and Mia said in unison.

"I'm sorry, what?" Belle asked, extremely lost.

"Do you want to fuck him?" Jasmine asked.

"I . . . no! I mean—maybe, but no." She shook her head,
getting a hold of herself. "I'm not looking for that kind of
relationship."

The women stared at her blankly.

"I'm lost. Don't all relationships eventually lead to sex?"
Mia asked.

"The good ones do," Remy added.

"She means she doesn't do one-night stands. Right?" Jasmine asked for confirmation.

Belle nodded.

"Ahhh." Mia nodded.

"I've never seen my brother interested in anyone long-term before. But from what I hear, you've piqued his interest," Jasmine said.

All the women's eyes were on her. She pulled the collar of her T-shirt away from her neck, suddenly feeling flushed. "Look, I don't really know what to tell you. There's nothing going on between us. So, you have nothing to worry about."

Remy placed her hand over Belle's. "Oh, we're not worried—we were gettin' excited. Bently is such a good man and he deserves to find happiness after all he's been through. You seem like a great person from what we can tell."

"Oh." It was all she could say.

"He's taken care of me my whole life, and I would be remiss if I didn't check out his potential interests. Make sure you won't break his heart." Jasmine winked, but Belle got the feeling that the woman meant business.

What did Jasmine mean Bently had taken care of her? Did she have even more in common with Bently and his family than she'd realized? Before she could ask, the door burst open and the men filed in.

"I want a rematch!" Mikel said.

Bently chuckled. "Nope. Not my fault you underestimated my buddy here." He rose his fist and TJ bumped it.

Belle swallowed. The sight of her brother and Bently getting along so well made her stomach flutter.

Mikel wrapped his arms around Remy. "I got all I need right here. I'm still a winner if I come home to you, baby." He leaned in and kissed Remy.

Andre splayed his hands over Mia's cheek. "Me too." His

lips crashed to hers with so much passion that Belle looked away, giving them a bit of privacy.

"Ahhh, come on, ladies. You deserve real men, not these two losers." Bently chuckled.

Andre pulled back and said, "You're just jealous I get to go home to this fine woman in my bed every night."

Bently's eye's clouded over before he glanced at Belle.

"*You're* just lucky I was there to help you pull your head out of your ass in time," Bently teased, grabbing another beer from the fridge and walking out to the fire.

Something tugged her out after him. The mix of emotions she'd seen reflected in his eyes was something familiar and recognizable. For the first time, she could see past the jokes and smiles. His mouth said one thing while his eyes told another story. The real question was, what was he hiding underneath the facade?

She walked out into the cool night air towards the crackling fire. She crossed her arms and shivered, having left her jacket in the house.

The tether between them pulled her onward. He sat on a log. Red flames reflected in his blue eyes. Heat from her core spread through her, warming her from within as she sat next to him.

"You okay?" she asked, studying him.

"Why wouldn't I be? TJ and I won a hundred bucks each," he answered, not looking up from the fire.

"Why do I get the feeling that wasn't the first time you saw my brother in action?"

Bently shrugged. "Sometimes we happen to both be at the same court at the same time."

A burst of gratitude bloomed in her chest. "He seems to like you."

Bently tipped back his beer, taking a sip. "Most

people do."

A pang of guilt swept through her at the insinuation. "Can I ask you a favor?"

He turned to face her. Half his chiseled face was hidden in the shadows of the night. The corners of his eyes creased. "What do you need?"

Need? *Someone to extinguish this fire inside me. Someone to take all these complicated feelings and uncomplicate them.*

"I'd like to start over. I made some mistakes and assumed I knew you. That was wrong and unfair. I would like to become friends. If that's okay with you?" she asked, laying it all out there. She sat in her vulnerability, waiting patiently for his answer.

He blinked a couple times before the corner of his mouth quirked up. "So, this is what it feels like."

She furrowed her brow. "Like what feels like?"

"To be friend-zoned."

She laughed, happy to see the humorous glint return to his eyes. "It's all I have to offer."

"Then I'd be happy to be your *friend*, Belle." He rubbed his hand against the rough stubble on his chin. Something about the way he said it sounded more like he was accepting a challenge.

She licked her lips—his eyes darted to the movement. The tension between them grew thick with anticipation. He leaned in a little closer, his woodsy scent melding with the campfire. She shivered, frozen in place, all thought leaving her head except one. *What would his lips feel like on mine?*

"Are you cold?" he asked, his gravelly voice bringing to attention just how much closer he was now. He pulled off his jacket and put it around her shoulders before she could answer.

"Thank you." Now that oak scent was intoxicating her, cloying to every cell and coating it in desire.

"You're welcome, *friend*." He smirked.

The sight sent a shock of wanton lust through her. She clenched her thighs together. She began to tremble from a mixture of hazy need and fear over how her body reacted to him. Something deep inside her whispered, *he's safe*. That voice had never misled her before. That intuition was the only reason she was alive.

"I think you're going to like being my friend," he said.

"Why's that?"

"Guess you'll just have to wait and see, beautiful." He winked.

A flutter of butterflies erupted in her belly. Excitement she wasn't used to feeling knotted her stomach with nerves. She didn't like being this off-kilter. She was always in control—she'd had to be. That was what scared her most about him—the disarray he thrust her into.

He's safe.

But was she?

14

BENTLY

After walking up the steps to Belle's house, Bently took a rallying breath and knocked. The way she'd come to check on him, asking if they could be friends, it had given him the first spark of hope he'd had since everything went south at the gym.

The door opened and TJ looked up at him, unsure and hesitant. He obviously still had a long way to go earning this guy's trust.

"Hey, is your sister home?"

TJ's mouth split into a knowing and almost relieved grin. "Sure is. Come on in." TJ walked in, leaving the door open as he went to the array of books at the kitchen table.

"Belle, it's for you!" he hollered.

Bently shut the door and cleared his throat as Belle came down the stairs with a basket full of laundry in her arms.

Her full pink lips opened into an O. It was the first time he hadn't seen them coated in that sinful red lipstick. A mouth he'd almost kissed the other night, until good judgment had won out.

"Hey, *friend*. Feel like having lunch on this fine Sunday with me?"

She bit into that delicious bottom lip and set the basket on the couch, giving him a nice view of her perfect ass in those red high-waisted leggings. She turned around, the tiny half T-shirt showing off the strip of soft stomach. He put his hands into his jean pockets, controlling the itch to touch her.

"Do you take all your *friends* to lunch?" she asked, her eyes narrowing as if she could see right through his plans.

"Only the best ones." He smiled.

"You seemed pretty chummy with TJ. Is he invited on this . . . excursion?"

TJ quietly laughed as he watched their exchange.

Ideally, Bently wanted this woman alone, but they were a package deal and he'd come prepared. "Of course."

Belle's shoulders relaxed. "It's kind of last minute."

"I like to think of it as spontaneous."

A ghost of a smile turned up the corner of her mouth. This woman was a challenge, and damn if he didn't like it.

She looked over at her brother before nodding. "Alright, we'll go."

"Great. We can take my truck. You'll want a pair of sneakers." He glanced at her small naked feet as she wiggled her hot-pink toes. Everything about this woman was tiny compared to his six-foot-three stature.

"Okay. Anything else? Where are you taking us?"

"A warm jacket, and as far as our destination goes, that's a surprise." He shrugged innocently.

The corner of her mouth turned up again in an almost smile.

She grabbed a pair of Converse sneakers and tied them before slipping a coat off the rack next to the door. "Come on, TJ."

"As much fun as spending the afternoon babysitting the two of you sounds, I have plans. Rain check?" TJ smirked, and Bently liked the kid a lot more in that moment.

Belle's eyes widened, but Bently swept into action, opening the door. "Well, we better get going. Don't want to miss our reservation." He winked.

Her brow furrowed as panic flashed in her expression. Bently spoke in his most soothing tone. "We don't have to go if you're not feeling up to it, but I would love your company. If we're gonna be friends, we should get to know each other a little better, right?"

She swallowed, the action drawing his attention to her exposed neck and a small light scar that zigzagged right above her collarbone. "Okay. Let's go." She passed him and walked down the porch towards his truck.

He shut the door and ran to catch up to her before opening the car door for her. Belle needed a boost in because it was so high up. As she took the hand he offered, her soft touch sent a zing of energy buzzing around his body. She pulled herself up, as he reached out his hand to the back of her thigh, steadying her. Liquid heat rocketed through him. He bit back a groan. He'd barely touched the woman and his cock was pressed into his zipper so hard he might have a permanent imprint. He cleared his throat and shut the door as she buckled in.

Bently climbed in the driver's side and started the engine before he pulled out. He drove through town and turned the music on low. The band Grandson played on the radio, filling the silence.

"I had you pegged as a country music fan." She smiled sheepishly.

He winced. "I mean, I can stand to listen to some, but it's definitely not my go-to."

She chuckled.

"What about you?"

She scrunched her nose. "Country music? No way."

He laughed. "What's your preference?"

"This is nice. I listen to a mix of things."

"So, we seem to have music in common. What's your favorite food?"

"Italian. What's next? You want to know my favorite color?" She giggled and fuck if it wasn't the sweetest sound he'd ever heard.

"I already know your favorite color."

She swiveled her head to look at him as he turned down the road towards the state line separating New Hampshire and Maine.

"You do?"

He nodded as he stopped at the stoplight. Swiveling his head to face her, he said, "Red."

She sucked the tiniest amount of her bottom lip into her mouth, and a shot of lust burned his veins. He wanted to be the one to do that.

Someone honked behind them and he focused his attention back on the road, pressing the gas and continuing on to their destination.

"How did you know?" she asked, a little quieter.

"You wear a lot of it. It's one of the first things that drew my attention to you. Those red lips."

"Oh."

The sexual tension in the car was stifling. He cracked his window, letting cool October air into the cab, but it offered no relief.

"Your family and friends seem like good people. They look up to you."

They do, but should they? "They're special."

"Jasmine said you basically raised her," she pressed.

He cleared his throat. "TJ said the same about you."

"I did. I guess that's something else we have in common. Both having to protect and care for others long before we were meant to."

He wanted to ask about her life, but that would leave him open for her return questions. And there was no way he was going there.

"What made you become a nurse?" he asked instead.

She waited a beat before she answered. The road they traveled turned into gravel as they wound through the forest, up the mountain path. "I like helping people. Where are you taking me? Is this where you murder me and leave my body for the bears? I have to warn you, I know self-defense," she joked, though her voice was tinged with uncertainty.

He laughed. "I thought it might be fun to hike to our lunch spot."

"Hike? Here in the woods? Aren't there like bears and other wild animals?"

He pulled into the lot and parked the truck. Turning to face her, he tried to hide his grin. He patted her knee, need and want blistering from the touch. "Don't worry, city girl. I'll keep you safe."

She looked down at his palm and back to him. The lure of her dark brown eyes wavered his defenses. Bently jerked his hand away like it was on fire. He was too exposed and vulnerable with her. He needed to get himself under control. Bently opened his door and walked around to her side. He held out his hands and she gripped his shoulders before sliding herself slowly to the ground. Her soft curves pressed against him, sending white-hot flames splintering through him. He set her on her feet and stepped away before she could feel what she did to him.

He'd promised her friendship, and anything more would scare her off for good, he was sure of it. The problem was, there was no way he could just be platonic with this woman. He craved her, desired her with every cell in his damaged body. But she needed slow. She'd only offered him friendship and he'd take what he could get. Someone like her would never want him long-term—not after she found out what a failure he truly was.

"Mount Agamenticus," she read off the sign.

"It's got a great view of the White Mountains and the ocean at the top." He pulled the backpack from his truck bed and slung it over his shoulders before leading her towards the trail.

They walked in silence at first, passing other hikers every now and then. It wasn't too busy this time of year. Most of the leaves had already fallen, covering the floor of the forest in the bright yellows, reds, and oranges. The trail was steep in many places. He slowed to stay in pace with Belle.

The farther they hiked, the closer she got to him. "Are you sure we won't run into any bears?" Her hands touched his arm, and instinctively he wrapped his palm around hers and squeezed.

"No, we'll be fine. This is a well-traveled area. I've hiked this mountain hundreds of times and never seen more than a squirrel or chipmunk."

"Okay." She seemed to breathe a little easier, but she didn't let his hand go.

He'd protect her, even if it meant risking his life. That was part of his job—every day there was a risk he might not make it home because he'd sworn to protect and serve. But nothing about the softness of her hand entrusted in his felt like just another day. The ache in his chest at the fear in her eyes told him that whether he was a cop or not, it was more important to protect this woman than the next beat of his heart.

He was the one in danger.

15

BENTLY

They were out of breath by the time they reached the summit. He led her to a wooden lookout, his leg muscles aching with every step. When he guided her to the top, he pointed out in the distance. "There are the White Mountains."

"Where?" she asked.

He stepped behind her, one hand on her shoulder as he leaned in and pointed with the other one. "They're easier to see when they have snow caps on them."

She turned to face him. "And that other side is the ocean?"

He nodded, not taking his gaze off her. He leaned the tiniest bit forward, testing the waters.

Her stomach grumbled.

He chuckled. "Guess we better eat."

She smiled bashfully. "I skipped breakfast."

"You should have said something. We could have stopped for food."

She shrugged as he led her towards a picnic table. "I just got busy and forgot. It's not a big deal."

"Do you do that a lot?"

"Skip breakfast?" she asked.

"Forget to take care of yourself?"

She opened her mouth to say something and then closed it. Belle remained silent as he pulled out the water bottles and handed her one.

"So glad we could make the reservations." She cast him a skeptical look and twisted off the cap before taking a long gulp of water.

He smirked. "Wouldn't want to miss the best seats in the house." He laid out the sandwiches and fruit and veggie platter he'd packed on the wooden picnic table.

"Wow. You've really outdone yourself," she said, unwrapping one of the sandwiches.

He shrugged. "Didn't know what you'd like."

"This is perfect," she said before biting into the turkey sandwich.

After they'd finished eating, Belle said, "Tell me about yourself."

He drained the rest of his drink before answering. "My favorite food is also Italian and my favorite color is green. I am the oldest of three and I like to hike in my spare time."

She shook her head. "Is Jasmine your half sister?"

An uneasiness tumbled in his belly. "Yeah, same mom."

"Are your parents still alive?"

He shifted in his seat and picked at the wrapper of the water bottle. "No."

After a beat of silence, she shared, "I have no idea who my father is, or TJ's for that matter. I was seven when he was born. My mother wasn't exactly capable of taking care of us, so I stepped in. I have no idea if she's dead or alive, but she's not in our life and that's a good thing."

He swallowed. She'd said so much and yet left so many questions swirling in his mind. He'd experienced personally how incapable and downright toxic some parents could be. His gaze flashed to the collar of her jacket where he'd seen the scar earlier. The thought of this beautiful woman being hurt made his body hum with anger. His fists clenched, crunching the plastic.

"Was your situation similar?" she pressed.

Yes. No. "You want to know my childhood story so you can figure me out, Doc? Are you really a nurse or a shrink?" He forced a laugh. When he glanced up, she wasn't smiling.

"How do you ever expect to get to know someone if you always hide behind that mask of humor?"

His breath stalled. She'd scared the shit out of him. He slipped into the role that came so easily. His voice dropped lower as he gave her a look that usually worked on women. "Oh, I could think of a few creative ways to get to know you."

She shook her head, disappointedly. For some reason the idea of letting her down made his stomach sink like a rock. But the look that flashed in her eyes grated across his skin. *Pity.*

"I'm sorry."

"What's that supposed to mean?" he asked defensively.

"If you can't be vulnerable with someone, how do you ever expect to share a lifetime?"

"Isn't that kind of like the pot calling the kettle black?" he snapped.

She crossed her arms over her chest. "I already admitted my faults. This is me being open with you, sharing about my past. I haven't had many friends before, but isn't this what friends do—share?"

He swiped a hand through his hair and sighed. "It doesn't matter. I'm not the marrying kind."

"What makes you say that?"

He needed to get her off his back. To stop asking him questions he didn't want to answer. The woman had an uncanny ability to push his buttons and find the weak spots in his defenses. Bently had to push her away, keep her at arm's length. "I'm the playboy of Shattered Cove, or haven't you heard?"

She shook her head, disappointed with his answer again.

"Why does this matter to you anyway?" he asked.

"Because no matter how many times you say you're my friend, the way you look at me says different."

He leaned in, his eyes locked on hers in this battle of wills. "And what exactly do my eyes tell you?"

She moved closer so that their faces were only a few inches apart. Her sweet breath whispered across his lips. "That you want to strip me down. See me like so few men have."

His jaw clenched at the thought of another man touching her.

"You want my body, and I'll admit . . . I want you too."

He swallowed, hope and lust swirling inside. *Yes*. He needed to have her and get this out of his system. This woman was driving him mad with desire. Spinning him so out of control, he gripped her face just to ground himself. That was the wrong thing to do. Her soft skin against his rough palms was gasoline onto the burning chaos raging inside him. Her breath quickened, lust and want darkening in those brown-sugar eyes. She wanted him just as badly as he wanted her.

"Bently."

His name on her lips was his breaking point. He leaned in, swiping his lips across hers softly, gently at first. Energy crack-led, want obscured his vision as he kissed her like he'd never kissed before. Overpowering and staggering. Roaring need lit him up, his body glowing red hot from the inside out. Fireworks and explosions rocked through his body as she moaned. He cursed the wooden table between them as he pulled her face closer, tasting the seam of her lush lips with his tongue. Lust blanketed him as he tore his mouth away, searching for a hidden alcove. He needed this woman right the fuck now. If kissing her was this beautifully devastating, being inside her was imperative.

She looked up at him, dazed and glassy-eyed as if lost in the smoky fog of lust herself. He shot to his feet and tugged her hand. Belle resisted.

"No." She shook her head. "I can't do this, Bently. We can't . . ." The fear flashing in her eyes poured over him like a bucket of ice water.

Shit. He'd moved too fast. "I'm sorry. I thought you wanted . . ."

"I did."

A rush of relief washed over him.

"But that's the problem," she said.

"I don't follow. If you want me and I want you, then what's the issue?" he asked, confused.

She licked her lips, no doubt tasting the traces of him. "You've made it clear you're not a relationship type of guy. But I can't separate feelings from sex." Her voice trembled. She wiped at her eyes before the tear that had welled there could fall.

What have I done? He ran a hand over his rough stubble. "I'm sorry. I really didn't plan on trying to . . . I . . ." For once in his life, he wished he could be that guy—the one who could love. The one who wasn't screwed up and damaged beyond repair.

She placed her hand on his cheek. "I wish I could."

The statement staggered him, nearly brought him to his knees. Belle was one of a kind. Strength and grace oozed from her pores, radiating from her like warm sunshine. Belle was too good for him. This woman was better off staying away. She'd only end up like him in the end—broken.

16

BELLE

Belle parked at the library, then texted TJ that she was there. Her thoughts drifted back to Bently and that kiss for the millionth time that day as she waited. His lips had felt like destruction and rebirth all at once. Her body had come alive in what seemed like the first time in her twenty-four years of life.

The back door opened and TJ threw his backpack in before climbing into the front seat.

"How was your day?" she asked, shifting into reverse. She backed out.

"Fine. Just can't wait to be done with all this." He sighed.

"You're almost there. Then you have college to look forward to."

"Do you mind dropping me off at the Hope Facility in the city? I can take the bus back," he asked.

"Is that the place that Bently suggested?"

TJ nodded. "Yeah, I'd like to check it out."

"Okay."

He plugged his earbuds in and rested his head against the seat, closing his eyes.

He worked so hard. They'd never had another choice. Seeing him become such an incredible man after all they'd been through brought a swirl of pride to her chest.

She turned the radio on. The same band played that she'd heard in Bently's truck.

After their lunch, he'd kept his distance—careful not to touch her unless he was helping her in and out of the truck. The unease was eating at her. She may not be able to repeat that incredible kiss, but she still wanted to remain his friend.

Something about the man tugged at her heart. His hidden scars only evident for those that knew what they looked like personally, those like herself. Belle might not have all he wanted, but she could offer him what he needed most—a friendship from someone who knew what it was like. She smiled as a plan took form in her mind.

An hour later, she walked into the sheriff's office, cup of coffee in hand, and a box in the other. An officer came over to her with a blank stare and scowl on his face. "Bail bonds are one floor down."

"I'm not here to post bonds. I'm here to see the sheriff."

His gaze narrowed on the items in her hands before shifting back to her.

"Do you have an appointment, dear?" an elderly woman asked from a desk to her left.

Belle turned to the woman. "No. But would you mind telling him Belle is here to see him?"

The officer to her right scoffed. "Listen, lady, this is a place of work. What are you doing here?"

Who the fuck did this man think he was? Sneering at her like she was less than the dirt under his feet? She turned and eyed his name tag. "Officer Parsons, exactly what do *you* think I am doing here?"

His face reddened as Betsy spoke into an intercom.

"What *are* you doing here?" Parsons repeated.

A door opened and Bently's surprised voice asked, "Belle?"

She turned from the officer and walked to greet Bently. She smiled. "I brought a peace offering."

He ushered her into the office, closing the door after her. A beat-up antique of a wooden desk sat in the center. A small bookshelf lay against the wall in between several metal file stands. Warm sunlight filtered in through the large bay windows off to her left. A few plaques and commendations hung on the wall in the otherwise sparse room.

"What can I do for you?" he asked, taking a seat across from her at the desk.

She handed him the coffee and box of pastries with the yellow sticky note on top that read *Cop food*.

His eyes studied the note and a grin broke through the nervous air in the room. "Ahhh, she can be funny too." He chuckled.

"Cops like donuts, right?"

"One assumption you got right about me." He winked.

She relaxed into the chair across from him. "I just thought I'd return the favor. Remy told me which ones you liked."

"Oh, great. Now I'll never hear the end of it."

"I made it clear I needed a treat for my *friend*." She waited for his reaction.

"Coffee was a good call. Thanks." He sipped from the paper cup, his expression giving nothing away.

"I was wondering how the investigation over Charli was going? Have you seen her since?"

His brows drew together and his tone grew serious. "I can't really share any details about an ongoing investigation with the public. I can assure you I take what happened very seriously. I don't stand for women being hurt and the perp getting away with it."

Something about the way he said it told her Bently Evans took those sorts of crimes personally. Why did he feel the need to be everyone's knight in shining armor?

"As a friend, I can tell you she's managing. Reed is coming home soon, and I think she's just waiting to really fall apart until then."

"He's deployed, right?"

Bently nodded. "Army."

"That's got to be tough." She looked down.

"How's TJ?" Bently asked.

"I dropped TJ off at the Hope center you mentioned."

"Oh yeah? I think he'll like it there."

"I wish he could make some friends. I've seen him with this one kid at school, but something about him is just . . . off."

Bently squinted. "What do you mean?"

"Being around those types long enough, it becomes second nature to spot. You learn real quick to trust that gut feeling."

His eyes darted to where she rubbed the small scar on her neck absentmindedly.

She dropped her palm to her lap. Questions reflected in his eyes, but he held back. *Again.*

"Tell me the guy that hurt you got what he deserved."

Belle looked at her hands before focusing on him. "I think you know that in real life the bad guy doesn't always get his deserved judgment."

His gaze darkened. The silence between them was almost deafening, the air charged with warning.

"I'd better go." She stood at the same time he did.

"I'll walk you out," he said, coming to her side and opening the door. "Thanks again for the coffee and donuts."

She smiled and walked out on shaky legs, wishing she'd never known what his lips felt like on hers. Then she could pretend it wasn't the most world-shattering experience she'd ever had. Then she wouldn't be longing for his touch. Then she wouldn't be disappointed with the reality that she'd never get to feel it again.

17

BELLE

"Take that!" TJ's voice rose, waking Belle from her nap. She shifted the covers to glance at the clock. *Five o'clock.* She'd slept for two hours.

TJ's laugh echoed up the stairs as she walked to the bathroom to relieve herself and brush her teeth.

A low chuckle accompanied his. *TJ has a friend over.* She glanced at her reflection in the mirror. Her sleep-mussed hair was wild. She wiped under her eye, erasing the last trace of makeup from her skin. Her finger pressed against the thin scar on her neck. Shame and helplessness washed over her like a rogue wave. Spinning, she tumbled back to the ghosts of the past, the men who'd used her.

"You belong to me."

Voices rose downstairs, overshadowing the ones in her mind.

She clamped her eyes shut, taking a deep breath. "I'm safe. I'm free. I'm calm," she repeated the affirmations until the heaviness lifted from her shoulders.

The memories were like a dark shadow looming in the

background, waiting for the opportunity to jump out and try to drag her back down into the abyss. She couldn't afford to be depressed. TJ needed her. She was all he had. She'd learned early on that, in order to survive, you had to keep going—no matter what.

"Ahh, you think you're so slick hiding back there. I see how it is." TJ was in some sort of competition, probably playing the video game that hardly ever got touched. She'd got it for him in hopes it would help him take a break from always studying. He deserved to be a teenager without the weight of the world on his shoulders.

Belle's stomach grumbled. *Dinnertime.* She pulled on her black high-waisted leggings and adjusted the off-the-shoulder crop top—her go-to comfort clothes.

She grabbed her phone off the nightstand in her bedroom before heading downstairs.

"You in the mood for lasagna?" she asked, not looking up from her emails.

"A woman after my own heart."

Her head snapped up as she stumbled down the last step, awkwardly catching herself on the railing at the last second.

Bently winced. "You okay?"

Heat rushed to her cheeks. "What are you doing here?"

"Got ya!" TJ yelled triumphantly next to Bently on the couch.

"You cheater. I was distracted," Bently argued, standing and setting the gaming controller on the couch. His eyes caressed every inch of her body.

TJ shrugged. "Hey, a man has to play to his advantages. Not my fault you can't keep your eyes off my sister."

Bently smirked. His blue eyes shone as he winked at her. "I believe I heard something about lasagna?"

"Are you staying for dinner?" she asked, amused.

Bently placed a hand over his stomach. "Why, thank you for the invitation. I would love to."

Belle rolled her eyes and laughed.

"Need any help in the kitchen?" Bently asked.

A pang of something unfamiliar flitted through her chest. But if he kept looking at her like *she* was what he wanted for dinner, there was no way they could cook in that small kitchen without her combusting.

She shook her head. "No, I got it. You two have fun."

"Best out of three does the dishes after dinner," he said to TJ as he resumed his place on the couch.

Belle got to work, pulling out her homemade sauce as the oven warmed up. She layered the pasta, meat, and cheese with fresh herbs. Sliding it into the oven before she brewed a pot of coffee. The sounds of laughter and trash talk bounced between TJ and Bently.

A flash of movement in the window drew her attention. The reflection staring back at her was smiling. Her fingertips pressed against her cheek. She'd been doing that more and more lately. She bit her lip. *A crush—that's all this is.* He'd made it clear he couldn't give her a romantic relationship. Why did that feel like such a loss? Didn't you have to have something before you could feel it missing?

She poured herself a cup of coffee when it was ready and added some hazelnut creamer. She fixed two others, one with cream and sugar, the way TJ liked it, and then left one black for Bently. She brought it to the living room, carefully setting it on the coffee table out of their way.

"Thank you," Bently said, making eye contact before he focused back on the game.

TJ had a carefree grin spread wide on his face. He didn't ever get to do this—have a grown man giving him attention. She went back into the kitchen to grab her coffee and her book before returning to the living room to sit in the chair beside them. She flipped to her bookmark and got sucked into the book.

This story was riveting and real. The characters' emotions so raw, she'd felt like she *was* them. They'd both had so much to work through. Everything seemed to be designed to tear them apart, and it had. But as she closed the book on the last chapter, they'd found each other again and what's more —hope.

Setting the book aside, Belle drained the rest of her cold coffee and tucked her feet underneath her. Still reeling from the ending, her eyes stung from the tears that wanted to fall. She blinked to keep them at bay as she looked up. Bently stared back, the look in his eyes somehow different than any other time. There was lust there for sure, but also a flash of something else. His gaze was like quicksand, pulling her in deeper. Stirring and blurring the lines she'd so carefully lived her life by. The intensity of need coiling inside her was threatening to snap.

TJ hooted and hollered in the background and Bently blinked away, as if just realizing what he'd been doing, ending the trance.

Beep! Beep! Beep!

She grabbed her empty cup and went to the kitchen. After shutting the timer off, she grabbed hand mitts before opening the oven. The savory smell of pasta, meat, and cheese permeated the small house. She inhaled as she pulled the casserole dish from the oven and placed it carefully on top. Belle uncovered it, the steam wafting up.

The fine hairs on her arms and neck stood on end as if reaching out towards a source of electricity. She sensed him before he spoke. "Can I help set the table?"

She nodded and pointed without looking up. "Plates are in there."

He walked over, invading her space one step at a time. She used the spatula to cut the lasagna into pieces, pretending he didn't affect her. Pretending her body didn't hum with some unseen energy that crackled and thickened the air between them. Pretending her inner muscles didn't throb and ache with emptiness. She shook her head. This wasn't her. She'd never experienced this kind of attraction before.

Glass clinked as he set the plates next to her, his arm grazing hers. Her breathing hitched. She stood frozen, afraid if she moved, it would be into him rather than away.

He leaned his head in inhaling. His hot exhale tickled the exposed skin of her neck and shoulder.

"Smells delicious."

God, she wanted his mouth on her neck. She turned to face him. His eyes darted to her mouth. She bit down hard on her bottom lip.

"Don't do that," he grated. He reached out and pulled her bruised lip free with his thumb.

She shivered, need and want blazing like a wildfire within her.

Tension clamored, electrifying her insides. He was so close. Oak and coffee. Earth and musk. *Man.*

Her resolve was weakened by the way he was looking at her. Like he was awed by *her.* Like *she* was precious.

Kiss me.

Bently's other hand gripped her shoulder, pulling her against him. Her cheek pressed against his chest as his arms enveloped her.

"I'm sorry." His voice was ragged as his chest heaved with each sharp breath.

She wrapped her arms around him and squeezed as she

melted into him. Belle breathed him in. A different kind of warmth radiated in her chest. When was the last time she'd been truly just held by a man? *Never.* Bently's arms felt . . . safe.

He's safe.

He kissed the top of her head and backed away. Something about the exchange was so intimate. The way he'd touched her, so careful and gentle, completely opposite of the roughness she'd expected. The way he'd held her . . . he'd given her something rather than taking.

"What else do you need?" he asked, clearing his throat.

You.

* * *

As they devoured their dinner, TJ and Bently exchanged stories. The deep rumble of Bently's laugh vibrated through her, teasing her.

"Oh, I forgot to tell you the light came on in the car again for the oil change," TJ said before shoveling another bite of the pasta into his mouth.

She sighed. "Okay. I'll make an appointment and take care of it."

"So, I checked out Hope Facility," TJ said to Bently.

"What did ya think?"

"It's a cool place. Half the kids there are homeless. I met a guy whose family kicked him out because they caught him with his boyfriend." TJ shook his head.

Bently nodded. "Yeah, Aaron originally started Hope because his brother was in a similar situation."

"It's cool to meet other people who've gone through something similar to what we have. I feel like I can let them know there's a way out." TJ scraped the last bite into his mouth.

123

Bently's brows creased as he glanced at Belle, his questions written in his eyes.

Belle finished chewing and swallowed before washing it down with a sip of wine.

"At least I had my older sister to look out for me on the streets. Most of these guys only have themselves."

Belle picked up her wine again. She didn't mind Bently knowing about her past. She was proud of how far she'd come. But TJ saw her as a heroine, and *that* made her uncomfortable.

"You were on the streets?" Bently asked. His knuckles grew white around the beer bottle.

"Just for a little bit," she answered.

"More like a year or so," TJ corrected. "We had to leave our mom's because—"

"Does anyone want dessert? I've got ice-cream sandwiches," Belle interrupted.

Bently's eyes flashed before he nodded. "Sounds great."

She stood to clear away the plates, but he shot to his feet and took hers, stacking it on his own before reaching for TJ's.

"The cook doesn't clean. You just sit there and relax," Bently said as he took the dishes to the sink. He opened the freezer and pulled out three treats. He tossed one to TJ and then handed one to Belle.

She tore hers open and sunk her teeth into the frozen dessert, barely tasting it as Bently's eyes locked on hers.

"What made you want to become a cop?" TJ asked, seemingly oblivious to the tension between them.

Bently focused his attention back on her brother. "I wanted to protect people. I saw the need for it and figured it was a good way to help get some of the bad guys off the streets. Plus, I needed to do something to support my siblings. It was that or the military, but basic training in the military was longer and I could have been deployed. I was their guardian, so I needed to stay close to home."

TJ nodded, wiping his mouth with the napkin on the table. "I'm gonna go up and finish the reading assignment that's due tomorrow. Thanks for coming over and playing the game with me." TJ extended his hand to Bently who didn't miss a beat as he slapped his palm against her brother's, pulling it back before bumping his fist.

"Thanks for dinner, sis." TJ leaned in and gave her a side hug.

"You're welcome."

The creak of the stairs was the only sound as TJ made his way up to his bedroom.

"That was honestly the best meal I think I've ever eaten. Mia's tamales come in a close second." Bently chuckled.

"How is she doing?"

"Good. Keeping Andre on his toes. They're getting married in the spring." Bently smiled.

So, he'd be the only bachelor left in his group of friends.

"Do you play video games often?" she asked.

Bently shrugged. "Never really had time to play much of anything." He frowned as if he regretted the small confession. He shifted and tipped the beer bottle to his full lips. His Adam's apple bobbed as he swallowed.

"Thank you for hanging out with TJ. He doesn't have any grown men around him, and it means a lot that you take time for him. He doesn't get much opportunity to play either." She sipped her red wine.

He shrugged as if it wasn't one of the greatest kindnesses anyone had ever shown them. "He's a fun guy to hang out with. He's pretty good at ball too. Why doesn't he play for the school team? He's like, scholarship good."

She licked her lips and set her glass down. "He's got some

academic scholarships. He says he isn't interested, that he'd rather double up on work and get the whole thing over with so he can start college early. He was a year behind when we got him enrolled in school again after his guardianship was transferred to me. He buckled down and surged ahead. That's TJ for you. He's focused and a hard worker. He tries to play it down, but he's really smart and driven."

"I can see that." Bently nodded, watching her with rapt attention.

"Sometimes I wonder if I did something wrong. That maybe I put too much pressure on him, or he fed off my overachiever energy."

Bently reached out his hand, his warm palm eclipsing hers. "I think that boy is so amazing *because* of everything you've done for him. Despite . . . everything . . . you got out. You changed both of your life courses for the better. There's nothing to regret about that."

She swallowed. He may not know everything about her past, but he'd hit the nail on the head. He *saw* her.

His finger traced the skin of her wrist, sending tantalizing swirls of arousal spinning through her. He abruptly pulled his hand away, ending the contact. He stood and walked over to the sink.

"You don't have to do those." She got up.

He turned back to her, switching on the water. "You cooked, I clean. Now put your feet up and tell me about that book you were reading."

Her eyebrows rose. "My book?"

He nodded, squirting soap onto a sponge. "You seemed to be lost in another world while you read it. A million different expressions danced across that beautiful face as you turned the pages."

"You were watching me read?"

"Hard to look away. Why do you think I lost so badly to your brother?" He chuckled.

Heat spread in her chest and rose to her cheeks. She was flattered and confused and awed by this man.

"What was it about?" he asked, elbows deep scrubbing her dishes.

Was it possible to combust internally? Sparks and shimmers, like warm rays of sunshine, blossomed beneath her rib cage.

He'd given her something so much more than a physical release tonight. He'd offered her what she craved most— connection. Even if he didn't want it, how was she supposed to stop giving this man her heart?

18

BENTLY

"Give me the drip pan," Bently said, reaching his hand out.

TJ handed him the black plastic container as the asphalt bit into his shoulder.

"Now the socket wrench, and get down here and you can see what I'm doing better," he directed. The cold metal pressed into his palm, before TJ bent and crawled under the jacked Ford Focus.

"You sure it isn't going to fall and crush us?" he asked worriedly.

"Yeah, even if it fell, we got the tires to protect us. It's pretty secure though." Bently lined up the drip pan underneath the right location. "Okay, so take this socket wrench and put it on the oil drain plug there." Bently handed the tool over to the young man. "Pull it to the left."

TJ did as he was told and the bolt loosened.

"Perfect. Now unscrew it with your hand the rest of the way. But watch out, it drains fast."

Black liquid poured out into the plastic bin.

TJ's large grin highlighted his white teeth. "Now what?"

"After it's done draining, we'll put one of these new gaskets on to make sure it won't leak, and get it nice and tight."

Bently walked TJ through the rest of the process, taking time to answer his questions.

"Now it's done, we can put some fresh oil in from under the hood." He inched out from under the car, his eyes meeting the very fine legs of the woman he couldn't get out of his head. He took his time as his gaze lazily crawled up her curves, modestly hidden in those blue scrubs she wore. Her brown spheres slammed into his with so much force. Gratitude he didn't deserve radiated out of her, saturating the air between them. How long had she been watching them?

Bently wiped his hand on the rag and stood. "Almost ready for you to go to work."

"You changed my oil?" she asked, searching his face for an explanation. There wasn't one, except, something inside him drew him to her like a moth to the flame. He may not be able to give her everything she needed, but he could take care of her in these little ways.

"TJ mentioned it the other night at dinner." He hoped she'd drop it and they could move on with their day.

"And he showed me so I can do it next time," TJ said, patting him on the shoulder.

Belle looked between him and her brother, her eyes going glassy as she blinked.

"Aww, don't cry, sis." TJ wrapped his arms around Belle.

Bently's own hands itched to do the same. Why was she acting like this was a big deal?

"You need a shower." She laughed, pulling out of her brother's embrace.

"Yeah. Have a good night at work," TJ said, walking backwards towards the house. "Wanna order a pizza, Bently? Then I'll school your ass in Madden."

"Sounds good," he agreed as the young man disappeared inside. He bent and picked up the tools before placing them back in his toolbox.

"Thank you. No one's . . . I mean . . . this means a lot," Belle said, stepping closer.

Bently gathered the quarts of fresh oil and poured it into the dispenser. "It's not a big deal."

"It is to me," she said quietly.

He capped off the top and shut the hood of the car. "I'll get it off the jack and you'll be all set."

He did as he said and put his tools in the back of his truck, along with the old oil he'd drop off to Link to recycle at the garage.

Two arms wrapped around him as he turned, encompassing him in a hug. His chest squeezed tight, something snapping inside. Careful not to get his stained hands on her, he hugged her back. He breathed her in—cocoa butter and vanilla. He'd hang on to the moment as long as it would last, stealing it like a thief.

"You're a good man, Bently Evans." Her words unlocked something deep inside him. As much as he wanted to argue, having her think that of him put a little piece of him back together.

He leaned in and kissed the top of her head before she released him. He didn't know why he'd done it at dinner a few days ago, except that not putting his mouth on her in some way felt wrong. It wasn't sexual. It was . . . something deeper. *Friendship.* That's right. He was just being a good friend.

* * *

"In what year did slavery end?" Bently quizzed TJ on his history homework.

"Which one?" TJ asked.

Bently looked back to the list of questions on the paper. "Is there more than one?"

"The Emancipation Proclamation was issued January first, eighteen sixty-three. But the civil war between the confederate states of the South and the union soldiers of the North didn't end until eighteen sixty-five. However, news didn't reach Texas until June nineteenth, eighteen sixty-five."

Bently searched the notes. "It doesn't say anything about that date in here."

"It wouldn't." TJ shrugged. "Juneteenth isn't even a public holiday."

Andre and Remy celebrated Juneteenth—he'd heard about it from them when he was a young teen. "Okay—"

TJ held up his hand. "That's when they say slavery ended, but really it changed forms. Since you weren't allowed to own human beings anymore, they enacted Jim Crow, segregation. They created more laws in the eighteen nineties limiting what a Black person could do, where they could live, what they could own, and suppressed their votes."

Bently nodded. "Good thing that was a long time ago."

TJ met his eyes. "Jim Crow didn't end until nineteen sixty-four. Only fifty-six years ago. That means your daddy or granddaddy lived to see it."

Bently shook his head. Heaviness settled on his shoulders for his ancestors' crimes. His stomach churned. "Right, the civil rights movement."

"Bingo."

"Aren't I supposed to be quizzing you?" Bently forced a chuckle.

TJ lifted the can of soda to his lips and took a sip. He set it down and grinned. "I got a good one for you. What year were interracial marriages legalized?"

"Uh . . . I don't know. The same year?"

TJ shook his head. "Went all the way to the Supreme Court in nineteen sixty-seven. Loving v. Virginia."

Bently sat back and sighed. "I don't get how so many people could mistreat a group of other humans like that, like shit."

TJ was quiet, staring out the window.

"Can I ask you a question?" Bently asked.

TJ turned towards him. "Sure."

"Were you scared of me, that day with the bike?"

TJ's eyes clouded over as he nodded. "All I could think was I'm gonna be shot and Belle's gonna be all alone."

Bently ran his palm over his face. This conversation got heavy fast. "I'm sorry. I hope you know that you're safe here in Shattered Cove. My station is full of good officers who care about this community."

TJ grunted.

"You don't believe me?"

"I think you believe that. I've had a target on my back from the day I was born, simply for having more melanin in my skin than you. I can't afford the privilege of feeling safe, or not being conscious of where my hands are at all times when I'm out."

Bently cleared his throat. His mind reeled from TJ's honest and heartbreaking words. "What can I do to make it better?" he asked.

"Man, I'm seventeen years old. I ain't got the answers to world peace. Apparently treating each other with basic human decency is too hard for so many to grasp." TJ shook his head, reaching for his soda once more.

"I'm sorry. You're right." He grabbed the beer he'd set on

the coffee table and took a long gulp. "Alright, next question. What was the date Abraham Lincoln was killed?"

Bently sat on his couch, his computer open on his lap. TJ's words stuck with Bently long after he'd finished quizzing the young man for his test. An uncomfortable briar wedged deep in the back of his mind. The kid had a valid point. How could one man solve world peace? How could you convince another person to leave their bias in the garbage where it belonged? How could you change what was imbedded in the DNA of an entire country?

It had to start somewhere. Shattered Cove seemed as good a place as any.

Bently clicked open his browser and pulled up a list of books on racism and white privilege. TJ was right—it wasn't his job to give Bently answers. Change started from within. The first step in battling ignorance and prejudice was identifying your own.

19

BENTLY

Pain radiated along Bently's neck as his head snapped back from the blow.

"Stupid, good-for-nothing, pussy boy. Man up! Get off your ass and face me like a real man. You think you're so tough." The growl of his father's voice told him all he needed to know. If he didn't get back up, his father would take out his rage on someone else. His mother, his little brother, or possibly his baby half sister.

"Stop!" his little brother's tiny voice yelled.

Paul Evans turned his scowl onto Mikel's five-year-old body. Bently shot to his feet, ignoring the throbbing ache.

"Go to bed, Mikel!" Bently yelled.

Mikel looked back and forth as Jasmine began to wail in their mother's arms. She needed him to protect her too. Maybe if he was stronger, or smarter, he'd be able to get them to safety, away from the monster that was their father.

Paul Evans took a swaying step forward towards Mikel. Bently tucked his shoulder and rammed into his dad. The man's rage now focused on him, rather than the others.

"You son of a bitch!" Paul screamed as he brought his fist down hard on Bently's back again and again. Pain sliced through him.

A sweaty hand grabbed his neck and pushed him against the wall. His feet dangled helplessly, inches from the floor. Bently grabbed his father's wrists, fighting for a breath. Fear and anger mixed with the adrenaline pounding through his veins. The man's unforgiving grip only tightened. The alcohol on his father's rank body odor burned Bently's nose, tainting the tiny bit of oxygen he managed to gasp. Maybe this would be the day his father finally killed him. No. *He needed to live, if only to* protect *them.*

The ice-blue eyes of his father seemed to glow red with rage. "I hate you. You are good for nothing. Dirty bastard that you are, you'll never amount to anything. You hear me? You're nothing!" The edges of Bently's vision darkened. He wasn't strong enough. I'm gonna die and they'll be next.

The pounding blood in his ears didn't fully drown out Mikel's screams and Jasmine's crying. A small hand pressed down on his father's, making him release his hold. Bently crumpled to the ground, gasping for breath through his burning throat. He looked up in time to see his father's hand slap across his mother's face, leaving a scarlet handprint against her fair skin.

He'd failed her. Again.

Bently shot out of bed, gasping in fresh oxygen. His eyes scanned the darkened room, alert. His body buzzed from the adrenaline, and was slick with sweat. The only sound in the room came from the football game still playing on the television. He'd fallen asleep on the couch. *It was just a dream. Just a memory.*

He shut the TV off and ran upstairs. He needed to clear his head. He'd start with a shower.

An hour later, Bently sat at The Shipwreck downing his third whiskey for the night. He normally stuck to beer and limited himself to two drinks, wanting to be nothing like the man who shared half his biology. He'd prove that everything in life was a choice. Bently would be better. Despite what the monster had done to try to break him, he'd risen above.

But tonight, Bently just wanted to forget. Because for the first time in a long time, he wished he could be someone else. Someone who could love and be worthy of love in return. He was too broken.

Belle had made it clear she couldn't be with him in the way he wanted without getting her heart involved. Bently may have been an asshole, but he wasn't that selfish. He shook his head. He wouldn't use her like that. She needed someone deserving of her, who'd take care of her. Someone who could give her a full life with everything she wanted. He wasn't even fully a man thanks to fucking cancer. No woman who wanted a future would choose him if they knew.

The small voice inside him whispered, *She'll leave you, once she sees what a failure you are. You couldn't even protect those you loved most.*

His mother had killed herself, leaving them all alone with that monster. He hadn't been able to get her out in time. His brother had even left without a word. Yeah, he was back, having faced his demons and found his happiness with Remy.

Jasmine was the only constant in his life, but she needed him to watch over her, like he'd failed to do in the past. So many people depended on him, and he couldn't afford another. His grip tightened around the glass as his thoughts spiraled. So many reasons to stay away from *her.*

Claire Reed approached him, bottle of whiskey in her hand. "Would you like another?"

He nodded. "Just fill 'er up."

Claire's eyes crinkled at the sides. Her brow furrowed with concern, but she didn't ask questions and did as he said. That was one thing he liked about Claire Reed—she kept her thoughts to herself.

"How's Finn?" he asked as she finished pouring.

She smiled. "He's hangin' in there. Promised me some grandbabies when he gets back from deployment."

"He's a good man." Bently smiled, highlights of their shenanigans in high school playing a loop in his mind.

Lieutenant Finn Reed, dressed in his battle dress uniform, stopping by the station to say goodbye before he was deployed. "Take care of my girl while I'm gone."

Charli's swollen face flashed, sobering his thoughts. Another failure. He'd get the bastard eventually. "How's Charli doing?"

Claire sighed, wiping down the bar as she looked around them. He followed her gaze towards the few patrons with their backs turned away from them. "She's hanging in there. Any leads on catching the asshole who did it?"

Bently shook his head, drawing the glass closer. "Not yet. Camera catches the assault, but then he runs off out of view. Must have had a car waiting down the road. Too dark to make out his face or any distinguishing details. And the footage from inside had their faces obscured. The lighting in this place doesn't help."

Claire shook her head.

"I'll get him," he promised her, and she nodded once before she walked down the bar, tending to the other patrons looking for a good time.

Bently tipped the glass to his lips, drinking down the alcohol until it didn't burn anymore. The liquor's warmth buzzed through his veins, easing the ache in his chest and clusterfuck in his mind. He'd have to let Belle go. That was the only way to keep them both safe.

"Hey, baby. Looks like you could use some company," a husky voice said from his side. He turned and the room spun with him. Was there one or two women in front of him?

The old Bently would have said something witty and put his arm around her, or them. Then he'd go back to their place and fuck all night. But this Bently hadn't been with anyone since the diagnosis. That was well over a year without the company of a woman. He hadn't had anyone he was truly interested in, until Belle. She'd sparked something to life in him. If there was something he'd learned from the whole experience of being on death's door, it was that life was short, tomorrow was never promised, and regrets would eat you alive.

So, why not take a chance on Belle?

"You okay, handsome?" the woman asked.

"Yeah. Just tired. Gonna head home." He stood, wavering on his feet. He was drunk for the first time in . . . forever.

The blonde looped her hand through his arm. He hadn't been clear enough.

"I'm not in the mood for company tonight, but thanks for the offer." He pulled his arm away from hers, unsteady on his feet.

"You sure? I could do all the work." She winked, seemingly familiar. Tina? Tanya? Tonya?

"I'm sure. Have a good night," he said, walking towards the exit. He'd sleep it off in his truck and then drive home once he was sober.

Opening the door, he stepped out into the cold night air. He stared up at the dark sky, filling his lungs. Stars peeked out from behind clouds, defying the encompassing blackness with tiny sparkles of light. *Hope.*

"Bent, you're not planning to drive home like this, are you?" Mason asked.

Bently shook his head, immediately regretting the movement. "Nah, gonna take a little nap in my truck."

"I'm sorry about leaving Charli that night. I should have . . ." Mason trailed off.

"Ness time call me if you gotta leave. Let the other bouncssser know too. I don't want Claire or Charli walking out here alone at night."

Mason nodded. "Already done. Won't happen again."

Bently walked into the darkened parking lot, heading to where he'd parked his truck. He pulled out his keys as a burst of pain erupted across his back. He was shoved against his car from the impact before he fell to the ground. His head spun as he drunkenly tried to make sense of what was happening. Was this another flashback? He searched the darkness as he groaned in pain. A hooded figure stood above him, angry eyes boring into him, with a metal bat glinting in the moonlight.

"What the fuck!"

"You're gonna pay, pig."

He lifted his hand to block as the bat swung and met his head with a *crack*!

Everything went black.

20

BELLE

Belle stretched her neck out, easing the kinks as she approached the nurses' station. Sandy, the third shift head nurse, handed her a cup of coffee. "You're almost there."

"I could kiss you right now." She gratefully accepted the hot cup of blessed caffeine before she sipped it. The earthy warm liquid perked her up. Third shifts were killer when she was used to seconds. But she was the go-to woman when someone wanted their shift covered. She needed the money. TJ was going to get some grants and scholarships, but it still wouldn't cover everything. He'd need an outrageous amount for books, not to mention she hoped she could cover it all so he could focus on the classes rather than balancing a job and college like she'd had to.

"Patient in four needs an IV change and the one in two pressed the call button," Sandy said with a smile.

"So, the coffee was to butter me up, huh?"

Sandy motioned to her leg. "These old knees are trying to make me retire before I'm ready."

Belle took another sip of the warm drink. It would be cold by the time she next got a chance to drink it. "I've got it."

"And that's why you're my favorite nurse in this whole hospital." Sandy grinned.

Belle smiled.

"Though I'm not the only one it seems." Sandy nodded to Doctor Stanley across the hall who was walking towards them.

"I take my job seriously," Belle whispered, clearing up the insinuation.

"Good evening, ladies," he greeted them.

"Doctor Stanley." Belle nodded. He was tall and handsome. All the nurses loved him. But he didn't make her stomach flutter.

"Please call me Rick." He smiled.

Belle glanced at Sandy's smirk before she responded, "Sure. I've got some patients to attend to, but did you need anything before I go, Doc—uh, Rick?"

"Not at the moment."

She turned and walked towards emergency room number two. After getting the patient a cup of juice, she went to room four. A child snuggled against her mother, an IV sticking out from her tiny arm. Belle tried to be as quiet as she could so as not to disturb the sleeping duo. She exchanged the bags and turned the lights down in the room. The mother's arms held the child protectively, lovingly. A longing in Belle floated to the surface. She'd never had that, been the one to *be* held. She closed the door and made her way to the desk where Sandy still sat, rubbing her knee.

"Do you want some ice for that?" Belle asked.

"No. I'll be fine."

"Sandy, can you help me in six?" Doctor Stanley asked.

Belle patted her hand. "I've got it."

She made her way to the room and froze in the doorway. Her stomach turned to stone. Her heart pounded. *Bently?*

The gauze around his head was soaked red with blood. His cheek was swollen and bruised. His eyes opened, locking on her. Surprise and then shame clouded over those cerulean-blue pools. The wall slammed into place between them.

She swallowed. *Get it together, Belle. You're a professional.* She walked to his side as the doctor put his X-rays into the lighted area.

"Been a while since I've seen you in here, Bently. Wish it was under better circumstances," Doctor Stanley said.

"Me too, Doc," Bently said.

"Glad to hear you're cancer-free."

What? Bently had had cancer?

Bently didn't look at her. It was as if he was pretending she wasn't even there.

"You made a good call and caught it in time," Bently said.

"Looks like you got a few bruised ribs. No internal bleeding. But you do have a concussion," Stanley explained.

"I would say you should see the other guy, but then again, I didn't even get a good look at him." Bently chuckled as if anything about this was funny. Humor was his defense as usual.

"It's a good thing your friend found you when he did. A concussion is a traumatic brain injury," the doctor started explaining.

"I know, Doc. This is not my first rodeo."

Belle looked closer at the X-rays. Healed fractures from old injuries were scattered across his ribs. Surely he hadn't sustained all of those on the job.

No. Something more sinister had to be at play.

"You might have trouble with your vision, problem-solving,

motor skills, and reaction time for a while. You need to keep yourself in a quiet dark room with absolutely no TV or phone screens for forty-eight hours. You'll also need someone to help take care of you. No driving." Doctor Stanley crossed his arms.

Bently's fists clenched.

"Your CT scan showed negative acute injury and no orbital or facial fractures. You got lucky."

"This pounding headache doesn't feel so lucky." Bently winced.

"You might be nauseous and unable to walk unassisted for a while. Best to rest and let your body heal. You can't rush these types of injuries into getting better or you could end up worse in the long run," Doctor Stanley said firmly.

"Alright." Bently waved him off.

"Belle here will dress your flesh wounds and we'll monitor you for a few more hours. You should arrange for someone to pick you up. Did you want us to alert someone on your team?" Doctor Stanley asked.

Bently grimaced. "I'll take care of it."

"Alright. I'll be back to check on you." Rick left them alone.

Belle bit her lip, unsure of what to say. Anger rolled off him like waves lapping the shore, each one stronger than the next. She pulled out the tray and laid the items she'd need on the portable table. He closed his eyes, giving her freedom to study him as she prepared. Her heart ached seeing him like this.

"I'll need this off," she said gently, pulling open the hospital gown and lowering it to the bed. His broad bruised chest was exposed. The defined planes of his muscles rippled with strength. The ache in her chest grew. Angry black and purple bruises marred his olive skin.

"I'm going to wrap your ribs." She explained each step as she carefully took care of his wounds.

A myriad of other scars covered his body. Every time she touched his skin, he winced.

"I'm sorry. I'm trying to be gentle," she said softly as she peeled away the gauze around his head.

He remained silent. Jaw tense, and his face hard.

She leaned in to clean the wound on his head, preparing it for sutures. His breathing sharpened as she coasted the gauze over the dried blood. "What's your pain level?"

"I'm fine." His voice was scraping and raw.

"Your ribs are bruised and you have a concussion. I'd say you're far from fine."

His hand darted to hers, grabbing her wrist as his eyes snapped open. "I don't need your pity!"

She gasped, flames licking up her arm from his firm grasp. Was that what he thought she saw when she looked at him?

Belle had her fair share of stubborn patients, but no one spoke to her like that. Her eyes narrowed. "Well, it's a good thing I don't have any for you, then. As your nurse, I'm responsible for your care. Pain management is part of that."

He dropped her hand and sighed before nodding.

"On a scale of one to ten, what is your pain at?"

"Four," he grumbled.

Probably more like a nine, then. She shook her head. Stupid macho men.

"If I had known you wanted to play nurse and patient, I wouldn't have bothered with the hike. I can do role play." He winked.

A crack in his façade, his words pierced her heart nonetheless. Was he trying to cheapen their experiences? Those moments where his kind heart had shone through—was she supposed to believe they were all because he wanted to sleep with her? No, it was his brass reminder of where the lines were drawn between them. Bently was scrambling to find anything to distance her from him. As if she couldn't see how utterly shattered he was. Whatever he kept buried was eating him alive.

"Should I call your brother?" she asked.

"Nah. Don't want to wake the kids and Remy."

So that meant Jasmine was out too. "How about Andre?"

Bently shook his head and grimaced. "He and Mia are in California."

"Okay, who should I call to come get you, then?"

"I'll be fine on my own. I'll get a taxi or something," he grumbled.

"You can't go home alone with a concussion." She could help him. She might be the only one who could. He'd spent his life protecting others, but who protected him? If this man thought he could push her away when he needed her most, he had another thing coming. After all, what were friends for?

21

BENTLY

His head pounded like someone had put a jackhammer to it. The lights had been dimmed in Bently's hospital room, and the meds had kicked in somewhat, but it wasn't enough. He tried to sleep, but then he'd catch a whiff of her cocoa butter while she quietly checked his vitals or whatever the hell it was nurses did every hour. He could sense her nearness as she made her rounds through the emergency department like they had some sort of string tethering them together.

Now she's seen me at my fucking lowest.

She'd run, taking the choice he'd been struggling with away from him. He was powerless again. He'd been helpless when that person had beaten him, leaving him for dead. Why had he drunk so much?

Because I'm weak. I'm like him.

He was angry at himself for his lapse in judgment, lack of control. Furious with the man who'd jumped him. Was it the same one who'd smashed his windshield? His chest ached as he tried to suck in a tormented gulp of oxygen. The heavy weight on his chest made it impossible. He just wanted to escape. Needed to let this pain out before he burst. He grasped for some semblance of control as his world spun out of order. The craving to run away was like acid on his frayed nerves. It was all he could think about.

The machine next to him started beeping, aggravating his headache like tiny spears. Pain radiated and throbbed from his forehead to his neck.

Soft cool hands touched his. "It's okay, Bently. Just take deep breaths. In for four seconds, and out for four."

He tried to do as she said. The angel to his darkness. His guiding light. Everything hurt, but the ache in his chest overpowered them all. Belle had seen his charts—she'd know what cancer he'd had and the fact that he was now infertile. She'd have seen the X-rays, the record of years of abuse in black and white.

"How's our patient, Belle?" Doctor Stanley asked.

Bently opened his eyes, not wanting anyone else to see him in such a state. He shoved it all down like he'd always done. "Ready to go home, Doc."

The doctor nodded. "That's why I'm here. Belle has the paperwork about concussion care and for your stitches. I'll send you with a pain script, but as I said, you'll need someone to stay with you around the clock for at least forty-eight hours, longer if possible."

"No worries," Bently said.

"You might be nauseous for a while. The headache could last for a week or so. You feel funny or get concerned, you come right back here. Okay?" Doctor Stanley asked.

"Yes, sir."

"Alright, then. You're good to go. Did you have someone waiting to pick you up?" he asked.

"I took care of it," Belle interjected.

Stanley looked at Belle. His expression softened. "Of course. I never doubted your capable hands for a moment."

The man had checked her out every time they'd been in the room together—he could use a lesson in subtlety. Bently's fists clenched as the doctor left the room.

Belle pulled a wheelchair up to the bed.

"That better not be for me," he said, harsher than he'd intended.

Belle rolled her eyes and crossed her arms. "You heard the doctor. You can't walk unassisted."

"He didn't say I was an invalid. I can walk." Bently shuffled his feet to the ground, his head going dizzy with the abrupt movement. Belle's competent arms wrapped around him.

"Men," she grumbled, and he couldn't hold back the small smile that tipped the corner of his mouth up.

He stood carefully. She pressed her side against his as they took slow steps towards the exit. "Did you call Mikel?"

"No."

"Who's coming to get me?"

"You'll see. You like surprises, right?" she said.

He chuckled, but winced from the pain. His head was pounding and his balance off-kilter like he was swimming through a dense fog. Her closeness only added to the dizzying effect. They turned to the double doors to the well-lit parking lot. It was still dark.

He stumbled and swayed, but her grip only tightened.

"I've got you," she promised.

He searched the parking lot for any signs of his family. She led him to her beat-up Ford Focus and opened the door.

"Are you trying to kidnap me?"

"You need round-the-clock care, remember? Now, my

place or yours?" she asked in a no-nonsense tone as she opened the door and guided him inside.

He'd wanted to hear those words from her, but not under these circumstances. His head was throbbing and he shivered. His bloody stained pants and this flimsy scrub top weren't keeping him very warm.

He sighed. "Mine."

That way she could drop him off and go on her way.

She reached across him, her face inches from his. He closed his eyes and tried to relax his muscles, taking shallow breaths so as to not aggravate his sore ribs any further. He stole her exhale as Belle pulled the seat belt across his chest, carefully.

Belle supported him as they walked into his house. There was no way they could both fit up the staircase side by side, so he reached out to the wall to steady himself. Her soft touch grazed his back, blistering his skin. He got to the top of the stairs and tripped. His hands flew out as they landed on the wooden floor. He groaned as pain lit him up from the inside out, his ribs throbbing.

"Which bedroom is yours?" Belle reached out to his arm and helped pull him up.

At least she wasn't asking stupid questions like how was he doing. But damn! He didn't want anyone to see him like this, much less the woman he . . . *wanted*. Frustration built as he stood, grasping the edges of the doorframe to his room. She reached inside and found the light. He slammed his eyes shut at the visual intrusion.

"Fuck! Shut it off," he growled.

"I just need to see where everything is so I can help you.

Keep your eyes closed and I'll lead you to the bed." She was asking him to trust her.

He did as she said—it wasn't as if he had a choice. The back of his legs hit the bed and he sat down, gingerly.

"Do you have any candles?"

"Check Jasmine's old room. First one on the left."

Belle disappeared, rustling through what sounded like drawers before she returned. "Okay, you can open your eyes if you want. Which drawer has your pajamas?"

"Just go, Belle. I can take care of myself from here."

She huffed. "I'm not leaving you alone. You need help. You're my patient and my friend. You said yourself you don't have anyone to call at this hour, do you?"

She wanted to take care of him? The thought made his heart splinter. But his pride reared its ugly head, sending a new wave of anger. He was at his weakest, powerless and help-less. There was only one reason this woman would stick around—she pitied him.

His eyes snapped open. "I said to go. I don't want you here. I can take care of myself!"

Belle's features hardened under the soft light of the few candles placed around the room. Her golden brown skin glowed as she stepped closer. "You're human, Bently. Just because you need help, doesn't make you less of a man."

She'd fucking read his thoughts.

"We both know you won't ask for help, so I'm volunteering so you don't die in your sleep. You want to leave Jasmine and all your family alone because you were too damn stubborn to accept my assistance?"

"No," he grumbled.

"I knew you were a smart guy. Now, tell me where your clean clothes are or I'll start going through all of them," she said gently but firmly, all at the same time. This woman was fierce—a force to behold. She challenged him alright.

"I just sleep in my boxers. Top drawer. But I want a shower—to wash off all this blood caked in my hair."

Her eyes wavered only a moment before she nodded. "Okay, let me set everything up."

She left him alone, and a few minutes later, water swished, flowing through the pipes. Belle came back and wordlessly pulled the end of the scrub top he'd been given at the hospital after the EMTs had to cut his off. He gingerly lifted his arms as she maneuvered the shirt over his head, taking care of his injuries.

She wrapped her arm around his good side as he draped his arm over her tiny body, helping him stand. They walked together to the bathroom as the steam rose.

"Stand here," Belle said, pointing to the space right near the entrance to his walk-in shower. Shifting around him, she reached towards his pants button.

His hand shot out to hers. "Woah, just what in the hell do you think you're doing?"

She let out a frustrated sigh. "You can barely stand. How else do you think you're going to get in the shower?"

"Nah, darlin'. You ain't seeing me naked like this."

"Bently, I'm a nurse. I see naked bodies every day. It's really no big deal." She said it more like she was trying to convince herself. "Unless you're too shy," she teased.

"Fine, but boxers stay on."

She smiled. "That's what I was going to propose anyways." She pulled down his pants as he stepped out of them, grinding his teeth together from the pain.

She tugged her top off and his mind short-circuited. Did concussions cause hallucinations? She reached for her scrub bottoms before guiding them quickly over her legs.

Fuck, that tiny body was perfect.

"W-what are you doing?" His voice sounded like he'd swallowed a bucket of gravel.

She looked up at him. "I can re-bandage your ribs after, but you can't get your stitches wet. I'll keep the wound site dry and wash your hair. You'll need help to stand and not slip on your ass and make your head worse. And I don't have any other clothes."

It made sense, but not getting a boner when her half-naked body was wet and slick against his in the shower would be impossible.

"We're both adults," she said as if sensing his dilemma.

"That's the problem."

She smiled. "Don't worry. I'll keep my hands to myself."

This woman was going to be the death of him. Since when did Bently Evans, playboy, ever turn down being naked with a sexy-ass woman? *Never.* He walked into the shower, her bare skin against his as he kept his balance.

"Sit down there so I can reach your hair." She motioned to the plastic step stool he'd gotten for Lyra.

Careful not to pull on his ribs too much, he sat. The hot spray of the water reached his back. Belle stepped forward and closed the glass shower door, caging them in together. Steam rose, billowing upwards. A shiny sheen of water sparkled across the swell of her breasts. Two perfect curves peeked out over the thin, red lace bra. Her panties matched. He hadn't seen the back yet, but fuck he was having a hard time thinking about anything else besides tearing them off her —fucked-up ribs and all.

Soft hands smoothed his hair away from the stitches. He bit back a moan. There was no way he was taking his eyes off her and wasting this once-in-a-lifetime opportunity to memo-rize every shape and curve of Belle's perfect body. As she caressed his scalp, washing out the blood, her breasts were front and center in his line of view. A hint of her dark brown nipples poked through the red lace. His cock was already hard. Just when he thought he couldn't be in any more pain, this woman brought a new ache to his groin.

"I was really scared when I saw you in that hospital bed," she said.

He swallowed, not knowing what to make of her confession.

"I'm fine."

She reached farther, drawing his head down so close to her plump breasts, he could nearly taste her scent. He bit his tongue, reining it in so he wouldn't do something stupid like lick her cleavage. Warm hands mixed with hot water, massaging the back of his neck. His cock turned hard as granite.

Blazing lust overpowered him. Want splintered his control. He reached his hands out and grabbed her hips hard, no doubt leaving a bruise.

She gasped, startled. His eyes met hers, hazy and vulnerable. A moment suspended in time as they stared into the portals of each other's souls.

"Bently." Her voice was breathy and wavering.

"Tell me you want this." He smoothed his thumb over the lace, towards the juncture of her sex.

Her eyes drifted closed. She looked like a goddess, standing before him. Her tight little body could be the balm to his wounds. Fuck, he wanted her more than tomorrow's sunrise. His fingers trailed to the middle of her thighs, teasing the top of the flimsy fabric. He'd bet his life she was soaking wet underneath.

"What I want and what I actually get are two very different things."

Her words staggered him. Here he was, trying to steal a piece of her goodness like a thief. She wanted more than his body, but that was all he'd ever had to offer. If anyone in this world deserved happiness, it was Belle.

She lowered her gaze. "I'll give you a few minutes. Don't try to stand up without me."

She turned and opened the door before quickly exiting, closing the glass wall between them. He looked at his hands. What could he do? There was one thing he was certain of—he was done with this back-and-forth dance between them. He was standing at a fork in the road. It was time to make a decision. He was either all in, or he'd have to let her go.

22

BENTLY

Bently carefully laid his head on the pillow as Belle pulled his soft, cool sheets over him. Belle walked around the room in one of his T-shirts, blowing out the few candles. The woman was so tiny it reached mid-thigh.

Is she wearing any panties?

She'd probably gotten hers wet in the shower. Seeing her in his clothes brought a new wave of possessiveness over him. He wanted her. Needed her. But was he willing to risk the pain that would eventually come with having a relationship? Could he make an exception for Belle?

Next, she pulled his curtains closed, eliminating the remaining light in the room. The squeak of his chair made his body stiffen. "What are you doing?"

"I'm getting comfortable in this chair," she said deadpan.

"Don't you need to get home to TJ?"

"He's fine. I already texted him that I'd be gone until tomorrow." She yawned sleepily. She'd worked all night. She had to be exhausted.

"I'm just going to sleep. I'll be fine. You should go."

She sighed, as if tired of having this argument. "Bently, we talked about this. You could vomit in your sleep and aspirate. Or a whole host of other complications could happen. You can't be alone—not for forty-eight hours."

"I appreciate your concern, but—"

"Look. I need sleep. So, if you could just shut up, I'd be very grateful."

Damn this woman was something. "You're going to sleep on that chair?" *No fucking way.*

"I have to be in the room. I won't hear you if you need help otherwise."

"I'll take the chair." He pulled off the covers and sat. He hissed as the pain of his ribs protested the movement.

"No. You need to lie down," she snapped.

"No way am I taking the bed and letting a woman sleep in that old-ass chair," he argued. "The bed is big enough for the both of us."

She sighed again. "Fine. If it will get you to shut up, I'll sleep in the bed."

He smiled, thankful for the darkness. "I promise I'll keep my hands to myself," he repeated her earlier words.

"You better," she grumbled. The bed shifted under her weight as she lay next to him. Overtired Belle was cute.

She turned on her side, facing away from him. Her breathing slowed and evened out within minutes. For the first time all day, he could relax. Just having her near brought him a sense of calm. He drifted into sleep.

Flashes invaded his mind. His mother's lifeless body hanging from the rafters of the basement. His father coming at him with a fury of fists and boots. Jasmine's tear-stained face when she'd run to get him, warning him his father was attacking Mikel. The sight of his little brother, crumpled on the floor, his face so swollen he was unrecognizable.

You didn't save them. You should have been there. You weren't enough.

The voices taunted him as memory after brutal memory slammed through his mind. Each flashback felt as real as the moment it had happened.

"Bently."

Why was Belle here? *No. He couldn't get to her too.*

"Bently. Honey, it's just a nightmare," Belle soothed.

He cracked his eyes open. His heart raced against his chest as he gasped for breath. Her soft hands rubbed over his rapid pulse, grounding him with her touch. Sparse rays of light bled into the room between the curtains, illuminating her worried expression.

"It's okay. You're safe. You're free. You're calm." She repeated the words over and over until his breathing evened out.

Belle started to pull her hand away, but he grasped it. "Don't stop."

She leaned against his shoulder and resumed the calming swirl of her hand back and forth across his chest.

"Do you want to talk about it?" she asked.

"No."

"Okay."

Birds chirping outside the window were the only sounds in the otherwise silent room. Belle's hand rested against his pec. Her movement stilled as she fell back into her slumber.

He took the opportunity to study her closer—her long lashes brushing the tops of her cheeks ever so slightly. He got the urge to kiss her button nose, but refrained. A sleeping woman could not consent, no matter what Disney had to say about it. He brushed a dark curl from her face. Her lips parted slightly. She was breathtakingly gorgeous. A true queen in his bed. Strength and beauty emanated from every pore, all wrapped up in such a small body. No woman ever stood up to him the way she did, nor challenged him. No one had ever dropped everything to take care of him either.

I shouldn't need to be taken care of.

Anger roiled in his gut. She'd seen him overpowered and wounded, helpless and having nightmares like a child. Yet still, here she was, snuggled against him, trusting him. A woman like that . . . A spark of hope lit inside him. Belle was what he'd never been looking for, but always needed. He'd be damned if he let her slip through his fingers without trying everything in his power to keep her by his side—she was worth it.

Hours later, Belle stirred against his chest. He kept his eyes closed so she'd think he was sleeping. Her stare swept across his face, tingling his skin. He'd expected her to shy away from his arms once she realized how close they were. But instead, she lay there for a few minutes. Eventually, she shifted gently out of the bed.

The smell of bacon wafted upstairs a little later.

He sat, carefully, and rubbed his eyes. He needed coffee, stat. Bently glanced at the clock. Three in the afternoon. They'd slept the day away. He shifted his feet off the bed. His headache had dulled, but it still persisted. His body ached even more than the day before. Bently slowly got to his feet. His head swam, but there was no way he was calling her up here for help. Reaching out, he steadied himself on the wall as he made it to the bathroom to relieve himself and brush his teeth. He shuffled back to the bedroom to grab a pair of basketball shorts before starting down the stairs.

"What are you doing!" Belle gasped as she dropped the spatula and ran to his side.

"Coming for breakfast. What's it look like?" he grumbled, taking notice of the fact she hadn't changed out of his shirt. He shuddered as she wrapped her arm around his naked chest.

"You are not supposed to—"

"Walk unassisted. Yeah, I know. But I think the doc was overreacting. I made it just fine, didn't I?" After reaching to steady himself on the chair, he pulled it out before taking a seat at the table.

"You are the most stubborn man I think I've ever met," she snapped.

"That's what you like about me, isn't it?" He smirked.

She shook her head and walked over to the stove before shutting off the burner. "Well, it's your loss. I was going to bring you breakfast in bed."

Damn.

She opened the cupboards until apparently finding what she was looking for. The sight of her so comfortable in his home brought a tightness to his chest. He'd never wanted this before, but then again, he'd never met Belle Jones. She reached up on her tippy-toes, the oversized T-shirt rising over her bare thighs, the barest hint of the globes of her ass peeking out.

He swallowed hard. *No panties, then. Fuck.* He shifted in his seat.

She filled the mug she'd grabbed with coffee and brought it over to him, along with a plate filled with bacon, and an egg and spinach omelet.

"Looks delicious. Thank you."

"You're welcome." She went back to the counter for her own plate and mug before returning to the table. "You don't happen to have any hazelnut creamer, do you?"

He shook his head. "Sorry, Angel."

"I figured as much." The corner of her mouth quirked up before she tucked into her food.

Ding-ding. Ding-ding. She got up and retrieved her phone from the counter. "Hey . . . Yes. Okay. I'll be home soon. There's chicken and macaroni and cheese in the fridge for dinner with salad if you're hungry . . . Okay. Love you." She smiled before she clicked the button and rejoined him at the table.

"TJ?" he asked.

She nodded, taking another bite of her food. "Oh and try to avoid screens as much as you can for the next few days at least."

"Yeah, alright, doctor."

She rolled her eyes.

Damn that was cute. "I'll call Mikel to come over when you leave."

She smirked. "No you won't."

He smiled. "You're right. I won't."

"You know, asking for help isn't a sign of weakness, but of strength."

"Where'd you get that from? A fortune cookie?" He chuckled.

She set her fork down and sipped her coffee. Her delicate throat bobbed as she swallowed. "Your X-rays showed a lot of previous injuries."

His stomach hardened as a wave of nausea rose. Suddenly, he wasn't feeling hungry anymore. His body tensed. His shoulders grew rigid. His fists curled as the pain from each haunting injury burned his consciousness.

Her hand rested over his, bringing him back to the moment, chasing the ghosts away, if only temporarily. "If you were to examine mine, you'd find my bones in a similar shape."

He turned his hard gaze onto her. Anger boiling to the surface. *Who'd hurt her?* The fierce protectiveness clamored inside.

"Who hurt you, Belle?" If the son of a bitch was still alive, he'd . . .

Belle shrugged. "There were several people. Foster homes with over-interested daddies, some of whom liked to inflict physical pain. Then there were the countless boyfriends of our mother's revolving door. They didn't like when I got in the way to protect my mother. Of course, some from her too."

His body trembled as a low growl came from his mouth. The thought of some man's hands on Belle made his skin crawl and his rage boil over. However, he was powerless to do anything. *Again.*

"My point in telling you this is so that you understand that a past is nothing to be ashamed of. We did what we had to in order to survive. And we did survive. I'll never know what it's like to grow up in a loving home, or have someone protect me. But I can create that safe environment for myself now, and my brother. I can heal. The battle scars will always be there, but they're a reminder of what I've lived through and what's made me stronger."

Bently stared at the woman with awe. She'd been through hell and back from the sounds of it, but still she faced the world with positivity.

"Keeping it hidden inside only hurts yourself and anyone who tries to get close to you. Holding on to this pain only gives the perpetrators more power over you."

Let this out? Was she crazy? It would destroy him. His

anger was all he had to keep him going. Holding on to the anger gave him the motivation to always strive to be better. Talking about it was . . . no way. He swallowed. "I admire you for what you've done. You broke the cycle . . ." He ran a hand through his hair and shook his head. "But my situation isn't the same as yours."

Because I failed them.

23

BELLE

B elle placed the dish in the rack to dry before toweling off her hands. She'd refrained from driving over to Bently's for the fifth day in a row just to check in on him. After all, she couldn't help someone who wasn't ready to help himself.

Ding!

She pulled the phone from her pocket and smiled.

Bently: *Thanks for all the sticky notes. How did I ever survive before you?*

Attached was a picture of one of the many notes she'd left across his house. Little reminders to hydrate, not watch TV, or overdo it.

She responded.

Belle: *You're welcome.*

After another few seconds, her phone chimed again.

Bently: *Let me say "Thank you" properly. Come over for dinner tonight.*

She pursed her lips together. Excitement fluttered in her belly.

Belle: *What time?*

Bently: *Six.*

Belle: *Should I bring anything? You sure you're up to cooking?*

Bently*: I wouldn't turn you down if you wanted to come early and help.*

Belle: *See you at five, then.*

She slipped the phone back into her pocket. Now, what to wear?

* * *

At five o'clock sharp, Belle knocked on Bently's door. He opened it a moment later. His eyes lazily made their way up from the open-toed sandals she'd chosen to her white skinny jeans, and over the bohemian-style flowy crop top partially hidden by her leather jacket. When his gaze met hers, his wolfish grin widened. She swallowed.

"Can I come in or do you just want to stare at me all day?" she teased.

"I'm a multitasker. I am capable of doing both." He stepped aside to let her in.

She glanced towards the living room off to her right. The simple brown leather couch and coffee table sat in the center in front of a large TV. His bookshelf situated opposite. But there were no pictures hanging on the wall or any other personal décor touches.

"Shall we?" he asked, waving his hand towards the kitchen on her left. She walked ahead, taking in the clean counters and small table they'd shared their late breakfast at. He was organized, she'd give him that.

"What's for dinner?" she asked.

"My specialty—chicken Alfredo."

"Mmm. What can I do to help?" She shrugged off her jacket and laid it over the back of the chair.

"You can slice the chicken while I start the sauce. Pasta water is already heating up." He pointed to the cutting board and knife he'd laid out. "Oh, I almost forgot." He held an apron up for her to slip her head inside.

She smiled and bowed her head. His hands slid down her arms to her waist as he turned her around. She swallowed back the shot of lust that blossomed within her. The fabric tightened around her hips as he tied the knot.

"All set." The deep timbre of his voice made her inner walls clench. Maybe dinner alone wasn't such a good idea after all.

They got to work, side by side. Bently strained broccoli and poured heavy cream into another pan with butter. He added spices and cheese as he stirred. The timer for the pasta went off.

"Can you keep stirring this and I'll take care of the noodles?" he asked. Her hand swept under his to take the whisk, lightly brushing against him.

"Do you want some coffee? I got that creamer you like." He dumped the pasta in the colander.

He had? The small gesture brought warmth to her chest. "Sure."

After all the ingredients were ready, Bently shooed her away to prepare the coffee while he made their plates.

She sat at the table and sipped her java while he set the steaming plate of savory creamy pasta in front of her.

"This smells divine," she said.

"The noodles are gluten-free—it's all I had on hand. Lyra and Remy have celiac disease."

"Oh, I had no idea. Now it makes sense that her bakery is all gluten-free."

She twisted the pasta on her fork and took a bite. She moaned. The food was so good. Licking her lips, she glanced at Bently. His jaw was set and his brow furrowed.

"What's wrong? Is your injury bothering you?" she asked, worried.

"Oh, I'm definitely aching." He smirked.

She rolled her eyes. They continued eating their dinner and making small talk.

"That was delicious. No man has ever cooked me dinner before."

"I'm glad I could be your first," he teased.

She drained the last of her coffee as he cleared his throat.

"I've been thinking about what you said . . . I thought maybe . . . I could try to open up with you. You get my kind of past . . . and I trust you."

She took a deep breath, the weight of his words staggering her. *He* trusted *her?*

"Plus, we'd have doctor-patient confidentiality." He smiled.

She chuckled. "I'm honored."

"My mother killed herself."

Whoa. He was diving straight in.

"Mikel was almost beaten to death by our father because I wasn't there. Jasmine . . ." He ground his teeth, his eyes clouding over. "I failed to protect her too." His eyelids fluttered before he locked eyes with her and continued. "You got TJ out. You were able to make a difference in his life. I waited too long. I should have gotten them out faster. I failed them. That's my secret. That's what kind of man I am."

Was he trying to scare her away? She reached out and took his hand in hers. "How old were you when these things happened?"

"It doesn't matter."

"So, you were young, then, a child?" He didn't say anything, so she continued. "I'm sorry you had to go through that. I'm sorry that you felt all that grown-up responsibility on your shoulders as a boy. Would you expect Lyra to fight off a grown man from her mother?"

"No," he snapped.

"You have to realize that you are holding yourself to impossibly high standards. And the guilt you carry will eat you alive."

He shook his head.

"Grieving the loss is a process that helped me. The loss of childhood, of the naiveté I should have had, of the loving relationships I wished were there. Then you have to comfort your inner child. Let them know you have their back. That that little boy is safe inside you."

His brow furrowed as he stared at her.

She sighed. "I know I can tell you it wasn't your fault until I'm blue in the face, but the reality is, until you start to believe it, you're still chained to the past."

He nodded.

"You carry so much on these shoulders. Even now that your brother and sister are grown and on their own."

"Jasmine still needs me."

"Yes, I'm sure she does. But just not as her protector anymore. How would it feel if you were to only be her brother, rather than caretaker?"

His brow furrowed. "I don't even know what that would look like."

"You could talk to her and find out exactly what she needs from you," she suggested.

He sat back in his chair, rubbing his thumb along the soft flesh of her hand.

"The thought of not being needed anymore is terrifying,

isn't it? When you've built the foundation of who you are around taking care of others' needs, it can be hard to figure out what *you* really want."

He nodded solemnly.

She reached out her other hand, pulling his face towards hers. "But it can also be the most freeing thing you could ever do."

"How do you know all this?" he asked.

Her lips turned up in a sad smile. "I learned the hard way. Went through it all so that I wouldn't make the same mistakes as my mother. I wanted better for TJ and myself."

"You're really brave—you know that?" He glanced down to her lips.

The tension in the room thickened, making it hard to fill her lungs.

"Bravery is not about not being afraid. It's doing what scares you in spite of the fear." Her words came out in a whisper.

He leaned in, searching her eyes.

Every cell in her body screamed to kiss him. But what if that finished this friendship between them? She liked Bently— a lot. She didn't want that to end just yet for only one night that was sure to be incredible.

She released his face and reached for her empty coffee cup. "You can live your own life now, Bently. White picket fence and all." She hoped to lighten the mood.

He released her hand and stared at his empty plate. His body turned rigid once again.

"What's wrong?"

He shook his head. "Didn't you read my file?"

She searched her brain for what he could mean, but came up short.

"I had testicular cancer. Between that and the chemo, I'm . . . a family isn't an option for me anymore."

He's sterile. "There are many other ways to make a family, if you want one."

"What kind of woman would want a man who shoots blanks? It's in your DNA to want to reproduce and nurture life."

She straightened her shoulders. "That's a pretty ignorant opinion. Not all of us want to carry a baby for nine months and then take care of it for the rest of our lives. Just because it's society's expectation, doesn't mean it's ours. I've been in the mother role since I was seven years old. I've never known anything but. I love my brother, but I'm ready to have some freedom—not have to worry about if he's eaten enough vegetables, or make his doctor appointments."

He turned to her. "You don't want biological children?"

She shook her head. "Maybe someday in the future, after I've had time to do everything I've put off, I'd consider foster care and eventually adoption."

He leaned in, a small smile quirking up the side of his mouth. "So, what you're saying is, we'd be perfect for each other."

She chuckled. "That's what you got out of all of that?"

"Nah, I hear what you're saying. Not all women want or are meant to be mothers, whatever their reasons, and that's okay."

"Exactly."

"What do you want to do for yourself?" he asked, changing the subject.

"Like, my bucket list?"

"Sure."

"I want to sleep under the stars and have s'mores." She smiled.

"You've never gone camping?" he asked, surprised.

She shook her head. "I want to travel, and see some of the world."

"What else?"

"A picnic."

He shook his head in disbelief. "We had a picnic on the mountain, didn't we?"

She laughed. "I mean a real, checkered blanket, basket-full-of-goodies kind."

"Tell me more." Bently leaned in, as if captivated by her words.

Something deep inside fell into place as Belle listed off all the things she'd tucked away in the treasure box of "someday." She felt connected to Bently. He'd bared his deepest hurts, and listened to her advice like he respected what she had to say. Now he was asking her about her dreams—things she'd held inside for so long, waiting until she could make herself the priority for the first time in her life.

She was falling. But would he be there to catch her? Or was this just temporary?

24

BENTLY

Shuffling the papers on his desk, Bently looked through the stack of messages Betsy had left while he was out on medical leave.

"Evans, you're back." Vargas walked in, taking a seat across from him.

"Miss me?"

"I won't miss the desk duty I had to do in your place." She laughed.

"Any leads?"

"On your attack? No. Cameras caught the dark figure with the bat. Mason didn't see anything identifiable when he rushed over. But he said the assailant was definitely a teenager or smaller-built man."

"He should have chased the fucker down," Bently grumbled.

Vargas tipped her head to the side. "He was more worried about you. There was a lot of blood and you were unconscious. Mason did the right thing."

"Who would be targeting me, and why?"

"That's what I want to know." She studied him.

"As sheriff, I'm bound to piss someone off. It's part of the job description. But I really have no idea who would want me dead."

"You think this is related to your truck windshield?" she asked.

"Could be."

"Watch your six, Evans." Vargas stood.

"Yes, ma'am."

"Oh, we got DNA evidence back from Charli's evaluation. Perp is unknown, but it's not the first time someone has reported this guy. I got six matches from the whole East Coast."

Bently shook his head and clenched his fists. "Any hits on the sketch?"

"Not yet."

"Keep me updated," he said.

"Will do."

Bently got to work on the mountain of paperwork Vargas had left for him to check over. He glanced at the clock. It was going to be a long day.

25

BELLE

A bouquet of deep red roses was nestled in the corner of Belle's front door. She set down the bags of groceries and reached out to inspect it closer. No one had ever gotten her flowers before. *Who would . . .*

Bently.

Butterflies tumbled in her belly. A flash of yellow caught her eye on the front of the gray ceramic vase. She peeled the note paper off to inspect the masculine writing.

Meet me at Green Park at noon. -B

She smiled and inhaled the fresh floral scent of the bouquet. This felt an awful lot like dating. Was it? Or was that wishful thinking? Bently would say so if he was ready for more, wouldn't he? Maybe this was just his way of saying "thank you" for her help.

* * *

Two hours later, she parked her car in the lot next to the sign for Green Park. Only a few parents played with their tots around the sandbox and play structure on this Wednesday afternoon. She got out and zipped up her coat against the slight chill in the air. She turned her face to the blue sky, and the sunrays warmed her. She took a deep breath. Clean, crisp air filled her lungs.

"Don't you know it's illegal to look that good?" Bently said from behind her. She turned as his molten eyes locked with hers. "I should give you a ticket, because you've got FINE written all over you."

Her heart rate sped up and fireflies tumbled haphazardly in her belly. She laughed. "Come on, Bently. I know you've got better lines than that."

He smirked, eyes flashing with amusement. Bently stepped closer, reaching out to tuck a stray curl behind her ear. Her chest hitched from his gentle touch as he brought his face closer to hers.

"I think you're the most beautiful woman I've ever laid eyes on."

God damn. She swallowed. A mix of emotions warred inside her. Was he serious? Was this more? She couldn't be sure. "Th—that one was better."

He looked at her mouth before returning his gaze to her eyes. "Come on. I've only got an hour for my lunch break." He took her hand in his, pulling her along beside him as they walked up a dirt path.

"In the winter, kids use this as a sledding hill," he pointed out.

She nodded, taking in the green grass-covered mound. Several trees reached out their naked limbs towards the blue sky at the top. A plaid blanket with a wooden basket sat underneath one.

Her eyes darted to Bently and then back. "What is this?"

He held out his arm and gave a slight bow. "Your picnic, my lady."

Emotion welled in her chest, stinging her eyes. She blinked, trying to hold back the tears that threatened. He'd listened to her the other night and taken time out of his busy workday to make one of her dreams a reality. Bently had put in the effort and hadn't expected anything from her in return.

Bently cleared his throat. His brows drew together in concern. "Are you okay?"

She stepped forward, placing a hand on his chest, looking up into his eyes. "You did this for me?"

He shrugged. "Everyone should have at least one fancy picnic in their lifetime."

Didn't this man know just how amazing this was?

"I—I don't know what to say . . . Thank you, Bently. This means . . . it means the world to me."

His brow furrowed as he looked away, almost as if he was embarrassed.

She instinctively wrapped her arms around his neck, as he secured her waist. The air thundered with anticipation between them. She reached up on her tiptoes. His pulse beat frantically against her chest as her resolve splintered.

He'd been so gentle with her—she could do the same for him. If labels seemed to scare him, she could avoid them for his sake. There was no way he just wanted to be her friend. Yes, he flirted with everyone, but the things he said to her, the way he'd trusted her with his demons, the effort he put into taking care of her—he was wooing her, dating her, no matter what he wanted to call it.

Was she ready to do the same? He hadn't said he was ready for a relationship—but his actions spoke loud enough. Did she really care about the label enough to pass up this once-in-a-lifetime opportunity based on her fear?

"Bently?" Her voice came out needy.

"Yes?" he asked, pained.

"Kiss me."

He hesitated only a moment before he leaned the rest of the way, his soft lips caressing hers gently, slowly, as if savoring the delicious connection. She traced the seam of his lips with her tongue, tasting him. His kiss turned hungry and seeking as he squeezed her closer, stealing the breath from her lungs. This kiss gave as much as it took. This kiss had the power to heal her, or break her. The connection was like a riptide, sucking her under and leaving her powerless to stop it. She sighed, pressing herself against his hard planes. One of her hands wove into his hair and gripped. He groaned, possessive fire slamming through her at the hypnotic sound. Calloused hands cupped her face before he slowly pulled away, resting his forehead on hers.

The world around them came back into focus. The sound of their heavy panting was the only exchange between them as a million thoughts raced in her mind. Is he going to be mad and shut down like before? Does this mean he wants a relationship? Did she just ruin their friendship?

"You're under arrest," Bently said.

What the hell? Her brow furrowed as she pulled back.

He was grinning. "For taking my breath away."

She burst out laughing as he joined her. "You just can't help yourself, can you?"

"Where's the fun in that?" he asked, sitting on the blanket and patting the spot next to him.

She got comfortable as he opened the wooden basket and pulled out a whole charcuterie with an array of dried meats, aged cheeses, and marinated olives. Inside was also a bottle of wine, water, and chocolate truffles.

"There's only one glass?" she asked.

"I'm on duty. It's all yours, Angel."

She picked up a cracker, piling it with meat and cheese before she took a bite. As he ate, he seemed to be more interested in studying the people below them playing at the park than speaking to her.

"This is a nice town," she said.

He nodded. "For the most part."

She'd seen her fair share working in the emergency room, and being a SANE-certified nurse, to know just how far the reach of violence was in the world.

"How are your injuries feeling?" She studied the healing cut by his hairline.

"Getting better every day. How's TJ? I've missed working out with him on the courts this week."

She smiled. "He asked about you. He's good. He'll graduate in December." He'd already shown he trusted her by sharing his past. How could Belle show Bently she believed in him? She inhaled shakily. "I know it would mean a lot to him if you came."

He took another bite, chewed, and swallowed before replying. "I'll be there. But is this your way of asking me on another date?"

"Is this a *date*?"

Bently coughed and grabbed his bottle of water before taking a sip. "Is TJ all set for college in the spring semester?"

"Yes. But you didn't answer my question."

"It's a friend-date." He smirked.

Belle shook her head with a smile.

Bently shifted to face her. "You feel like going with me to see Remy's friend Emma and her band play at The Shipwreck Saturday?"

"For another *friend-date?*"

"Of course. What kind of friend would I be if I didn't spend time with you?"

She sipped the sweet wine before teasing him. "Sure, that sounds fun. But it's so unlike you—giving me notice of more than a few hours."

He shrugged and smiled. "Got to keep you on your toes. I can't be predictable if I want to be spontaneous."

She chuckled.

"It's a Halloween costume party, by the way. I was thinking you could come as a sexy nurse." He grinned.

She shook her head. "I bet you were."

"Well, you could go as an angel and I could be the devil." He winked.

"A little cliché, don't you think?"

"What do you suggest?" He stuffed an olive into his mouth.

"I think you'll just have to wait and see."

"Ooh, intrigue. I love it. Okay, then I'm not telling you what I'm going as either."

"I do love a good surprise." She smiled, their eyes meeting. She hoped he really understood just how amazing he was.

He sighed. "Unfortunately, duty calls. I gotta get back to the office."

She downed the rest of the wine in her glass and put it in the basket. "Thank you again for this." She stood and helped him fold the blanket and put it on top of the picnic basket he was carrying. She slipped her hand in his as they walked back to the parking lot.

"You good to drive?" he asked.

"Yes, but I'll probably go for a walk anyways before I go home. My shift doesn't start until three today."

He nodded. She looked up at him, her eyes darting to those perfect lips. She wanted another taste. Just one more moment where everything else disappeared and she could just be a woman, just experience. He leaned in slowly. She tilted her mouth towards him expectantly, willingly. He grabbed the back of her neck and pulled her in, kissing her forehead before he turned and walked away.

"See you Saturday at nine." He waved.

Disappointment flooded her, clouded by confusion at all the mixed messages.

"It's a date," she called after him, hoping to gain some semblance of control.

He kept on walking towards his truck without looking back. He motioned goodbye to her again as he drove past.

She bit her lip. He'd kissed her—holy hell, he'd used those magic lips on her. But then he'd gone and distanced himself again. Or had he? The forehead kiss was sweet, undoubtedly so. But she'd wanted the heat. The line drawn between friend and something more was now so blurry she didn't know where they stood.

He hasn't ever done this as far as you know. Cut him some slack.

Could she be all in and risk the rejection she feared so much without any guarantee from Bently? It didn't really matter if she was ready, because she was jumping over the line between friendship and more with two feet. No more living in the gray area. It was time she put it all on the line. But would he?

26

BELLE

Belle turned and checked her reflection in the mirror. It wasn't easy finding a costume so last minute, but she'd finally settled on the perfect one.

A knock sounded at her bedroom door.

"Yeah?"

TJ peeked his head in. "You look awesome. Bently's here."

"Thanks."

"He seems like a good guy," TJ said, putting his hands in his pockets and looking off to the left.

"He does," she agreed.

"He's nothing like the other guys."

The grim reminder from TJ was like a slap in the face of the last time she'd trusted a man, given him everything, just to have him use her and throw her out like garbage when he was finished.

She nodded, speechless. Her stomach knotted. Would Bently do the same? Was she stupid for assuming a leopard could change their spots? How could she be sure he hadn't been with anyone else while she'd been spending time with him?

"You okay?" TJ asked.

She nodded and grabbed her leather jacket and whip. "I'm just fine," she lied.

TJ walked down the stairs ahead of her.

Bently stood by the door. The tight material of his costume showed off every hard ridge of his muscles and there was no missing the bulge between his thighs. The black mask covered most of his face and matched his cape.

"Batman?"

"Wonder Woman." Bently nodded his approval. "Looks like we are better matched than we thought." He smirked. His white teeth flashed in contrast with the dark mask. "Damn, you look good enough to eat."

"Hey, now! There are some things I really don't need to know about my sister." TJ made a disgusted face.

"Sorry, bro. You got your own hot date tonight, don't you?" Bently asked TJ without shifting his gaze from hers as she approached.

That was news to her. She looked questioningly towards TJ. "You do?"

He shrugged, a small smile playing on his lips. "Mark is coming over with a date and his sister, Cam."

"If you're thinking of trying anything—"

TJ held up his hands. "I promise I won't."

She shook her head, unease building. TJ was seventeen, but he had so much on the line.

"Condoms in the drawer of the bathroom sink."

"It's not like that."

"Mm-hmm. You got too much to lose to go and knock someone up in high school. You better use your head. And I mean this one." She tapped his temple lightly.

TJ shifted uneasily on his feet as he looked down, as if embarrassed. But it was better to be upfront about these types of things. He was a young man with raging hormones and a huge crush on this girl.

"I'm gonna go upstairs. Have fun, guys." TJ took the steps two at a time like he couldn't get out of there fast enough.

Bently chuckled.

She turned around with her hands on her hips. "I don't find anything about this funny."

He shook his head. "You never cease to surprise me."

"Are we going to this party or not?"

"I don't know if I should let you out of the house looking that good." He smirked. His voice deepened as he continued. "Lots of dangers out there in Gotham City."

She chuckled. "Well, it's a good thing I can take care of myself." She tied the whip onto her belt.

Bently's hands gripped her hips and pulled her against him. "And I've got your back." His fingers trailed lower before squeezing a handful of her ass.

Electric lust shot through her. Heat blanketed her core and her breath hitched. His touch burned her in the best of ways, igniting a yearning within her. But was she ready for that? She swallowed and pressed against his chest.

He released her before opening the front door. "The Batmobile awaits."

She chuckled as she slipped her jacket on. Following after him, she locked the house behind her. When they got to his truck, he opened her door and lifted her up. His hands glided over her thighs as she climbed the rest of the way in. She shivered. Something about tonight was different.

The way he touched her, and the emotions he stirred up inside her.

He climbed in the cab next to her, stealing all the air. She stifled a laugh at the ridiculousness of their costumes. But damn, he looked hot. Maybe it was because of the role play, or perhaps the cover of darkness, but her imagination was running rampant with all the bad things she wanted this man to do to her. Pure primal need overwhelmed her rational thought. It was easier to relax and enjoy this if she wasn't Belle with her past, but someone else—in this case Wonder Woman.

He drove them into town, the low music the only sound in the truck. When they parked, he had her door open before she'd managed to unbuckle her seat belt. His strong arms stretched out to catch her. He set her onto her unstable feet. She slipped her jacket off and put it on his seat. It was sure to be warmer inside.

Bently nodded to the bouncer at the door before they entered. He placed his hand on the small of her back and a shiver ran through her as he guided her in. Music thumped. Bodies pulsed to the beat on the dance floor off to the left as the band performed on stage. The bar was packed. Bently ushered her through the crowd. Heads turned, women casting hungry gazes towards him. She didn't blame them. The man was too good looking for his own good. Still, a slight burn of jealousy lit in her belly.

"Drink?" he yelled the question.

"Beer," she yelled back.

He nodded and took her hand before he pushed over to the bar amidst the throng of people. Women reached out and grabbed his arms, trying to strike up conversation. Bently smiled politely and pulled Belle in front of him, pinning her against the bar. The women seemed to catch his message loud and clear. The action sent a burst of relief and pride through her like he was telling everyone he was with her. It calmed the anxious knots inside her.

She recognized Charli behind the bar, expertly making drinks faster than she'd ever seen anyone do. Bently ordered their beers and Charli glanced at her, faltering only for a moment before turning back to her task.

After they had their cold beverages in hand, Bently led them to a table in the corner where Remy, Mikel, Andre, and Mia sat. Jasmine was the only one missing from their small group.

The women's faces lit up as Bently sat in the one and only empty seat. He pulled Belle onto his lap, his hands resting on her bare thighs. Tingles reverberated through her and heat spread from his touch. There was no doubt she was wet. There was nothing between her short skirt and his legs but a pair of red lace panties. She shifted, trying to pull the edge of the dress down farther, worried she would leave a wet spot on Bently's costume. His hands shot out to halt her movements. His erection poked against her now throbbing core.

Oh fuck.

He leaned in and spoke in her ear, his voice gravelly and heady. "This costume doesn't hide much. You keep moving against me like that and I might have to punish you."

The logical part of her wanted to flee his touch and the hurricane of sexual yearnings he awakened within her. The woman in her wanted to grind down on him, see how much it took to send him over the edge.

"How are you, Belle?" Remy asked, interrupting her salacious thoughts.

"Yeah, fancy seeing you here." Mia smiled knowingly.

"I'm great." Belle choked as Bently's hand spread out over her thigh. Heat blossoming, spreading, pooling in her center.

"Is this a thing now?" Remy asked, motioning between Bently and Belle.

Belle gulped down her beer, buying some time. She didn't know how to answer that. *I hope so.*

Bently tapped her thigh. "Let's dance."

Avoiding the question again. She got off his lap, setting her beer on the table before he whisked her to the dance floor between the writhing bodies. The volume grew louder the closer they got to the stage. Bently waved to the blond woman singing—she must be Remy's friend Emma. Her voice was so light compared to the heavy music.

Bently jerked her body against his. His arousal hadn't tampered in the least. If anything, it had grown. She looped her arms around his neck as he swayed her back and forth.

His breath tickled her ear as he growled, "Do you have any idea what you're doing to me?"

She swallowed, her mouth suddenly dry. The music drowned out the squeak that had surely come out of her mouth. She pressed against his erection. "I think I have a pretty good understanding."

"You make me want things. Things I shouldn't want. Things I shouldn't have." His grip tightened.

Her body shuddered as he grasped the back of her neck, pulling his head away far enough to gaze at her.

He dipped his mouth to hers, consuming her with his kiss. Sparks and shimmers built into fireworks of need. She gripped his shoulders as he deepened their connection, stealing, staking claim. His hands roamed to her ass, squeezing before trailing down her thighs and leaving goose bumps in their wake. Lust-fire burned her from the inside out, scorching her restraint and silencing her fears, filling her with urgency. All that mattered was this moment. This need that had her ready to throw caution to the wind and burst like an active volcano.

The ground itself seemed to quake from the raw power of his touch. Her legs shook, and her body trembled. His kiss made her feel unstable and volatile. His tongue invaded her mouth in an erotic dance. He tasted like beer and sin. Risk and temptation. Tonight and forever.

He broke away, leaving her breathless. His chest heaved against her breasts. Her hard nipples brushed against his muscles, fueling her ache with the friction.

"Let's get out of here," he ground out as he dragged her from the bar into the chilly night. The blast of cold air swept over her, dulling the lust-filled haze enough for her to come back to her senses. Panic gripped her as he led her to his truck. *What if this is just like before? Does he want me, or my body?*

"Bently."

"I know, Angel. I know."

Despite what she'd thought, Belle couldn't let this go any further unless she knew for sure. She wouldn't risk it all and give her body to him without assurance. She wished with everything in her that she could be less complicated. But the fear that this would all end once he'd had her body was paralyzing.

She bit down until she tasted blood. "Bently?"

"My place?" He opened the door, his hands immediately gripping her waist.

"I—I don't think that's a good idea."

"Okay, we can go to yours." He leaned in.

She pressed her hand against his chest, turmoil raging inside her. As much as she wanted him, she needed to make sure her needs were clear. She'd made the mistake of giving pieces of herself away in the past for fleeting attention and false love. She wouldn't betray herself like that again.

"No, I meant . . ." She searched his eyes in the moonlight.

He furrowed his brow. "Do you not want this?"

"I do, more than anything."

He smiled, relief painting his features.

"But . . . unless something's changed for you and this can be more than one night . . . I really care about you, Bently—more than I probably should. Which is all the more reason that I need you to make your intentions clear. Is this more than sex to you?"

He opened his mouth and then closed it, seemingly struggling with her question. Fear flashed in his eyes. Her hope fell like a rock in her stomach. He wasn't ready.

"I wish it could be."

It could, if you let it.

"It's okay." She turned to climb in, hoping he wouldn't see the tears glistening in her eyes.

She had fallen in love with Bently Evans. The man had his faults, but leading her on and lying so he could take advantage of her was not one of them. Of course, when she finally found an honest man she could trust, he'd be incapable of loving her back. Why did life have to be so unfair?

27

BENTLY

Sighing, Bently opened the door to The Stardust Café. Remy was busy helping a customer ahead of him, but she flashed him a smile.

He scanned the room—a habit—searching for potential threats and gauging where the exits were. For the safety of himself and those he loved, he'd had to maintain a constant alertness his whole life. There was no way to turn it off or slow the adrenaline surging through his blood stream. It left him fatigued and on edge.

His head pounded. The few drinks he'd had last night hadn't helped. He'd been so close to taking what didn't belong to him that evening with Belle two weeks ago. Even in a club crowded with people, she'd been so responsive to his touch. The woman would be a fucking masterpiece to watch fall apart. The way her tiny body ground against him. The way she tasted when those succulent lips locked with his. He'd forgotten anything else existed outside Belle. His sole focus had been *her*. She had a way of making him forget his place.

"Bent, what can I get y—you look like crap. Are you

okay?" Remy asked, bringing him back to the present where fantasies died and Belle could only ever be a friend.

"Thanks for the compliment, beautiful."

She shrugged. "*Are* you okay?"

"Large coffee. You know what, you better make it two." He pulled out his wallet.

"Should I add a shot of hazelnut to one of them?" she teased.

"No," he grumbled.

She filled two cups and pushed a paper bag across the counter. "You need to get that blood sugar up, mister grumpy pants. Cookies are on the house, of course. Seven fifty for the coffee."

He handed her a ten-dollar bill. She entered it in the cash register as he sipped from the first paper cup. His sister-in-law might be nosy, but she had a gift straight from the caffeine gods for making the best coffee around.

"Thanksgiving is coming up in a couple weeks," she said.

"Mm-hmm." Like he didn't know. It happened every year.

"Well, I was just thinking that Belle and TJ don't have any other family around here. Maybe you should invite them to ours." Remy wiped down the counter.

Ulterior motives or not, Remy was right. Belle and TJ would be alone. Unless they'd made plans with one of her friends from the hospital. He could ask TJ tonight at the courts. In spite of avoiding Belle like the plague, he'd kept up with her brother, though avoided one-on-ones in favor of a lighter hoops regime.

"I was going to ask her, but I haven't seen her in the last couple weeks," Remy added.

Maybe Belle was avoiding him too. His stomach hardened. He'd seen the hurt in her eyes before she'd turned away and climbed into his truck. It had been like a spear thrown through his heart. It was better they ended whatever was between them now before he really did her damage.

You good-for-nothing piece of shit. You're nothing! You'll never amount to anything.

"Earth to Bently." Remy's eyebrows drew together.

"Sorry. I uh—I'll see if they don't already have plans. I guess make me one of those coffees she likes too."

Remy smiled like the cat that ate the canary. "My pleasure."

Bently drank his java. He needed to act like nothing had changed and they were still *just* friends. Even if everything inside him screamed *liar!* But the real question was, was he lying to Belle or himself?

He closed his eyes. Everything was so mixed up inside. What he should do and what he wanted to do were at war. But which would win in the end?

* * *

"I'm looking for Nurse Belle Jones?" Bently asked the older woman at the desk.

"Down that hall. She was making her rounds." The kind lady studied him cautiously.

"Thanks." He walked over the way she'd pointed, searching for any sign of the woman who made him unravel at the seams. He adjusted the sticky note on the coffee. Just a little something to put a smile on her face.

Her throaty laughter caught his attention first. He swiveled his head towards an empty patient room. Doctor Stanley had his hand on her shoulder and was telling her some story about an enema tube and a patient. Bently tensed, his veins burning green. He wanted to walk over there and rip that man's hand off Belle. He had no business touching his woman.

Fuck. My woman?

Every muscle was rigid. His jaw flexed. His teeth ground together threatening to break. This could not happen. Maybe he was a selfish asshole after all, because Bently didn't want anyone else touching her, kissing her, even making her smile like that. That was his job! Was it worth risking everything? Could he put his doubts aside and be what she needed?

He fucking hoped so.

"Belle. There you are, Angel." He walked in.

Doctor Stanley looked up, surprise flashing at his intrusion. Belle blinked as if she couldn't believe he was actually there.

He wrapped his arm around her and pulled her into his side before kissing her cheek. "Brought you some coffee, sweetheart."

Doctor Stanley's forehead wrinkled as his gaze jumped between Bently's hold and Belle. "Oh, Bently. So nice to see you. Looks like you're recovering well."

"Sure am, Doc. Had the best hands to care for me." He squeezed Belle's shoulders. She tensed.

"Well, I'll see you around," the doctor said before leaving them alone.

Belle whirled around, her face a mask of confusion lined in anger. Fuck, even that turned him on.

"What the hell is this?" she whisper-yelled.

"Coffee, and an apology?" He said it more like a question and shrugged, feigning innocence.

She shook her head and stepped back. "If we're just friends, maybe you should lay off the PDA. It . . . confuses things."

Bently sighed and set the coffee on the counter in the exam room. He reached out his hands to her arms. "I've been thinking a lot. I don't know if I can be what you need, but I'll be damned if I don't try. I couldn't stand seeing another man's hands on you. I just . . . I want to try . . . to be more than friends."

Understanding flashed in her brown eyes before a small smile quirked up the side of her mouth. "You were jealous of Rick?"

Belle was on a first-name basis with this guy? "Yes," he grit out.

She looked at the note and smiled. "Another cheesy cop pick-up line, huh?"

He smirked. "You don't like 'em?"

Belle chuckled. "Only you, Bently Evans, could take something so corny and make it endearing."

Warmth blossomed in his chest, radiating to the hidden recesses of his heart. This woman was truly an angel—an embodiment of love and light and all that was good in this world. He was in trouble.

"I can't promise you everything, but I'd like to see where this goes. I like you, Angel. And I don't want to end up hurting you, but it's more than just one night for me. I understand if that's not enough for you."

She stayed silent, studying him for a few moments as if considering his offer. That's just one more thing that set her apart—her ability to think through things with a level head. The way she chose what was truly best for herself over temporary escape. It took a fierce woman to do that.

"Okay. We can see where this goes without a label. But . . . I need to know you'll, at the very least, be committed to this. I mean . . . that you won't have sex with other women."

He nodded. "That won't be a problem."

She looked up at him curiously. "Okay, then."

"Can I kiss you now?" he asked.

She giggled. "I'm at work, Sheriff."

He pulled her against his chest. "When do you get off?"

Her eyes darkened. "I don't think how I *get off* is any of your business."

All the blood drained straight to his cock. Fuck, now all he could think about was her touching herself. He liked this new side to Belle.

"From work, dirty girl." The timbre of his voice deepened. "Six."

"How about you meet me and TJ at the courts and then we get dinner together?"

She smiled. "Sounds good."

"It's a date." For the first time in his life, the words held weight. The fear was still there, but the alternative was to let her go. And maybe his father was right after all, because not being able to let her go would be his weakness.

28

BENTLY

Bently swirled, swatting his hand out to reach for the ball. TJ was quick, but not quick enough this time. His fingers caught the tip, sending the basketball bouncing off the backboard and missing the rim. Bently winced and rubbed his side at the lingering stiffness.

"Foul!" Belle's sweet voice called from the sidelines.

Bently rested his hands on his hips, catching his breath. "How was that a foul?"

"Hey, don't argue with the ref or you're out!" She laughed.

He shook his head. "You believe this?" he asked TJ.

TJ dribbled the ball. "Man, I learned a long time ago, life is much better when I don't argue with my sister."

Bently chuckled. "Alright, you get in here, *ref*. You can be on TJ's team."

"Nah, I'm just an observer." She waved dismissively.

He stalked over and grabbed her hand, pulling her onto the court.

"Bently, I'm still in my scrubs and work shoes," she protested.

"Doesn't bother me any." He swatted her ass playfully.

Her brows knit together, but amusement lit in her eyes. "You're gonna get schooled, old man."

He slapped a hand over his heart and grimaced. "Old man? Well, tell me how you really think of me."

"You're what, thirty-five?" She giggled.

"Try thirty-two."

"Eight years older than me." She smiled.

His breath stalled. "You're only twenty-four?" How had this not come up before?

"You thought I was older?" She narrowed her eyes at him.

He held up his hands, placating. "No, no. I just. Damn. I didn't realize I was so much older than you."

She smiled. "It doesn't bother me. It just means you'll be easier to take down."

He chuckled. "Let her start with the ball," he said, before TJ bounced the ball to her.

Belle caught it and dribbled it awkwardly at the half line. Bently held his arms up to block any chance of a pass. She looked at him as if he intimidated her, before a mask of determination schooled her features.

She turned around, facing away, dribbling as she backed into him.

"Over here!" TJ called from her left. Bently quickly pressed his body against hers, blocking the path.

He reached out, trailing his hand down her hip and over her ass.

"Hey! That's definitely a foul." She giggled.

"Oh yeah? You mean this is distracting you?" He squeezed.

She pushed back, grinding her ass against his hard-on. "Two can play this game."

He wrapped his arms around her and picked her up. She screeched. The ball was thrown over his shoulder where TJ caught it and dribbled towards the hoop before it swished into the net.

"We won!" Belle cheered.

He bent to her ear. "Nah, I think I'm the real winner."

She turned, surprise and wonderment lighting her features. She leaned in, drawing her lips against his, tasting him, tentatively. He kissed her back, nipping at her bottom lip.

"Ahhh. Come on, guys. Get a room!" TJ yelled.

Belle's body stiffened.

He pulled back, laughing and pretending he didn't notice. That was information he'd have to earn. He of all people understood what it was like to want to keep your demons buried.

"You guys in the mood for pizza?"

"Yes!" TJ quickly agreed.

"Sure." Belle smiled.

He was starving, but it wasn't food he was craving. But he'd be fasting until Belle gave him the go-ahead.

The three of them sat around the checkered tablecloth, enjoying their pizza at Pirate's Pizzeria.

"How did Cam like the tickets?" Bently asked TJ.

TJ sipped his chocolate milk before answering. He smiled, eyes glimmering. "She loved them. I can't wait to take her."

"Bently, are you giving my brother dating advice?" Belle teased.

He shrugged. "I don't want to brag, but I know a thing or two about how to woo a woman." He winked.

Belle shook her head and smiled.

"Do you guys have any plans for Thanksgiving this year?"

"I work until three," Belle answered.

"Well, consider yourselves invited to Remy's. She said not to worry about bringing anything unless there's something special you wanted. And, since my brother doesn't drink, it's kind of BYOB," he explained.

"Okay. I think that would be nice. We've never actually celebrated before." She smiled.

He swallowed. He had always had Mr. and Mrs. Stone, Andre's parents, who invited them to their family events. To think of Belle and TJ all alone, holiday after holiday, made his chest ache.

"Well, now's your chance to see what all the fuss is about. What about you, TJ?"

"I don't know. I wouldn't want to crash their party." He looked away.

"You're invited, no crashing needed. Plus, the more the merrier. They're good people."

TJ shrugged. "Will there be more of that casserole your sister made last time?"

Bently chuckled. "She makes a lot of food. I promise you won't be disappointed."

"I'm in." TJ smiled.

* * *

Later that evening, Bently walked Belle and TJ to the car.

"Night, Bently," TJ said, climbing in the passenger side.

"Night, buddy."

He grabbed Belle's hand, weaving his fingers through hers.

He led her to the driver's side, pinning her back against the car. He supported his hands against the roof as he leaned down and kissed her. He dipped his tongue inside her mouth, savoring her sweetness. She moaned, sending a direct bolt of lust through his dick. The woman was pure temptation— nothing but seduction wrapped in lace and coated in allure.

She was the one to pull back first. Her hand rested against his cheek, rubbing her thumb against his overgrown stubble. She licked her lips. His body pulsed and throbbed. *What is this woman doing to me?*

"I had a nice time tonight," Belle said.

"When is your next night off?"

"I have a mini-weekend. Saturday and Sunday," she answered.

He grinned. "Pack an overnight bag. I'll pick you up Saturday at ten. Tell TJ not to wait up for you."

Unease flickered through her expression. Bently caressed her cheek before lifting her chin to look him in the eyes. "I'm not expecting anything. I just have a surprise for you is all."

She smiled. Hope sparked back to life in her dark brown eyes. "Okay."

He breathed in her trust like the life-saving grace it was. He'd do anything to put a smile on that gorgeous face.

"I'm in this, Angel."

He kissed her forehead before backing up.

She struggled to straighten, as if she'd been as shaken to her core by his admission as he had. For the first time in his life, he was falling headfirst into some unknown abyss. Hopefully the darkness wouldn't destroy him.

But he should know better. Since when did he deserve a happy ending?

29

BELLE

Belle reached out to the door to steady herself as the truck bounced through the potholes on the dirt road. Tall trees surrounded them as far as her eyes could see. It had been what seemed like miles since she'd seen evidence of other civilization. *Where is he taking me?*

She was more curious than afraid, even way out here where who knew what lived in the shadows. It struck her like a bolt of lightning. She *trusted* Bently.

His big strong hands gripped the wheel. His arms were only half covered by a long-sleeved thermal, hiked up and exposing his sexy sinewy forearms. The shirt clung to his broad chest. Her eyes flicked from his corded neck to his devastatingly handsome face. Strong jaw. Dark stubble. And those eyes. Bright blue and vast like the ocean. A strand of his black hair fell against the side of his face. She reached out and tucked it back.

He turned, a warm smile aimed at her. "We're almost there."

"Are you gonna tell me what we're doing way out here?"

His gaze focused ahead on the winding road as he spoke. "You said you'd always wanted to spend a night under the stars."

She blinked and searched the woods around them, fear trickling down her spine. "I meant like somewhere safer. You know, without wild animals looking to me for their dinner."

He reached over and enveloped her hand in his. His thumb rubbed soothing circles over her palm. "Whatever happens, I'll always keep you safe. That's a promise." He turned down a smaller road, this one only big enough for one car.

The forest opened and a glimmering lake sparkled in the sunshine. A small log cabin with a stone chimney was situated at the end of what she could now tell was in fact a driveway.

Bently shifted the truck into park and got out. He opened her door and helped her down. "I'll get the bags. Code to get in is five-seven-four-two."

"We're staying *here*?" she asked, stunned. "In this tiny cabin?"

"Unless you want to try a tent?" He smirked.

He grabbed the bags while she walked to the door. Brown pine needles and scattered cones covered the soft earth of the forest floor. Geese honked somewhere in the distance. Trees and bushes rustled as squirrels and chipmunks raced around the forest. She grabbed the key box and entered the numbers before opening the door.

Notes of cinnamon and clove hung in the air as she walked in. Thick woven rugs adorned the floor. A stone fireplace with a stack of wood next to it was the focal point of the living room. The worn brown leather couch faced it and was decorated with colorful pillows. She reached out and ran her fingers over the various novels stacked neatly into a built-in bookshelf in the far-left wall. She turned towards the open-concept kitchen and small dining table.

There was a sign across the first door with a crescent moon that read "outhouse." She cringed, hoping she didn't actually have to go without indoor plumbing. Opening the door, she let out a breath of relief. The small but clean bathroom had a giant tub, porcelain sink, and a regular toilet.

She relieved herself and washed her hands before going back out to search the last room. Bently came in behind her, heading straight for the last pine door down the small hallway. A bedroom. The fireplace opened on this side too, though here it was covered with glass. Bently had set the bags onto one of the wooden dressers. A bedroom with a king-sized bed with a red plaid comforter took up most of the room. Bently's body stretched out across it, making the space seem that much smaller.

He tapped the spot next to him. "Come here. And no, this isn't me making a move." He winked, and she laughed. "I just wanna show you something."

She kicked off her shoes and snuggled to him. His arm wrapped around her, pulling her closer. She shivered.

"I'm gonna start a fire, but I wanted you to see this first." He pointed upwards. A large picture window replaced a good portion of the ceiling above them, giving them unfettered access to the sky above. "We're far enough from the city lights that tonight, you'll be able to see thousands of stars all from the safety of this warm bed." His deep voice rumbled in his chest against her ear.

What did I do to deserve this man? I can't believe this is real.

"Why are you doing this for me?" she asked, not looking at him.

He took a deep breath before replying. "Because I care about you. And I want you to have all your dreams become a reality."

Who supports his dreams?

"What are some of your dreams?" she asked.

"To stay healthy. To keep everyone safe. To make a difference . . . To be nothing like my own parents."

He was holding so much back. "You've already made a difference."

He scoffed.

Belle sat, her hand resting against his cheek, hoping he saw the man he was in her eyes. "You've changed my life. Given me hope. Taught me that I can't necessarily judge someone based on appearances. That not every man is the same. You've made me feel not so alone."

His gaze darkened. "You make it really hard to control myself around you. I want you so bad it fucking consumes my thoughts, day and night."

She swallowed, fear and uncertainty mixing with her own desire. Her body trembled. She wanted him too, but . . . "I'm afraid."

His brows drew together as he brought his hand to cup her face. "Of what, Angel? You know I'd never pressure you to do anything you weren't ready for, right? What are you worried about?"

She nodded. "Every time a man got his fill of sex with me, whether it be one time or more, it would end. Just like that, I'd be thrown out like yesterday's trash." *Or worse.*

His jaw tensed.

"I don't want this to end. Not yet," she whispered.

He pulled her against his chest tightly as if trying to erase the hurt from her past. "I'll admit, I don't know what this is between us. I've never felt anything this . . . strong before. And I know I have a reputation. But I want you to know I've never done for another woman the things that I have for you. And I never expect *anything* from you that you are not ready to give."

His deep voice was like a tattoo on her soul, branding her with promises that glowed of hope and possibilities.

"I haven't actually been with a woman since before my diagnosis, more than eighteen months ago."

His confession floored her. After all the rumors, she'd thought for sure . . .

"Why not?" she asked.

He sighed. "No one caught my interest until you. You sparked something in me, shocked me back to life."

She craned her neck and kissed him, infusing her admiration and awe for this man into every brush of her lips and tangle of their tongues. He held her gently as she rubbed the tip of her nose against his and kissed his cheek.

"I trust you, Bently. And that doesn't come easily for me."

"I know, Angel."

Awareness spun around her. She was nearly bursting at the seams, overrun with emotion, falling so fast. Could she ever enter into a partnership with a man like him? Could she feel safe enough to be vulnerable and share her body again? Could she rely on Bently when things got hard? Only time would tell.

"I better go start a fire to keep you warm," Bently said kissing her forehead before he unwrapped himself from her.

"Do you need help?"

"Nah, I got this. You feel free to relax. You can go for a walk to the edge of the lake, but don't go too far. There are bears around here. Shouldn't bother you, but just to be safe, don't wander off without me."

She had no intention of setting foot outside the door

alone. But the concern he voiced for her brought a surge of intensity inside as another piece of her broken heart locked into place.

At least for now, he was her protector.

30

BENTLY

"S'mores?" Belle asked excitedly.

"Of course." Bently smiled, handing her a stick with a marshmallow on the other end. They sat side by side facing the crackling fireplace.

He placed his marshmallow into the flame, gently browning the outside. She eagerly followed his example.

Flames lit up around her confection. "Oh no!"

He reached out, enveloping her hand in his, guiding the marshmallow out of the fire before he blew on it.

She laughed. "Is that supposed to happen?"

He shrugged. "You gotta keep it moving not too close to the flames or else it will burn. But some people like the charcoal taste."

He held the cracker and chocolate out to make her s'more before preparing his own. "Ready to taste?"

She nodded, and he bit into the crunchy, gooey, chocolatey goodness as she did the same.

Sweetness and richness exploded on his taste buds. She smiled and licked the sticky treat from her lips, sending a bolt of lust through his system. Want and need throbbed within him. "Is it as good as you'd hoped?"

She grinned. "Better."

He brushed his thumb across her chin, wiping away a string of marshmallow. He sucked it off. "Delicious."

Her eyes darkened. She cleared her throat. "So, uh, how's your family doing?"

He chuckled. "Good. Well, Andre seems to be avoiding me lately. Either that or Mia is keeping him busy."

"She seemed like a spitfire when I formally met her at the harvest dinner."

"Yeah. And Mikel and Remy are great. Jasmine . . . well, she's just taking life one day at a time."

"Does the baby's father help her at all?" Belle asked.

Bently sighed.

"I'm sorry. You don't have to answer that. It's none of my business." She shook her head and stared back into the fire. The shadows of orange flames danced across her brown skin, painting her in soft lights. She was stunning. Breathtaking.

He weaved his fingers through hers. "It's fine. Jaz won't even tell me who the father is."

"She probably has a good reason, then."

He looked up at her, his eyebrows rising. "Maybe you're right. I just wish she'd tell me if the bastard hurt her." His grip tightened.

"Sometimes, it isn't that easy." Her voice soothed him.

He nodded.

"Let's go see those stars you promised me." She led the way into the room, climbing under the covers.

Bently lay next to her, pulling her against his chest like that was where she'd belonged all along.

He'd been right. Thousands of stars scattered across the dark sky—wisps of clouds like ghosts haunting the heavens.

"Do you know any constellations?" she asked.

"Nah, that's Mikel's territory. All I know is the Big and Little Dipper."

Her head rose ever so slightly with each of his inhales. Her breath synced with his as if they were one. His hand stroked her back. They lay like that, enjoying the view in silence. He closed his eyes, savoring the moment. Her closeness blanketed him with peace, lulling him into sleep.

After preparing a tray with eggs, bacon, and toast, he added a cup of coffee with the creamer she liked so much. He walked into the room as she stretched out her arms, yawning. Warm sunshine cascaded down on her, making her glow as if she was truly an ethereal creature sent to earth for his redemption. Since when did he believe he was worth saving?

"Good morning, beautiful."

She sat and adjusted the silk cap on her hair. "Is that for me?"

"Breakfast in bed." *For the woman who occupies my heart.*

She smiled and held out her hands. "I don't know what I did to deserve all this, but thank you."

The woman gutted him. Staggered by how humble and pure she was, he set the tray on her lap.

"I'm just going to grab mine and I'll be back."

And take a minute to get a hold of myself.

Bently returned with his own tray and joined her on the bed. It was like they were a couple, but without the sex. They hadn't gone far besides a few light touches, and molten-hot kisses. And he was perfectly content just being next to this woman, sharing her space.

"How'd you become homeless?" he asked the question that had been burning the back of his mind.

She sipped her coffee before answering. "One of my mother's boyfriends, also her drug dealer, tried to get his payment from me."

His fists clenched around the cup in his hands as his stomach turned to stone.

"I heard him coming and told TJ to hide in the closet. He was only ten at the time. All I could think about was his safety. I just hoped he wouldn't see or hear anything. Once he was tucked away, I fought with everything I had. I knew my mother wouldn't come to help. It had just been me and TJ against the world since he was born."

She stared off like she was witnessing the scene play out on a screen.

"I was so tired of fighting, of being taken advantage of, of being hurt and used. I knew if I just lay there and let him do what he came to do, it would be over eventually. It's like I floated above myself, watching my teenage body be abused by this grown man. I thought, what chance do I have? This is all that I've ever known, so I know exactly how this ends."

He didn't move. Every muscle tensed with anger. He ground his teeth together, forcing control.

"Then I saw the closet door open. TJ ran out. I was so scared for him. He lunged at the man, clawing and hitting his head with his little fists. This force surged through me, snapping me back into my body as I freed myself long enough to grab the lamp. TJ's body was thrown against the wall as I lifted it over that man's head. I swung as hard as I could and the man crumpled to the floor. I raised my hand and did it again and again." She looked up at him, tears in her eyes. "I just wanted to make sure he'd stay down and leave us alone."

Bently nodded. No longer able to contain himself, his

arms shot out and pulled her against his chest. "You did what you had to in order to survive. There's no shame in that."

"I checked on TJ and told him to pack only what he absolutely needed. We didn't have much anyways. I grabbed a couple blankets and clothes and ran out of there while my mother was strung out on the couch watching TV like her own children were not being attacked. I never looked back."

"You were runaways."

"Yes. And as soon as I turned eighteen, I went back and had her sign over parental rights to me. Two hundred dollars and she sold her son. I had found a lawyer willing to . . . willing to do the paperwork for a . . . uh . . . trade." She faltered.

He gripped her tighter. The idea of teenage Belle alone on the streets of New York City, afraid and unprotected made vomit rise in his throat. Agony sliced through him that she'd had to make that choice. That her only option had been to be used.

"I would do anything for my brother. *Anything*." Her whisper was coated with shame.

He kissed her forehead. "You amaze me."

She looked up at him with watery eyes. "How can you say that?"

"Because when everything in this world tried to break you and tear you down, you defied gravity. You're still fighting. You got free, and you saved your brother in the process. You know how many cases of domestic violence I see? It's more common for the products of abuse to continue the cycle. You're the exception. You're the most beautiful, *pure* soul I've ever known."

She wiped the tears that dripped down her chestnut cheeks. "Then I guess we're a lot alike, you and me."

His brows knitted together.

"Because I feel the same way about you." She reached her hand up to cup his jaw—her softness against his roughness.

The fact that she thought so highly of him would have brought him to his knees if he'd been standing. He was weak when she'd been strong. They were not even in the same stratosphere. She was from heaven and he from the depth of Hades—or so he had thought. Maybe she was right. He'd only been a kid himself. As soon as he found out what his father was doing, he'd acted.

After their heavy conversation, Bently had brought out the fishing poles and taught her how to fish. They'd only caught a couple of little pumpkinseed fish, but her excitement was contagious. Bently had held her hand as they walked along the shore, talking about their likes and dislikes, about what they'd been learning. They'd kept the topics light and he'd savored the drive home. He wanted to enjoy every minute he had with her, for however long that was.

He walked Belle to her door, and set her bag down. "When can I see you again?"

She smiled. "Aren't you getting sick of me yet?"

"Quite the opposite actually." He stared at her—beauty radiated from every pore.

She stood up on tiptoes, bracing her hands against his chest. He wrapped his arms around her and lifted her. She giggled before he slanted his mouth to hers—tasting, teasing, taking everything she offered like the greedy bastard he was.

Her touch was like a live wire to him, a sensory overload. Unable to resist the pull between them, he squeezed her tighter, eager to hold on to whatever this was a little longer, greedily taking the scraps he could. She tipped her head back, and reluctantly he released her.

"I'm beginning to like you a lot, Sheriff," she said, breathily.

He groaned and set her onto the ground. "Me too, Angel. Me too," he said as she walked towards her door.

Her absence in his arms immediately fueled the longing. This woman was like an addiction. Each time he tasted her, it got harder and harder to walk away. And not just because his dick was throbbing, begging for release. But because being with Belle was like being whole for the first time in his regretful existence. She gave him hope. Maybe he could be worthy.

31

BENTLY

Thanksgiving had become one of the holidays Bently looked forward to the most. Each year the noise level grew as more children were added to their small family. When they walked in, they found Mr. Stone watching the football game with Andre and Mikel who was holding baby Phoenix.

The men all turned at their arrival. Andre's gaze narrowed on TJ.

What is his problem?

Bently needed to sit down with Andre and hash all of this out because this wasn't like his best friend.

"Oh, good. You're just in time." Remy appeared from the hall, taking the casserole from him.

He leaned in and gave her a kiss on the cheek as she wrapped one arm around his waist. "I always am." He smiled.

"Well, you and TJ go join the guys while I steal Belle away to the kitchen." Remy winked at Belle who seemed a little nervous, but she smiled back.

"Ain't gotta tell me twice," TJ said, walking into the living room and taking a spot next to Remy's father.

Remy leaned in and whispered, "We're just drinking wine and sampling the dessert while the food finishes heating."

"Good thing I brought a couple more bottles, then." Belle held up the wine in her hands.

"See? You fit right in here with us." Remy beamed.

Belle's smile faltered only for a moment before she glanced at him.

"You gonna be okay?" He checked with her to be sure.

"Of course." She nodded.

He leaned in and brushed his lips against her cheek, breathing Belle's scent. Vanilla and cocoa butter. She trembled. *So responsive.* Going slow with her was pure torture, but he would do whatever she needed. If he could only be in the shadow of the sun, it was better than the utter darkness of his life before Belle.

"You two are so cute together." Remy winked.

Belle smiled at him. "He is pretty handsome, isn't he?"

A bark of laughter escaped from him. Belle was loosening up, integrating into his circle, and he was loving every minute of it.

"Well, I'm partial to his brother." Remy sighed as Mikel walked up behind her and wrapped two arms around her.

"You better be," Mikel teased as he kissed her neck.

Remy giggled. "How's my baby boy?"

"His grandpa is spoiling him." Mikel kissed her cheek before eyeing Bently and Belle.

"Glad you could finally make it. Good to see you again, Belle. You keeping this guy out of trouble?" Mikel joked.

"I'd like to think so." She smiled.

It was the uncertainty in her eyes that did him in.

"Come on, Belle. Let's pop some bottles and get you a glass of wine." Remy nodded and Belle followed.

Mikel waited until they were out of earshot before he turned a knowing gaze on to Bently. "I never thought I'd see the day."

Bently shoved his brother on his way into the living room. "I don't know what the fuck you're talking about."

"That's a bad word, Uncle Bently! You owe me one dollar." Lyra held her hand out as she appeared from the corner of the living room with a crayon in the other. A coloring book was sprawled out at her feet with several pages ripped out and arranged in a circle.

A hard slap reverberated across his back as Mikel smirked. "Yeah, Uncle Bently. That's a bad word."

"Since when does it cost one dollar? Last time it was a quarter. That's highway robbery," he said as he dug into his wallet.

"No, it's flatulence." Lyra shrugged.

Bently's eyes furrowed as he looked to Mikel who was trying hard not to crack up.

"Inflation, baby. That's inflation," Mikel corrected.

Lyra rolled her eyes and held out her hand. Was she six or sixteen?

Bently pulled out a five and handed it to her. "Alright, here. It's all I have. It should cover me for the next four times I slip up, princess."

Lyra's eyes lit up. "Five dollars?"

"For your college fund," Mikel reminded her.

"Okayyyy. I'll go put it in my piggy bank." Lyra stalked off.

"You have your hands full."

"It's fucking terrifying having a daughter, man." Mikel's complexion grew a little whiter.

"That's one dollar for the college fund," Bently teased.

Mikel smacked his shoulder. "Only counts if you get caught."

"Jasmine in the kitchen?" Bently asked.

Mikel nodded. "Yeah, Zoey's sleeping in that thing she wears."

"Touchdown!" Mr. Stone and Andre yelled together.

"You notice anything off with Dre lately?" Bently asked.

"Something's been on his mind, but he won't talk to me about it. I figured it had to do with Mia's paperwork. Probably just stressing about their interview with ICE coming up." Mikel shrugged.

"Yeah, maybe."

"Dinner's ready! Shut the TV off and find a seat," Mrs. Stone called.

Bently waited for TJ as he was the last to file into the dining room. He wanted TJ and Belle to feel welcome, to know they had a place they were wanted.

As they sat around the table, Mr. and Mrs. Stone did what they did best—brought everyone together in conversation. They laughed as a group, they teased. Mr. Stone was talking to TJ about the college where he was a professor. Mia, Jasmine, and Remy were laughing with Belle. She fit into his life like she had been made to all along. TJ helped himself to a third plate. Bently remembered what it felt like to be a bottomless pit as a growing teenager. Though he'd had to go hungry more times than not so his brother and sister could eat.

He'd come so far, despite the circumstances he'd been born into. For the first time in his life, he wanted to share his life with someone else. No, not someone—with Belle.

"So, Belle. What made you so hesitant to be friends with

our friend the sheriff here? Was it because he's a cop?"
Andre's hard gaze leveled on her.

"Man, what's your problem?" Bently asked, a slight edge
to his voice for the first time that night.

What the hell has gotten into Dre?

Belle placed her hand over Bently's thigh, instantly
injecting him with calm.

"Absolutely. As a Black man, I'm sure you know that you
have a one in one thousand chance of getting killed by the
police. It's survival to be weary of those who have been given
the ability to wield power in a way that is so harmful for
minorities and other groups of vulnerable people," Belle said.

Andre bit his bottom lip, looking between TJ and her.

"I know all about that," Mia said. "But Bently's one of the
good ones."

Belle smiled and looked up to him. "I know that now."

Bently put his arm around her and kissed her temple.
"Most of us in the force are. I don't see color."

Every adult at the table cringed simultaneously.

What did I say wrong?

Andre shook his head. "So, I look white to you?"

Bently's brows furrowed. "That's not what I mean."

"What *do* you mean, then?" Mrs. Stone asked.

He shifted in his seat. "I guess I'm just trying to express
that I'm not racist or prejudiced. That I see us all as equals, no
matter what color our skin is."

"In order to explain that you're not sexist, would you say
you don't see gender?" Remy asked Bently.

Bently sighed and shook his head. "No. I wouldn't."

"Color blindness isn't what we need. We should celebrate
our differences and what makes us unique. But by saying you
don't see color, it's like saying you are ignoring us and our
reality, and diminishing our experiences. Whether you see it or

not, we experience everything in life differently. We're judged as criminals for our melanin, seen as outsiders, or uneducated and dangerous," Belle added.

Bently scanned the faces surrounding him. Remy and Mia nodded. Andre looked impressed. *Damn. I never thought about it that way.* "I see what you're saying. I'm sorry if I've ever made any of you feel that way. I'll do my best not to in the future."

"Thank you," Belle said.

He reached his hand out and gently ran his thumb up and down her jean-clad thighs. Her hand covered his, returning the gesture, sliding those soft fingers over his hot skin. It wasn't sexual. It was . . . more. Something deeper. He felt . . . connected to her. But how could that be without sex?

Her warm throaty laughter spilled out, rushing over him. Her lips turned up, and her eyes sparkled. The intense emotion couldn't be contained, and it was as if his own heart exploded. A gush of liquid sunshine spread through his chest.

Oh my god.

The air was ripped from his lungs. He'd done the impossible and fallen for Belle. He was in love.

32

BENTLY

"Do you want to come in for coffee?" Belle asked as Bently followed her and TJ to their entrance.

"Yeah, I'd like that," he replied as she unlocked the door and led them in.

"I'm gonna listen to this new album and get to bed. All that eating wiped me out," TJ said, giving his sister a hug before walking away.

"Don't stay up too late," Belle said.

Bently chuckled. "Good night, bud."

TJ turned and looked him in the eye. "Thanks for inviting me, Bently."

"You're more than welcome." Bently nodded before the young man wandered up the stairs.

Belle opened a cupboard, reaching over her head to grab the bag of coffee grounds. He stepped behind her, pressing his body to hers as he retrieved it for her.

The drumbeat of his heart was frantic. He set the container on the counter and dipped his nose into the curve of her neck. Anticipation thickened in the air, coating it with the fire of a thousand suns. His lips met her warm, naked shoulder. She shuddered.

He inhaled her, craved her, wanted to devour her. The building pressure of months of waiting bore down on him like a vise. His hands gripped her hips, turning her to face him. Her eyes met his, dark and alluring. They were filled with her own want, but it was the vulnerability flashing in them that cut straight to his heart. He'd show her just how much he loved her. He'd show her she was safe with him. That he would take care of her every need.

He leaned in, sucking in her shaky breath before he pressed his mouth to hers, soft and undemanding, coaxing her tongue with his own. She gripped his shoulders as a tiny moan slipped from those sweet lips. He dug his fingers into her hip as the other hand glided up her back to her neck. He pulled her closer as his mouth trailed the low neckline of her blouse. He bent, lifting her shirt a few inches. She wrapped her hands around his neck, pulling him closer, locking him in.

She sucked in a sharp breath. "Bently."

The way she said his name was like gasoline on the fire raging within him.

"Let me take care of you, baby," he said, waiting for her permission.

She swallowed and nodded. "Not here."

TJ. He'd forgotten they weren't alone. It took all his remaining strength to back off. He picked her up in his arms as she shuddered and trembled. He carried her upstairs as fast as his feet would carry him. Loud music bled into the hallway from TJ's room as he passed.

"That one." She pointed to an open door at the end of the hall. He kicked the door shut behind them and gently set her on her feet.

She helped him get the thin, silky fabric over her head,

leaving a strapless red bra pushing up her breasts. His tongue dove between them, tasting, kissing, sucking as his hands pulled the fabric away exposing two dark nipples. He swept his mouth over one while he gently massaged the other. Pinching the hard peak on one side while scissoring his teeth over the other. He sucked, as she whimpered.

Raking her fingers through his hair, she pulled him closer, urging him on. Little whimpers and moans escaped from behind those lush lips, making his dick pulse and beg to be let out. But this wasn't about him. This was about letting the woman he loved know that no matter what, he was there for her. That he would take care of her. That he could give without taking.

"You're so goddamn perfect, Angel." He kissed along her belly, unbuttoning her pants. "I want to taste you. Make you come on my mouth. Drink you up as you explode all over my face."

"Bently."

"You want that, Angel?"

She bit her lip and he held his breath. He'd wait until the end of the world for Belle, but this needed to be her decision.

"Yes." She nodded. "I want that, Bently, more than you know."

He pulled the zipper down before tugging the skintight jeans to the ground, until she was in nothing but those damn red panties. He pressed his nose against her cleft and inhaled. Her scent intoxicated his senses, flooding his body with overwhelming desire. His mouth watered. He licked over the lace, giving in to the overpowering need to taste her. Sweet musk tantalized his senses. He was hungry for more. One hit would never be enough.

Bently kissed his way up her belly and neck, ending on her

lips as he guided her backwards onto the bed. Her tiny gasps and whimpers only stoked the burning need within. He sat and pulled her to the edge of the mattress, kneeling once again. Slipping his fingers under the band of her panties, he tugged them down her legs. She unhooked her bra, letting it tumble to the ground. She was bare before him. A bronze angel of perfection. His hands spread out, tracing the dips and curves of her breasts. He sucked them each one more time before he moved south, exploring, worshiping as he'd promised. He spread her thighs as she shivered. Circular scars and burn marks peppered her inner thigh. His grip tightened and she stilled.

"I'm sorry—"

"No. You have nothing to apologize for. You're beautiful." He kissed one scar, and then another. "Perfect just the way you are." He made sure to caress each one with his lips before he looked up at her again.

Tears welled in her eyes as she focused on him. She sucked him in like a black hole, relentless and complete. His chest squeezed. "You are not your scars. You're not your past. They're just reminders that you're a warrior. They're beautiful. You're so fucking stunning you take my breath away. You make me . . ." He choked up. He wanted her to know just how truly amazing she was.

He dipped his head to her sex. His tongue darted out, licking between her hot slick folds. She was dripping wet for him. She tasted like honey from the gods. He groaned and she pulled on his hair until the pain only highlighted the pleasure. His cock was rock hard, the zipper teeth cutting into his flesh painfully.

"You taste so good," he said before diving back in for more. He licked and sucked as her legs began to tremble, clamping around his head. He pressed them apart, spreading her thighs open to him as he used his fingers to fuck her and sucked her clit into his mouth.

"Fuck!" she gasped, her eyes widening before she squeezed them shut.

"Open those eyes, Angel. Want you to see me worship you. Want you to see how responsive your tight little body is. Want you to see who's making you feel this good. Don't hide from me," he begged.

Belle's eyes rolled. Her thighs clenched around him and he raked his teeth ever so gently over her pulsing nub.

"Oh, god. Yes!" she grit out, no doubt trying to be quiet.

How loud could she be if they were alone?

A flush of wetness dripped down his chin and fingers. He lapped up her juices as she came down, her body growing limp. Her fingers released his hair as she lay back on the bed. He tucked himself in next to her, pulling her hot naked body against his. He was still fully clothed, but he'd never felt so naked with a woman before in his life. Her gaze had penetrated his soul, leaving him exposed. Too vulnerable. Belle *saw* him. *And she didn't run away.*

"That was . . ."

"Beautiful," he finished for her. He'd never seen anything more stunning than witnessing her come.

"Earth-shattering."

He chuckled and held her closer. "My ego appreciates the compliment."

"Bently . . ." Her voice wavered.

He considered her eyes, worried. "What's wrong?"

"Nothing's wrong."

Relief swept over him as he exhaled.

"I've never . . . I mean . . . I've never experienced that before."

She'd felt it too. "I know. It was intense." The hurricane of emotions that had swept through him while worshipping her on his knees was staggering.

"No—I mean, yes, it was. But I meant, I've never had an orgasm that wasn't self-induced before. I had no idea it could be like that."

He was stunned speechless. His brows knit together. This beautiful creature had never had an orgasm from a partner? "That was your first?"

She nodded, looking down as if ashamed.

He smiled. "Then we have a lot of time to make up for."

He sucked her nipple into his mouth as she gasped. His hands found her slick entrance, searching out the spot that was sure to send her over the edge again.

He was going to make her come, over and over. Until she begged him to stop. Because his angel deserved to see heaven.

* * *

Bently squinted his eyes open, jolting upright. Warm sunlight trickled in through gray curtains, shining onto the red-rose bedspread. *This is not my bedroom . . .*

Belle.

He settled back, replaying the long night they'd had together, orgasm after orgasm that he'd given her before she'd fallen asleep in his arms. He shifted, adjusting his throbbing cock in his boxer briefs. He'd need a cold shower soon, that was for sure. He'd never gotten so worked up and not at least given himself relief. But she'd looked too peaceful to move his arm from under her as they'd lain in bed last night. Where was she now?

The door opened and Belle walked in carrying two cups of coffee. "Good morning, sleepyhead."

Her shy smile only made his grin widen. He accepted the

cup and took a sip in an attempt to hide his morning breath, before he said, "Good morning to you, gorgeous. Thanks for this."

"It's the least I owe you." She sat next to him on the other side of the bed.

He set his cup on the nightstand and held out his arms to her. "Come here."

She set her own mug down and moved closer.

He wrapped his arms around her, lifting her chin to meet her eyes. "You don't owe me anything."

"You're not upset because I didn't . . . return the favor?"

What! That's what she thinks of me? No. That's what she's known all her life. She deserved so much more. And he was just another selfish bastard getting in line. "Last night wasn't a favor. It was a gift. No strings attached. Last night was for you."

She nodded, her neck bobbing as she swallowed.

"Fuck, I want you more than I ever thought was possible. But I will never pressure you to do anything you're not ready for. I'll wait as long as you need to be ready for that." He rubbed her cheek with his thumb.

She sighed and leaned her head against his. "I know that. It's just . . . you're so much more than I was ready for."

"Is that a good thing or a bad thing?" He chuckled.

"It's the best thing." She leaned in and kissed him.

When they pulled apart, he pressed his lips to her temple. "Now, how about I take you to breakfast and then I'll drop you back off here before I go into work?"

She smiled. "That sounds like a great idea."

After relieving himself and freshening up in the bathroom, he followed her downstairs. The warm feeling in his chest grew. Love for Belle overflowed like a well, spilling over and soaking his every cell. She'd come into his life and stolen parts of his heart he hadn't known existed. He was going to do whatever it took to protect her, to care for her, to love her.

TJ was sitting at the kitchen table scribbling away in a sketchbook. He looked up as they passed the kitchen. "Sleeping beauty finally awake?"

"Smart-ass," Bently replied playfully.

TJ smirked, mirth flashing in his eyes.

"You coming to get breakfast with us?" Bently asked.

TJ shook his head. "Nah."

"Your loss." Bently shrugged as he grabbed his jacket. His arm snaked around Belle's as she laughed. "And my gain."

A warm smile spread across Belle's face as her eyes sparkled like she couldn't believe how good and right this felt either. She leaned in and kissed his cheek. "Come on. I've worked up an appetite."

"Uhhhh, too much information!" TJ grumbled.

Bently and Belle burst out laughing as he opened the door for her. But the laughter died as soon as it had started. The blood drained from his face. Belle's body stiffened. Her gasp was the last thing he heard as blood rushed in his ears. Adrenaline and instinct kicked his body into high alert.

Words were written in blood across his windshield. *"You'll pay."* A gallon or more of red liquid had been sprayed all over the hood of his truck. There in the center lay a lifeless pig.

The fuck? What happened?

Violence stained his life. *Belle.* Belle wasn't safe. Not with him. He opened the door and shoved Belle back inside.

"Lock the door," he barked.

His eyes greedily searched the neighborhood. The fucker would want to see him find this. Whoever this was knew he'd be here. *Or he followed me.* Did that mean his family was in harm's way too? Either way, it meant Belle and TJ were in danger because of him. He'd promised to take care of her, be her protector. He'd put them in harm's way. He'd failed.

Bently dialed dispatch. He needed Vargas to help him sort this out.

Several minutes later, Officer Luke Parsons and Rife Owens pulled up, lights flashing.

"What the fuck?" Rife asked, surveying the damage.

"I want to find out who this fucker is," Bently growled.

"Well, at least we know it ain't gonna be one of those Muslims." Parsons laughed.

Bently and Rife both turned to him. Bently's fists clenched, his nails biting into his palm. *The fuck!?*

"Oh, come on. Pigs, pork, Muslims . . . Get it?" Parsons didn't take the hint.

"We're not laughing because it's not funny," Bently snapped.

"Geez, tough crowd." Parsons chuckled.

Rife shook his head. "I'll get every inch of the truck dusted for fingerprints."

"I'll talk to the neighbors and see if they saw anything," Parsons said, before heading to the house to the left of Belle's.

"Sir, you should see this," Rife called him over.

Bently walked to the open driver's side door. Rife held a photo in one gloved hand. Bently's eyes widened, taking in the photograph shot of him and Belle together from no more than a hundred yards away from this very spot as he helped her into his truck. But that wasn't the outfit she'd worn last night. That was weeks ago—on one of their dates.

His pulse raced and his ears rang, drowning out all the other sounds around him. His vision grew hazy at the edges. Gasping for breath, he turned back to the duplex. Belle's worried gaze focused on him from behind the window inside. His stomach tipped and his heart sank. This was why things would never work between them. Because sooner or later, he wouldn't be able to protect her. He'd fail her like he'd done with everyone else, every time it mattered before. Everything was spinning out of control. He couldn't risk it.

He couldn't risk *her*.

33

BELLE

Raindrops pelted against the roof of her idling car as Belle checked her phone one more time while she sat across the road from Bently's house.

11 a.m. Belle: *Are you okay?*

1:30 p.m. Belle: *Can I bring you some lunch?*

Both texts were marked as read, but he'd not bothered to reply. She glanced at the digital clock. 8:06 p.m.

When they'd discovered the horror outside her house the previous morning, real fear had shimmered back in those cautious blue eyes of his for the first time since she'd known him. He had to be hurting. He wouldn't ask for help, *and* he'd pull away. But there was no chance she'd leave him when he needed her. Like it or not, she was in this with him.

She slipped the keys in her pocket and opened her door, glancing around the quiet neighborhood as she got out. Thunder rumbled overhead, the gray storm clouds ominous. She locked her car and jogged over to Bently's house before knocking with more confidence than she felt. Because there was always a small chance that he'd reject her, now more than ever. But she could do this. She could put herself out there for the only man who had ever truly shown her what it was like to be honestly cared for.

Bently cracked the door open, his dark gaze widening when he met hers. He quickly averted his eyes, seemingly searching the otherwise empty neighborhood.

"What are you doing here?" he growled, opening the door and pulling her inside. He slammed the door shut and flipped the deadbolt. Something dark flashed in his hand as he moved.

Oh my god. It was a gun.

Fear leapt, strangling her chest. Of course he had a gun— he was a police officer. But the fact that he was answering the door with it confirmed her suspicions. The man was terrified and in real danger.

He set the gun on the small table by the door. "What are you doing here?" he repeated.

Her eyes flicked up to his, hidden behind an emotionless mask. The dimness in the entryway only added to the charged air. Lightning flashed, illuminating the vulnerability in his eyes. Anger and fear crashed off him in unsettling waves of unseen energy. She could *feel* him. Feel the ache of his terror, his worry, his guilt. She blinked, licking her lips. "I was worried about you."

He scoffed. "You shouldn't be here."

The wall was back, erected even stronger between them. Why was he shutting her out again?

Because that's all he's ever known.

"You can talk to me. I'm here for you."

Silence. His shoulders inched higher with tension and his breathing grew ragged.

She pressed on. "I'm sure it's scary having someone doing

this to you. Are you worried it's the same guy who attacked you?"

"I'm not scared!" he roared as thunder outside boomed.

She flinched at his outburst. Anger boiling over, she snapped. "Then you're not human! Experiencing anger, fear, happiness, and sadness are all part of having a beating heart." She pushed her finger against his chest. "Do you think it makes you less of a man to talk about your emotions? To admit you are worried about this?"

He captured her hand in his and backed her into the door, caging her in. "Angel, I want to prove to you just how much of a man I really am so bad it aches."

His hot breath tickled her tingling lips. Bently's gaze was dark and needy, like he was on the verge of coming undone. The man was pure chaos, smelling of the unflinching honesty of oak and the depravity of sin. The air hung heavy with anticipation and knowing. She might not be able to take away his pain, but she could be here for him. He needed an outlet. He needed *her*. More than that, she wanted to show him she trusted him and loved him, enough to give him the thing most precious to her.

"So do it." Her voice was breathy.

He blinked as if in disbelief.

"Take me upstairs, Bently."

"I'll ruin you," he growled his warning. His grip on her wrist tightened. Lightning flashed, and the lamps flickered. The storm's energy grew as the wind whipped and whistled through the old house.

She searched his face. As much as this man wanted to believe he was the devil, didn't he know he could only ever be her savior?

He glanced at the door. He was going to tell her to leave.

"Do your worst." She pulled her wrist free and reached down before quickly pulling her shirt off.

His gaze raked over her exposed flesh, searing her skin with his lust. The cool air on her damp flesh made her shiver, as goose bumps prickled across her torso. His jaw ticced and his eyes roamed. She swallowed, waiting for him to do something. *Anything.* Bently's fists balled at his sides as if afraid to touch her.

She leaned in and pulled the hem of his shirt up. His muscled torso was chiseled to perfection. Lightning flashed again, highlighting the dips and ridges of his abdomen, heaving with each bated breath. It was as if he'd sucked all the oxygen up in the room, leaving her with nothing but thick, sticky, wanton gasps. He helped her get the rest of the fabric over his head and then he was shirtless before her.

His body trembled as she lightly traced over his scars. She'd seen them before, but this was much more intimate. It was like he was letting her see him for the first time. Like he was baring it all to scare her away, send her running in the other direction.

"I'm not going anywhere, Bently."

He picked her up faster than she'd thought possible. Her legs wrapped around his waist. His hard bulge pressed against her ass. He carried her upstairs as the lights went out—a blackout eclipsing them in total darkness.

Her stomach tipped as he laid her on the bed. His hands roughly pulled her pants and panties off all at once. She couldn't see anything in the darkness, but it only amplified her other senses. The sound of his zipper and rustle of clothing melded with the pounding of rain on the tin roof. Thunder boomed, and a second later lightning streaked, illuminating Bently in shadows and heaven's light. Those blue eyes glowed for a moment in time, locked on her, filled with a hurricane of emotions, with so much passion. She trembled in apprehension as he leaned in. Hands pressed her wrists to the mattress as hot lips met hers. He dove his tongue into her mouth, taking, ravaging, stirring any hesitation left into burning need.

He licked her neck, and then sucked hard.

"Bently," she gasped.

His hands moved to her breasts, and he took his time to suck and tease her. His touch was rougher than last time, but still so perfect. His want bled into his every caress. His movements frantic and desperate.

His fingers dipped inside her wet pussy as he groaned. "You're so fucking wet for me."

"Only you," she panted.

Thunder rumbled, chills skating across her skin as his hot body lowered onto hers.

"I need you," he grated.

"So, have me." She reached out and stroked his hard cock as he pulsed and twitched in her hand.

He groaned. "Not going to last if you keep doing that."

Lightning flashed, creating a snapshot of the pleasured agony of his face—brows drawn, eyes focused, teeth biting.

She lined him up at her entrance, both of them gasping in the same breath at the connection.

"Are you sure?" he asked with a pained breath.

Tears welled in her eyes, because even now, he was thinking of her. No matter how out of control he felt on the inside, he was still putting her first.

"I've never been surer of anything in my life. Fuck me, Bently."

He plunged inside her. She sucked in a staggered breath. He rocked into her, hard and slow, as if savoring every second. Brutal and gentle. Reckless and inevitable. She squeezed her eyes shut in utter rapture.

The man felt like he was meant to be inside her, like this was the piece of her heart she'd been missing all her life. His hands held her ever so gently, exploring every inch of her body and sending shivers and gooseflesh erupting over her nakedness. She'd never felt as alive as she did right now. They were no longer two people, but one soul, connected in the most intimate of ways. His thrusts, hard and savage, claimed her, branded her with a delicious burn. The pressure built. Flames licked and teased with each bated breath they shared.

"You're so fucking perfect. So sexy," Bently whispered in her ear before kissing her, deep and long. Their bodies were lost in humanity's most ancient dance. Tears spilled over her cheeks towards the bed as he reached between them and swirled her pulsing clit, making her cry out.

"Bently!"

"That's it, baby. Come for me. Let me feel that pussy shudder." His voice coaxed, pouring gasoline onto the raging inferno inside her. She came apart, and was put back together all at once. He pinched her nipple as another wave of pleasure crashed over her.

He gripped her hips and flipped her over. She lay flat on her belly as he plunged harder inside her. His fingers dug into her hips as he leaned down, brushing the scruff of his beard over the sensitive skin of her shoulders, kissing gently as he pounded harder and deeper.

"Fuck! Yes!" It was all she could say, over and over, as he grunted and drove her into oblivion again and again.

"That's it, baby. Come for me, Angel. So fucking perfect. So beautiful."

It was too much pleasure—she was drowning in it. Unable to draw breath, she surrendered, growing limp as she shattered again and again. He bit down hard on the back of her neck, sending a jolt of pain laced in surrendering lust shooting through her. He eclipsed her body and soul in euphoria.

Bently roared a moment later, emptying inside her, filling her with his release. He wrapped his arms tighter around her, staying close, holding on to what they shared just a little longer, like he too never wanted it to end. Nothing but the sound of their heavy breaths mingled with the steady beat of rain pelting the roof.

She was boneless and more satisfied than she'd ever thought possible. This man had given her one of the best gifts in the world. He'd shown her that she wasn't broken. There wasn't anything wrong with her—she'd just needed the right man in her life. A man whom she could trust. A man whom she loved.

"I love you," she said, before she could filter the words in her sex-hazed brain.

Bently's body stiffened before he slipped out of her and said, "I'm sorry. I'm so sorry."

34

BENTLY

Alarm bells blared in Bently's head. A heavy weight settled over his chest. He'd just majorly fucked up. Panic squeezed his rib cage. For the first time in his life, he'd had sex with a woman and it was so much more than just a physical release. He'd made love to Belle.

And everyone I love gets hurt because of me.

He couldn't let that happen to her. He should have kicked her out as soon as she came to his door. But . . . he'd been too weak. What if whoever was harassing him turned their sights on to Belle? *Fuck!* Once again, he'd messed up. She'd never forgive him for this.

"What do you mean? I wanted this," Belle said, sounding confused.

She had every right to be. He was a selfish bastard and he'd used her like he'd sworn not to. Taken what he couldn't give back, just like the thief he was.

He'd never thought he'd be capable of loving a woman. *What did I do?* What if that demented prick was outside right now? What if . . .

"I'm so sorry. I never meant . . ." *. . . to put you in the middle of this.* He found his sweatpants on the floor and pulled them on.

"You never meant what?" she asked, her voice tinged with rising anger.

His dick pulsed—the traitor wanted another round with this sweet angel. But that would never happen. Because he loved Belle, and that meant the best thing to do would be to let her go. She'd be safer without him in her life.

"This. I never meant for it to get this far." *I never meant to fall in love with you too.* He stood, searching in the darkness for his shirt. Thunder rumbled in the distance as the rain began to die down.

She let out a choked sound. "Are you pushing me away again? I got too close and now you're running scared like you have every other time?"

"No!"

"Bently?"

"You need to leave. Right now." *So you'll be safe.*

The lights flicked back on, and the look in her eyes shattered what was left of his damaged heart. Anger, pain, and finally resolve. She stood, every inch of her naked glory tense and rigid. She reached for her clothes.

His heart ached. He wanted to wrap his arms around her and hold her until the morning. He wanted to take it all back and wipe that agonized look off her face. But instead he stood motionless as she held her chin high and got dressed like the warrior she was.

She gazed back at him, opening her mouth and then snapping it shut. She shook her head. He was the biggest asshole.

You're nothing but a failure. You ruin everything you touch. You're weak. His father's voice played in his mind. He'd been right after all. But not anymore. He'd do the right thing and keep the woman he loved away from him so she'd be safe.

Belle turned to leave, and he followed her downstairs in torturous silence. She unlocked the deadbolt and stopped, turning to face him with watery eyes. His heart lurched.

"If I walk out this door, whatever this was between us is over. I won't be treated this way again. So you need to think really hard if that's what you truly want, or if this is just your trauma talking."

She staggered him. Couldn't he just . . . The message written in blood and the dead pig flashed in his mind. He hadn't told her about the picture they'd found in his truck.

He shook his head. She wasn't safe.

"I don't want you to come back." The lie burned his throat.

She blinked, those dark eyes flinching. If he told her why, she'd only try to stick by him. He couldn't have her hurt because of him, or worse.

"I trusted you. Guess I should have followed my first instincts after all." She turned and ran out the door through the sprinkles of rain. Heartbreak and grief weighed heavily on the wet air.

As soon as she was behind the wheel, he grabbed his gun and keys and slipped from the house. He tailed her from a distance, following her home. She had to be safe. Her car pulled into the drive. He texted TJ from a few houses down the street.

Bently: Make sure your doors and windows stay locked.

TJ: Why?

Bently: Keep her safe.

Because I can't.

He sat in his police truck as the rain dripped over the window. His personal vehicle was still being searched for any traces of the stalker. They'd gotten lucky with a fingerprint, but it wasn't in the system. Unknown. So now, he'd wait here in the shadows until morning.

He picked up his phone to call Vargas. Maybe she could trail Belle to work. But then what? He couldn't find someone to watch her at every moment of every day. All it would take was one lapse in concentration, one opportunity, and she could be hurt. *Or worse.*

His chest squeezed. His lungs constricted. He gasped. *Oxygen, damn it!* Where had it gone? Each damaged beat of his ragged heart shot vicious pain spiraling through him. He slapped his hand across his chest and bowed over.

I'm having a heart attack.

He sucked in air, squeezing his eyes closed as everything came crashing down on him. The weight of pain and guilt he'd carried for so long became more than he could bear.

No, this is a panic attack.

He forced himself back to sitting and started to count, slowing his breaths. Each shaky inhale was like filling his lungs with shards of glass. In and out. Over and over until the tightness in his chest relaxed. But his heart still ached like a herd of wild horses had just trampled over it. Or maybe, whatever was left of it had been ripped to shreds the moment he let her walk out that door for good.

But it was too late now. He'd have to live with this loss.

35

BELLE

Belle's secret places no longer ached. His scent no longer invaded her bedroom. Two less reminders that Bently had been inside her less than two weeks ago. But her heart felt like someone had cut it into ribbons and left her to die from the internal bleeding. The hot water sloshed over her tired body. Her eyes felt like sandpaper. Why was she still crying over this man?

Because you fell in love with him and he ripped your heart out.

He'd made love to her, connected with her emotionally in a way she hadn't known was possible. Bently had given her the best sexual experience of her life and then pushed her aside so cruelly. It felt as though he'd left her alone in an ocean, no longer helping her tread water. Nothing was left but the lead weights of her fears to drag her into the darkness. She'd given him everything, all that she had left, and he'd kicked her out as soon as it was over. Her stomach revolted at the memory. Bile rose up the back of her throat.

"I don't want to brag, but I know a thing or two about how to woo a woman." His words came back to haunt her.

Had this all just been a ploy to get her into his bed? *No.* It couldn't have been. Could it? Was it all a lie?

After she'd dried and gotten dressed for the day, she headed downstairs.

TJ looked up from his book. "Hey, just made some coffee."

"Thanks." She forced a smile.

"Are you and Bently, uh . . . okay?" TJ asked cautiously.

Belle turned to pour herself a cup, afraid he'd see the pain in her eyes.

"I'm in this, Angel." But he'd never clarified what "this" was. He'd always been vague. She was surprised TJ had waited this long to say something.

"Why do you ask?"

TJ sighed. "He won't respond to my texts and he hasn't shown up to the courts in weeks."

Right. TJ was losing a friend too. A man he looked up to.

Anger boiled inside her. Bently had been just like the men of her past—using her brother to get to her. Rage curled in her belly as she grit her teeth. "I'll talk to him and find out what's going on. I know he was busy with work."

Even if he was a coward, TJ looked up to the man. Her brother deserved better.

Belle waited until the evening. She pulled her car across the street from his house, glancing at the driveway. His truck was all clean of the blood. It had been erased, like the vandalism had never happened. *Just like us.* She inhaled long and deep, bolstering courage for what she needed to do. As she exited the car, she left it unlocked. If she was in a hurry to leave, it would make for a faster getaway.

Her steps were determined, but her knees wobbled and

her belly flipped with a mixture of anxiety and nerves. She held up one shaky hand to knock on Bently's door. Feminine laughter drifted from behind it. Her stomach lurched as her chest squeezed tight. Was he with another woman? The blood drained from her face as she forced a cold breath into her lungs. Her heartbeat hammered against her chest as she forced herself to knock.

The door opened, and warm green eyes met hers. *Jasmine.* "Hey, Belle. How are you?" she asked, smiling.

"I told you not to answer the—oh. Belle." Bently halted. He had dark circles under his eyes, and looked as if he hadn't shaved since the last time she'd seen him. An unkempt beard only highlighted his perfect jawline. Her inner muscles clenched. That scruff had felt like heaven between her thighs . . .

No. She was angry at this man.

"I was hoping I could talk to you for a minute," Belle pressed.

"Good luck with this asshole. I was just heading out anyways. Remy has Zoey for the afternoon while I run some errands. Just wanted to make sure this guy was still alive. Now that you're here, I'm sure he'll get in a better mood." She winked.

Belle swallowed and shifted uncomfortably. He'd obviously not shared anything with his sister.

"Bye, big brother. Don't be a stranger. Zoey might forget what you look like." Jasmine zipped up her coat and waved to Belle before she shut the door behind her, leaving them in deafening silence.

Bently swiped the curtain over and peeked outside, watching his sister get into her car, no doubt. Ever the protector. *Except when it comes to my heart.*

"What are you doing here?" he asked as though his throat

was full of gravel. He turned to face her, still keeping his distance.

"Are you okay?"

"You came to check in on me? What a good *friend*." His tone was sarcastic.

She furrowed her brow. "Still trying to push everyone away I see. I'm not here because of us, Bently. If you want to live in fear and let your ghosts win, that's your choice. I'll move on." *I'll survive you, because that's what I do.*

His gaze darkened, blue fire blazing in those eyes locked on her. He was holding so much back. A prisoner in a jail of his own making. The irony was that he was the only one with the key. It wasn't any good unless he chose to use it.

"It was just sex." He winced as though his words were assaulting him at the same time as thousands of tiny arrows pierced her already battered heart.

"That's all it ever is." She shook her head. "Look, I came here to tell you that no matter what happened between us, my brother looks up to you. You need to man up and stop being a coward. Tell him to his face that you don't want to hang out with him, that you were using him to get to me, or continue playing ball with him and responding to his texts like nothing is different. I don't care which you pick. But don't punish him to avoid me, or we *will* have a problem."

Bently's shoulders slumped as his eyes shifted to the ground. He nodded.

She opened the door, the burst of December air not even making her shiver—she was already numb inside. And nothing and no one would ever persuade her to open up to a man again. This time, she was surely broken for good.

Bently had told the truth. He'd said he would destroy her, and that was one promise he didn't break.

36

BENTLY

"You look like shit," Mikel said, staring across Bently's desk at him.

"I feel like it too," Bently confessed. He was too exhausted to put up a front. He was barely holding it together.

"What did you do to mess things up with Belle?" Mikel asked, going right for his sore spot.

"What I always do," he deadpanned and scratched his overgrown beard.

"You cheated on her!" Mikel growled, jolting forward.

"No! I've never cheated on a woman in my life, asshole." Bently frowned.

"Because you've never been in a relationship before." Mikel eased back into his seat.

"We weren't . . ." It was a lie. Fuck the label. Belle had been his, if only for a short time. And she would always have a piece of him.

"So, what happened?" Mikel asked, rubbing the back of his neck.

"I failed her . . ." He took a deep breath. Perhaps it was time to speak his truth. "Like I failed you and Jasmine." The confession was like a gasp of fresh oxygen.

Mikel's brows drew together. "Come again?"

The old Bently would have found some sort of sexual innuendo to retort with, but he was at the end of his rope. He was tired of carrying this burden and pretending that everything was okay. That he had everything under control when in truth, every single thing in his life was falling to pieces, including him. His fists clenched as he ground his teeth together hard enough to snap bone. "When I found you in a pool of your own blood and that sick fucker was nowhere to be seen . . . I should have been there."

"Bent—"

Bently held up his hands. "Then, when you told me what you'd seen. What he'd been doing to Jasmine. Why hadn't I known? Why did I wait so long to get you guys out of there?"

Mikel blew out a breath and shook his head.

"I went there to kill him, you know." Bently's voice sounded dead, even to him.

Mikel's eyes widened before he looked around the small office, eyes narrowing on the closed door. "You did?"

Bently nodded and stared at his brother. He knew what Mikel had done. Mikel shifted uneasily under his gaze.

"I never got to thank you for doing what I'd been too weak to do before."

"Th—thank me?" Mikel asked, jaw ticcing.

"I was there. I came in the back window with a fucking hammer. But he was already convulsing on the ground and you were standing over him with that needle in your hand."

Mikel swallowed and looked down at the desk. "You knew. All this time . . . I thought . . ."

"I figured if you wanted me to know, you'd have told me.

You saved my life that day. Because If I had followed through with my plan, I'd be in jail."

Mikel blinked and met his gaze. "I thought you'd turn me in. Always Mister Righteous, following the rules. You're the fucking sheriff." He lowered his voice and shook his head in disbelief.

"Ironic, isn't it?"

"Someone needed to put that monster down," Mikel agreed.

"I wish I could have done it sooner, protected you both." Bently rubbed his eyes.

"It was never your job, you know? You took that upon yourself."

Bently sighed. "How could I not? Who else was going to do it? Mom abandoned us, leaving us with that horrible man. Maybe if I'd been better, stronger, she would still be alive."

Mikel shook his head and sat forward. "No. Don't fucking take that on. That's on *her*. She put us in that situation. But she was also sick and never got the help she needed. And Dad, what that bastard did is on *him*. You can't fix everyone's problems, Bently."

"Who else will?" he shouted, anger rising.

"I never realized you thought so highly of yourself, that you actually think you have the ability to save the world," Mikel said.

"That's not what I mean," Bently denied.

"Isn't it though?"

No. Because I'm nothing. I'm unlovable. I'm a failure.

"So, you're having a pity party instead of going after the happiness you could have with the woman you love?" Mikel asked.

Bently frowned. "I'm not having a pity party."

"If anyone knows what self-loathing is, it's me, big brother.

Don't fuck it up and waste your chance at happiness like I did," Mikel said sympathetically.

Bently remained silent. He'd already ruined any chance with Belle. She'd told him her worst fears and then he'd gone and done just that. He'd sabotaged their only chance. "It's too late." The words felt like the last breath he'd ever release. Like inhaling without at least a spark of hope was too painful.

"True failure isn't in failing, but in not trying at all. You can still fight for her. Just talk to her. Tell her what you told me. Except, maybe leave out the murder part. Might want to work up to that later." Mikel smirked.

"Does Remy know?"

Mikel swallowed and nodded solemnly. "I told her when I returned before we got back together. I wanted to lay all my cards on the table. I'd held everything from her before. I knew this time, I couldn't hide the worst parts of me. That she needed to know what she was getting into."

That sounded terrifying.

Bently opened a file on his desk and pushed it towards his brother. Mikel looked down at the picture of Bently and Belle climbing into his truck. He still got chills knowing that the stalker had been this close to them and he hadn't even suspected anything was off.

Mikel frowned. "Is this from . . ."

"Yeah. One more reason I need to keep my distance from Belle."

Mikel sighed. "I think she deserves to know. She needs to have all the information so she can be vigilant and protect herself. Don't make the same mistake I did."

That made sense. So why was he holding back?

Because I don't want her to walk away from me. I'd rather leave before being left.

"I'll think about it."

246

Mikel stood. "Good. And while you're at it, get some sleep and maybe have a shave." He laughed.

"How did you know that I loved her?" Bently asked.

Mikel met his eyes. "Because you're different since you've been with her. You're better. You seem more . . . peaceful."

Wow. Hearing those words was like a blow to his chest.

"Not to mention the hearts in your eyes whenever you look at her or talk about her." Mikel chuckled. "It's about time you met your match. She knows how to put you in your place."

Bently laughed. "You think I need to be put in my place?"

Mikel smiled. "I think every man does. We just don't know it until it happens."

* * *

Bently jolted awake. The hair on the back of his neck and arms stood on end. He was on his couch, and the TV was muted, so what had woken him?

Smash!

Beep! Beep! Beep!

He jumped to his feet, sending the empty beer bottles clattering to the ground all around him. He ran out the door barefoot. His body pulsed with adrenaline. Every nerve was on edge. He was ready for a fight. He was going to catch his tormentor once and for all.

He yanked the door open and ran across the fresh snow, not even registering the cold as his eyes focused on the hooded figure wielding a wooden bat. *Not my truck again!* The perp swung, smashing his other headlight as Bently increased his speed and tackled him with full force to the ground.

"*Oomf!*"

"You sick fucker! I got you, you piece of shit!" Bently wrestled the bat free, as the person underneath him staggered to suck in a pained breath. Rage coated his insides. This was the one who'd broken his windshield before. The same asshole who killed a pig and left the message written in blood. The same one who had been following him and Belle. *Why?*

"Get off me!" the young man yelled.

"Not a chance in hell." Bently ground the perp's head into the asphalt and pushed his arms behind his back until he groaned in pain. Broken glass glittered in the moonlight all around them.

"What I want to know, is WHY?" Bently ripped off the back of his hood and froze. Shock shivered through his body as he looked into the familiar face. Horror filled him as his stomach tipped and convulsed. *No.*

"It was you? All along, you're the one who's been following me? You left that message and killed the pig? You attacked me outside the bar?" His grip tightened as he yanked TJ up. Blood dripped down his face from the cut and embedded glass below his right eye. Neighbors' lights flicked on as his car alarm continued to beep.

"No!" TJ shook his head. "None of that was me."

"Why would you do this? I thought we were friends, TJ," Bently said in disbelief.

"I thought we were too. But you just used me to get to Belle," TJ grit out as he took a swing at Bently's face.

Bently evaded the maneuver and locked TJ's hands behind his back. "No, I didn't. That wasn't . . ." He struggled to find the words.

The fury emanating off TJ reminded him a lot of himself. This boy was fighting to protect the only woman who had ever cared about him. He couldn't fault a kid for doing what Bently had promised to do before he'd fucked it all up.

"You're worse than the asshole who used her, kept her like a fucking slave in exchange for me to have a roof over my head and food in my belly. At least he was honest about what he wanted from her," TJ spat.

He staggered backwards, the earth tilting. Violence slammed into him, filling his rigid muscles with bloodlust. He wanted to kill the fucker who had done that to Belle. But wasn't he just as bad? He'd promised to be there for her and then he'd left her after she'd shared her vulnerability.

"Let's go," Bently grated.

"You going to read me my rights now, Sheriff?" TJ asked, chin up, the young man ready to face the repercussions for avenging his sister.

"No, we're going to take you to the hospital and get you stitched up," Bently said.

TJ's eyes widened.

"Despite what you believe, I never tried to use you to get to her."

He'd also never intended to put her in danger.

37

BENTLY

Bently leaned against the wall in the corner of the emergency room as Doctor Burton put the last stitch under TJ's eye.

The curtain yanked open as Belle ran into the room, halting as soon as her eyes focused on her brother.

Bently's heart squeezed as the ache he'd grown accustomed to since she'd been out of his life became overwhelming. The air was ripped from his lungs merely by her presence.

Her eyes shimmered with unshed tears. Her face was a mixture of fear and shock. She covered her mouth with her hand as she stepped closer to her brother.

"TJ?" Her voice was like a plea. Like she was asking him to tell her this was all a dream.

"I'll give you a few minutes," Doctor Burton said, before glancing to Bently and leaving the room.

"What happened? Where are you hurt?" Belle asked, holding her brother's face in her hands, inspecting him.

Regret flitted through TJ's features before he looked at

Bently. Belle stiffened and turned, her eyes meeting his for the first time.

Her mouth opened and closed like a fish as realization flashed in her gaze. "You did this?"

He remained silent. His mind reeled with a thousand things he wanted to say to her, but none of them were set free.

She lifted a trembling hand to her chest as she staggered back, putting herself between him and TJ. She was looking at him like he was a monster, like he had done this on purpose. He was paralyzed with regret. A lifetime of paying penance, of punishing himself for not being enough weighed on him. *Say something!*

"Why?" she croaked.

"I busted up his truck," TJ confessed.

Belle's head snapped to her brother. Her shoulders rose as her eyes narrowed. "You did what?"

TJ looked down ashamedly.

"I raised you better than this, Thomas Nigel Jones! You . . ." She staggered back, her words stuck as she crumpled to the floor.

Bently stepped forward, reaching towards her, his instincts overriding his fear. The need to comfort, to take some of her burden, drawing his lead feet towards her. His fingers grazed her shoulder as she flinched away from him. Her eyes were a mixture of betrayal, confusion, and fury.

"Don't touch me," she growled like a wounded animal.

He held up his hands and backed away. He'd thought the pain when he told her to leave had been the worst thing he'd ever seen, but he was wrong. Belle looked, destroyed now.

I've done this.

You destroy everything you touch. You're good for nothing. You're weak!

Belle stood on shaky legs, straightening her back and

crossing her arms over her chest. She spoke to TJ. "Everything I did. All the sacrifices I made so you could have a life, so you wouldn't end up in jail or dead. And you just throw it all away? All for what?" Belle's voice was unnaturally calm. All emotion drained from her face except the tears that dripped down her beautiful face.

TJ's shoulders slumped. "I was just trying to protect you. To stand up for you."

She shook her head. "That is not your job, TJ."

"No one else will!" TJ snapped, his eyes narrowing on Bently.

The accusation hit its intended mark. Shame and guilt swept over Bently like a rogue wave, pulling him under. He was drowning in it.

Belle turned towards him, wiping the tears from her face. "Can I speak with you, privately?"

"Of course." Anything to take even a fraction from the riot in her eyes.

Belle walked briskly past him, the scent of cocoa butter drifting over him. Another violent twist of longing for her creaked and splintered inside him. He followed her into the hallway on shaky legs and over to an empty room with only a few chairs and a coffee table with pamphlets on grief and loss sitting on it. *Fitting.* There was most definitely a part of him that had died after Belle left. He was hollow without her.

She turned to face him, staring straight ahead at his chest. She seemed so broken and vulnerable. He wanted to wrap his arms around her and promise everything was going to be okay. But he knew better. He'd lost that privilege the moment he'd let her walk out the door.

"I know I have no right to ask anything of you." Her voice was shaky and empty, as if she was hanging on by a thread. As if she had nothing left.

Because of me.

She looked the kind of tired that reached the marrow of your bones, not from lack of sleep but the exhaustion from a lifetime of having to struggle to survive. She'd done everything in her power so that both she and her brother would not have to end up like their parents and repeat the cycle.

How can I fix this?

"But is there any chance you'll let me pay the damages and not press charges? I'll keep him away from you—"

"Belle?" Bently clenched his fists at his side so he wouldn't reach out to her.

She blinked and turned her eyes towards his, steady and unwavering. Her strength was one of the things he loved most about her. She'd challenged him in so many ways. A woman he could count on through thick and thin. A woman who'd been through the fires of hell and come out stronger. His angel. He wanted to be the lucky bastard who got to live life by her side. He'd get her back. Bently would make this right, or die trying.

"I'm not pressing charges. I brought him here to get stitched up. I had no idea it was him. I thought—I thought he was the one who'd been harassing me. I *never* would have laid a hand on him if I'd have known it was TJ." He hoped she would see his honesty.

She swallowed and nodded. "Thank you. Just send me the bill."

He held up a hand. "I'll take care of my truck."

Her tiny nostrils flared as anger sparked in her brown-sugar eyes. She glanced at the door and then back to him. "I always pay my debts. We both know nothing in life is ever free. So, send me the bill."

He was going to argue, to tell her he was sorry for so much more, but Doctor Stanley walked in.

"Oh, Belle. I just heard your brother was brought in. Are you okay?"

Belle nodded and walked towards the door. "I'm fine, Rick. Thanks for asking."

Bently ground his teeth together and forced himself to stay put as Rick put his hand on Belle's shoulder. Chaos broke out inside him. He wanted to be the one to comfort her.

"If you need to reschedule tomorrow, let me know," Rick said as they disappeared around the corner.

His chest was heaving as if he'd just run a marathon. Jealousy burned his guts and they twisted into a million intricate knots.

There was no way he was going to give up. He loved her, and he'd prove it. He'd beg for a second chance, or whatever number they were on now. Maybe they had been doomed from the start. Maybe not. Perhaps he'd gotten in his own way and sabotaged this.

Failing was not attempting to try—wasn't that what Mikel had said?

You're nothing. You're weak. His father's voice echoed in his mind.

No. Maybe I once was, but not this time. Not for her. I'll be better. I'll get back up. For Belle, I'll do anything.

The bounce of the ball got louder the closer Bently moved to the near-empty basketball court. Two other kids dribbled down the opposite end. TJ shot and made the basket with a swoosh of the net before he jogged to grab the ball.

"Nice shot."

TJ faltered, his head snapping towards Bently. The boy's gaze filled with apprehension as the ball rolled off the court.

"Can we talk for a minute?" Bently asked, motioning towards the metal bench on the sidelines.

"Do I have a choice?" TJ didn't move.

"Of course. But I hope you'll hear me out." Bently sat and waited.

TJ hesitated a moment longer, glancing around before he joined him.

"I owe you an apology," Bently started.

TJ snorted.

"I never used you to get close to Belle. I liked playing ball with you and hanging out. I just happened to fall in love with your sister along the way."

TJ jerked his head to face Bently, brows drawn together. "You got a fucked-up way of showing your love."

"It . . . scared me," Bently admitted. The only way he was going to win her back was to give her everything he'd kept inside.

"My tiny sister scared you?" TJ scoffed.

"Terrified is more like it. I was afraid I'd . . . mess it all up. I thought she'd leave me anyways once she saw I wasn't . . . enough for her. That she'd want more someday and I'd never be able to give her that."

TJ studied him.

"We found a picture in my truck the same day the blood was spilled all over it. The photograph was one of Belle and me. Someone is coming after me and I don't want her caught in the crosshairs."

TJ nodded. "You didn't think she deserved to know?"

"She did—does. And I'd really like to try to make it right." Bently held his breath. He needed things to be okay between him and TJ.

"What if she doesn't want you back? My sister doesn't give out second chances, and you've already had one. Statistically, you have no chance to get back with her." TJ shrugged.

"Even if she won't accept me, I just want her to understand why I did what I did. So she won't think it was anything to do with her. I don't want her second-guessing and thinking she's anything less than perfect the way she is." Bently's throat burned as emotion choked him up.

"So, what's the plan?" TJ asked.

"I'm gonna figure out how to get her to talk to me, and then I'll tell her . . . everything." Bently shrugged.

"Good luck with that."

"I have your approval?" Bently asked, surprised.

TJ shrugged. "I mean, if what you say is true, then you're exactly the man I thought you were. But . . . right now it's just words."

Bently nodded. "You're right. But I promise, I'm in this for the long haul. I'm gonna be there from now on for both of you. Even if she doesn't want me, after all is said and done, I'm still here for you, TJ."

TJ cleared his throat. "Means a lot. And thanks for not, you know, arresting me."

"You're a good kid. We all make mistakes, and we all deserve some grace. You have your whole life ahead of you, and you don't want to do anything to jeopardize that in the future," Bently warned.

"I won't. I've never seen that look on her face before. Not even when the worst of the worst happened to us. I can't believe I almost . . ." TJ covered his mouth with his hand. Conflict flashed in his eyes, as if he wanted to say something more.

Bently clapped a hand on the young man's back. "We all fuck up sometimes. All we can do is get back up and try harder next time."

"Your life's motto, I'm assuming?" TJ chuckled.

"Something like that." Bently laughed. He'd honestly thought he'd lived his life by that statement. In truth, maybe he'd always been keeping one foot on the other side of the fence while sinking deeper into self-pity. He'd been weighted down by guilt he shouldered out of self-imposed obligation. He'd figure a way through it somehow. Because from now on, he was all in.

And he'd start with winning back the woman he loved.

38

BELLE

Turning down her street, Belle glanced out the window as "We Wish You A Merry Christmas" played on the radio. Big snowflakes fell from the dark sky, reflecting in her high beams. The holiday lights of her neighbors lit the street like something out of a Norman Rockwell painting. Decorated Christmas trees sparkled from windows. Red and silver candy canes reflected off streetlamps. This was supposed to be the most cheerful time of year, yet she was anything but. She pressed her hand to her chest to stifle the twinge of longing. The back of her eyes burned as she swallowed the emotion down.

"TJ is safe and healthy. I have a great job. TJ graduated with honors."

Three things she was thankful for. Gratitude was her buoy when she was drowning in pain. She'd had a lifetime of hurt, but this time was different. For the first time in her life, she'd experienced true heartbreak.

Figures. The one time I actually open up enough to love someone, my heart chooses the most unavailable man on the planet.

Seeing him in the school's auditorium a few days ago during TJ's graduation had brought her relief and devastation. He'd come through for TJ after all. She'd taken the coward's way out, shuffling towards the exit with the crowd and texting TJ to meet her in the car once he was done saying goodbye.

All she wanted was someone to be there when she needed them. A port in the storm. Someone to help shoulder the burden, who would understand that she was not her past. She'd thought Bently was that man. But maybe she was better off alone. It was better to be lonely than feel like this again.

She switched her blinker on and pulled into her drive. Her headlights illuminated a hunched-over figure on her porch. She sucked in a breath. *Bently.*

He looked up as he stood, causing her belly to flicker and tip. Fluffy white snowflakes stuck to his head and shoulders as he waited. Her core ached. The man was as sexy as ever. His black hair was a disheveled mess, sticking out over his forehead like he'd been running his hands through it. His beard had been trimmed since she'd last seen him. Why did he have to look so good?

Why is he here? What does he want? Maybe it has to do with TJ.

She took a deep breath, steeling herself against the dangerous yearning within her. Belle grabbed her bag and opened the door. The blast of chilly wind blew against her skin, sending a shiver through her. The crisp clean air changed the closer she walked to him, growing heavy with anticipation —with unspoken pain and dashed hope, with broken trust and warning.

She stopped a few feet in front of him. The porch light behind him edged him in shadows, much like the man she'd come to know. Maybe that was part of his allure. Maybe she'd been drawn to him because of the pain she'd recognized in him—a kindred spirit. How many women fell for the same fallacy? The hope that they could save the boy from the darkness, but instead it consumed them both? *Like it did my mother.*

"Hey." Bently's voice cracked.

At least she wasn't the only one knocked off her axis.

"Why are you here?" The tension wound thick between them, coiling tight. She stuffed down the need that burned inside her to be in his arms.

Bently licked his lips and shifted on his feet. "I, uh. I was hoping you'd be willing to talk to me. I have some things I want to say. I didn't want to involve TJ, so I waited out here. I hope that's okay."

"Did you come to talk about TJ?" She crossed her arms in front of her, a poor attempt at protecting herself from the devastating allure of this man. Her jaded heart pounded in her chest. Just being this close to him was too much.

"About us." Pain and uncertainty flashed in his stormy blue eyes.

Belle's resolve wavered. Her first instinct was to go to him, to comfort him, but she fought the urge. Clenching her hands into fists, she snapped, "I thought there was no us. It was *just sex.* That's what you said, right?"

He winced and glanced at the floor. "I lied."

"Yeah, I'd say. Everything was a lie. The only truth was that sentence. And I should have known it was all too good to be true." She pushed past him, pulling her keys out to open her door.

"Angel, please—"

She spun around, anger blazing. "Don't fucking call me that!"

His jaw ticced as he blinked rapidly. He searched the air around them as if the magic answer to this mess between them was there.

"Leave me alone. Don't ever contact me again. Get off my property and don't come back." Her voice shook as she turned away, blocking him out. Belle inserted the key.

"I was terrified. You scared the shit out of me, making me feel things I never knew I was capable of. I thought—I thought I was broken, unable to love someone."

Bently's confession ripped the air from her lungs. She turned the knob. Her mind was reeling, hope and rejection warring inside Belle's battered heart.

"I thought if I ever did love someone, the way I love you, I'd end up hurting them. I'd end up failing them like I failed my family." Bently's voice shook and wavered.

The air vibrated, the ground beneath her seemingly quaking from his confession. This was what she'd wanted all along. She'd just needed him to be vulnerable with her. Should she listen, or should she walk away? Was it too late?

She pushed open the door and stepped inside, dropping her bag on the floor before she turned to face him.

His eyes glimmered with unshed tears. Pain was etched across his beautiful face. Shadows of doubt and fear highlighted his chiseled jaw. Those clouded spheres reflected the scared little boy locked deep inside him. He was breaking her heart all over again. But was this how her mother had felt as she'd let her boyfriends come back in her life time and time again after they'd beaten her? Was she weak for hearing him out? Was it the same thing? *Am I like her?*

The small flame of hope in his gaze dimmed until nothing was left. He dropped his head, shoulders slumped. "I just want you to know that being with you meant everything to me. It was the only time I'd ever truly been me. You're so amazing, and everything that happened was all my fault. It had nothing to do with you. You're perfect the way you are." His gaze met hers, honesty glowing back.

He continued. "I'll leave you alone. But there's something else you need to know. Whoever was following me took a picture of us together. They know you're important to me. I don't know if they'll try to come after you, but I've had everyone at the station taking turns patrolling by a few times a day."

What? This psycho had pictures of them? She was in danger?

"When did you see the picture?"

He looked down. "Same day as the blood message."

All the pieces started to click into place. Why he'd been so upset and pushed her away. His overwhelming desire to protect her. She shook her head in disbelief. "Why didn't you just tell me?"

His gaze flicked back to hers. "I—I thought I could handle it. I'm sorry."

She took a deep breath. Everything inside her spun and tipped, tumbled and plunged. "You made the decision for me. You never stopped to consider that I could be trusted. For weeks some psycho could have been watching and waiting outside my house where I live alone with TJ. I'm a shift worker! What if he tried to attack my brother when I wasn't home? What if he came in when I was alone?" She shook her head and clenched her fists before she could do something she'd regret—like slap him.

He blinked, a tear slipping down both sides of his cheeks. "I'll regret that for the rest of my life. But it wasn't because I didn't trust *you*. It was because I couldn't trust *me*. I failed to protect you the moment that guy got you in his sights. I put you in danger just by being near you. You were not alone though. I had officers driving by a few times a day, and I . . . stayed close, but out of sight."

"Get in here." She opened the door wider.

He hesitated only a moment before he walked in, his scent invading her space, oak and sin twisting her up. She shut the door and took off her coat, then hung it on the hook.

TJ came down the stairs and halted, looking between her and Bently. "I see you got her to listen." He smiled.

Belle looked to Bently accusingly.

Bently hung up his coat and explained. "I ran into TJ yesterday and wanted to apologize about everything. Needed him to know I never used him to get to you."

Belle cut a hard look towards her brother.

"I'm just gonna, uh, go back to my room," TJ said, disappearing up the stairs.

Belle walked into the kitchen shaking her head. Memories of Bently kissing her trampled over her wounded heart. She pulled out a chair at the table and sat. The muscles in her body ached. Every part of her felt tired and sore. Her nerves frayed as a million questions swirled in her mind like a tornado.

"Can I make you some tea, or coffee?" Bently asked quietly as he approached.

"I'd rather you explain what you meant. You're a police officer. I understand your job is dangerous. I also understand the risks of being *with* a cop." *Of loving one.* Whatever his fears were, this went deeper. "Why didn't you just tell me? I had a right to know."

He took the seat next to her and faced her. "I've never told anyone this before." He cleared his throat and took a deep breath as if mustering the courage. "My earliest memories as a child were of my father beating my mother. Once I got a little older, I mean like three or four, I'd try to make him stop. I'd yell or go at him."

Belle's gaze never wavered as she listened to a story not

unfamiliar to her own. Her heart broke for the boy Bently had been as he recounted the trauma.

"I was never strong enough. I begged my mother to leave him. But she said to me, 'Bently, you don't understand. I love him. I can never leave him. Even if I did, there's no way I could take care of you kids alone.'" He shook his head. "I never wanted anything to do with love after that. Not if it could hold someone captive, against all better judgement. She chose him over us. The woman who was supposed to love us and care for us."

His parents had picked everything else over *him*. Destruction and chaos over love and peace. The picture of Bently Evans was becoming clearer. Belle reached out and put her hand over his.

He looked up at her, pain and conflict evident in his expression. He wrapped his warm hand around hers as he continued. "I told her I could get a job and support them, but she said I was just a child. I wasn't strong enough when they needed me. She . . . she took her own life when I was sixteen. Jasmine found her."

Belle sat forward, her need to support him pulling her closer to him like a magnet. No words of comfort would erase the pain of losing a parent, much less one who left by choice. The only thing she could do was sit with him in this heartache while he released what he'd held inside all his life.

"A year later, Jasmine came running into the mechanic shop where I worked—Link's place. It's off Main Street. Anyways, I'd never seen her more scared in my life. I dropped what I was doing and told her to go to Dre and Remy's and raced home." He closed his eyes and wiped a stray tear from his eye that hadn't yet fallen.

"I thought Mikel was dead." Bently choked out. His expression was grim. "There was blood everywhere. His face was so swollen, I barely recognized him. My father had almost killed him. I knew in that moment that I needed to end the bastard myself before he could hurt them any further. I thought that was my only way. We'd had CPS involved before but that meant separation and group homes. Jasmine wouldn't be safe without me. Last time we'd spent time as wards of the state, she'd been hurt by the family that took her in. I couldn't chance it."

Bently shook his head. "We stayed in some abandoned factory while he healed. Jasmine remained at Dre's parents' house. I asked Mikel what set Dad off. He'd always hated Jasmine more—if that was possible. Because our mother had an affair with another man. My sister was the product of that. The look in Mikel's eyes when he told me what our father had done to Jasmine . . ." Bently's voice cracked as his expression crumpled in utter devastation.

Belle sucked in a sharp breath. She knew better than to ask for details. She knew firsthand what that look meant.

He cleared his throat, his eyes snapping to hers. "I waited for Mikel to heal and plotted the million different ways I'd do it." He searched her face.

He wasn't looking to her to absolve him—she knew firsthand how trauma changed your brain, how it made you consider things you wished you never had to in order to survive. She understood too well the deepest darkest depths of the wickedness of humanity. Sometimes there was no good choice. Sometimes it was kill or be killed.

"I'm still here," she said, placing her hand over his, assuring him she wouldn't be scared away by his darkness, that they were alike in more ways than he could ever imagine.

Maybe they were both broken. But just maybe their shattered pieces could come together and make something whole.

39

BELLE

"I went there to do it," Bently said.

Belle held her breath. Was she ready to find out if he had in fact murdered his father? Would she be able to look at him the same?

Yes.

She nodded, urging him to continue.

"But I was too late. It was already done." Bently's brows drew together and his shoulders sank.

"And you feel guilty that it wasn't you?"

His eyes snapped to hers. "How did you know?"

"I'd feel the same way in your position, but only for one reason," she said, her mind racing and her heart pounding. That wasn't just guilt over wanting to murder his own flesh and blood glinting in his eyes. It was failure.

"What reason?"

"If someone I loved, someone I was supposed to protect, did it instead." She searched his eyes for the answer.

His gaze flashed as he sat straighter. His head bowed

forward as if his body was subconsciously nodding in confirmation. "Do you think I'm a monster?"

She shook her head. "Not even close."

"I failed them. I was all they had to protect them and I fucked it up. The very woman who was supposed to have unconditional love for us left us to a wolf. That monster happened to be my father."

"I'm really sorry that you had to go through that. It isn't fair. It isn't okay. And it's absolutely terrible that you were put in that position." She said the words she had once longed to hear. She was able to empathize and validate his feelings.

He swallowed and nodded. "Thank you."

"Do you feel better? After sharing this with me?" Belle asked.

Bently blinked and took a deep breath. "I feel . . . exhausted."

"Understandably." She glanced at the clock. The hand ticked toward eleven. "Talking about past trauma is emotionally draining."

"I just wanted . . . I hoped that by telling you this, you'd understand that when I realized you were in danger, I freaked out. I thought . . . I couldn't let you get hurt too because of me." His thumb grazed over her wrist, soothing her with his gentle touch.

"I want to forgive you, Bently. But I told you that if you let me walk out, that I couldn't keep going back and forth like this." She pulled her hand to her lap and cleared her throat. As much as her heart broke for this man, as much as her body craved his touch, she needed to stand up for herself. She had her own demons in her past, and becoming like her mother, giving in to a man while having to sacrifice parts of herself was not going to happen.

"I know, baby. I'm so sorry." He sounded utterly broken.

She straightened her shoulders and lifted her chin, tears welling in her eyes. "I need someone who will be with me when life gets hard as well as the good times. Someone who will sit in the pain with me and be my rock when I fall apart. Who understands why it's hard for me to get out of bed some days. Who won't make decisions for me. Someone to be my partner in all things. I need a man who can love me, and let me love him in return." Fat droplets splashed over her cheeks. Tears of hope and regret. Of choosing the right thing for herself regardless of how much it hurt.

I'm not like her. I'm stronger.

Bently pushed off his seat and her heart froze. *This is when he walks out the door for good.*

Instead of standing, he knelt in front of her, taking her hands in his as he stared into her eyes. Emotion fell in teardrops from his own pained gaze. "If you give me the chance I don't deserve, if you let me try one more time, I promise I'll do everything in my power to be that man. I promise that rather than turning away, I'll face my fears. Instead of pushing you in the opposite direction, I'll hold on to you."

Her hands trembled in his as his beautiful promises grated from his lips, like he was digging to the depths of his soul to find the courage to voice them.

"I love you, Angel. You're the one good, pure thing in my life that's just for me. Let me spend the rest of my life making things up to you. Let me love you and show you that love every single day. I'm in this, with my whole heart. It's all yours —you've had it since that first day you stole my breath away. You consume my thoughts, and take up all the space I never knew I had in here." He tapped on his hard chest. "If you need me to love you from afar, as much as it will kill me to do that, I will. Whatever you need, it's yours," Bently finished, looking in her eyes.

Belle choked on a sob. Could this be real? Could she give him another chance? Could she really have her happily-ever-after?

He's safe.

He waited, vulnerable and patient, gazing at her as if he cherished and adored her.

She reached out her hand to his cheek, the jolt of electricity burning brighter than a thousand suns. "I love you too —I tried not to. But I can't stop. You're impossible not to love." Her voice cracked, as hope burned in those blue eyes staring back at her. "I want you to be that man, Bently. But I can't go through this again."

He flinched as if her words had been a physical assault. He nodded solemnly and looked down. "I understand."

No, you don't. That much was clear. She took his face in both hands, forcing his attention to her once again. "So, don't fuck this up. You get scared, tell me. You want to run, tell me. You want to push me away . . ."

"Tell you," he finished.

"Can you do that? Can you communicate with me?" she asked.

He nodded. "Yes."

"Will you speak to a therapist? Regularly?" she asked. He had to have help for the trauma, and therapy had been beneficial to her healing. She couldn't be with a man who thought seeking help was showing weakness. This was her test. Would he do this for his own good?

He hesitated and swallowed hard. "Yes." His voice was scraping and raw. "I'll do it."

She let out the breath she hadn't realized she'd been holding. Relief blew over her, a light, warm breeze on a summer day. She blinked the remaining tears away and smiled. "Then, yes for me too."

He wrapped his arms around her and pulled her closer, his kiss hungry. His lips melded with hers, releasing the floodgates of passion. She burned bright and hot like she'd swallowed a flame. His tongue danced with Belle's. She dug her nails into his shoulder as he crushed her against his hard ridges.

"I need you." She panted.

Bently froze. "Are you sure?"

"Yes." Belle grabbed his hand and led him up the stairs to her bedroom. He shut the door behind them as she moved towards the bed. She lifted her shirt over her head before reaching for her pants.

His eyes took their time, drinking her in. His hands clenched at his sides.

"Don't hold back," she said.

"I don't want you to think this is all I want from you," he ground out, his self-control seemingly hanging by a thread.

"Is it?" she asked, unhooking her bra and letting it fall to the floor.

"No!" His voice was sharp.

"Okay, then."

He swallowed as she hooked her fingers under the elastic of her panties and tugged them down her legs, leaving her bare.

"You exposed your deepest darkest secrets to me. You let me in and I sat with you through the pain. Now, I'm standing here, naked and vulnerable. I'm asking you to join me. I'm asking you to connect with me in a way that I've never done with any man but you. I'm asking you to make love to me, Bently." A chill skated across her skin as he stepped closer. He reached out, tracing the line of her jaw before he tipped her chin up. His hulking frame towered over hers. She felt so tiny next to him, and yet so safe.

"You're truly the most beautiful creature I've ever seen, both inside and out. You must have been sent from heaven, my sweet angel, because there's no one else on this earth who holds a candle to you." He bent his head and kissed her, long and deep. Taking his time as he explored her body with his hands, he left no inch untouched. His rough palms skidded over her skin gently, a perfect contradiction. Belle was cherished and loved. Adored and worshipped. Frantic and needy.

She reached out and pulled his shirt over his head as he undid his pants, leaving them in a pile on the floor. He dropped to his knees and spread her legs. Her stomach clenched as his gaze turned dark, focusing on the juncture of her thighs. He leaned in, his pink tongue darting out and licking through her already slick folds. Fire bloomed like a flower, blossoming and growing. Her skin tingled. Her knees trembled and wobbled weakly.

"Bently," she gasped.

He gripped her ass, pulling her closer, spreading her wider as she tugged on his hair, seeking balance in the erotic chaos.

"I missed your taste. Never going to give this up again. You're so perfect. So fucking beautiful, every part." He licked again, spreading her wider. Bently pressed two fingers inside her, and curled them. The pads of his fingers knocked the sensitive spot deep within her. Her body vibrated and her core clenched in a tortured blend of pain and pleasure.

She whimpered.

He sucked her clit, teeth grazing, sending her over the edge as white-hot bliss consumed her body.

"Bently! Oh god! Fuck!"

He licked her gently as she came down before he kissed her thighs. Trailing up her belly, he pressed her gently onto the bed, crawling over her. She pulled his boxers down, and he helped, leaving him completely naked. His hard cock jutted out between them, nudging the apex of her thighs.

Belle reached over, stroking the hard velvet length as his muscles bunched and tensed. A drop of precum beaded at the end. She pressed his chest, pushing him onto his back before she climbed on top. Belle bent to lick the tip of his cock. The salty taste incited a primal fever inside her.

"Fuck," he swore.

She reached her hands out to his hard abdomen, dragging her nails over his toned six-pack as she took him all the way into her mouth. He throbbed and pulsed inside the well of her lips.

"Jesus, fuck! Belle . . . Angel," he pleaded before he groaned. His breaths became shorter as she pumped him in and out of her mouth. She swirled her tongue over the tip.

Two hands of iron gripped her and pulled her up. "I need to be inside you, right now."

His tone left no room for argument. Her core throbbed with an empty ache. She wanted him more than her next breath. She lifted her hips over his swollen cock and slid down, taking him in from root to tip until he bottomed out. She hissed. He felt so good. So right. Stretching her, filling her all the way to her womb.

His hands gripped her hips roughly. Her skin burned hot. Awareness prickled through every nerve ending with a hurricane of sensation. She began to move, thrusting up and down, riding him as pleasure tumbled through her. His half-lidded eyes focused on hers as one hand played with her breast and the other gripped her neck, pulling her to his mouth.

"Your pussy feels so good. So tight."

She kissed him, nipping at his bottom lip as she increased the pace. His pubic bone hit her clit just right as she whimpered. A sheen of sweat formed between them. Belle rocked back and forth, moving, grinding against him. His hot tongue stoked the all-out blaze inside her.

He pinched her nipple, fueling the pressure building. Strong merciless hands gripped her hips, pushed her up, and slammed her back down. She cried out. The pleasure overwhelmed and overpowered her senses. She was not in control anymore, or maybe she'd never been. It was too much—all-consuming. Fire and ice. Dark and light. The violent euphoria took over her. She flushed with heat. Her orgasm quaked and splintered inside her. She was soaring, enveloped by the stars and heavens above that glimmered and flashed in her eyes. Souls merged. Breaths mingled. Bodies tangled. She wasn't sure where he ended and she began.

His brows drew together. His gaze focused and intent as he bit his lip. "I love to see you come apart, Angel. It's the most beautiful sight in the world," he gritted as she rocked faster.

He smacked her ass. The burn mingled with the pleasure sent another orgasm rocketing through her. Her eyes rolled back in her head. She bowed from the intensity, tucking her face in his neck. "Bently. It's too much."

He flipped her over onto her back, never breaking the connection as he slipped between her legs. "Then let me do it for you. Let me carry you."

Bently grunted as he slid in and out of her, holding her as she came apart again and again. She surrendered to him, boneless and limp as he thrust her towards the heavens once more. He was there, each time she came down, to catch her, encompassing her with awe and reverence as everything else ceased to exist.

"I love you so fucking much," he said, kissing her cheek and neck before locking his eyes on hers.

"I love you too." She clenched her inner muscles.

Bently thrust twice more, roaring as he released inside her. Bently held her, body and soul, while she floated back to earth.

"Thank you," he said.

"For the orgasm? I think I should be thanking you." She chuckled as he slid out of her.

He tucked her against his chest, his mouth by her ear. "Well, that too. But I meant for giving me the most amazing gift. For loving me."

Tears sprang to her eyes. Her emotions were all over the place. Sex with Bently wasn't just amazing—it was transcending. She'd been destroyed and put back together. He'd exposed and protected all at once. Elation lit every cell in her body. She was happy, truly and incandescently blissful.

For once in her life, she could let go, and without a doubt, she had someone who loved her enough to catch her when she fell.

40

BELLE

The scent of peppermint and chocolate wafted over Belle as she followed Remy into the café. Jasmine and Mia trailed behind, and they shook off the chill as they browsed the menu above the counter.

"This place is cute," Mia said.

"I love coming here whenever we visit the city," Remy replied.

"Their chai latte is to die for," Jasmine agreed.

When Belle got to the counter, she ordered a peppermint latte with extra whipped cream. She joined the ladies with their drinks at a table, their shopping bags set underneath.

"I can't believe I've been so last minute this year. I've just been so busy." Remy sighed, unwrapping the scarf from her neck.

"*Dios mio.* I know. It's impossible to shop for your brother." Mia chuckled.

"I'm sure Dre would appreciate you in something lacey . . . or is he a leather kind of guy?" Jasmine teased.

Remy covered her face with her hands and shook her head

with a grimace. "Ugh! You guys, he's my brother! Stop. I don't need to know that answer."

Belle laughed.

All three women turned to look at her.

Remy reached out her hand to Belle's. "I can't tell you how happy I am to have you with us today. It's so good to see Bently *committed* to someone finally."

Jasmine set down her tea. "I'm just glad you're a genuinely good person. You make him smile."

"Bently is always smiling. I swear those Evans boys have a devilish smirk permanently plastered onto their faces." Remy laughed.

Jasmine met Belle's eyes, knowingly. "Yeah, but now it's for real."

Belle grinned reassuringly. "He's definitely changed my life."

"Aww, she's totally smitten." Mia giggled.

"And now we have another sister!" Remy cheered.

Belle tapped her cup against the others' before she sipped her peppermint coffee. The warmth started in her chest and blossomed. She glanced around at the small group of women. *Sisters.* She was being welcomed into their family. She'd never had anyone but TJ, now it seemed she had been adopted into the fold.

On Christmas morning, Belle turned down "Let it Snow" as Bently pulled his truck into Jasmine's parking lot.

"Christmas by the sea," Belle mused.

"Jasmine was so excited to host this year." Bently turned the ignition off.

"Did you get the gifts I picked out for Mr. and Mrs. Stone?" TJ asked.

"Yes. They're in the back," Belle said.

"Good." TJ sighed with relief. He almost seemed as nervous to impress this family as she was.

Bently leaned across the console and kissed her as if sensing her unease. "Come on. Let's go have some good food and laughs."

He opened his door, sending a rush of cold air inside the cab. She smiled as he came around to help her down. TJ climbed out after them.

"You go on in and I'll get the gifts." Bently kissed her cheek. He could barely keep his hands off her and she loved it.

"I'll bring the wine in." She reached into the floor of the truck and grabbed the three bottles.

Bently shut the door behind her. Belle walked up to the front of the inn, the sound of laughter and revelry bleeding out into the snowy afternoon. She closed her eyes, tipping her head upwards, listening to the sound of the waves crashing in the distance. The air was salty and crisp, carrying the essence of the ocean in the breeze.

TJ and Bently chatted and joked as they came closer and her heart squeezed. She opened her eyes, her joy spilling down her cheeks. This was everything she thought she'd never have. Everything she had been afraid to hope for. A lifetime of Christmas wishes, of lonely Decembers, of darkness and pain had brought her to this moment.

Concerned blue eyes met hers. "Are you okay?"

She nodded. "Just happy tears."

Bently leaned in, his woodsy scent caressing her senses as he kissed her forehead and then her lips. "I love you."

"I love you too." She smiled.

"Yeah, yeah. We get it—you're both sappy in love," TJ joked as he pushed past them to the front door as it swung open.

Belle and Bently laughed.

Jasmine greeted them. "Come on in, guys. You're the last to arrive and Lyra is getting more impatient by the minute to open her gifts."

Bently gestured for Belle to go first. She held up the bottles of wine. "I brought a little something to spread the cheer."

"Ooh, looks like the good stuff too," Jasmine approved as they filtered in through the inn and made their way back where the kitchen was.

Belle greeted Remy with a hug and Mia lightened her load by taking two bottles from her arms.

"Mama, you remember Belle," Remy said.

The dark-skinned woman turned her kind brown eyes on Belle.

"Mrs. Stone, merry Christmas."

"Call me Tilda, or Mama T, please. And my husband goes by Mathew. No need for formalities here. You're family now." Tilda held out her arms.

Belle set down the bottle of pinot on the counter and walked into the tall woman's embrace. She was still so over-whelmed with gratitude. Everything was so much better than she'd ever imagined it could be. It was hard to believe this was her life now.

Tilda released her with a squeeze. She spoke low enough for only Belle to hear. "I'm so glad Bently found his happiness finally. That boy is like a son to me. I knew it would take a special woman to reach his guarded heart. Take care of him."

"I will," Belle promised.

"You will what?" Bently asked, sweeping his arms around

her and pulling her back firmly against the front of his chest as he kissed her cheek. "Hey, Mama T."

Tilda's eyes shone with joy. "How are you doing, son?"

"Better than ever. How are you?"

"You look like a man who's finally content." She smiled. "I'm good."

"Uncle Bently is here! Gramma, can we do gifts now?" Lyra ran into the kitchen.

The adults chuckled.

"Yes, sweetheart. Let's go."

Belle sat between Bently and TJ as the family gathered around the large tree in the sitting room. They exchanged gifts. Lyra tore her presents open with glee and excited cries. Mikel held Phoenix and helped him slowly tear at the paper, taking care not to let him eat it. Jasmine held Zoey close, letting her gifts pile up.

Belle nudged Bently, nodding towards his sister. He took her cue and reached over to grab his niece. "Open your gifts, Jaz."

Jasmine looked towards them before she nodded. Some unnamed emotion flitted through her features. The girl seemed to keep so much inside.

Jasmine got to her feet. "I'm just going to get a drink."

"I'm worried about her," Bently said quietly after she passed by.

"It seems like something is troubling her."

"I just wish she'd talk to me." Bently sighed.

"Let me try?"

Bently leaned in. "I'd appreciate that." He kissed her cheek.

Belle stood and walked into the kitchen. Jasmine poured the remnants of a bottle of wine into an empty glass as she approached.

Jasmine grabbed another glass and motioned to it.

"Yes, please," Belle answered the unasked question.

Jasmine filled the glass halfway with wine before sliding it towards her.

"Are you okay?" Belle took a sip.

Jasmine swallowed, turning towards her and nodding. "Of course. It's Christmas. I'm surrounded by family and people who love me. I have a healthy baby girl. What else could I ask for?"

Despite her words, sadness flickered in her green eyes.

"I don't want to overstep. But I just wanted to let you know that it's okay if you feel sad even though you have everything you listed. It's okay to want more."

Jasmine looked down and nodded. "I'm so happy you and Bently found each other, as well as Mikel and Remy. I'm happy my brothers and my friends are blissfully in love. Some days it's just harder than others to go it alone. I feel like maybe I'm depriving Zoey of what she could have. Of what she *needs*."

"You mean a father?"

"Yes. I want to give her everything I never had. Maybe it's stupid, but I hate that I won't even be able to tell her his name when she asks someday." Jasmine took a long chug of the wine.

"I don't know my father's name either. I like to think I turned out okay, despite . . . everything." Belle searched for any words of encouragement to lighten the heaviness in Jasmine's eyes.

Jasmine glanced at her, drawing in a deep breath. "I'm sorry to dump this on you."

"It's really not a problem at all. We all need someone to listen to us . . . someone who can understand. Someone who knows from experience how overwhelming and hopeless things can feel."

"Thank you." Jasmine's voice was just above a whisper.

"I'm here if you ever want to talk, or just to sit in the silence with you so you don't have to be so alone."

"I appreciate it." Jasmine forced a smile, hiding her scars with false cheer.

A peal of laughter erupted from the other room, drawing both of their attention.

"We better get back in there," Jasmine said, leading the way.

After the gifts were opened, they all sat around a long table sharing a festive meal. There was so much food and all made with love. The dessert table was filled with every cookie known to man, several pies, and tins of homemade fudge.

"I think if I eat another bite, I'll burst." TJ patted his stomach and pulled out his phone.

"Well, you certainly ate your weight in ham," Bently teased.

"Hey now, he's a growing boy. Don't let this guy fool you." Tilda pointed towards Bently. "He used to be the same way."

Bently shrugged and TJ beamed.

"Are you all set for classes to start in a few weeks?" Mathew Stone asked TJ.

"Yes, sir. I got my books and the welcome packet. Bently and Belle took me to tour the campus already so I know where my classes will be."

"Good. Make sure you stop by my office to say hi every now and then," Mathew said.

"Yes, and you come to us if you need anything." Tilda smiled.

Belle's heart was about to burst. Truly, she could not handle any more happiness.

"Sure thing, Mrs. and Mr. Stone. I appreciate all the help." TJ smiled.

"Oh, call us Gramma and Papa Stone. You're a part of this family now," Tilda said.

"Okay." TJ's phone pinged. He tipped the screen before he looked up. "Cam is here to get me. You okay if I go?" he asked Belle.

She nodded. "Sure."

"Text when you're on your way home," Bently said, wrapping his arm around her on the plush couch.

"Who's Cam?" Mikel asked.

"My friend's sister," TJ said, standing.

"The girl he likes," Bently added.

Mikel elbowed Andre in the gut playfully as he said, "Ahh, best friend's little sister, huh? Good luck with that, my friend."

Andre shoved Mikel. "Yeah, don't do what this idiot did and keep it a secret from him."

"Hey, I was up front about it once I realized I was in deep." Mikel pulled Remy onto his lap as she giggled.

Andre shook his head. "After I caught you two together you mean."

Mia snuggled in close to him. "Ooh, I haven't heard this story."

"See you all later. Thanks for everything," TJ said as he shrugged on his coat and grabbed his bag.

Belle stood to give him a hug. "Be safe."

"Always am." He smiled and left.

Belle sat again. Bently pulled her against him. She stared into the crackling fire as the holiday lights glittered over the mantle and the giant decorated tree. She was warm and relaxed. Christmas music drifted from a speaker, and for the first time in all her life, she understood what it meant to be truly at peace.

Bently nuzzled into her neck. His voice was a harsh whisper. "Move in with me."

She blinked and turned to face him. His cautious smile tipped the edges of his mouth up.

"A week ago, you were begging me for a second chance."

"I told you I was in this. I want to wake up to you in my bed, and fall asleep next to you every night. I've wasted enough time. I know what I want, and that's you. I want you so deeply imbedded in my life, I don't know where you stop and I begin." Bently searched her eyes.

Her heart raced. Could she do this? Was she ready for such a big step? "What about TJ?"

"He's all for it if you are."

"You already asked him?" She was well and truly stunned.

"I figured you two were a package deal. I've got the room."

She'd been wrong before. Her heart could apparently hold more than she'd thought possible. Was it a risk? *Yes.* Was she willing to take the plunge?

"What are you two lovebirds talking about over there?" Mikel asked.

Bently smirked. "I'm asking her to move in with me."

Dre's smile slipped as his eyes darted between them.

"What did you say?" Remy asked.

Bently turned to her. "Well?"

"Yes."

Bently's grin widened as he pulled her in and crashed his mouth onto hers.

"Uncle Bently's kissing Belle!" Lyra exclaimed before they broke apart. The little girl approached her uncle before grasping his face in her tiny hands. "Your spell can be broken now."

His brow furrowed. "What spell is that, sweet pea?"

"You used to be the beast, but now you can be the prince with a happy heart." Lyra smiled.

Bently glanced at Belle knowingly as he answered his niece. "You're right, sweetheart. Belle saved me from myself."

"Can we watch the movie now? I love *Beauty and the Beast*. Are you a real princess, Belle?" Lyra asked in rapid succession.

Belle laughed. "I've never seen it."

"What?" Lyra gasped. "Mommy! Did you hear that?"

"I did, sweet girl. We'll have to watch it with her sometime." Remy looked adoringly towards her daughter.

"Yes. We can have a girls' night!" Lyra said excitedly.

"I'll bring the juice boxes," Remy said.

"I'll bring the wine," Mia added.

"And I'll bring the chocolate." Jasmine winked.

"Then I'll have to bring the ice cream." Belle tapped Lyra's nose.

The little girl's eyes grew wide. "It will be the bestest girls' night ever!"

Belle looked around the room, a warm glow settling within her chest.

Mikel nudged Andre. "Guess us guys will have to take Phoenix and have a guys' night, then."

"I'll bring the beer and poker chips." Bently's laugh rumbled against her side, sending a shiver through her. This was her life now. She had family and true happiness. Acceptance and love. Finally she had everything she'd been too afraid to hope for. Nothing could take this away from her.

41

BENTLY

January brought a fresh blizzard to the coast, and several feet of snow. Vargas was leading the investigation on who had been after him. But all the leads had dried up, as had the incidents. Bently had thanked his lucky stars that he'd had peace from his likely stalker.

He'd spent the last few weeks helping Belle move her things over to his place a little bit at a time. Now that most of the snow had cleared from the storm, he would be able to make a trip with his truck to get the big items.

Knock. Knock.

Bently looked up from the stack of paperwork on his desk. "Come on in."

Andre walked through the door, his brows knit together.

"Hey, man. What's up?"

Andre sat in the chair across from him. "You busy?"

"I'm always busy." He chuckled and closed the folder in front of him. "You available Saturday to help me move some of Belle and TJ's stuff to my house? She can't get out of her lease until February, but we're gonna start bringing things over."

Andre shifted in his seat. "Don't you think it's kinda soon to be moving in with them?"

Bently furrowed his brow, bewildered. "You asked Mia to marry you only how many short months after meeting her?"

"I know." Andre sighed. "But that was different."

"How?" Bently asked, hackles rising.

"How well do you really know them, Bent?"

"Why don't you just say what you gotta say," Bently snapped.

"The kid who mugged me and Mia in the alleyway . . ." Andre started.

What the hell?

"What about it? I haven't got any more leads."

Andre held up his hands. "I told you the kid looked scared, said he didn't want to be there. But the other one with the knife threatened to hurt his sister."

"What does this have to do with me moving in with Belle?" Bently growled. He was out of patience.

"TJ is the one who mugged us."

The air was sucked out of the room. *No. No way. He couldn't* . . . "Are you sure? There's no—"

"I'm positive. Remember when you first brought them to Remy's?" Andre leaned forward.

"Why didn't you tell me then?"

"I tried but Mia stopped me." He sighed. "TJ and Belle found her that day. When Mia woke up, he apologized and gave her back her mother's ring. I guess he was forced to commit the crime and didn't have a choice."

"Why did you hold that back? Why didn't you tell me!"

"Did you hear her go off on me at the harvest dinner? I know which battles I can win with that woman, and it definitely wasn't that one. You know how she feels about the authorities," Andre said.

The memory of Mia yelling at Andre in Spanish came back to him. All Andre's concerned looks and scowls directed at Belle and TJ suddenly made sense.

"But I'm your friend!"

Andre looked down as if ashamed.

"Why are you telling me this now?"

Andre rubbed the back of his neck. "I didn't know you were that serious about her. Women come and go in your life—none of them stick. I figured maybe you just needed to get her out of your system and it wouldn't matter. But now that it's more serious . . . I just wanted you to know everything."

The pieces clicked into place. "The kid held a knife to you? The other one, right? He was young, around TJ's age? Same height and build?"

Andre shrugged. "I talked to Mia and she said he was taller and broader, but not much older than TJ. He was white. Light hair."

A chill ran down his spine. Hazy pictures became clearer. A flicker of a memory before the metal bat swung and knocked him out. Ice-blue eyes and a somewhat familiar face. He shot up from his desk and grabbed his coat.

"Where are you going?" Andre stood, holding out his hands.

"To talk to TJ."

* * *

Bently burst through the front door. Belle and TJ both jumped at the table. A cup of coffee spilled between them.

"Shit!" She ran to grab a paper towel and mopped it up,

moving the notepad and pens out of the way. "What's wrong?"

Bently slammed the door and stalked to the kitchen. "Did you know?" His voice boomed. If she'd kept this from him, he didn't know how he would handle it.

"Know what? What's wrong? Are you okay?" Belle asked.

Bently searched her face—there was nothing but genuine concern there. He turned a hard gaze on TJ. "You mugged Mia and Andre."

TJ looked worriedly between him and Belle.

Belle's mouth opened in an "O" and her eyes grew wide as she shook her head. "What? No. TJ would never do such a thing. Are you kidding me right now?" Her voice rose with hurt and anger. "Tell him you didn't, TJ . . . Tell him!"

TJ looked down, biting his lip. "He said if I didn't, he'd come after Belle."

Belle gasped.

Bently didn't need to look to know her face was painted with horror and disbelief. The urge to run and comfort her grew inside him. Bently tampered his rage and let out a defeated sigh. He forced himself to sit at the table. "Start from the beginning."

TJ shifted uncomfortably. "This kid at school was the only one who was nice to me when I first got there. He took an interest. Got a few bullies off my back. He seemed cool at first. He gave me music gift cards sometimes. That's mostly what we talked about. Then he introduced me to a few of his other friends. They were older. They played pranks on people and it was fun at first. But then they started doing other stuff."

Belle's body trembled as she sat across from them.

TJ continued, his eyes glued to the table. "They broke into some cars, houses. I didn't want to do it, but Junior told me that I owed him for dealing with the bullies at school. Said all

I had to do was be the lookout. I did it a few times, but I felt so guilty. I told him I was done. But they just laughed at me. He pulled a knife on me and told me that if I didn't fall in line, he and his friends would come visit Belle. They'd take turns . . ."

Bently's fists clenched and he ground his teeth. "Keep going."

"That night in the alley, that was the last time. He kept getting bolder. I thought he was gonna kill Dre . . . I didn't have a choice." Tears spilled from TJ's eyes. "I'm so sorry."

"Why didn't you tell me, TJ? I could have helped." Belle's voice choked.

TJ shook his head. "I knew you'd be disappointed in me. I figured I would do whatever it took to protect you, like you did for me. Then Bently showed up and I thought maybe he could keep you safe. I knew I had to go to college, and having him around would be good for you."

"What does Junior look like?"

TJ blinked, turning his gaze to Bently. "Few inches taller than me. Blond hair, blue eyes."

"Did you know he was the one that attacked me?" Bently pressed.

TJ shook his head vehemently. "No. I thought maybe it was him, because he hated cops. Loathed them. He specifically talked about the sheriff. I didn't think anything of it until I met you. But I was never sure."

Could this be the same guy? His gut told him yes.

"You stopped hanging out with him and he's just left you alone?" Bently asked.

"Yes. I haven't hung out since Mia and Dre. He's come up to me at school a few times . . . Uh . . . left a dead rat in my locker. Stuff like that. Haven't seen him since school let out. I just steered clear of him and ignored it."

Belle covered her mouth and squeezed her eyes shut as she shook her head.

Bently wanted to comfort her, but he was torn in two. TJ had known this whole time who was most likely behind this danger and he hadn't said anything. The kid was as slow to trust and quick to protect as his sister.

"Why didn't you say something sooner?"

"I thought the message on the truck was for me. I thought Junior wanted me to pay, not you. I was trying to wait it out. But then you told me about the photo and I realized I'd been wrong . . . but he'd stopped. I figured he moved on after the prank."

Silence descended on them as Bently struggled through the warring emotions. "You need to tell me everything you know about this Junior. Where does he live?"

"I only know where he hangs out. It's like his clubhouse," TJ answered.

Bently shifted his gaze, searching for any sign of dishonesty. "You gotta be honest with me. If there is anything else you know, you have to tell me now."

"That's everything I can think of."

"Is his real name Junior?"

"Uh, I heard a few teachers call him Joseph before," TJ answered.

Bently pushed a pen towards him and stood. "Write down the address."

TJ nodded and picked up the pen as Belle stood and walked towards him.

"What are you going to do?" she asked, her voice wavering.

"I'm going to take care of it."

"I'm sorry, Bently. I didn't know." She bit her lip.

He pulled her into his arms, kissing the top of her head. "I know, Angel."

"What does this mean?" she asked, fear flashing in her brown eyes.

"For us?" he asked.

She nodded.

"Nothing's changed."

She sighed, relief flitting across her features. "What about TJ? Is he going to be in trouble for this?"

Bently looked between the woman he loved and her brother. "He's a cooperating witness. If this goes to court, I'll need him to make a deal with the prosecutor. He was under duress during these crimes, and was acting in fear of his life, and yours. I'll figure this out. Okay? I'll keep you both safe."

She crumpled into him. He held her, wishing they could solve this mess and be done with it.

"I love you." He pulled her chin up to kiss her on the mouth.

"I love you too."

* * *

Bently motioned to Deputy Vargas as he quietly slipped through the sheet of metal hanging open in the run-down factory building. The place had been condemned years ago. The smell of mold and decaying wood was pungent.

He walked through, his flashlight shining from end to end. Light reflected off the heaped piled of old rusted machinery abandoned throughout the room. At the far end were a set of metal stairs. Bently kept his gun extended as he motioned for Vargas to follow.

Bently climbed the stairs, careful not to make too much noise. The layout was just as TJ had described. Bently ignored the trickle of sweat down his forehead. His body was on high alert as he navigated his way to the upper room. Supposedly the space was an old office. Bently counted down with his fingers as Vargas got into position.

"Shattered Cove Police Department, put your hands up!" Bently yelled as he swung the door open. He searched the dim room like he'd been trained, his flashlight and gun aimed where he looked as Vargas covered his six.

"Clear," he said, walking in. A dirty mattress lay in one corner with a newer sleeping bag and pillow heaped on top. A cooler sat next to it. Empty snack bags were scattered across the floor. A few folding chairs leaned on the other side of the area, along with an old wooden desk. He swiped his finger over the top. No dust.

He let out a breath, fogging up the space in the cold dingy room. One of the drawers was left partially open. A glint of something shiny reflected from the beam of his flashlight.

Bently pulled the drawer open and his blood ran cold. A chill skittered up his spine.

No fucking way.

There was a picture of a young boy with cold blue eyes with a man who looked just like him. *Joe Canoby.* The man he'd shot and killed to protect Remy during a home invasion. Joseph *Junior.* He was Canoby's son.

And now it was clear why this kid was after him.

Junior was out for revenge.

42

BENTLY

Bently walked up the steps to Belle's porch with lead feet. His shoulders ached and he hadn't had a decent night's sleep in weeks. He turned, waving a hand towards the officer on duty in the patrol car across the street.

Rife waved back before Bently grabbed the doorknob. It twisted as he leaned his head against the cold metal frame. Steadying himself, he drew in a breath and pushed.

The warmth and comfort of her home enveloped him, melting some of the numbness. Soft music played from the kitchen to his left. He shut the door and shrugged off his coat as he eyed the stack of boxes. They'd held off moving her into his home at his request. Anything to try and keep her safe. He slept at his house alone with his gun next to his nightstand and a knife under his pillow, waking and wondering about each creak and thud in the old house.

"Honey, I'm home," he said, forcing a playful tone in his voice to hide the utter exhaustion and fear riddling his body. Maybe he should just leave now, send Belle away somewhere safe.

She turned and flashed him a welcoming yet cautious smile. He'd done this to her. Brought danger to her doorstep. She didn't deserve this.

"Hey, stranger." Her brown-sugar eyes met his as she wiped her hands on a towel.

He took off his boots before he walked in, reaching his fingers out to trace the shape of her face, tempting fate. He'd stayed away as long as he could. But he needed to be grounded. She was the only one who made him feel safe. Like a thief, he was here to take some of that light and peace.

She reached her palm around his before she walked into him, resting her head against his chest. He wrapped his arms around her, though he wasn't sure who was holding who this time.

"I missed you." Her voice wavered.

He leaned and kissed her head before weaving his fingers in her dark curls, tipping her face towards him. "Couldn't stay away." It was an apology.

The last thing she needed was him to cause her more trouble. He'd promised to take care of her and TJ, and the only way he knew to do that was to keep his distance and try and draw the fucker out.

"I know you have a job to do, but you can sleep here. Or I can come to your house—"

"No." His answer was harsher than he'd intended.

Her brows knit together, rejection flashing in her gaze. He leaned farther and whispered against her lips, "It's not safe."

Her arms clung tighter to him as she stood on tiptoes, melding her sweet mouth to his. This girl, always giving. But how much more could he afford to take before she had nothing left?

Her nipples hardened against his chest and he groaned. He

wanted nothing more in the world than to get lost in her tight little body. His palms swept to the backs of her thighs, lifting her up. He carried her over to the counter without breaking the kiss. Their hands moved, pulling, cinching, burning. Their tongues tasted, warring, searching. She gasped as he pinched her nipple through the thin cropped tee she was wearing.

"TJ?" He panted, his breath stolen by the heavenly creature in his arms.

"Upstairs." She moaned as he kissed down her neck.

"Dinner?"

"Keeping warm in the oven." She sucked his earlobe into her mouth, raking her teeth over it.

It'd been almost a week since he'd had her. The pressure built, need and want overpowering him. He fisted her dark curls and kissed her, hard and unrelenting. Her hands ripped up the hem of his shirt as he ground against her center. She moaned, gripping his hips, rocking into him, taking what she wanted.

"You're so fucking hot," he growled.

"I need you, Bently. Please."

He forced himself away, every cell screaming in protest. His body was an all-out inferno of desire.

"Upstairs," he ordered. His restraint was only holding on by a thread. But the last thing they needed was her brother walking in on him fucking Belle on the kitchen counter.

She smiled and hopped down. "Give me a few minutes. I got you something special."

His cock screamed for attention, pressing hard against his zipper. He smirked. "You've got five minutes."

She giggled and swayed that perfect ass out of sight and up the stairs as he took a few deep breaths. He glanced at the clock on the stove before opening the fridge. Bently pulled out a beer. He drank the whole thing in a few gulps. *Time's up, Angel.*

He stepped up the stairs, pulling his T-shirt off and unbuckling his belt before he got to her bedroom door. He knocked before he opened it and froze. Belle lay on the bed facing him with her eyes closed and blood trickling from her head. Every muscle in Bently's body went rigid. Adrenaline pumped through his veins as his hair stood on end. A dark figure hovered behind her holding a gun to her head. Bently grabbed his gun.

"Nah ah ah. I wouldn't do that unless you want her brains all over this room." Joseph Canoby Jr's blue eyes flashed with amusement.

Bently swallowed and kept his palms open in front of him. "Alright, man. This is between you and me, right? Why don't you let her go and we can settle this?" Bently stepped to his right. Joe pressed the barrel of the gun into Belle's temple. His heart raced as he searched for any sign of life, exhaling with relief at the steady rise and fall of her rib cage.

"How about you move over there next to the window. Put your gun on the floor and kick it to me."

Bently lifted his weapon carefully, doing as Junior instructed. He was completely powerless. Fear wound tight, constricting his chest as his breaths grew shallow.

I need to draw his attention away from Belle.

Junior walked around and picked up his gun, shifting it to his empty hand. He smiled. "Maybe I should kill your girl with your own gun. How would that feel, Sheriff?"

"You want to hurt someone? Hurt me," Bently pleaded.

Junior chuckled, his eyes burning with hatred. "Oh, I will. First, I'm gonna start with your girl here. She looks like a good fuck."

Bently stepped forward, his fists clenching. Rage burned him from the inside out.

"Stay back, lover boy, or I put a bullet in her," Junior warned, his evil smile widening.

Belle groaned and reached for her head, coming to. He needed to find a way to get her out of here. But one false move and she'd be dead. He had to keep Junior talking.

Belle's eyes fluttered open and she jolted upwards only to gasp and lie back down.

"Now the real fun can begin." Junior chuckled.

"Bently!" Belle called, her confusion turning to panic.

A knot formed in his chest. "I know, baby. I'm here. You're going to be okay."

"I wouldn't make promises you can't keep," Junior snapped, pressing the barrel of the gun to her cheek as she winced.

"I'm the one who killed your father. I'm the one you want. Point the gun at me." Bently stepped closer to the bottom of the bed.

"So, you know who I am. Took you long enough."

Bently risked another step closer to the window.

"Get up, bitch. You and I are gonna go somewhere a little more *private,*" Junior said, directing Belle.

She pushed to her elbows, but winced at the attempt of movement. She held her head and dry heaved.

"I said get up!" Junior yelled.

Bently's fingernails cut into his palm as he restrained himself. He softened his voice. "Just do what he says, baby. You can do it."

Belle's eyes flashed to his—a mix of fear and trust reflected back. Her eyes darted to the door to his left. Her worried gaze conveyed her unspoken message.

Where is TJ? Did Junior do something to him?

Belle stood slowly on shaky legs. Her balance tipped as Junior climbed over the bed, one hand on her shoulder and the other holding the gun to her head. There was nothing Bently could do with the weapon pressed against her. It was too risky.

"Stand over there, Sheriff." Junior motioned to the windows past the bed as he shuffled Belle towards the door. He couldn't let them leave.

Junior stepped backwards, towards the hallway. "Tie yourself up with those zip ties on the bed."

"Let her go and I'll do whatever you want. Leave her out of this," Bently begged.

"You took someone I loved. The only person who ever gave a shit about me. And now, you're going to know exactly how that feels. I'm gonna start with her. Then I'm gonna go visit that pretty sister of yours."

Bile rose in his throat. He'd done this. He'd brought this on his loved ones. *No.* No way was he going to let this boy destroy everyone he loved.

"I love you. This isn't your fault," Belle said as if reading his mind. This brave woman, facing death and still trying to ease his guilt.

"Your father cried like a fucking pussy before I put a bullet in him," Bently snapped.

Junior glared at him. "You're lying!" His hand wrapped tighter around Belle's throat, squeezing.

Junior would leave bruises like his father had on Remy. Bently used the anger to fuel him on. "He tried to go after my family and he failed. What makes you think you're going to do any better?"

The gun shook as Junior's face reddened.

"You want to know what his last words were?" Bently pressed, stepping forward, willing the gun to aim at him rather than Belle.

"W-what were they?"

Bently took in a breath, time slowing as he savored one last look at the woman he loved. The woman he would die protecting. "Not a fucking thing. He never had a chance. After I shot him, he choked, drowning in his own blood. The last thing he saw was me making sure the fucker was dead!" Bently poured salt into the festering wound.

The gun shifted, aiming at him as a flicker of movement behind them flashed. *TJ!*

Bently lunged forward.

Boom!

Glass shattered and pain split his chest before he tackled Junior to the ground. He pulled the gun from his limp hand, tucking it in the back of his waistband. He kicked the other away before grabbing the zip ties by the bed. He rolled the teen, the back of Junior's head sticky with red blood. Bently bound Junior's hands behind him.

His gaze darted up. TJ still held the wooden bat, standing over them.

"Is he dead? Did I kill him?" TJ's chest heaved with each breath.

The door crashed open downstairs. No doubt Rife had heard the gunshot.

"Shattered Cove PD!" Rife's voice boomed below.

Bently stepped into the hall with his hands up. "All clear, Rife. Perp's been apprehended and restrained. Call a bus."

Rife picked up his radio and nodded from the bottom of the stairs.

Bently took the bat from TJ's trembling hands, dropping it to the ground before answering his question. "No. He's still breathing."

Belle grabbed TJ in one arm and him in the other,

collapsing against them. Tears poured down her cheeks. He winced, pain burning his ribs.

"You're safe now." Bently's voice shook. He'd come way too close to losing her, to losing them.

"You're bleeding. You've been shot!" Belle said, pulling up his shirt to reveal the bullet wound. Her fingers traced the tender flesh around the injury.

He winced. "It's just a graze. I'll be fine." He patted TJ's shoulder. "You saved us."

TJ blinked. "No, I—"

"If you hadn't acted, this would be a lot more than a flesh wound," Bently said.

TJ nodded solemnly. "I heard him yell and I didn't know what to do. I grabbed the first thing I could and waited in the hall for my chance."

"You did everything right. You saved us."

TJ swallowed.

Bently took Belle's face in his hands, studying her head wound. His anger boiled over. He turned towards Joe Junior. Like father like son. A chill shivered through his body.

He and this kid were both born from devils. All his life, Bently had been terrified of being anything like his father, fighting from birth not to make the same mistakes. Everything revolted inside him when he came close to being similar to his father. He'd hated his own face because it was too much like Paul Evans's. Why would anyone want to repeat their father's same mistakes?

Junior's finger twitched. The boy had chosen to follow in the footsteps of a monster. Why? Was evil something you were born with? Or was it bred into you? Why had he made it out of hell and Junior hadn't? The only thing that separated them was a choice.

"It's over." Belle's voice brought him back.

He took her in his arms and kissed her gently as blaring sirens drew closer. He held her as close as he could without hurting her. The sweet relief of having them safe was tainted by guilt. "Are you sure you want this? With everything that comes with being with me? My baggage, and the dangers of my job?"

Belle met his eyes. "I've never been more sure of something in my life."

Her words pierced his heart, ripping and mending. Retribution and atonement.

"Do you want to run?" Her voice came out in a whisper.

"Never again. I'm not letting you go." His lips slanted across hers. He wished they were alone so he could take care of her—bullet wound be damned. He'd wash every inch of her body with his hands and then kiss away any trace of this nightmare.

She kissed him back, as if surrendering. He succumbed to the energy that pulled them with a force unknown to man. He was going to marry this woman. She was his forever. She was his gravity.

43

BELLE

A week later, Belle opened the door. Bently's woodsy scent made her weak in the knees. He leaned down, his scruff scratching her cheek as he kissed her.

"Is it here?" she whispered excitedly.

"With a big red bow." He chuckled, pulling her against his hard frame.

His arousal pressed against her. Need blossomed in her belly.

Will I ever get enough of this man?

His arms enveloped her, squeezing her tighter. "How about we go for round two?"

She swatted him away. "We'll have time for that later. I can't wait to surprise him. TJ!" she yelled, barely able to contain her glee.

"I'm coming," her brother called down.

"I was hoping you'd be the one saying that," Bently grumbled in her ear as she spun around, wiggling her ass against him, knowing it would drive him wild.

"You play dirty." He chuckled.

"You haven't seen anything yet, Sheriff," she teased.

Bently groaned as her brother descended their stairs, probably for the last time. *I can't wait to move in with Bently, and have both the men I love under the same roof.*

"Why is that look on your face?" TJ asked suspiciously.

Belle shrugged, motioning to the stack of boxes in the living room. "Just happy to be taking this step. Grab your boxes—we'll load them into the truck."

She spun around, zipping up her coat and opening the door before the secret burst from her lips.

A couple of minutes later, TJ and Bently walked out, boxes in hand. She turned the camera on her phone on and pointed it at TJ, excited to catch his reaction. "Go ahead and put them in the blue truck."

TJ peeked around the cardboard square, his eyes widening and darting to Bently, confused. "New ride?"

"Do you like it?" Bently asked, playing along.

"Yeah, it's dope."

"Good, because it's yours." Bently smiled, holding out a set of keys.

TJ set the boxes in the truck bed before glancing between Belle and Bently. "You messing with me?"

"No way. We thought you could use your own vehicle to get to classes." Bently smirked, pressing the keys into TJ's palm.

TJ's mouth opened and closed like a fish, seemingly bewildered. He shook his head. "You did this?" He searched Bently's face.

"*We* did this. You've earned it. You kinda saved our lives. I'd say we owe you one." Bently chuckled, always trying to lighten the mood.

TJ glanced at Belle, affection and gratitude shining from his eyes. It hit her right in the solar plexus. Happiness radiated from the boy who had worked so hard to elevate himself from the gutter they'd been born into. The boy she'd raised as a child herself.

"Thank you." TJ hugged Bently around the waist and the man she loved embraced her brother, slapping him on the back.

TJ came over to Belle next, swatting the camera away. "Enough of that. You get over here." He squeezed her tight, his strong arms holding her as she'd done for him so many times. He'd been her reason for living, her driving force to choose the hard road. She wiped the tears from her eyes.

"Don't cry, big sister."

She laughed. "You know I'm just so happy for you. You are going to start the rest of your life today. And now, you've got your own wheels and are in college classes. Soon you'll bring a girl home to meet me. I'm just so proud of you and everything you've accomplished, TJ. I love you so much." She hiccupped.

"Love you too, mama." He held her as she fell apart again from the endearment. Warm happiness and elation brimmed from her every pore like she was soaking in a river of golden sunshine. This was the kind of joy she'd only read about in books, the kind she'd believed only existed in fairy tales.

Bently wrapped his hand around her waist. "Hey now, give the boy some air. I'm starting to get jealous."

TJ and Belle laughed. She looked up into the face of the man she loved, the man who had faced his past and taken the hard road to be vulnerable with her. The man who had breathed life into her for the first time.

"Now it's your turn for a gift." Bently's smile wavered as if he was nervous.

Her brows knit together. "My turn?"

"You didn't think I'd leave you out, did you?" Bently pulled a leather box from his pocket.

The breath shuddered in her lungs. *No way. Is he? Oh my god!*

Bently got down on his knee, not seeming to mind the cold snow on the frozen ground. "Belle, I know it's really soon. But I decided that when it comes to you, I'm done waiting. I'm never holding back again."

She glanced to TJ. A wide smile lit his face.

"I have already given you my heart, but I'm hoping that you'll do me the greatest honor of letting me share my life with you. We don't have to do it now. I'll wait until you're ready, whenever that is. I want you to be mine in every sense of the word. My lover, my best friend, and my wife."

Fresh tears spilled over her cheeks. She didn't bother to wipe them away this time. There was so much she wanted to say to him, but everything jumbled up and stuck in her throat.

"Show her the ring," TJ said.

Belle's eyes darted to her brother who now held his phone up, capturing their moment.

"Oh, right." Bently opened the box.

A dark red ruby glinted in the morning sunlight, the square-cut stone set in a delicate silver band. It was simple and elegant. It was perfect.

"I got you a ruby because it's the queen of all stones. Uh —" Bently cleared his throat nervously. "The ancients believed its value surpassed that of all other stones in virtue, even the diamond. There are a lot of other meanings, like protection, and it symbolizes the sun. I chose it because to me, you are the sun. You're everything good in this world. You're valuable and precious, and powerful. And I want to have the privilege of standing by your side forever."

Belle's heart pounded in her chest. Disbelief and butter-flies swirled in her belly.

Fear and uncertainty flashed in those cerulean-blue eyes.

Say something!

She nodded vigorously and pulled him to standing. "Yes, Bently. I-I want that too. Yes!"

Bently let out an audible sigh as he pulled her tight against him, kissing her. "You scared me for a minute there."

"Did you think I could walk away from you? From the only pure love I've ever known?" she asked, kissing his jaw.

"I fucking hoped not." Bently chuckled.

TJ finally spoke up. "I've always wanted a brother."

Bently released Belle enough to pull TJ into the group hug. "Well, you've got a lot more than just me now."

Of course. His family was now their family. Belle's heart swelled. That was the thing about love—just when you thought it wasn't possible to have room for more, your heart expanded and grew to accommodate the new demand. And maybe all those times she'd had her heart broken, left in shattered pieces, it was for this moment. To be able to re-piece it all together to form something much bigger and better than she could have ever had on her own.

"Alright, you two. I'm gonna go stop in and see Cam." TJ smiled and slipped the phone into his pocket.

"Drive safe," Bently said as TJ shut the tailgate.

"I will. See you guys at home for dinner."

"I'm working until seven," Belle reminded him.

"Love you."

"Love you too!" Belle blew him a big kiss as he shook his head and pulled the red bow off before climbing into his new ride.

TJ drove away.

Bently rested his arm over her shoulders. "That's one happy boy."

"Yes, it is."

"Can I put your ring on now?" Bently asked.

"Of course! It's so beautiful." Belle focused on the red stone as he slipped it over her ring finger.

"You sure you want this? Even though I can't . . . we could never have biological children?" Bently asked, a shadow clouding those pure eyes.

She lifted her hand to his cheek, narrowing her eyes at him. "I've never been surer of anything else in my entire life. As long as you keep working on you, and being open and honest with me. As long as you stay rather than run. I told you —I don't care about having biological children."

He blinked. "I just don't want you to regret anything."

"I could never regret you," she said against his mouth.

His lips caressed hers hungrily as his tongue traced the seam. Teeth raked across her soft flesh igniting the fire within her. Passion and lust swirled inside her, mixing and melding and forming something much deeper and unbreakable than what she'd known before—the truest love.

Bently broke the kiss and leaned his forehead against hers, groaning. "I'd better get you to work before I can't stop myself."

"I could be a few minutes late." She panted.

"We have some celebrating to do tonight. I'm gonna take my time making your sweet body come all over my face." Bently squeezed her ass.

Electricity shot through her core. "I like the sound of that."

"That's just the appetizer. Gonna see just how many orgasms it takes until you beg me to fill you with my cock," he growled the words in her ear, ramping up her desire.

"Mmmm. Please don't make me wait." She reached between them, cupping the steel rod in his pants.

"Fuck." Bently checked his watch. "Alright, just a preview. Then I'm taking you to work where you can show off that ring to Doctor Stanley so he knows you're all *mine*."

"Rick?"

He scowled.

"Why, Bently Evans, are you jealous?"

He tugged her back into the house as she suppressed a giggle.

"Maybe I need to remind you who that pussy belongs to."

Her body shivered as he swept her up the stairs towards her bedroom. Her inner walls clenched at the feral gaze that scorched her skin through the layers of clothing. He looked like a man possessed. His wild gaze stirred something inside her, something dark and possessive. *He's all mine. Bently is going to be my husband.*

Belle accepted the cup of coffee from Katy as she glanced at the clock. Only two more hours to go and she could go home and have Bently make good on his dirty promises. He'd been kind enough to deliver not one, but two orgasms before her shift. He'd created some sort of greedy monster in her. Belle's sexual appetite had never been so insatiable.

"Thank you."

"You're welcome. Oh. My. God! That's gorgeous." Katy grabbed her hand and eyed the unique stone. "Is this what I think it is?"

Belle couldn't contain her smile and nodded.

"You are the worst friend in the world! How could you not tell me first thing? You managed to nail down *the* Bently

Evans? Is this a joke? Am I stroking out right now?" Katy exaggerated her eyes as she slapped a hand over her chest.

"Shhh. I don't want the whole hospital knowing," Belle scolded.

"Girl, the whole town is gonna be buzzing. One of the most eligible bachelors of Shattered Cove is now off the market. You will be small-town royalty to some, and the most hated by others," Katy teased.

"Poor Tina." Belle laughed.

Katy joined her and then sighed. "You two moved awfully fast. Didn't seem like you thought much of him when we had that girls' night."

"Well, we certainly got off on the wrong foot."

"Mm-hmm. Must be that magic cock that won you over." Katy smirked as her eyes flashed coyly.

Belle burst out laughing. "You're terrible . . . but not wrong."

"I knew it!" Katy giggled.

The head nurse on shift waved them over. "We've got incoming. Officer-involved shooting. Five minutes."

Belle's smile quickly faded. Her heart lurched. *Is it Bently?* Would fate be so cruel? Was all of this just the high before the lowest of lows?

No. He's okay. I would know if something happened. They'd connected more than just physically. She shared her soul with the man.

"I'm sure he's fine," Katy said, seemingly reading her mind as they rushed to prep.

Belle nodded, a sick feeling twisting in her stomach. This was just part of being with a police officer. She'd have to get used to it. She was going to marry the sheriff for fuck's sake.

"Ambulance radioed in. Looks like a DOA in the first bus." The rest of the words were drowned out by ringing in her ears. Time slowed down as Belle faced the ambulance-bay doors. Red lights flashed as she forced air in and out of her lungs.

Get it together. He's fine. Bently's fine.

The doors opened and two men pushed a stretcher inside, a white blood-stained sheet covering a body. Bile rose in her throat. Her heart screamed at her that something was wrong. The hair on the back of her neck stood on end as Bently's ashen face came into view behind the stretcher. All the color had drained from his complexion. His bloodshot eyes had turned dark. His brown uniform was saturated in crimson.

Oh my god. Bently!

44

BELLE

She sucked in a breath, tears burning her eyes as she tried to pull herself together. She was going to make a terrible sheriff's wife.

"Are you okay?" she asked.

He dragged his gaze to hers as if they'd been weighed down by something heavy. She reached out, checking him with gloved hands for injuries, taking care over the site of his gunshot wound from a few weeks prior. None of the blood seemed to be his. His body was tense and trembling. His chest heaved. Blood-stained hands gripped her wrists as tears shimmered in his eyes.

"I'm fine." His voice cracked and broke as if he'd swallowed shards of glass.

"No, you're not."

Bently's body quaked as a storm of energy bellowed from him, swirling and swallowing up all the attention in the room. It had grown silent as she stared up at him worriedly. Fury radiated from him.

Fear slithered around her spine. A warning blared in the

back of her mind. Something was very wrong. "Bently? Was it one of your officers?"

He grimaced. "I'm so sorry."

"What?"

He gripped her face in his hands, his gaze steady and unwavering despite the fear bleeding from his eyes. "I love you. Please don't forget that I love you."

"You're scaring me, Bently."

"I tried—" His voice choked. His eyes darted towards the room with the sheet-covered body and time stopped. The pieces clicked into place. *Officer-involved shooting.* Air ceased to exist, ripped from her lungs as she shook her head.

No. No. No!

Belle turned and ran to the room before pulling back the blood-stained sheet. Hands gripped her, tugging her back as TJ's open eyes stared up from the stretcher. Empty. Vacant. He was no longer here. Her brother. *My brother! No!*

A guttural scream pierced the air as her lungs burned. She floated high above her body in the corner of the room, watching herself struggle against the nurses who tried to drag her out, away from the dead corpse of her brother. Bently stopped them, holding her up. His touch jolted her back into her body.

Screams tore from her throat as her knees buckled. Her stomach emptied itself on the floor. She panted, gasping for oxygen as her body shook. Bently's arms wrapped tightly around her. His mouth moved, but his words went unheard. She pounded her fists into his chest, relentless and unforgiving. The glint of his badge was the source of her aggression. She ripped it from his shirt, pushing him away. He just held on tighter.

TJ was *gone*. Her sweet boy had been murdered. He'd had his whole future ahead of him. He was going to be a doctor.

He was going to be a dad someday. He was going to fall in love. He was going to . . . No. He wasn't going to do anything now. Because someone had stolen his future with a bullet and a badge.

She gasped, trying to suck in oxygen despite the heavy weight crushing her chest. It hurt too much. The agony of her heart being ripped from her sternum was overwhelming. She screamed, wailing from the loss. It was all too much. She needed to escape. Belle gave in. She held her breath and closed her eyes, chasing the darkness. She wanted to switch places.

Let him live. Take me.

Her prayers fell on deaf ears, swallowed up by the empty space that took everything good in her life. All that was left were death and destruction. Emptiness and horror. Devastation and darkness. And she wanted none of it. Without TJ, she didn't have a reason to keep going. Without him, life wasn't worth living.

* * *

Belle's eyes fluttered open. She winced in the harsh light. Her head pounded. Machines beeped. *Where am I?* She gasped. It wasn't just a bad dream. TJ was really gone. Her life was now the real nightmare.

Bently's worried expression was grim and somber as he held her hand. Pain etched in the shadows on his face, but something more sinister lurked in the darkness of his eyes. *Guilt.*

Could he have? No.

"Who?" One word was all she was capable of. She wanted the name of her brother's murderer. She wanted to know what had happened.

Bently's jaw ticced as he swallowed and looked down. "One of my neighbors called nine-one-one. Reported a break-in at my address."

She swallowed the emotion down. She couldn't fall apart again. She owed TJ this.

"They saw him moving the boxes." Bently's voice broke as tears streamed over his face.

She watched as they dripped along his jaw, falling to the bed. *Drip . . . Drip . . . Drip.*

"Officer Luke Parsons was first on the scene. I'd been at Remy's getting coffee." His grip tightened, the shame so thick and heavy in the room it was suffocating.

Parsons. Officer Parsons was the dick who had given her a hard time at the station. The one who'd looked down at her like she was scum.

"By the time I heard the radio—it was too late." He choked up.

"He was shot in *your* house. Moving boxes in. By one of *your* officers. One of *your* neighbors called the police because a Black boy was in their neighborhood."

"I'm so sorry, Angel. I don't know what to say. I can't fix this." His voice was tormented.

"Why did they shoot? TJ wasn't a threat. He's a good boy. He was going to save lives. He—he was—"

"I know, baby. I know. I'm so sorry."

Had TJ been scared? Had he died alone? Did he suffer?

Stabbing pain radiated in her chest. She winced.

"Did you arrest the murderer?" Her voice was cold and dead like her heart.

This was where the line would be drawn. Maybe she'd been naive enough to think this day would never come, that she and Bently could exist in a world together.

"There will be an internal investigation. He's been suspended until further notice." Bently cringed.

"An investigation? A fucking suspension! Why is he not in handcuffs? You know he murdered TJ. Why isn't he being treated like the cold-blooded killer he is?" she shouted.

"I'm too close to this case. It's been taken out of my hands. I'm also suspended until further notice because I . . . attacked him."

Her eyes fell to his torn fists for the first time. He'd chosen. He'd already chosen what was right rather than to help the man hide behind the badge. She should have felt relief, but beyond the numbness, there was only agony. And if she let herself feel anything, the pain would destroy her.

"He just started classes. He was going to celebrate with us at dinner. He—"

"I know, Angel. It isn't fair."

Fair. Equal. Freedom. Words thrown around this country like a pretty dress worn to hide the ugly reality. America the beautiful. America the brave. America the murderer. TJ had been killed for the perceived threat, not because of fact but bias. He'd been assumed to be dangerous because of the color of his skin.

No. It isn't fair.

But when had life ever been fair for a Black man?

45

BENTLY

Grief was like being drowned above water. Like having your heart stop while your body continued to live on. Grief was all-consuming. A million emotions all compounding inside you at once, and just when you thought you'd reached your limit, they doubled down again. Bently's body hummed with rage, with shame, with guilt, and terror.

Belle was a shell of the woman he'd asked to marry him only twelve hours ago. The joy in her eyes had been replaced with emptiness. And TJ's life had been stolen by a man he'd once respected.

This was why he should have stayed away from Belle. Everything he touched turned to ruin. He destroyed everything good in his life. Happiness was never supposed to be his. If he'd stayed out of her life, if he'd never asked her to move in, her brother would still be alive. TJ should be laughing with Cam, falling in love for the first time. He should be worrying about his first exams, not lying in a cold morgue, alone, with five bullets in his back.

Guilt ate at his insides until his guts burned with acid. *I could have prevented this.*

Maybe if he'd heeded Andre's warning. Maybe if he'd stood up to Parsons more. Maybe if he'd looked past his own blind spot and recognized that his whole team needed some sort of de-escalation and sensitivity training, TJ would be walking through the front door any minute.

How could Parsons do this? He'd taken the same oaths to serve and protect as Bently had.

Belle picked at the dried blood on her wrist as she stared at the steps.

"You need a shower," Bently said, helping Belle inside her house. They were supposed to be at his tonight, but that was a crime scene now. She'd never be able to return there without the reminder of what happened. He wouldn't either.

Belle didn't respond. She hadn't said a word since before they left the hospital. She was like the walking dead.

His heart lurched. He picked her up, needing to have her in his arms. He wanted to take on all her pain for her. He'd carry her until she could find her footing again. And then, when she was ready, he'd walk away so she'd never have to be hurt by him again.

Taking one step at a time, he climbed her staircase. After switching the shower on with one hand, he set her down. He stripped off her clothes, leaving his own blood-stained uniform in a pile on the floor. Bently helped her into the shower. The hot water rained down on them. He pulled her against his chest, not knowing what else he could do except hold her while she broke apart.

The water washed away the blood from his skin, but it could never take the regret. Belle trembled, staring off vacantly as he washed her body with the one bottle of soap they'd left next to the basin to use as they went back and forth.

Thankfully Mia had been kind enough to rush to his house and pack Belle some things in a suitcase that was now sitting in her bedroom. A bottle of soap rested against the tile. He squirted some into his hands and lathered it over her body, taking care to wash her gently.

"I've got you." Bently tried to soothe her.

His own eyes burned. His stomach was hard and his chest felt as though he'd had open-heart surgery without pain medication. It tore him up to see Belle this way, nothing he could do could fix it. He obsessed over all he could have done to prevent it.

He'd raced home, praying to a god he didn't believe in that TJ's truck wouldn't be there when he arrived. Fate was never that kind. He'd charged inside. Vargas had tried holding him back as he barked orders. Parsons had been standing next to the body. TJ's arms had been handcuffed even though he no longer resided on this earth. Even in death, Parsons deemed him a threat. Bently's stomach had roiled. The next thing he'd known, Parsons was underneath him and his fists were heavy, pounding into the man's face until the satisfying crunch of bone rattled through his arm. Vargas and Owens had to pull him off and handcuff him until he'd calmed down enough to ride in the ambulance.

He'd probably lose his job, but what did that matter when TJ had lost his life while heating up a bowl of mac and cheese, listening to music? TJ had been a hero. And no matter how Bently tried to look at it, his gut told him that Parsons would not have barged in and shot an unarmed boy in the back if he'd been white.

When the water ran cold, he shut it off. He grabbed a towel that Mia had most likely left for them. He bundled Belle up and carried her to the bed.

The suitcase sat on the floor with a few bottles of water, a box of tea, a few cans of soup, and a bottle of tequila. A pang stabbed in his chest. Belle had a lot of people who cared about her, whether she knew it or not.

My family is her family.

Bently pulled back the covers and laid her down gently before sliding in next to her. Silent tears leaked from her eyes as she stared off into space. She was lost in grief and devastation. *Come back to me, Angel.*

He wrapped his arms around her and held on tight as if he could will her back to life. If her heart was too damaged to beat, he'd do it for the both of them. He'd take care of her. He'd be here for her no matter the cost. He laid his hand across her chest, counting her heartbeats until he fell asleep.

Bently jolted awake. His heart raced and sweat trickled down his brow. The room felt empty. A sick feeling twisted in his chest. *Where is Belle?* He shot out of bed, not bothering to grab his clothes as he left the room in search of her.

He opened the door to TJ's room and breathed a sigh of relief. She was curled up on his mattress. An old quilt lay over her. He backed out of the room and went for a pair of sweatpants that Mia had packed before going down to the kitchen.

He carried the cup of chamomile tea upstairs once it was ready. The sunlight was only starting to peek over the horizon. He walked into TJ's room and swallowed hard. It still didn't feel real that TJ would never enter through those doors again. He'd never smile again, or laugh.

Bently blinked away the warring emotions that rose up as he rounded the bed. Belle's eyes were open and unfocused. He knelt by the side of the mattress, next to her face.

"I brought you some tea." He gently caressed her forehead, tucking the mess of curls aside.

"I don't want anything. What's the point? He's gone." Fresh tears streamed from her swollen red eyes.

"You have to take care of yourself. Even though it hurts." His voice softened and his heart broke more.

"I have no one left." Her voice was so quiet he barely heard her.

"You have me. You're my family now." Didn't she understand just how much he loved her? How much she meant to him?

A spark lit her dark eyes. Anger blazed in Belle's pained gaze as she sat up. "You're one of them!"

Her words were a shot to the chest. She blamed him. *Because I could have prevented this somehow. Maybe.* "I'm sorry—"

"Sorry doesn't bring my brother back." Her voice was cold and dead like she must have felt inside.

This time, his soul cracked and splintered with it. Blinding pain shot through him, breaking him apart.

"Leave me alone. I can't even look at you."

"Angel." It was a prayer. A plea with the universe.

"Go, Bently. GO!" she screamed.

Bently stood, his hands itching to reach out and touch her one more time. Torment eviscerated his insides. He'd lost her for good. He'd been clinging on to a false hope and empty faith. All good things must come to an end. He should have known better than to believe he could have more. After all, he was Paul Evans's son. The one who'd failed to protect those he'd loved. And he'd done it again.

He staggered back before he turned and ran out of the room, down the stairs, and out into the ice-cold twilight. It didn't matter that he was still shirtless in the January morning because he was already frozen and numb inside. The tether between Belle and him cinched and tightened the farther he walked away from her. He struggled to gasp in a breath. One more step and it would snap. He'd be separated from her for good.

He took one last glance towards her duplex, the finality of it all weighing down heavily on his shoulders. He lifted one leaden foot and walked away like she'd told him to do. He clutched his chest. Searing pain slammed through him. He staggered backwards as he fell to the snow. Desolation poured over him as his heart pounded against his rib cage. The red predawn sky glowed above.

Even the heavens were bleeding.

46

BELLE

hat did I just do? It wasn't Bently she was mad at, but the system that had taken her brother from her. She was furious at the cop who had pulled the trigger. At society for fearing her smart, amazing brother who'd overcome more adversity than most of them would ever know in a lifetime, all before he was eleven years old. He had been going to save lives and change the world. Now he was a hashtag.

Belle sucked in a pained breath. Every cell in her body ached, down to the marrow of her bones. Devastation wracked her. She was locked in a prison of grief. Hot tears stung her chapped face as the weight of everything crushed her. She was suffocated by anguish, asphyxiated by anger, strangled with regret.

Could she ever live with the fact that the man she loved was a cop? That he'd vowed to uphold unjust laws that had racism pounded into their very fiber?

She gasped for air.

I just blamed him for an entire country's fault.

And now he was gone when she needed him most. She'd pushed him away.

She let out a guttural scream and began to sob until no sound came out. She pounded her fists into the mattress. Her lungs depressed, locking in place, burning. She couldn't breathe. The edges of her vision darkened.

The bed dipped and a cold, hard body melded against hers as two strong arms held her.

"Shhh. It's okay. Just breathe. In one, two, three, four. Now out, one, two, three, four. Five things you can see. Name them," Bently's voice commanded gently.

"Window. Wall. Hand. Bed. Blanket."

"Five things you can feel."

She listed off sensations as he guided her back from her panic attack. He held her while she calmed down, the emotional strain overwhelming her with exhaustion. Her heavy eyelids drooped closed.

"I'm here. Sleep, Angel. I'm not going anywhere. Not when you need me."

Her heart beat for what felt like the first time since she'd seen her brother's body. But just once. A flicker and then it was gone.

Bently's voice rumbled in his chest. "I can't leave you like this. Give me your hurt. Give me your anger. Cast it all on me. I can take it. I can be strong for the both of us for now. Hate me, but let me love you."

47

BELLE

Belle pushed the eggs around on her plate. More food she wouldn't be able to stomach. Her appetite was as absent as her brother.

Bently's pacing was the only sound in the otherwise silent room. The worry in his eyes was always aimed at her. He hadn't left her side in days—making calls, taking care of the funeral arrangements.

Her inhale was shallow, her chest aching too much to take in a full breath. Her eyes felt like sandpaper. And her muscles ached from all the tensing she'd done while she sobbed into TJ's mattress night after night. She had no energy left. She was depleted of everything. Her life had been snuffed out along with her brother's. Her reason for fighting through the pain was gone. What was she doing here?

Why bother if life is more painful than death? Why not just lie down and never get up again?

She was exhausted from fighting to see another day. Everything she'd ever done was for TJ to have a better life. So she'd not repeat the mistakes her mother had made. And what good had it done her? TJ was dead.

The floor creaked under Bently's weight as he set a cup of tea in front of her. He'd been careful to keep his distance, only touching her when he absolutely had to. *Like when I need to shower. Or when I cry so hard I can't breathe. Or when the panic attacks come.*

He's my lighthouse in the storm. My gravity. And I fucked it up.

Was he here out of obligation now?

She glanced at him from the corner of her eye. His shoulders sagged, as if he carried the weight of the universe on them. Overgrown stubble was now more of a short beard on his jaw. He ran a hand through his messy and unkempt hair. The dark rings under his bloodshot eyes would have caused her heart to ache, if she was capable of feeling anything anymore but grief. She was paralyzed with it. Disbelief that TJ was actually gone switched to anger, and then hopelessness. A constant erratic cycle that consumed her. Sucking her into this dark pit of despair. It was as if she was being buried alive. There was no light here. No oxygen. No hope.

But he was here with her through it all. She'd screamed at him. She'd blamed him. She'd pushed him away. But he'd stayed.

Her gaze met his as he sat across from her at the table.

"How about some soup?"

She shook her head. She'd just throw it up anyways. There was no point.

"You gotta eat something. He wouldn't want this." Bently's voice was gentle and true. A compass in the desert. A guiding light in the darkness.

"I can't."

"What about the tea?" He motioned to the mug.

Her stomach rolled. Her mouth was parched, but it didn't

feel right. She couldn't go on without TJ. He was more than her brother. He was like her child. She'd lost him.

"Just a sip," Bently pressed.

She reached for the handle, sealing her lips to the edge of the ceramic as she sipped the dull liquid. Food had lost its taste. The day had lost its brightness. Color had lost its vividness. Nothing was the same. And everything was wrong.

Bently relaxed in the seat, his shoulders lowering. He didn't deserve this. *I don't deserve him.*

Knock. Knock.

Belle's head swiveled to the front door as Bently stood. He cleared his throat and walked over to open the door.

"*Dios mio.* Bently, I'm so sorry." Mia's accent drifted in as Bently widened the door. She walked in with Andre trailing right behind her.

"You doing okay?" Andre asked.

Bently nodded before glancing to her. His friends turned their gazes on her. She didn't want company. She wanted to be left alone. Irritation boiled.

"Belle, sweetheart." Mia came over to her, setting a bag on the table before she wrapped her arms around her.

Belle's chest tightened and her eyes burned.

Mia released her and sat in the chair next to her, gripping her hand. The gesture provided a flicker of comfort.

"You guys, give us some privacy," Mia called to Andre over her shoulder.

Bently's brows formed a triangle, looking to Belle as if to make sure she'd be okay.

Belle nodded as Andre wrapped his arm roughly around his friend, pulling him outside the door.

"Not hungry?" Mia asked.

Belle shook her head.

"This will get better. I know you're in the thick of it right now. It's all so fresh. But I promise you, it will get easier." Mia patted her hand.

Anger rose, heating Belle's veins. "How would you know? All my life I've fought for something better. I finally got there. TJ was about to start a life on his own and—and—" Belle choked on the words.

Mia pulled out a bottle of clear tequila and two glasses. She poured them each some and pushed one cup to Belle. "My father was killed in front of me when I was a child by the cartel. My mother . . . she died a little over a year ago, violently, by the hands of the same group. I know what it is to lose someone. To wonder why you should even bother to go on with life. To want to give up." She shook her head. "But then I realized how selfish that was. That the best way to honor their lives was to live my life to the fullest for them. To laugh three times as hard. To wake up each morning and greet the sunrise for them." Mia leaned forward. Her brown eyes peered deep into Belle's soul. "It will take time, but you'll get there. You'll want to live again. You'll feel again. But only if you process this grief. Only if you give yourself the chance to heal."

Belle was speechless. She'd had no idea that Mia had experienced such loss herself. "It hurts so much." Belle's voice cracked.

Mia wrapped her arm around her. "I know, sweetheart. It will for a long time. Some of that hurt will be with you for the rest of your life, but someday you will be able to turn that pain into something beautiful. The ones we loved and lost don't leave us completely. Every time you feel the sunshine on your skin, it's him embracing you in a warm hug. Every time the wind rustles through the trees, it is TJ letting you know he's there. He's all around you, but most importantly, you are carrying him inside your heart. You loved him. He is a part of you. You'll always have him with you." Mia squeezed her shoulder.

Belle blinked back tears. Was he still with her? She'd never been one for religion, or fairy tales of golden gates. But something lifted inside her. The weight bearing on her shoulders lightening just a fraction at the thought of TJ's spirit watching over her, staying close. "When will it stop hurting?"

Mia gave her a sad smile. "That depends on you. Grief is different for everyone. But the only way to get past it is to go through it."

"I'm so scared. And so tired. I don't think I can do it," Belle admitted, utterly defeated.

"You have a guardian angel watching over you. Let him carry you when you're too weak to stand. Let him hold you when you fall. Eventually, you won't need to lean on him so much. But for now, let him be there for you." Mia's voice was understanding.

"I can't feel him here. I'm all alone." Belle shook her head.

"That man is not going anywhere. Andre dragged him out to make sure he was getting a good meal and some support. He'll be back."

Bently? Mia had meant let Bently be here for her, not the ghost of her brother. But he couldn't. "I don't deserve him."

Mia chuckled. "Of course you do. You deserve the world. And that man wants to give it to you. You have to make a choice. Are you going to let this tragedy rip you apart, or use it to make you stronger as a unit?"

Belle remained silent as she contemplated her life. Everything she'd fought through to get here, all the things she'd sacrificed. If she gave up now, they would all be in vain. She imagined TJ sitting in the empty chair next to her, his headphones in, scribbling in his notebook. His goofy smile as he looked up at her, admiration shining in his eyes. Her chest squeezed. She wanted to make him proud. She needed to make his sacrifice count. She'd do right by him. "I want to live for TJ."

Mia picked up the glass and lifted it to her with a kind smile. "To TJ. May he rest in peace and never be forgotten. We celebrate the time we had with our loved ones. May we honor them with our lives."

Belle picked up her glass and clinked hers with Mia's before swallowing the liquid. She coughed as the liquor burned her throat.

"Another?" Mia asked.

Belle nodded. She'd drink to TJ. She'd take another breath for him until she could do it for herself. She'd push forward and never give up.

And she wouldn't let his death be in vain.

48

BELLE

The hot water sluiced over Belle's raw skin. She stood, pushing through the aching emptiness with the hope that someday it would dull. For now, she'd allow herself to fall apart. Then, she'd get back up. Just as she'd always done.

She turned off the water and wrapped herself in a towel. Her things had slowly begun to be unpacked, returned from Bently's. She dried off and brushed her teeth and hair before walking into the bedroom. Bently was sitting at the edge of her bed, his face in his hands. She'd never seen him look more defeated. *And part of it is my fault.*

"I keep going into his room expecting him to be there," she said, just above a whisper.

Bently looked up at her, devastation written across the shadows of his face.

"Sometimes I swear I hear music. Or that damn basketball bouncing . . . It still feels like I can call his name and he'll answer me." Her voice shook and fresh tears streamed down her cheeks.

Bently grimaced, his jaw clenching. "I'm sorry——"

"No." She shook her head. "I'm the one who's sorry. I said things I didn't mean. I blamed you because you were here."

Bently shook his head.

She drew closer, kneeling in front of him. She placed her hands on his knees and looked into blue eyes coated in shame. "It wasn't your fault."

"Yes, it was!" His voice cracked, tears glistening.

"How? Did you pull the trigger?"

"I failed him. I promised to protect him and now he's dead. I tried so hard to be everything, to be the best leader, to run my unit—but I couldn't—I should have . . . maybe if—"

"There was nothing you could have done."

"I knew Parsons . . . that he was biased. He'd make jokes about women or minorities. It was just ribbing, locker room talk. I'd grown up hearing the same comments. I never thought it was a big deal . . . Now I see how wrong I'd been. How my silence made it acceptable. By not speaking up, maybe I encouraged his behavior. I should have stopped it." Bently's shoulders slumped.

She placed her hand on his cheek, his rough stubble scratching her skin. "It's not your fault. You brought TJ friendship and happiness. He'd never want you to beat yourself up over this. You spent your life carrying guilt and responsibility that wasn't yours. Don't take this too. This isn't yours to bear. This is on Parsons."

He jerked, shaking his head violently.

She grabbed his face in both her hands, forcing his eyes to meet hers. "Don't do this. Don't run from me. Choose me."

"I'm no good for you. I come from the devil himself. Everything I touch gets destroyed. I'm not enough." His words said one thing, and his eyes another. "But I want to be, Belle. I want to be so bad it hurts."

"You're nothing but good, Bently Evans. You've been surrounded by darkness your whole life and still you shine so much brighter than you realize. You're not the devil—you're the moon. You're my guiding light."

He blinked as a single tear fell down each side of his face.

"Give me your hurt. Give me your guilt. Cast it all on me. I can take it. We can be strong together, leaning on one another. Let me love you." She pressed her lips to his, halting his reply.

He hesitated only a moment before his hands pulled her tighter against him. She tore at his shirt, letting her towel fall to the ground. He pulled down his pants, leaving them in a pile on the floor. His body slammed onto hers. Their touches were frantic and needy. They were kindred spirits, stuck in a storm of grief, tumbling and plunging through the darkness they'd been born into. But together, they burned bright and hot. United, they lit up like a thousand suns.

His hands gripped and roamed, burning, searing her skin. Need enveloped her, washing away everything with its cleansing fire. Lips caressed hers, taking and giving all at once. Kissing him made it hurt a little less. She raked her fingernails over his back, pulling him closer, greedy and desperate. Electricity flashed and splintered through her as he thrust into her in one quick surge.

"Yes!" she cried out. Discord and chaos spun within. A wildfire of rapture shattered her. Pressure built until it crested. He rocked her hard and fast. His sinewy muscles were taut, curling and bunching over her as he pounded deep inside her. His blue eyes locked on her, as their bodies danced. She quaked. She cried out with whimpers and wanton words as he drove her towards the light. Warmth flooded her body as every nerve ending tingled with awareness just before another orgasm blasted through her. He'd taken her pain and replaced it with euphoria. He'd taken her darkness and given her glimmering, sparkling, blinding light.

"I love you," he said, over and over. He grunted, sweat beading on his forehead. His eyes locked on to hers as he charged his own release.

Bently pressed his cheek to hers. Their tears melded together as one. Her pulse raced. Breaths came in gasps. And a small piece of her heart fluttered back to life.

Bently held her hand. She was tucked against the side of his body, warding out some of the chill as they stood on a ledge overlooking the gray-green ocean as waves pounded against the black cliffs. The March wind whipped and whistled through the evergreens. She shivered and tucked her chin against Bently's chest. He swept his lips across hers before she lifted her head to the sunshine. Warm rays caressed her face. *TJ.*

Today was the day she'd say goodbye. She looked around at the small group of familiar faces. Bently's friends and family. Katy was there. TJ's friend Mark and the girl he'd liked, Cam. Everyone who cared about her brother.

They'd all taken turns saying something about him, and now it was her turn. "My brother was the best human on this earth. He was kind, and smart. He was the bravest person I know. He wanted to devote his life to helping people. He was going to become a doctor to save lives . . . but he saved mine when I was seven years old and he was born. He'd rescued me every day since. He'll always be with me. I'll carry him in my heart. And I'll honor his life by not wasting mine."

She opened up the jar of ashes, spilling the contents as the waves crashed against the rocks below. The wind blew, carrying his remains out to sea where he'd be forever immortalized in nature.

Her knees buckled and her chest squeezed as she let the last of him go. Bently's arm steadied her. She looked up at him, offering him a watery smile. They'd been through so much together in the eight months of knowing each other. Highs and lows. Mountains and valleys. He'd taken her to the tallest of heights, and held her hand as they navigated the lowest pits of grief and despair. Some days she needed to lean on him, and others he borrowed her strength. Together, they'd get through this. Together, they would build a future that was brighter and better. Together, they were unstoppable.

49

BENTLY

EIGHTEEN MONTHS LATER

Bently replayed the body cam footage over and over in his head as the wooden bench bit into his back in the packed courtroom. Parsons had peeked in the window, seeing TJ moving around in the kitchen. He'd assumed it was a break-in and decided that was probable cause. He'd opened the front door, announcing his presence. TJ's back had been to him, bobbing his head up and down, obviously lost to the music flowing through his earbuds. Five seconds. That was all it had taken for Parsons to open the door and open fire into the back of an unarmed teenager.

"All rise," the bailiff said.

Bently stood as Belle's trembling hand wove into his. He gave her a squeeze. Today was the day they would find out if TJ received justice.

"Please be seated," old judge Robertson said, after taking his seat.

Bently's ears rang, drowning out everything as his heart pounded in his chest. He wrapped his arm around Belle, holding her close as he'd done every day since the shooting.

They'd had such a long road of working through their grief. But each day got a little easier.

One of the jurors passed a piece of paper to the bailiff and then it went to the judge. This was it. The moment they'd waited twenty months, three days, and seven hours for.

"On the count of murder in the second degree, how do you find the defendant?" Judge Robertson asked the juror.

"We find the defendant, Luke Parsons, *not* guilty."

An audible collective gasp sounded throughout the courtroom. Belle's hand tightened around his. His heart lurched in his chest.

Come on.

"And on the count of manslaughter, how do you find the defendant?" Mathews asked.

"We find the defendant, *guilty*."

Bently let out the breath he'd been holding. TJ would get some justice, though nothing would make up for his precious life that had been stolen.

Luke Parsons sat stone-faced. He'd never even offered them an apology. He'd sworn he was just doing his job, that he'd feared for his life.

Bently glanced at Belle. She was so brave in the face of adversity. Her eyes shone with unshed tears. He reached into his pocket and pulled out a pack of tissues before handing them to her.

She smiled and took one from the packet before wiping her eyes. Her silver wedding band glinted in the light. He pulled her against him and kissed her head. His angel, sent from heaven. She'd endured hell and still managed to hold on to her goodness and light.

They burst through the doors of the courthouse as cameras clicked and flashed. A crowd of reporters thrust their microphones towards Belle.

"Mrs. Evans, are you happy with the verdict?"

"Mrs. Evans, do you think justice prevailed today?"

Instinctually, he stepped in front of her, protecting her from the surge of people. Thousands had gathered outside, holding their signs. After the body cam footage had been released, and the media had found out about yet another shooting, the *Black Lives Matter* movement had caught wind and the national news coverage exploded.

"It's okay," Belle assured him, squeezing his hand.

He stood by her side as she spoke, holding one hand on her lower back.

"Officer Luke Parsons received seventeen years. One year for every one my brother was alive. My brother will never be able to achieve the dreams he had. Am I happy with the verdict? I'd be much happier if my brother was here with me today. But nothing will bring him back. Continue to say his name and the thousands of others who've been unjustly targeted by the justice system and had their lives stolen for their only crime—being born Black. TJ had so much potential. He was so full of life, and all that was violently stolen by the internalized prejudice and systemic racism that plagues this country. It needs to end now!"

The crowd chanted, "No more! No more!"

Belle took a deep breath, as if drawing in courage. "The one thing I can do is try to make this world a better place. Make this country safer for people of color. I can do my part so that not one more Black man will suffer at the hands of police. We can hold those accountable who steal their lives out of misguided fear and racism. But I can't do it alone. I need your help." Belle took a breath, searching the crowd.

Pride glowed in Bently's chest as his wife called a nation to action.

She continued, "white people, allies, I'm talking to you. There will never be a world in which racism doesn't exist, unless we're willing to come together. Black, white, brown, we're all humans. We all love. We all have dreams and hopes, and families we care for. Start by talking to your children about their privilege and racism. Don't be afraid to speak up when you see something. white silence is white consent. Stop the hate by stopping the hate speech."

The crowd cheered.

Belle held up her hand, quieting them. "Educate yourself, read books, talk to people who've lived it. And don't get defensive when we tell you something is hurtful. Acknowledge your privilege. Be better, America."

"Mrs. Evans, what do you have to say to those who would accuse you of sleeping with the enemy? Your husband being both a white man and a cop?" a reporter asked.

Bently's spine stiffened.

Belle's chin rose. "The police are not the enemy. My husband is not the enemy. It is not them versus us. Many of those in blue are good people, risking their lives every single day to protect strangers—my husband included. The only way we're going to win this war on racism is to work together to weed out the ones who misuse their power, and those who stand by and do nothing to stop them. We have to rewrite unjust racist laws and make diversity and sensitivity training mandatory, as well as de-escalation instruction. My husband, Sheriff Bently Evans, has implemented it in our state and is working with our senators to introduce new legislation nationwide that will rewrite the structure of accountability for officers, along with stricter guidelines of their use of force."

The crowd applauded and cheered again.

"Mrs. Evans—"

"That's all I have to say. Thank you for your support."

Bently wrapped his arm around Belle and kissed her cheek.

"I'm so fucking proud of you," he said, leading her away from the crowd towards his truck.

Her smile made his chest tighten. There had been such a long period of time when she'd not been able to find happiness. They'd waded through the pain together and come out stronger because of it. He'd stuck by her side, and he knew without a doubt that Belle was the only woman for him. He loved her, body and soul. She owned every part of him. And he'd spend the rest of his life earning those smiles.

"You amaze me." He opened her door.

"Because of the speech?" She chuckled.

"No. Because when everything and everyone in your life tried to drag you down, you didn't stay there. You rose amidst the thorns."

She spun around and hooked her arms over his neck, pulling him towards her mouth. She kissed him, pressing her lush curves against him. "I could say the same about you."

Bently soaked in the sight, memorizing every line and curve of her light brown face. His bronze angel, glowing in a halo of sunlight. Love radiated through every atom. They were bound together by the energy that crackled between them.

"Why are you looking at me like that?" she asked.

"Like what?"

"Like I'm the only woman in the world."

"Because to me, you are." His lips descended on hers, soaking in her warmth and goodness. Happiness and gratitude tumbled and tangled in his chest, pressing against his rib cage. He'd found true joy after a lifetime of grief. Not the kind that fairy tales were made of, but the real, raw, love that was forged in fire and reborn in hope. The kind of partnership that he could count on. A wife who'd be by his side no matter what they faced. A woman who accepted him as he was while also pushing him to be better.

They were just two broken people, with jagged edges and sharp ridges, pieced together to make something whole—bound by the bonds of the truest love.

EPILOGUE - BELLE

ANOTHER 8 MONTHS LATER

The spring breeze blew lightly against Belle's skin as the sunshine warmed her, reminding her of TJ. She sipped her iced coffee and walked out to the back porch of the large house she and Bently had bought right after they were married. Her heart squeezed with a pang of sadness. She inhaled long and deep as she set the cup on the patio table. "My husband. My family. My friends." The three things she was most grateful for.

"What, Aunty Belle?" Zoey asked from her side.

Belle turned and gasped.

Big gray upturned eyes looked up at her guiltily. The little girl was covered in mud from head to toe.

"I gots the garden watered." She smiled, her white teeth standing out even more against the brown splotches all over her face.

Did she take a mud bath?

Belle burst out laughing and Zoey's sweet giggles were not far behind. "You certainly did. Looks like you need a shower."

Belle reached out and picked up a piece of dark hair caked in mud.

"I made a mud pie. Do you want some?" Zoey asked.

"Mmmm. Sounds delicious."

"What does?" Bently's deep voice asked from behind. She turned around, her heart stuttering at the sight of those brilliant blue eyes, amused and hungry and aimed at her. His uniform fit snugly showing off hard-earned muscles. He'd shaven his beard that he'd kept for the winter, leaving dark, rough stubble. She squeezed her thighs together, the rashes he'd left from said scruff tingling.

Will I ever get enough of my husband?

No.

"Uncle Bently! Do you want a mud pie?" Zoey asked, holding out a glob of dark brown sludge.

Bently wrapped his arms around Belle and kissed her cheek. "Hmm. That looks mighty tasty. You know what I *really* love?"

"What?" Zoey asked.

"Mud cupcakes. Those are my favorite." Bently smiled.

"Oh! Great idea. I do it!" Zoey got to work, busily plopping mud in smaller piles on the green grass.

"I missed you," Bently said next to Belle's ear, his hot breath tickling the fine hair on her neck.

"Same here, Sheriff."

His hands dropped to her waist, pulling her tighter against him as he peppered kisses down her neck, his scratchy chin making heat pool in her center. The tiniest whimper escaped from her.

He chuckled.

"Stop. Your niece is right over there."

"I don't know what you're talking about. I'm just saying

hello to my *wife*." Bently's deep voice reverberated through her.

"You know exactly what you're doing." He knew her body better than she did. He'd spent countless hours mapping every pleasure point.

"It's all done!" Zoey proclaimed excitedly. She held out a small clump in her hand towards him.

"Yum!" Bently accepted the handful from her before bringing it to his lips.

Zoey made a face. "Don't really eat it! It's just pretend."

"Now you tell me," he teased, reaching out his other hand to tickle her. She giggled.

"You know what's even more fun to do with mud cupcakes?" Bently asked.

Zoey shook her head.

"This," Bently said before he raised the clump of sludge and sent it flying towards Belle.

Speckles of mud pelted her chest and splattered across her face as she gasped.

"What—oh you're going to get it, mister!" Belle dove for a handful and sent it flying in his direction as he dodged and weaved.

Zoey giggled, grabbing two globs, and joined the chase.

"Let's get him, Zoey!" Belle tackled Bently to the ground, rubbing her handful across his forehead as he smeared some over hers. She was out of breath from laughing so hard. Tiny clumps pelted them from the side as Zoey joined in.

"Do you surrender?" Belle asked.

Bently chuckled. "Only to you. Only ever to you." He slanted his mouth over hers, kissing her as energy crackled between them.

"You're lucky I love you."

"I sure am." He smirked.

She turned her head, checking on Zoey who'd gone quiet. *Too quiet.*

"Time to wash it off!" Zoey yelled as she aimed the hose at them.

Belle gasped as she was flipped to the ground, Bently hovering above her taking the brunt of the ice-cold spray of water as it dripped onto her. "Ahhh! Zoey! It's too cold. Shut it off!"

The shower from the hose stopped as Bently got to his feet and reached out to help her up.

She examined her clothes—wet and muddy. Belle glanced at the two of them, Bently was even worse off than her. "Look at us."

They all burst into laughter until her stomach ached. She sucked in a breath and tipped her head towards the spring sunlight. Joy overflowed. Some days were still hard. She'd always miss her brother. But the winter made the spring that much more special. She'd cherish each day. She'd laugh, she'd love hard and embrace life, living for the both of them.

"We better get you cleaned up before your mommy gets here to get you," Belle said, holding out her hand to the little girl.

* * *

After they'd showered and changed, Belle put a plate of fruit and veggies on the table. Zoey's little fingers grabbed a cucumber first, chewing on all the edges before plopping the middle in her mouth. "Mommy made sandcastles with me after we had ice cream for bre-fast."

"You had dessert for breakfast?" Belle's eyes widened as she smiled.

"Mommy said Mother's Day is a special cajun." Zoey grabbed another veggie and chomped her little teeth into it.

"Your mommy is right. It is a special occasion."

Bently set a cup of coffee in front of her.

"Thank you."

"You're welcome, Angel." He winked at her.

His phone rang on the counter. He picked it up, glancing at the screen before answering with the speakerphone. "Hey, Jaz, you on your way?"

"Uh, no, actually. I need you to keep Zoey overnight."

His brows knit together. "Is everything okay?" He glanced at Zoey before turning to Belle.

Belle offered Zoey another cucumber as worry clenched her gut.

"I have everything under control, Bent. I just need you to do this and not ask me any questions, okay? I'll owe you one," Jasmine's voice said through the speaker.

"Okay. Fine. Anything you need," Bently said.

"Thank you. I'll call before bed to say good night to her."

"Sounds good." Bently ended the call. "Guess what, princess? You get to spend the night with us tonight. Would you like to have a sleepover with Aunt Belle and me?" Bently asked.

"Yay!"

"Why don't you go pick out a movie to watch until dinner is ready." Bently nodded towards the living room.

"Otay!" Zoey shoved another cucumber in her mouth before she ran out of the room.

"Is she okay?" Belle asked.

Bently rubbed a hand through his dark hair. "Something's up, but you know Jaz."

Belle chuckled. Getting information out of Jasmine was an impossible feat—she was worse than her brother.

Bently shrugged. "She said she was going to handle it. Whatever that means."

Belle got up and wrapped her arms around him. "It will all work out. Maybe it's a good thing."

"I want to watch Elsa!" Zoey came in holding the remote.

Bently kissed Belle's forehead before he walked away to help his niece. "Alright, the ice princess it is."

"Do your reindeer voice, Uncle Bently," Zoey pleaded.

Belle bit back a smile as the man she loved made a complete adorable fool out of himself, all to make a little girl laugh.

* * *

Later that night, after Zoey was sound asleep in one of the five bedrooms of the house, Belle turned the baby monitor on and slipped into bed next to Bently. He frowned at his phone and then set it on the small table.

"What's wrong?" Belle asked.

"The lead on Charli's attacker was a dead end. And we still have no hard evidence to connect Carelli to Canoby's drug dealers." He rubbed a hand over his face.

She rested her palm on his chest. "You'll find him."

"I hope so." He pulled her against his naked chest and she kissed his smooth skin.

"The princess is asleep?" he asked.

"She is. It only took four stories and two songs this time."

He chuckled and traced her shoulder with his fingers, leaving gooseflesh in their wake.

She looked up at him as his gaze shifted towards the ceiling.

"Are you worried about your sister?"

He sighed and turned towards her. "Actually, I was thinking about all the empty rooms in the house."

She smiled. "Oh yeah?"

He nodded. "I got a call today. Had to assist CPS in taking two young children from their home." He cringed. "The place was filthy. The kids were . . . neglected and scared."

She could tell by the flash of anger in his eyes that it had been *bad*. "And you want to start those foster parenting classes we've been putting off?"

That was why they'd bought such a big house after all. Someday they planned to use it to give children and teenagers a port in the storm. Somewhere they would get love and care for however long they needed.

He nodded. "If you think you're ready."

She smiled. "I might have already signed us up for next month's class."

"You did?" His eyes widened.

She bit her lip and nodded.

His lips quirked up at the side. "Do you know what this means?"

"What?"

"That we better take advantage of all the loud sex we can before we get kids filling up these rooms," he growled.

She giggled as his hands scorched over her belly. "Zoey's here tonight."

"Well, I mean, tonight you'll have to be quiet, but *tomorrow* . . ." He smirked.

"Will you ever get sick of having the same woman in your bed?" she asked.

"Impossible. Not if it's you. I can never get enough of these sweet lips." He crashed his mouth to hers at the same time his hand dipped inside her panties, parting her slick folds with his fingers.

She arched her back off the bed. Her gasp was swallowed by his mouth. His tongue tangled and dipped between her lips, matching the rhythm of his finger on her pulsing clit. Electricity shot through her as her body flared with white-hot heat.

"Need you. Now." She panted, sitting up.

Belle climbed on top of him, pulling the covers down to reveal his thick, hard cock jutting straight up. Lining him up to her core, she sat on top of him. She sucked in sharply at the same time he hissed. The pleasurable filling, stretching sensation would never be anything less than amazing.

She began to move, grinding her hips each time she slammed onto him. He ripped off her shirt before he sat up and leaned against the headboard. The position added extra friction. Lining his pubic bone against her clit sent sparks and shimmers shooting through her vision as she came.

"Bently!"

He clamped a hand over her mouth, stifling her moans. It only added to the building pleasure that crashed through her a second time. Lost in euphoria, she was unable to do anything but clench around his perfect cock. Her nails dug into his shoulders as his hands moved, sweeping over her skin, settling on her hips. His fingers kneaded into her naked flesh, lifting her off him as he climbed behind her. He grabbed her waist and spread her legs, slipping inside her from behind. She was on all fours as he pounded faster, deeper, harder.

"Yes. God, yes!" she gasped.

Bently leaned forward, raking his teeth over her shoulder and shooting a pleasured mix of pain curling through her core.

"Gonna take you to heaven, Angel," he said.

"Come with me."

He reached around and swirled her clit, sending her rocketing towards the universe as intense bliss shattered through her, curling her toes. She pressed her face into the mattress, stifling her scream. Bently's muscles tensed and bunched over her, his cock pulsing as his hot cum filled her. They came together as one.

Just two individuals who'd been born into darkness and lived through hell. But they'd found heaven together. They'd formed an intimate partnership. They'd built a life for themselves filled with joy and purpose. Their love was that much deeper, that much stronger because of all they'd had to endure. She'd finally been able to turn her pain into something beautiful.

They were two lonely souls who had fought the odds pulling them down, and done the impossible by defying gravity.

The End

"I wish I could say that racism and prejudice were only distant memories. We must dissent from the indifference. We must dissent from the apathy. We must dissent from the fear, the hatred and the mistrust . . . We must dissent because America can do better, because America has no choice but to do better."

- Thurgood Marshall

Thank you! We hope you enjoyed reading *Defying Gravity*.

Want more of Bently and Belle? Visit the website below to join our newsletter and get an exclusive bonus scene of their wedding today.

WWW.AMKUSI.COM/DGBONUS

You can also turn the page for your sneak peek of Chapter One in the next book, **The Lighthouse Inn** (Book 4, featuring Jasmine and Atlas's story).

Or visit the website below to order Book 4 in the Shattered Cove series right now.

WWW.AMKUSI.COM/THELIGHTHOUSEINN

SNEAK PEEK OF THE LIGHTHOUSE INN
CHAPTER 1

Jasmine

J asmine pulled the sheet over the two fluffy pillows, smoothing out the wrinkles before reaching for the soft pink comforter. A paper card fell off the nightstand. Picking it up, she smiled. *Happy Mother's Day mommy!* The script no doubt belonged to one of her sisters-in-law, but the shakily scribbled Z's all over the card were from her favorite person in the world. Zoey had drawn two smiling faces on the card; one for Jasmine and one for herself. Jasmine set the card back on the night stand before running her hand over the bedspread once more. Never in a million years would she have imagined having such a soft feminine color in her space. Motherhood had changed more than just her body.

After tucking the edge under the pillow, she moved across the small room she shared with her four-year-old daughter. She pulled open the old and worn dresser, wiggling it side to side at the same time so it wouldn't stick. Like everything in her life, it had been used almost beyond its limits. She placed

Zoey's carefully folded clothes inside before wriggling it closed again. She scanned the room, catching on the few dolls scattered across the floor. Jasmine bent and picked them up, opening the wooden doll house that Mikel, her brother, had made especially for Zoey. He'd painted it bright pink at her request. Jasmine bit back her smile. Only she would end up with such a girly girl for a daughter and be terrified.

She sighed, tracing the edge of the doll's expression. The two smiling faces on Zoey's Mother's Day card flashing in her mind. Her chest tightened. *Would Zoey have had a better life if I'd let someone adopt her? Would she have two parents who loved her, rather than just me? I can barely keep a roof over her head and used clothes on her quickly growing body.*

Maybe it had been selfish to keep Zoey, but the moment she'd seen that little heart beating on the ultrasound she'd known: she'd never be able to give her up. *But will I be good enough? Will I be able to protect her? Will she resent me when she knows what I've done? Who I was?* Life would be so much easier if Jasmine was someone else with a different past.

The walls seemed to be closing in. Her ribs squeezed and the back of her eyes burned. She gently placed the doll inside the wooden house and straightened. Taking a deep breath, she steadied herself. *I just need to keep doing better. For Zoey.* Her phone chirped, jarring her out of her mind. She had one guest checking in today, and that was what she should have been focusing on. She needed guests to keep her inn—her livelihood—alive.

She wiped her hands on her ripped jean shorts that had seen better days and opened her door. Walking down to the desk, a tall figure caught her eye. His back was to her, all attention focused on the painting of the crashing ocean waves on the wall.

"Good morning. You must be Mr. Remington."

A low chuckle sent a shiver through her. "My father is Mr. Remington. I'm just Atlas."

She smiled politely as her eyes darted up to his face and she froze. Time stopped. The air evaporated as terror gripped her heart and squeezed it like a vice. His tall frame filled out an expensive-looking suit. His black hair was short at the sides with flecks of grey, and longer at the top. Dark scruff peppered his perfect chiseled jaw. She shivered, remembering the way it had felt brushing across her shoulder. And those eyes. Grey and bright. She only knew one person with the same cloudy orbs. *Zoey*.

He'd changed some in the last four years since she'd seen him. Not that she'd had much time to really look at him before she'd nodded towards the dingy bathroom in the bar where he'd followed her and bent her over the sink. Flames of embarrassment lapped at her skin. She'd been looking for an escape that night, and the stranger had been more than willing to help.

Atlas. Atlas Remington. She finally had a name for Zoey's biological father.

"What are you doing here?" She gasped. Was he here to take Zoey from her? Had he known all this time? *No.* That wasn't possible. No one knew what had happened in that bar bathroom except them.

His eyebrows furrowed. "Uh, checking in. I should have a reservation for two weeks."

Did he not recognize her? Was it possible? He'd smelled strongly of whiskey that night. Maybe he had no idea who she was.

"Right. Sorry. We don't know each other, do we?" She held her breath.

"I think I'd remember if we did." He smiled. Was he flirting with her?

"What are you in town for?" She asked carefully, finding his paperwork.

He looked around the room, at the high white patched ceiling and then over to the paint chipped furniture, rather than at her before he answered. "Just needed a little vacation."

"And you chose my inn? Was it my two Yelp reviews that convinced you?" She couldn't hold back her smile.

He chuckled again, those grey eyes flashing as they focused on her. "I like the location, and wanted to see it for myself. The pictures didn't do it justice though."

Her eyes flicked down momentarily. "Well, someday I'll hire a professional photographer."

"Oh, no. The pictures were great. I just meant, it's even better in person." He smiled, showing off his perfect white teeth. Good god, was he a toothpaste model?

"Do you need my credit card?" he asked.

Shit, she'd been staring. "Uh, no. It's all on file. Just sign here—" She pointed to the space on the form ready and waiting on the counter. "You have the Lighthouse suite like you requested. There are extra towels in the closet in the bathroom. I'll come in to clean every three days unless you need it done sooner—just let me know."

He nodded and scribbled his signature on the paper. Jasmine held out the lone key ring with a lighthouse keychain and his receipt. "I'll charge the card you provided when booking with any incidentals. Your room is just up the stairs to the left." *Across from mine.* "There's a sign on the door. The silver key works for the front door, and the brass key is for your room. Did you need more than one set, or will it be just you staying with us?"

"Just me. The one is fine." He took it from her hand and reached down to grab a duffel bag she hadn't noticed in the shock of seeing the baby daddy from her one-night stand—

if you could even call it that. Were ten-minute stands a thing?

"Enjoy your stay. I leave my number at the desk here," she pointed to the folded card stock sign right next to the one stating *No cash kept on premises*. "And it's also on the copy of your receipt. Just text me if you need anything and I'm not at the front desk."

"You run the inn by yourself?"

She smiled with pride. "Yes, I do."

He nodded and grabbed the papers before walking towards the stairs. She waited until the sound of his door closed to let out the breath she'd been holding.

"Holy fucking shit." She placed a shaky hand over her racing heart as if it would help to calm the panic.

She whipped out her phone and stepped into the large kitchen, dialing her big brother Bently's number.

He picked up on the second ring. "Hey Jas. You on your way?"

She swallowed hard before answering. She didn't need her brother freaking out and showing up over here to make things worse. She didn't even know what the hell was going on yet. "Uh, no. Actually, I need you to keep Zoey overnight."

"Is everything okay?" The concern in his voice brought a rush of guilt crashing over her.

Not even close to okay. Of all the people in her life, Bently had been the one constant, the only person she could count on. She hated to lie, but she'd brought enough trouble to their family. No. She'd handle this on her own.

"I have everything under control, Bent. Okay? I just need you to do this and not ask me any questions. Okay? I'll owe you one." More like a million, but who was counting?

"Okay. Fine. Anything you need." Bently said.

"Thank you. I'll call before bed to say goodnight to her."

"Sounds good." Bently ended the call.

Jasmine opened her contacts. She needed to talk to someone about this. But her best friend, Remy was married to Mikel, and she was shit at keeping secrets from him. The last thing Jasmine needed was her two over protective brothers jumping in to save her. *Again.* She'd caused them all enough trouble. This was her doing and she would fix this. *Somehow.*

She scrolled through her contacts until Emma's name popped up, and hit call before she could back out. It rang and rang until her friend picked up.

"Jazzy! Hey Mama. I got a quick break from the studio. How are you?" Emma asked as background music filtered through.

Jasmine covered her mouth with her hand, trying to quiet the sob that surprised even her.

"Jas? What's wrong? Are you okay?" Emma asked. The noise grew quieter, as if she'd moved away.

"He's here." She managed.

"Who's there?"

"Zoey's father. He's staying at my inn."

Emma was silent for a few beats. "Is this a good thing or a bad thing?"

She couldn't blame her friend for not knowing. There were several things Jasmine kept locked away in a vault of topics she wouldn't talk about. Zoey's biological father was one of them. She was too ashamed.

"I don't know, honestly." Jasmine wiped the tears from her eyes and walked out to the back deck. Salty sea air blew gently over her skin as waves crashed in the distance.

"Okay. Does he know about Zoey?"

"I don't even think he remembers me."

"Oh, sweetie."

"I—I don't know what to do." Jasmine shook her head.

356

"I wish I could offer advice, but you have never said anything about this guy."

Jasmine sighed. "I know. It's a part of my past that I'd like to forget. I did a lot of fucked up things, and I'd just rather forget the girl I used to be."

"I get it…So, can you explain how you made a baby with him, but he somehow can't recognize you?" Emma asked carefully.

Flashes came back of that dark bar. Those grey eyes had burned her skin with awareness making it clear exactly what he'd wanted from her before he'd ever even offered to buy her a drink.

"He was just a guy from a bar. We never exchanged names, just…body fluids."

"Thanks for the mental image." Emma said and laughed. "Is he hot?"

Jasmine rolled her eyes. "On a one to ten scale, he's an eleven."

"Damn, girl. So, how can this god-like man not recognize you? Tell me it was something kinky like a sex party with masks."

Jasmine laughed. Only Emma could take something like this and turn it into something to laugh about. "It was less than ten minutes in a bathroom and I never saw him again… until today."

"Was it a good ten minutes?" Emma asked.

Jasmine blew out through her nose. "It was…okay." Achieving orgasm with a partner was pretty rare for her. Zoey's father hadn't been one of those unicorn moments.

"Hot but not great in the sack. Got it. Well, we can't all be perfect. Maybe you should try sleeping with a woman; I've never not had an orgasm with a woman. With guys, it's fifty-fifty."

"I wish I could be sexually attracted to a woman." They seemed safer.

"Okay, so maybe this is a good thing your baby-daddy is back in your life." Emma suggested.

Jasmine paced back and forth over the long porch. "How exactly is this good?"

"You can get to know him and see if he's a good guy. Maybe Zoey can have her dad in her life after all."

Jasmine stopped, a rush of dizziness spinning though her head. She sat on the ground with her head lowered to her knees. "I'm scared. What if he tries to take her from me? What if he says I'm a bad mom? What if—"

"What if he's a great father? What if Zoey could have two parents in her life? What if he can help provide for her and take some of that stress off you?"

Jasmine blinked back more tears. She hated showing her emotions like this, but that was something else that motherhood had changed. She couldn't hide anymore.

Emma had a point. She couldn't let fear stand in the way of Zoey's chances of happiness. If Atlas was a good father, and she didn't try, then she'd be robbing Zoey of something Jasmine herself had never had but always wanted. She couldn't hold the man's sexual history against him. After all, she'd done the same thing—more than once.

"You're right. I'll get to know him. I'll see if he's a safe person, if he can be good for Zoey. Then, I'll tell him."

"I'm here for you. Whatever you need." Emma offered.

"Thank you. I appreciate it. Can you keep this between us for now? I don't want Remy to find out just yet. She'll tell Mikel and then— "

"And then you'll have two big brothers and their best friend knocking on your door getting into the middle of your business. I got you."

Jasmine laughed. "They probably wouldn't even knock. They'd bust the thing down."

Emma giggled. "True. Well, I know they have your back, but I also respect your right as Zoey's mother to do what you think is right."

"You're the best, Em."

"Tell that to my step-brother the next time you see him." Emma laughed again, but this time it sounded forced.

"I'll tell Link next time I talk to him." Jasmine promised, knowing it was a hopeless cause, much to her friend's dismay.

"Okay, well, I gotta get back. Almost done with this album and then I start my tour next week," Emma said.

"I'm so happy that your dream is becoming a reality. Soon you'll be too famous to be my friend."

"Never!"

"Talk to you later." Jasmine smiled.

"Love you, bitch."

"You too."

Jasmine slipped the phone in her back pocket and got to her feet once more. Taking a deep breath, she stared past the salt water grass and rose hip bushes towards the expanse of green-blue waves. They crashed against the rocks to her left and licked up the sandy coast to her right as the ocean tide worked its way in. She could do this. For Zoey, she'd do anything. If that meant giving her father a chance, she'd do it. And if it meant keeping who he was a secret for the rest of her time on earth, she'd do that too.

Because Zoey would not go through the shit she'd been through. Jasmine would work through the pain of the past so that her daughter didn't have to have one tenth of the trauma in her life that Jasmine had. She'd protect her daughter, no matter what it took. Because Jasmine knew better than anyone that of all the people in a child's life, the father figure could be the most dangerous.

To continue reading Jasmine and Atlas's story, visit the website below to get your copy of *The Lighthouse Inn* today:

WWW.AMKUSI.COM/THELIGHTHOUSEINN

ACKNOWLEDGMENTS

We want to send out a huge thank you to our diversity editor, Renita McKinney of *A Book A Day*. Her belief in this novel, us, as well as her hard work getting this story out into the world, means the world to us! She's been with us since the beginning, and her unflinching honesty has been wonderfully helpful and motivating.

Our editing team Lauren Clark and Anna Bishop from *CREATING ink*. We've learned so much through our sessions together. Thank you!

To Curtis Evans, and everyone from *CREATING ink's* team, thank you for all you do.

So much gratitude for Danielle Sanchez of *Wildfire Marketing Solutions*, thank you for having so much belief in this series and all your hard work to get the word out!

To the family and friends who supported us, thank you so much for letting us gush about our stories and characters. To our daughters, for your patience and inspiration.

And every ARC reviewer and reader who left reviews, thank you from the bottom of our hearts!

Ash and Marcus
A. M. Kusi

JOIN OUR NEWSLETTER

The best way to get updates about new releases, sneak peeks, pre-orders, giveaways, and more is by joining our newsletter. You'll also receive a FREE short novel that's not available on any retailer to read.

Visit the website below to join now.

WWW.AMKUSI.COM/NEWSLETTER

THANK YOU

Thank you for reading *Defying Gravity*. We hope you are emotionally satisfied with Bently and Belle's love story. If you enjoyed this novel, please consider leaving a review on your favorite retailer and sharing it with your friends and family.

Also, you can start reading the other books in *The Shattered Cove Series* right now!

Mikel and Remy in **A Fallen Star (Book 1)**. eBook FREE on all retailers.

Andre and Mia in **Glass Secrets (Book 2)**.

Atlas and Jasmine in **The Lighthouse Inn (Book 4)**.

Finn and Charli in **His True North (Book 5)**.

Link and Emma in **In The Grey (Book 6)**.

Lastly, if you haven't read our first complete series, **The Orchard Inn Romance Series**, make sure you get your copy so you don't miss out on three wonderful love stories.

Thank you again for reading *Defying Gravity!*

Cheers,

Ash & Marcus.

ABOUT A. M KUSI

A. M. Kusi is the pen name of a wife-and-husband author team, Ash and Marcus Kusi. We enjoy writing romance novels that are inspired by our experiences as an interracial/multicultural couple.

Our novels are about strong women and the sexy heroes they fall in love with, are emotionally satisfying, and always have a happy ending.

Discover more about us at:

WWW.AMKUSI.COM

To receive updates about new releases, giveaways, sneak peeks, pre-orders, and more, click the link below to join our newsletter today:

WWW.AMKUSI.COM/NEWSLETTER

After you join the newsletter, we will send you a FREE novella to read.

To contact us, use this email address amkusinovels@gmail.com.

Happy reading!

tiktok.com/@amkusi.romanceauthor

facebook.com/amkusi

instagram.com/amkusinovels

ALSO BY A. M. KUSI

A Fallen Star (eBook FREE on all retailers)

(Shattered Cove Series Book 1)

Glass Secrets

(Shattered Cove Series Book 2)

The Lighthouse Inn

(Shattered Cove Series Book 4)

His True North

(Shattered Cove Series Book 5)

The Orchard Inn

(Book 1 in The Orchard Inn Romance Series)

Conflict of Interest

(Book 2 in The Orchard Inn Romance Series)

Her Perfect Storm

(Book 3 in The Orchard Inn Romance Series)

For a complete list of all our books, visit:

WWW.AMKUSI.COM/BOOKS

Made in the USA
Coppell, TX
29 January 2022

72644899R00225